I0525379

BAD BEHAVIOR

JACQUELINE VICK

ISBN-13: 978-1-945403-29-3 (Ebook)
ISBN-13: 978-1-945403-38-5 (Paperback)

Classical Reads 1st edition 2019

Cover Design by James, GoOnWrite.com

To Foster, with love.

"Clothes and manners do not make the man; but, when he is made, they greatly improve his appearance."

Henry Ward Beecher

CHAPTER 1

"Nicholas? What is this? A bad joke?"

My brother, Edward Harlow, author of the Aunt Civility etiquette books and columns, did a slow turn so he could take in the entire community room of the Babbitt & Brown Bookstore located on a downtown street corner of Citrus Grove, California, about twenty-five miles northeast of San Diego.

Admittedly, the room lacked character, being large and plain with cheap, beige carpet and off-white walls that looked a little dirty. The organizers had set up two long folding tables in front of a swinging door that led to the kitchen facilities and covered them with white paper tablecloths, the kind you'd find at a dollar store. Table number one held snacks provided by the Sweet and Sour Book Club, a group of enthusiasts who liked to read about food. Me, I prefer to eat it.

The second table held an assortment of desserts brought by Edward that related to his talk. Until my brother invited the crowd to partake, Mrs. Regina Robbins, a stout woman with short, gray hair who had the shoulders of a butcher, would guard the eats. Why make the audience members wait? Because Edward thought it was disgusting to watch people dribble crumbs down their shirtfronts and listen to lip-smacking noises while he lectured them. For around twenty-five minutes, they would be his captive audience, and by gum they could just suffer in polite silence.

Already attendees were slipping resentful glances at the woman who stood between them and free food since that was probably the only reason they showed up tonight.

I was more interested in the table directly across from the display of desserts. Stacks of Edward's latest masterpiece covered this table—*Conquering Shellfish and Other Messy Meals with Confidence* written under the pseudonym of Aunt Civility. My brother's sales were fine but, as one who depends on those sales for my paycheck, I wanted to keep a close eye on the book table. I hoped it would be empty by the end of the evening.

Bodies packed rows of folding chairs that filled the center of the room. It was an evening in early March, so most people had on sweaters and light jackets along with jeans and slacks, but a few stubborn sun-lovers, convinced that California's reputation for fair weather depended on them, wore shorts and sandals. Those people, especially the middle-aged man wearing the backward baseball cap, were the cause of my brother's irritation.

As Edward's secretary, my responsibilities include the usual chores of a personal assistant as well as duties not included in the job description: bucking the author up when he's feeling a typical writer's insecurities, calming him down when he has fits over silly details, and ignoring him when he doesn't like something that's for his own damn good.

I had arranged the event, and to say he wasn't pleased with the turnout would have been an understatement. A normal author would fret over a low head count, but

Edward's complaint revolved around the large number of people. At least, the wrong sort of people.

My brother thinks his advice books on manners, etiquette, and general civil behavior are for those who share his opinion that barbarians have taken over the world. He only likes to give lectures to pre-qualified groups made up of members who would rather shoot themselves than interrupt or chew gum.

I deal in reality. Why would someone already on their best behavior bother with one of his books? So, I'd lied. I told him he would give his presentation on dining to the Citrus Grove Culinary Arts Council.

It wasn't a bald-faced lie. They were here. All seven of them. I mentioned in passing that the council members would invite a few guests and, when that didn't incite a tantrum, I had given them the go-ahead to open the event to the public.

I shrugged. "What can I say? They must have seen the event posted on your Facebook page."

He narrowed his eyes at me. "I don't have a Facebook page."

My grin held a hint of malice. "Yes, you do. I put it up myself last month."

His lips pressed together under his trim Van Dyke beard, and he took a deep breath through his nose, which made his nostrils flare like a bull getting ready to charge. Fortunately, Jeffrey Babbitt, a white-haired gnome and the owner of the Babbitt & Brown Bookstore, chose that moment to thank Edward for coming. He gazed around the room, taking in the crowd with a reaction very different from Edward's. Jeffrey's eyes shone with delight, and he hooked his thumbs under the armpits of his green sweater vest.

"I haven't had such a popular signing since we had Whitney Sparks."

If Jeffrey were trying to get on Edward's good side, he blew it. Whitney Sparks was the antithesis of good manners. After the release of her book, *Whatever*, which was based on a blog of the same name, her popularity had soared among grungy twenty-somethings who felt that good manners were overrated. Mere mention of her name was enough to give Edward heartburn.

"I'm sure her crowd wasn't this big," I said with an encouraging glance at Edward.

"Actually," Jeffrey gushed, "it was enormous. Around the block, I believe."

"Vulgarians," Edward hissed.

Jeffrey beamed at him. "Vulgarians with money. I made an enormous profit that day." Profit reminded him of practical matters. "The books are on the table so you can stop by and greet Aunt Civility's fans after you're done. Customers seem to purchase more when there is an opportunity to shake hands with the rich and famous, even if it isn't the actual author. But you are related, and that's a plus."

When people thought of Aunt Civility, they got an image of a seventy-year-old grandmother type. Edward, at six-feet-two, with the physique of a football player, a head of black hair that kept trying to curl, and a trim beard, looked more like her arrogant, fat-headed nephew. The publicity department at Classical Reads had spread the word that poor Auntie suffered from agoraphobia, and her alleged favorite relative, Edward, traveled to events as her official representative.

My brother looked over Jeffrey's shoulder toward the table and his eyebrows joined in a frown. "What the devil is that?"

Jeffrey, surprised by my brother's tone, turned his head to look. "What is what?"

Edward would never point in public, but I knew exactly

what was offending his finer sensibilities. Next to the book table stood a cardboard cutout of him smiling, and the cartoon bubble coming out of his mouth said, "Win your free copy here!" In front of Cardboard Edward stood a kind of ballot box on stilts.

"He means the raffle." I knew all about the raffle. I'm the one who emailed Jeffrey the photo of Edward smiling, and I thought he did a good job of blowing it up. Edward's likeness stood about six inches shorter than the real man.

The bookstore owner spun back around with his hands clasped at his chest. "Isn't it marvelous? I'm sure half the people here showed up because they heard about the raffle. People love free stuff."

Edward cocked his head and frowned. "I look ridiculous."

I leaned close to him and lowered my voice. "Not half as ridiculous as you would have looked if I had sent the photo of you in your bathing trunks. Now behave."

Jeffrey patted Edward's arm and said, "Nonsense, dear boy. You're lucky. Very photogenic. One authoress had a huge mole on her chin. When we enlarged her image, it looked like she was being attacked by a giant tick."

He gave a small shudder.

Across the room, an elderly woman with a walker struggled to stuff her raffle ticket into the slot on top of the box. Jeffrey excused himself and trotted off to assist her.

"A man who understands business," I said with approval. Edward grumbled something unprintable in response.

Call me an optimist, but I had extra books in the trunk of our car in case the bookstore ran out. Since nobody but me and Edward's publisher knew he authored them, the books came already signed by Aunt Civility. He wouldn't have to sign them, but he would have to make nice with the public.

I scanned the potential buyers and wondered if this was the kind of crowd that would purchase Edward's books, or if most of them had shown up to kill an evening and get free food. The majority were over forty. In my experience, people between forty and, say, sixty usually had disposable income and weren't yet panicked about saving every penny for retirement. Unfortunately, it also meant they had enough life experience to be choosy about where they spent their dollar bills, and a book on fine dining might not make the cut.

There were a few younger people. Ms. Hattie Channing, spokesperson for the Culinary Arts Council, was probably in her early thirties. It was hard to tell. She dressed and carried herself as if inhabited by the spirit of her great-grandmother. Her high-necked blouse ruffled around her neck, and her polyester suit in yogurt pink matched the horn-rimmed spectacles that perched on the end of her nose. Black ortho-pedic shoes and a string of pearls added the final touch.

The rest of the council consisted of a grumpy old man named Ned, spinster sisters Dora and Flora, a former mili-tary man they referred to as The General, a short, balding banker, and a woman with a stylish, snow-white bob dressed in designer jeans and a peacock-blue sweater who carried a bag that said *Don't anger a knitter. We carry sharp objects.*

A man in his late thirties or early forties wearing a rumpled blue shirt and khakis, an impressive-looking camera hanging from a strap around his neck, approached Edward with his hand held out. My brother hesitated before proffering his own hand, taking a moment to eyeball the stubble on the man's face with disdain. When it comes to facial hair, Edward believes a man should be decisive.

"You must be the author's representative. I'm Charlie Grant, the reporter for *The Citrus Grove Courier.*"

Edward shook with him and murmured a lie about it being a pleasure.

Standing behind Charlie, so close he was practically

clinging to his leg, was a boy around five. Charlie saw me noticing and grinned.

"This is my son, Zachary. I couldn't find a sitter Say hello, Zack."

The kid held his hand up but didn't wave. Edward, who thought he knew something about children since meeting Claudia's niece and nephew at Inglenook, bent his head down and smiled.

"Are you helping your father?"

Zachary nodded. "I'm going to take pictures when I grow up."

"I'm sure you shall."

The photographer settled his son on a chair next to the dessert tables and handed him a peanut butter kiss from the Sweet and Sour Book Club stash.

"You stay here and be good."

When Charlie returned, he suggested Edward pose holding up Aunt Civility's latest book. This type of request always causes a dilemma. If Aunt Civility existed, would she appreciate her nephew holding up a copy of her book in a proprietary manner? Edward didn't think she would, but he agreed to stand next to the table with a book perched on a display stand to show the cover. Charlie agreed, and he took a few shots of Edward alone and some with him standing next to Jeffrey Babbitt, who showed more enthusiasm for the publicity. When the reporter suggested Edward throw a friendly arm around Cardboard Edward, my brother declined.

"I'd like to interview you for the paper after your lecture," Charlie said.

My brother gave a brief nod. "Certainly."

Edward enjoyed hearing himself talk, so that was all right. I had hopes that his mood would take a turn for the better, but then his body went rigid. I followed his line of sight to a man wearing an orange t-shirt, sky-blue linen suit, and white tennis shoes who was sauntering in our direction. He was *Miami Vice* a few decades late and without the good looks of the lead actors. His skin had that weathered, dry texture that comes from too much sun exposure, his gray hair needed combing, and the beady, pale-blue eyes behind his glasses went fine with his smirk. To be fair, his bone structure hinted that he might have been handsome once, but age had finally had its way with him.

I didn't like him on sight. First, he had an arrogant saunter. Guys who saunter think they're doing you a favor by being in the same room. Second, he carried a metallic-blue aluminum water bottle in his hand as if it was a fashion statement. As he got closer, I could see it was personalized with an etching of a book and the initials JT, which gave me a third reason not to like him. Finally, his lips smirked. I dislike smirking lips.

When he made it to us, he clapped my brother on the shoulder. "Edward Harlow."

His voice surprised me. It boomed.

Edward strained his lips into a smile. "Professor Taylor."

Our parents separated when I was a kid, causing my mother to move with her boys from Chicago to San Diego. Even with child support, which my father faithfully paid, by the time Edward and I were ready for college, we were short of the kind of cash it takes to continue an education. Fortunately, a private school, G.W. Marston College, had a Division II football team and offered partial scholarships that allowed both Edward and I to get our bachelor's degrees. It was a small campus, and I had a vague recollection of a dreaded teacher named Taylor.

"I see my guidance has paid off." Professor Taylor nodded toward the table stacked with Edward's books. "I'd say you're doing well."

"You give us both too much credit," Edward murmured. "I'm merely the official representative."

Taylor scooted close to Edward and clutched his arm with long, bony fingers, and I moved in to make sure that my brother didn't lose his temper. Another of my duties. He doesn't like to be handled, and his reflexes can respond before his thought process kicks in. It was an asset on the football field and made him a formidable player. Here and now? Not so much.

"I recognized your writing style," Taylor said. "Pompous and verbose." He grinned, something he shouldn't do often as it showed a missing tooth next to his left canine. "You can't kid a kidder."

"I wouldn't dream of it," Edward replied between clenched teeth.

On Professor Taylor's approach, Charlie had melted back into the crowd to show his son how to photograph easier subjects than Edward, so I didn't have to worry about a headline in tomorrow morning's paper calling Edward out as the author of the Aunt Civility books.

"How much is your secret worth to you?" Taylor winked. Maybe he shouldn't have because that started him blinking. He took off his glasses and cleaned them with his jacket, but when he put them back on his face, he frowned as if the exercise had been a waste of his time.

Although I thought readers would love to hear the male perspective on polite behavior, and I regularly told Edward he should go public as Aunt Civility, it was his decision. And I dislike people who share other people's secrets on principle. I reached for his arm to escort him to the door, but the professor held up his hands in mock self-defense.

"Kidding. Only kidding."

He stuffed his hands into his trouser pockets to affect a

casual pose, but to do it, he had to hold the water bottle under one armpit and wound up looking silly.

"You've got quite a turnout," he said, scanning the room. His gaze rested on someone by the snack tables behind us. "I think I'll mingle. It wouldn't hurt to promote my own book."

"You're an author now?" Edward stressed the now. "I seem to remember you were a stellar example of those who can't, teach."

"Edward," I said in warning. It wouldn't do for Aunt Civility's official representative to get into a public shouting match. Fortunately, the professor took it as a joke, and he threw back his head and laughed. I got another look at the gap in his teeth.

Just then, Miss Channing approached the microphone and tapped on it with one long fingernail as if she thought it might explode. The microphone, not her finger.

"Ladies and gentlemen. If I could have your attention."

Miss Channing's breathy, high voice didn't carry well, and she had to repeat the request several times before the remaining standees took their seats. Taylor jabbed a thumb in Edward's side and grinned.

"Talk to you after the show."

My brother watched him go with a contemptuous sneer, took a last look around the room, made a face, and, forced to admit defeat, settled onto his reserved chair in the front row. To leave now would be unspeakably rude.

After taking a seat in the chair next to him, I leaned my head in and whispered. "You don't think he'd spill the beans, do you?"

He didn't answer me, unless you count a low growl at the back of his throat as a response.

"We are so pleased to have a guest speaker tonight at the monthly meeting of the Citrus Grove Culinary Arts Council," Miss Channing began. "We are an interesting group and we're always looking for new members who share our passion for all things related to cooking, so please feel free to sign up at the table in the back. We'd love to have you."

A few people craned their necks to look at the table, but I would bet money none of them took her up on the offer. She then launched into the history of the council, and Edward leaned into me and growled, "We will talk about this later."

I held up a finger. "Shh. I think she's getting to your introduction."

She wasn't. She was talking about the suburbanization of Citrus Grove, which led to the annihilation of farmlands and a general decline in the tone of the place. Now that fast-food chains had taken over the outskirts of town leading to the freeway, a citizen's only defense was to bring fine dining into their homes. Mr. Edward Harlow, the official representative of that famous author, Aunt Civility, would help them reclaim that lost tradition, the family meal, and by gosh, armed with the correct etiquette, they wouldn't have to settle for hamburgers and meatloaf. Or if they did, they could do it with style.

I knew his talking points—the importance of the dining room in family meals, how to train your teenagers to be the perfect servers, how to eat finger foods without making a mess, and, for an exciting finale, the importance of adding color to your meals by serving brightly decorated confections for dessert. He thought it would thrill the crowd to mention some deadly ingredients that Victorians had used to brighten things up, including arsenic, iron, and lead.

I wondered how Edward would respond to people who weren't blessed with separate dining rooms. What about those who lived in tiny apartments, or lofts that were one big room? I glanced around nervously, searching the faces of the friendly townsfolk for any signs of disgruntled activists. I wouldn't have missed it if a person had dragged in a sign declaring white males with dining rooms as the pinnacle of privilege.

When the people applauded, I realized that Ms. Channing had introduced Edward. He approached the podium and glared at the crowd. I coughed several times, and when he looked my way, I plastered on a big, fake grin as a hint. He adjusted his features into a friendlier expression and launched into his lecture.

Edward is rarely boring, at least not to first-time listeners, but I had gone over his talk with him at least ten times, so I settled back, closed my eyes, and let my thoughts wander. There had to be two hundred people here tonight, and I fully expected four, possibly five, to spend money on the book. Maybe, with Edward's added surprise of special desserts, he might lull three more people with sweet tooths to buy. Or would that be sweet teeth? That would make...

Before I knew it, they were applauding again. I had dozed off for the entire talk. Jerking straight, I craned my neck toward the back of the room. The volunteers had put out the final additions on the dessert table, and they had followed my instructions without a reminder from me. I thanked my stars for the efficiency of women over fifty and turned back to see how Edward had taken his audience.

My brother looked gratified by their enthusiastic response. The left corner of his mouth curled up, and his eyebrows were relaxed instead of pulled into a frown. He held up his hand to quiet them so he could deliver his grand finale.

"To celebrate Citrus Grove's fine history, I've brought with me several citrus-based desserts. You can find recipe cards on the book table, courtesy of my beloved aunt. I've brought a Victorian treat called Kisses as well as lemon squares and sugared citrus peels. Lemon-barley water is available for anyone who's thirsty." He raised a finger. "And I promise you, any color in the desserts results from safe, modern color additives or nature."

They giggled and gasped, and the big showoff couldn't resist doling out additional tidbits about poison.

"If you think current makeup fashions are a pain, ladies used to use a couple of drops of arsenic to make their skin pale." The women shrieked, and the men guffawed. He nodded. "Gentlemen. Don't be so quick to laugh at the ladies. Victorian men regularly plastered bright green wallpaper in the family home—perhaps in the dining room—which also contained arsenic."

The women got a laugh out of that, and then Edward, finally out of steam, nodded again and thanked them. The applause this time was scattered, since most of the crowd was already on their way to the dessert tables. Edward stepped away from the podium and I stood and joined him.

"All caught up on your sleep?" he asked.

"Did I snore?"

He handed me his speech, and I packed it into his briefcase. The chairs were empty except for a few couples. His gaze moved toward the exit.

I shook my head. "Nuh-uh. You are required to mingle for ten minutes minimum."

Just then, the council members rushed up with hearty congratulations. The retired banker's name turned out to be Morton. Mort for short.

"I can't thank you enough for making the drive," Mort said with a smile that encouraged his fellow council members to agree. They did, which was funny since it only took us forty-eight minutes in rush-hour traffic to get here.

Grumpy Ned said, "I gotta get to the membership table," and he left us to join the Knitting Woman who was seated there and clicking away at a bulky project.

"You're right about teenagers," The General said. "They

need a firm hand and something to keep them busy. If they pay attention to your instructions, they may be able to find employment at a restaurant."

Dora and Flora twittered at my brother and grabbed the opportunity to regale him with stories of what it was like to grow up in Citrus Grove before the town had condescended to allow people without livestock or crops to move there. They were both in their seventies with white fluffy hair and floral print dresses. The sisters weren't twins but they were interchangeable except for the mole on Dora's left cheek.

The story ended with the delights of drinking warm milk straight from the cow's udder, and then they joined the rest of their group in a procession to the snack tables.

My brother shot me a glare, but when he saw the line at the book table, his features softened into his typical expression of mild irritation.

"They seem to be enjoying themselves."

"You're a hit. There's a cake club in San Diego—"

"Don't even think about it."

"Edward, you've got to branch out. You refuse to use social media—" I held up a hand to stop the coming diatribe. "I started your social media sites in self-defense."

"Sites?"

We hadn't yet discussed Twitter.

"It's for your own good. People want to connect with the author, and you're her gateway. In fact, I had a thought about starting an account for Auntie. She'd be a hit."

"She's supposed to be mentally ill."

"She has agoraphobia. She can write from home unless you want to give her another social disorder that prohibits her from going online, but I don't recommend it. If Auntie has too many problems, people might get disgusted." I snapped my fingers. "Unless you had her share her difficulties in a book. People love reading details about the horrors encountered by celebrities, and she might actually help people who share her diseases."

"Mental disorders are not diseases," my brother snapped. "I don't understand your obsession with the Internet. What's social about typing a message on someone's paper?"

"Page. It's called their page."

"Sharing intimate details with strangers to whom you haven't been properly introduced... It's madness!"

I rolled my eyes and turned toward the book table. The line had grown, and it pleased me to have proof that Edward was wrong. Public appearances were good for his sales.

To reward myself, I cut our conversation short and joined the others at the table with the snacks. Not the desserts we brought, since I could enjoy our housekeeper's baking any time, but the ones supplied by the Sweet and Sour Book Club. I took a few meringue kisses and popped one in my mouth. When I reached for a napkin, the table jerked. A startled cry was followed by the sound of breaking glass. I held my hands in the air.

"Wasn't me."

A glass pitcher, former home to the lemon-barley water, was scattered in pieces on the floor. Someone coughed, trying to smother a laugh, I assumed. Regina Robbins stooped over to pick up the pieces. Once she had gathered them up, she disappeared behind the swinging door that led to the kitchen.

"What did you do now?"

I tightened my muscles to keep from jumping. Edward had come up on me without making a sound.

"Nothing. Someone jarred the table, and the pitcher fell." I looked at the wet spot on the rug. "At least lemon-barley water won't stain. It could have been red wine. And why aren't you busy greeting book buyers?"

I glanced over my shoulder at the table. Jeffrey Babbitt sat alone; his grin gone. The crowd had transferred their interest from Edward's books to the free food. To make matters worse, Professor Taylor stumbled up to us. He put a hand on my shoulder for support, and when I firmly removed it, he leaned against the table to get his balance. I wondered if his water bottle held something stronger than $H_{2}O$.

"Did you enjoy the talk?" I asked him. Not that I was eager to engage him in conversation, but I wanted to set a good example for Edward, who was clenching his jaw muscles.

"Gave me a headache," Taylor muttered. He squinted and blinked at me. He looked confused, and I was about to give him some sympathy, but then he coughed in my face. He removed his glasses and rubbed his eyes. Whatever was wrong with him, I hoped he wasn't contagious.

Regina Robbins returned with a full pitcher and filled a few plastic cups. I gave a small shudder. To me, lemon-barley water looked like a cloudy, dirty puddle, and I couldn't think of anyone more deserving of a serving of it than the man who was still coughing in my direction.

I picked up a cup. "Here. This might help."

He nodded, took the glass, emptied it in a few gulps, and then handed it back to me. I took it to be polite, but since I wasn't his waiter, I turned my back on him.

As I set his cup down next to the other empties, I noted that most of the lemon squares were gone. A glance in the wastebasket at the end of the table showed me what had happened to the citrus peels.

"I think people sucked the sugar off and tossed them," I said to Edward, shaking my head. "Told you they were too sour."

"What a waste," Edward lamented. He looked around at the attendees, now stuffing their faces, hooked his arm through mine, and pulled me out of earshot. "And speaking of waste, let's not waste any time getting on the road."

He led the way back to our chairs to collect his briefcase. No way could I talk him out of leaving this time. He had made it seven minutes longer than I expected.

"Where you come up with these foolish ideas..."

I scanned the room and considered the crowd which had dwindled to half its original size. Still, it wasn't a bad turnout.

"Crazy!"

I held up a hand. "Fine. I got it. Foolish and crazy. I won't try to help you again."

He handed me his briefcase. "I didn't say anything."

"Crazy son-of-a—"

We turned toward the voice. Professor Taylor dropped his water bottle and folded his arm over his stomach as he doubled over. The other hand stretched out to point a bony finger at Edward. He gasped.

"You!"

And then he fell flat on his face.

"Someone call an ambulance," I yelled out as I crossed to him and knelt at his side. After rolling him over, I pulled at his shirt-collar to help him breathe and motioned the crowd back. His pale skin was clammy with sweat, and I thought *Great. Just great. I can't afford to get sick.* I forced a smile and told him to relax.

"Could everyone step back and give him room? Thank you."

A few people responded but most ignored me.

"Just relax," I repeated. "The paramedics will be here soon. You'll be fine."

His pale-blue eyes were fixed on something over my shoulder. I turned my head to look, but he clutched my jacket collar in a tight fist and jerked me to within a few inches of his face. I noticed an earthy smell that I assumed was barley and tried to turn my face away.

"Mwif." That's what came out. Then Taylor made a noise like "ack" and relaxed his grip.

I tried to find his pulse, but when you're panicked, it's not as easy as it looks on television. Resting one hand on his chest to feel the rise and fall of his breathing didn't get results, nor did putting my hand under his nose to feel an inhale or exhale. Nothing.

I searched the faces of the crowd for one of the volunteers. When I saw Miss Channing standing near the door with her hands clasped in front of her bosom, I said, "Did someone call nine one one?"

She nodded.

The professor's mouth went slack, with drool coming from one corner. "Get me a napkin." Someone shoved a handful at me. I swiped at the drool, placed one napkin over his mouth and started CPR on a dead man.

Jeffrey Babbitt crouched next to me; his impish expression gone. "Let me help."

While I handled the breaths, he pushed Taylor's shirt up so he could find the right spot and took over compressing the professor's chest. An hour later, or maybe five minutes, the medical professionals arrived and took over. Jeffrey and I moved out of the way and watched as they tried to revive him. Finally, they attached Taylor to a machine and took a reading. The female of the pair phoned the hospital, and a doctor pronounced the time of death.

I looked in the direction that Taylor had been staring when he made his last sounds. The council members stood in a huddle in front of the snacks, while Mrs. Robbins and her volunteers watched from behind the table. Maybe Taylor's last act was an attempt to complain about the food.

As the emergency personnel packed up their things, Jeffrey panicked. "You can't just leave him there!"

The female exchanged a look with her partner, who then concentrated on avoiding eye contact with anyone in the room. She looked up at me. "The medical examiner will be here shortly. And law enforcement. We'll wait until they get here."

Since I couldn't do anything for Professor Taylor, I returned to Edward's side. He demanded to know what was happening.

"I don't know how well you liked Professor Taylor—"

"I don't." He cocked his head. "Did you say liked?"

I nodded. "Dead as a doornail."

"Ye gads."

"You can say that again."

Edward searched the front of the room. "Where's my briefcase? Perhaps we should remove ourselves."

"Forget it. We're stuck."

As if to confirm my opinion, several San Diego County deputies walked through the door. The one in the lead, a tall blond man with a small belly, looked down on the late Professor Taylor and put his hands on his hips. "What happened?"

Miss Channing inched up to him and said, "I think he ate something that didn't agree with him."

CHAPTER 2

On the upside, the books sold out. While waiting for the deputies to send everybody home, the spectators had flocked to the book table to purchase a memento of the exciting event. I could hear them now, bragging about how they had been *this close* to the man when he dropped dead. My only concern was to get Edward out the door as soon as possible, preferably before he freaked out. The bad publicity was Classical Read's problem.

The man in charge, Detective Jonah Sykes, had shown up about twenty minutes after the first deputies arrived. He was every inch as tall as Edward, with broad shoulders and a barrel chest, short-cropped hair and a Van Dyke beard. In fact, he could have been Edward's twin except for the nutmeg-colored skin that seemed even darker against his crisp white shirt.

He conferred with the tall, blond deputy, jotting notes and nodding his head a lot. Their conversation was interrupted by a woman who I found out later was the medical examiner. After the detective had exchanged a few words with her, he slowly surveyed the room with eyes the color of topaz until they landed on us. He crossed over, introduced himself, and invited us to take a chair as he joined us.

"You're Edward and you're Nicholas," he said in a soft, rich baritone with a nod at each of us in turn. We confirmed with nods of our own.

"What time did you arrive?"

"We got here at six-twenty-two." I held up my wrist to show him my watch. "It never loses time."

"Your talk wasn't until seven."

Edward chuckled. "It's not as if I storm into an event and head straight for the podium."

That's exactly what he'd do if I wasn't around to control him.

"I always meet with the person who invited me, or in this case, the people."

"That would be the Citrus Grove Culinary Arts Council." Sykes listed them off by name, and I agreed those were the people who had issued the invitation.

"And I introduced myself to Mr. Babbitt, the owner of the venue. That reporter from the local newspaper asked to take a few pictures, which I did, and then he offered to interview me after the event." Edward looked to me for an answer to his unasked question.

I shook my head, irritated that he had even thought the question. The big egomaniac. "It's not going to happen tonight, that's for certain. Maybe Charlie Grant can interview you over the phone. You won't even have to leave your office."

So far, Sykes hadn't written anything down, but now he opened his notebook and readied his pen.

"And it's around then, after you'd taken the pictures, that Professor Jonathan Taylor showed up. Tell me about your interactions with him."

Edward made his contribution brief. "I exchanged a few

21

words with him after he arrived. I didn't speak with him again."

Sykes nodded at my brother as if to say that's a good start. Since he seemed to expect more detail, I picked it up after the lecture and offered plenty of description but without repeating the dialog verbatim until I got to the part where the professor died.

"He made noises, like *mwif* and *ack*." I lifted my shoulders. "Then he was gone."

"Are you being funny?"

I raised my brows. "If you want funny, I know some jokes, but they're off color and my brother wouldn't appreciate them."

"Nicholas! This is serious. Detective Sykes, you don't know my brother, but I assure you he wasn't being sarcastic. He has an excellent memory, and he told you exactly what he heard."

Sykes cocked his head. "Was he trying to say something?"

I waved a hand. "Think what you will. I say they were just noises."

He wrote in his notebook. I'm not sure how he spelled *mwif* and *ack*.

"How long did he take to die?"

Edward cleared his throat. "My brother is not a medical professional."

Sykes kept his eyes on me. "Let me rephrase it for your attorney. How long did it take from when you saw Professor Taylor show signs of distress until the moment he stopped breathing?"

I gave it some thought. "He collapsed about ten minutes after the talk finished. I asked someone to call an ambulance right away. Taylor stopped breathing before the paramedics walked in."

"The call came at approximately twenty minutes to eight. They took four minutes and thirty-two seconds to get here."

My brows went up. "That's it? It felt longer."

"We hear that all the time."

Sykes seemed like a nice guy. He was courteous and his questions were fairly benign. Still, his title was detective. In my limited experience, detectives didn't waste time at accident scenes.

I grinned. "Let me ask you a question."

He crossed his long legs and settled back in his chair. "Go ahead."

"A man has a fit, or maybe it was a heart attack, and he drops dead in a crowded room. Regrettable, but not criminal. I can see needing a deputy to take notes and gather the names of witnesses, but what's a homicide detective doing here? I beg your pardon, but you are a homicide detective, aren't you?"

"That's a fair question. To answer your last question first, yes. I work homicide. After speaking with a few of the witnesses, Deputy Harkness decided the situation required more attention."

He flipped a page in his notebook. "So, you knew the deceased?" He addressed the question to Edward.

"A long time ago. He was one of my college English professors."

"That *was* a long time ago." Sykes smiled to take the sting out, though there wasn't much sting to begin with since he was around Edward's age himself. "How about you?" he asked me.

"I didn't have any classes with Professor Taylor. I only knew him by reputation on campus. He was a stinker."

A brief smile flashed across the detective's face. "And he was blackmailing you?"

That caught us both by surprise. My mouth dropped

23

open before I could clamp my jaw. Edward hid it better. He leaned back and crossed his arms over his chest as if prepared to entertain a highly amusing but fictitious piece of gossip.

"Before tonight, I had not seen or spoken to the man since I graduated. In person, on the telephone, or through the mail." He slid me a glance that lacked amusement. "Or electronically."

"A witness told us the victim said," the detective flipped back a few pages, *"What's it worth to you?* Or words to that effect. Do you deny Professor Taylor said that?"

"Well, no." Edward was big on honesty. "He assumed that I was more than Aunt Civility's official representative. That I had written her books. An incredible insult to the industrious and intelligent woman who pens them. I told him he was mistaken, and then he said—what you said."

"But he followed it up by saying *just kidding,*" I added to clarify.

The detective cocked his head. "That's an odd joke."

"In very poor taste," Edward agreed.

"Before he collapsed, he pointed in your direction and shouted *Crazy!* Also, *How could you do this to me?* Why would he say these things?"

"Hang on." If the police were going to grill my brother, I wanted to get the facts straight. "Nobody said that second part. First, the professor shouted the word crazy. I thought my brother had said something. When he denied it, we both turned around. Next, Taylor yelled *Crazy son-of-a* and *You!*"

Edward's lips twitched with approval. "I told you he has a fine memory. So do I. That's what Professor Taylor said, verbatim."

The detective didn't appear to appreciate the clarification. "Again, why you?"

"I haven't the foggiest notion." Edward tugged at the bottom of his vest to straighten it.

Sykes turned those perceptive topaz eyes on me. "How about you?"

I had lost my desire to make up for Edward's lack of detail. "Same answer."

"That brings up an interesting point I'd like to cover. Not long before he died, you, Nicholas Harlow, gave the professor a glass of lemon-barley water."

"Sure. He was coughing. A lot. I grabbed the closest cup and handed it to him. He drank it. He handed it back. I set it on the table. End of story. What's your point?"

The detective closed his book. "Here's my difficulty. No one here knew the man. Citrus Grove is a small community."

"Population three thousand," I said. I'd done my research before the event. "No one person could know all the other two-thousand-nine-hundred-and-ninety-nine of his fellow citizens."

"True. But the man shows up at an event that your brother has advertised, it's clear he knows him, he threatens him, and now he's dead. And he dies not long after drinking the lemon-barley water you two brought with you. The lemon-barley water you took the trouble to hand him."

I sat up in my seat. "Now, hold on there. The man was hacking his guts out. It was the polite thing to do, not to mention he was annoying me. He didn't cover his mouth."

Edward's expression changed from one of disdain to one of disbelief, but not on my behalf. "Are you saying he died because he drank my lemon-barley water?"

"I'll leave that for the doctor to say, but we are looking into it. Witnesses said he grimaced shortly after drinking. Unfortunately, one of the volunteers made rounds to gather up empty cups. She rinsed them all out before she tossed them, so I can't have them tested."

"That means nothing," I insisted, spreading my hands. "So, he made a face. Come on. It's lemon-barley water. There's a reason it's not a favorite at parties."

Sykes sighed. "It may taste bad—"

"It's an acquired taste," Edward said. "That doesn't mean it's bad. It also has health benefits. It's good for the digestion. And for your information, Nicholas, plenty of people still consider it a refreshing beverage."

Sykes glared at him. "As I was saying, it may taste bad, but it wouldn't kill a man."

"Are you suggesting—" I had trouble getting the word out.

"I'm not suggesting anything. Not yet. Right now, I'm simply gathering information."

"Wait a minute." I looked to my brother. "Is barley a nut?"

"It's a grain," Edward said absently.

"Grain. Nut. Couldn't the professor be allergic? Maybe he died because no one thought of using an EpiPen."

"We're still talking to witnesses, but his symptoms tonight don't seem to correspond with an allergic reaction."

"Symptoms? Like what?"

Sykes smiled. I was beginning to dread his smile. "I'm reserving that information."

Edward came out of his stupor. "Do you honestly believe I poisoned the lemon-barley water on the chance I might run into my old college professor at a lecture? And how did I get him to drink it?"

"Your brother took care of that."

"To stop his coughing," I said. "Maybe the professor ingested whatever it was, meaning not the lemon-barley water, earlier in the night. Don't some poisons, if it was poison, take time to act?"

Sykes nodded. "Yes, they do. Depending on the poison and the amount the professor ingested. There is one curious thing. The original pitcher of lemon-barley water was knocked off the table while you were standing next to it."

"And I did that to destroy the evidence? Nuts. I gave him a cup poured out of the second pitcher."

"You could have broken the untainted pitcher to make way for the poisoned pitcher." He held up a hand. "These are just ideas until we know what killed him, but I want you to understand why it's so important to track Professor Taylor's movements." The detective raised an eyebrow at Edward. "What made you bring lemon-barley water anyway? It's an odd choice."

"It went with the theme," Edward muttered. "And it was available to everyone who attended tonight. Do you think I'm a madman?"

"Wait a minute." I snapped my fingers. "Did anyone else drink from the second pitcher?"

"That's the reason your brother is not being detained."

"You mean under arrest?" Edward sputtered. "For what? Murder?"

"Calm down. He said you're not under arrest. I'm sure the detective is just being careful and we can go—" I looked a question at the detective. "Are we allowed to go home?"

"For now." He narrowed his eyes at Edward. "Were Professor Taylor's allegations true? Do you write the Aunt Civility books?"

Edward froze. In his world, the truth came in black and white. It wouldn't occur to him to skirt an issue. I didn't have that problem.

"The publisher answers all questions about the series." I shrugged to show I was sorry, pulled my wallet from my inside jacket pocket and dug out a card. "It's in the contract. Here's the number."

I stood. "You know where to find us. C'mon Edward."

For once, my brother listened to me without arguing.

CHAPTER 3

I t isn't often I wish for material things, but tonight I longed for one of those old cars with the sliding panel that separates the chauffeur from his passenger. Though the purpose was to keep the prying ears of employees from hearing something untoward, the silence worked both ways. I was one sliding panel away from peace.

"Look at what you've gotten me into," Edward snarled. "All I want is to write my books and occasionally meet people who can appreciate them. You want me to hawk my books like a hot dog vendor."

"Offering a free hot dog with your books might increase sales."

"My sales are doing fine." He leaned forward and punched the back of my headrest, but I saw it coming in the rearview mirror and didn't flinch. "You lied to me. You said it was a private talk for the Culinary Arts Council."

"They were there."

"And so was Professor Taylor, who I assume was not a member of the council and therefore wouldn't have been there if you hadn't lied."

Squinting into the rearview mirror, I locked onto my brother's hulking shadow. "What's the deal with him, anyway? Why find you after all these years?"

Edward sat back and, from the tone of his voice, I could tell he had a satisfied smirk on his face. "Other than Daniel Pringle, someone I wouldn't expect you to recognize because he's a poet—"

I made a gagging noise.

"Other than Daniel and me, I don't think any of the professor's former students have forged successful careers in English."

"But how could he be sure you were Aunt Civility?"

Edward growled. "Weren't you listening? He recognized my verbose, arrogant style."

I drove in silence for the next few minutes, trying to figure out how to bring up an important point without suffering the backlash, but there wasn't a delicate way to say it.

"Not that I want to be the bearer of bad news, but if they prove something funny happened, you're a murder suspect. Apparently, I'm your accomplice."

"Don't make a crisis where there isn't one."

A metallic click-click sounded from the back seat as Edward toyed with the small passenger lighter from our older model Cadillac.

"You did understand what the detective said, didn't you? That part about letting you go only because he didn't see how you had the opportunity to poison the lemon-barley water? That's before I got rid of the evidence, of course."

Edward refused to talk for the rest of the drive, which suited me fine. After letting him out at the front door and garaging the car, I entered by the connecting door to the kitchen in time to answer the phone. In case it was the police, I used my secretary's voice when I answered. "Harlow residence. Nicholas speaking."

"Hello, Nicholas," a husky female voice said in my ear. "Why so formal? It can't still be business hours."

"Hello, Claudia," I said, still using my professional voice.

"Is Edward available?" she asked, oozing sweetness.

"He'll be available until they arrest him."

Admittedly, it was a snarky and unnecessary comment, but I was ticked that Edward wasn't taking the situation seriously. Before she could respond, my brother walked up to the counter and held his hand out for the receiver.

Edward and Claudia met last January when we visited Inglenook Resort in Northern Illinois, a converted manor owned by Claudia Inglenook and her brother Robert. One of the guests had been murdered. Initially one. The final body count came to three—two guests and an employee. There had almost been a fourth. Me. Apparently, there is nothing like a dead body to bring two lovebirds together. Edward and Claudia Inglenook had been exchanging phone calls ever since our return.

I didn't actively dislike Claudia, but I didn't care for her growing influence on my brother. Before Inglenook, I'd had to put up with his boneheaded, inflexible opinions and ways, but now I had to contend with *Claudia says* and *Claudia thinks*. It wouldn't bother me if Edward formed a relationship with a power-hungry activist because he'd get tired of that routine, but Claudia Inglenook was that dangerous female who wouldn't consider lowering herself to compete with a man. Claudia Inglenook understood that the exercise of femininity—real femininity—was the greatest weapon against the opposite sex, and she knew how to wield it.

"I miss you, too."

The words might sound benign, but the way Edward delivered them, sticky-sweet in his rumbling voice, was enough to make a normal man swear off women. I took an ice cream sandwich from the freezer and escaped to my bedroom.

Edward's Spanish-style house is decorated in neutral colors. The Maple hardwood floors spread throughout the house except for the diamond-shaped terra-cotta tiles in the kitchen and the plush cinnamon-colored carpet in the bedrooms. The furniture, which was wood and mostly Walnut, is thick and heavy, something I can attest to after having had to move a chair. The exceptions are the matching leather recliners that face each other in front of the fireplace and a white couch that provides a startling contrast. The latter is so deep that anyone shorter than my six feet has to struggle to keep his or her shoes on the floor.

My bedroom is decorated the same, since I sold everything including my furniture to pay off investors after my business partner ran off with our funds. He's enjoying a long vacation courtesy of the California State penitentiary. When my world crashed down around my ears, Edward happened to be looking for a secretary. I receive a salary as well as room and board that hardly compensates for my 24-hour on-call status.

I closed the bedroom door behind me and crossed to the sliding glass doors that opened onto a balcony. Outside, I leaned against the railing and looked out at a view that included a sliver of the Pacific Ocean. Not that this was beachfront property. We lived in unincorporated San Diego, a few miles from the water, but the grade of the land allowed us a good view. His house was probably the main reason I lowered myself to take a job as Edward's secretary and dogsbody. Dogsbody sounds much better than servant.

I unwrapped my ice cream and took a bite. It would be inconvenient if Edward were to land in jail, but first, I had to ask the obvious question and look at it with complete honesty. Assuming Sykes was right and the professor had been poisoned, would Edward kill a man to keep his secret safe? No. The only person Edward has ever seriously considered killing was me. That meant one of those Citrus Grove residents, including the members of the Culinary Arts Council, had both known Professor Taylor and disliked him enough to do a very naughty thing.

How did the poison get into the lemon-barley water? Was someone mad enough to poison a pitcher available to the public? Scratch that. Normal people wouldn't be tempted to try barley water, so there wouldn't have been much chance of killing off dozens of innocents. But the killer couldn't count on the professor sampling the beverage. It made more sense if the poison was in his glass. Maybe Sykes was on the right track, and the killer broke the pitcher intentionally so they could replace it with one containing poison. I snorted at the unlikelihood of that happening, because after they doctored the drink, they would have had to find a way to make him cough and then hypnotize me into handing him the right cup.

Who had served him his drink? I had. I was innocent, so someone else had introduced the poison into his glass. I remembered Mrs. Robbins pouring out several servings after replacing the broken pitcher. Were they all poisoned? The killer would have to be a magician to pull a trick like that without being seen, especially with me nearby. My observation skills are top notch.

That led me to wonder who would want him dead? Could one of those efficient kitchen volunteers be holding a grudge against the professor for a previous bad grade? She could have arranged to meet him there, but how did she happen to have poison on her? It wasn't as if stores sold arsenic. People used to soak fly papers to scrounge up a serving for use in murder, but I was pretty sure modern fly paper was simply sticky, not deadly.

Of one thing I was sure. He must have made an appointment to meet someone. Why else would a man who lived and worked in San Diego drive twenty-plus miles to listen to Edward babble at a rinky-dink bookstore? And where had he been between the time he left San Diego and his arrival at the event?

I finished off the sandwich, moved back inside, and dropped the wrapper in the wastebasket. Edward's volume had increased. Since the subject of conversation was most likely private, I cracked open my bedroom door to listen.

"I am not a murder magnet! The man may have died a natural death!"

Edward's silence must have been Claudia's response. She had a lot to say. Two minutes passed before he got in another word.

"We are separated by five states, so you should be safe from me."

When the phone slammed down, my eyebrows rose. Hanging up on a lady wasn't very nice and definitely not polite. I assumed Edward had been the one to abruptly end the conversation by acknowledging a simple rule. Women never willingly give you the last word, and there hadn't been enough time between *his* last word and the slam as the receiver hit the cradle for Claudia to fit in a final remark.

I decided to irritate Edward and walked to the living room but stopped in the doorway and stared. My brother had lost his mind. He sat in one of the recliners clutching a pipe. Little puffs of smoke filled the room with a sickeningly sweet, spicy odor.

"What are you doing?"

He sucked on the stem a few times and then held up his pipe, admiring it.

"I thought I'd take it up. Many of the great writers throughout history relaxed with a well-seasoned pipe. It's a civilized form of recreation."

"Did you just include yourself among the great writers?" I waved a hand under my nose. "It smells like a Turkish brothel in here."

He struck a match and held the flame to the bowl and puffed out a few more clouds of smoke, just to annoy me. I retaliated.

"How's Claudia?"

He choked on his inhale, so he grabbed the pipe by the bowl and punctuated the air with the stem.

"Women." He clicked his tongue against the front of his top teeth spoke in a philosophical tone. "The most unreasonable creatures ever created by God."

I took a seat on the couch and leaned back. This was going to take a while.

"She had the nerve to blame me. Me! As if I invited Professor Taylor to that fiasco and dispatched him as a form of amusement. The rantings of a deranged woman." He narrowed his eyes at me. "If anyone deserves blame, it's—"

"Professor Taylor for being a stinker." I stretched my arms across the back of the couch. "And until we find out who else felt he was a stinker, you're Sykes' number one suspect."

Edward straightened his shoulders. "That's ridiculous."

"Okay. Name me the top three suspects."

He gestured with his hand, pushing the smoke in my direction. "How could I hazard a guess?"

"There was the emcee, Miss Channing, the other members of the Culinary Arts Council, the ladies who helped set up and serve including Mrs. Regina Robbins."

"And Mr. Babbitt."

I cocked my head. "The owner of the Babbitt and Brown bookstore?"

Edward had a point. Jeffrey Babbitt had enthusiastically agreed to hold a lecture and signing revolving around my brother's book, which I found questionable. Maybe his excitement came from creating the opportunity to get rid of a pesky professor. I kept my face neutral to keep from giving Edward credit. His ego didn't need a boost.

"I suppose we could keep Mr. Babbitt in mind. Did you recognize anyone else in the crowd? Any of the audience members?"

"I wasn't looking at them," he snapped. When I raised my eyebrows in a question, he scratched his forehead with the pipe stem. "When I talk, I focus on the back wall. It keeps me from getting distracted."

"Unless you focus on this problem, you're going to wind up in jail."

He pulled on his pipe without producing results. He sucked in again. The insides of his cheeks were in danger of touching from the strain of trying to pull in air. With a growl, he flung his latest toy into the fireplace where it connected with the back wall and shattered.

I arched one brow. "Calm yourself, Edward."

He ran his fingers back and forth through his hair until it stood on end. "I could tell the detective suspected me of hating Professor Taylor, and I'm sure he wouldn't waste his time with us if he believed the cause of death was a stroke or a heart attack. He found the professor's death suspicious. Since he seemed intelligent, I assume he's right. I'm not a fool, but what am I supposed to do?"

"We didn't do a bad job of figuring out that trouble at Inglenook Resort."

"You mean I didn't do a bad job. You were busy flirting with the women and endangering your life. If I hadn't—"

"Yeah, yeah. I've thanked you. It's vulgar to keep bringing it up."

He slid his gaze in my direction. "It is? Yes, I suppose it is. Point taken." He folded his hands over his trim middle. "What do you suggest we do?"

Edward asking my advice? I hid my surprise. "At Inglenook, we didn't know the victim, but we listened and learned enough to get answers."

"We know something about Professor Taylor. He was my English professor, an untalented hack, and an egomaniac."

"That's old news. You haven't seen him in over twenty years. Maybe he's changed."

"Then I suggest we visit our alma mater tomorrow and find out all we can about his current circumstances."

Later that evening, Edward changed his mind. He had tried to call Claudia back to apologize, but her brother Robert had answered the phone instead. When my brother asked to speak to his own sweet love, Robert begged his pardon and explained he must decline to help. When Edward shouted, "What?" I picked up the extension in my bedroom and listened.

"I'm under duress, Edward."

"Just hand her the phone," Edward said in what he thought was his reasonable tone but was in fact just shy of a yell.

"I can't." Robert sounded stressed. "Claudia told me if I didn't hang up on you, she would instruct Mrs. Beckwith to limit my meals to runny scrambled eggs for a week."

Mrs. Beckwith was Inglenook Resort's cook.

"I've risked my stomach by taking the time to explain this to you. I'm sorry, but I've got to go."

"Don't you dare hang up on me."

"I have no choice."

After the click, the dial tone sounded in my ear. When Edward roared into the telephone, I gently replaced the receiver and made my way into the living room.

"What's up?" I asked with innocence.

Edward glared at me. "I suppose you heard that?"

"I heard you. Kind of hard not to when you keep shouting."

He picked up a hardbound copy of *Moby Dick* and settled into his recliner. He held the pose for a few minutes and then banged the book shut and tossed it onto the end table.

"I must get my word count done. You'll have to go to Marston on your own tomorrow."

I shook my head slowly. "Don't disappoint us."

"Who's us?"

"Me and every other red-blooded American man."

"My decision to write will hardly affect the entire male population of the U.S."

"I said American. That includes Canada, Mexico, and South America. We're all disappointed."

"Nonsense. I'm going to work."

"You're going to sulk and wait until your lady love relents and calls you back. Since she's female, that's not going to happen. She'll expect you to beg to speak with her several times before she allows you to grovel. I suggest you come with me tomorrow and let her stew. Show her you're not going to give in every time she gets snippy."

Edward stroked his Van Dyke beard. "It's possible."

"You don't want to set a precedent, Edward, or you'll pay for it the rest of your life."

He crossed his legs and appeared to consider my wisdom, but he needed a push.

"Women don't want spineless men. They just think they do, but once they successfully manipulate you, they lose all respect."

"Hmm. You may have a point."

After he turned in, I disconnected the land line and turned off his cell phone, just in case.

CHAPTER 4

That's how the two of us wound up strolling the pavement at G.W. Marston College the next morning. From now on, I'll refer to it as Marston.

The Arts and Letters building was close to where we parked, but we couldn't just storm in there and interrogate random teachers. Instead, we crossed the campus to the main office to get a starting point. Someone Taylor hung out with. A girlfriend he had on the side. Anything that might lead us to someone with a motive who we could pass on to Sykes.

The landscaping was pleasant without being ostentatious. There were a few trees throughout the campus and flowered borders along the cement walkway. There were also plenty of wooden benches available for those who wanted to take a load off their feet or eat their sack lunch while enjoying the scenery, but apparently the youth preferred grass. They clustered in groups on the vast lawns, some of them standing, others sitting, and a few sprawled out to take a nap. They resembled a herd of wild Homo sapiens enjoying the calm before a predator attack.

They weren't all young. There were older returning

students making their way to class, the occasional gray head sticking out of the crowd, but most of the population on campus were in their late teens and early twenties.

Edward stuck out like a sore thumb. He had dressed in a dark gray suit with a white shirt and a rose paisley print tie—too formal to be mistaken for a teacher or a student.

"So, what are we supposed to do?" I asked, stepping aside to let a blond woman pass me. She was headed in the direction of the Performing Arts Center, I assumed, since she had streaks of brown and green in her hair and wasn't wearing anything but body paint. She was disguised as a forest, I think, or maybe just one overgrown tree. Her plump rear end, painted to look like a bird's nest, bobbled up and down as she walked.

Without losing a step, Edward said, "Was that young woman naked?"

"As a jaybird."

"Whatever happened to modesty?" he demanded.

"It's not on the syllabus. Back to my point, are we supposed to go up to Taylor's fellow teachers and ask them nicely if they'd like to confess to killing him?"

"No. We're going to go to the administration building and we're telling them you are writing a story about him for a newspaper and we would like some facts about his life."

"Why me?"

"Because you look the part of a sleazy news hound."

Edward was miffed that I'd worn jeans today despite his rule I wear a suit when I work with him. I wasn't about to look like a stuffed shirt for my first appearance on campus since graduation. However, since I knew shorthand, I couldn't argue with his plan. When I looked through the glass walls as we approached the entrance and saw the brunette woman behind the reception counter, I embraced my role. I'm partial to brunettes. I pulled out the notebook I carried with me to jot down to-do items and clicked my pen.

"May I help you?" she asked as we walked in.

"I hope so." My gaze roamed over the black pencil skirt that hugged her hips and the gold silk blouse left open at the collar. She had a great collarbone. I gave the college a gold star for their public relations.

Edward nudged me aside. "I'm an editor with the—er —San Diego News, and this is my employee." He gave me a dirty look. "He's on probation."

She looked at me with interest. "Did you say San Diego News? I haven't read that one."

That was because it didn't exist. Edward didn't have the gall to name a real paper.

"It's a small press, though we have a decent circulation. We focus on the personal side of events. We'd like background information on Professor Jonathan Taylor for a piece we're doing regarding his death."

A shutter came down over her eyes as soon as he mentioned newspaper. She lowered her lids to half-mast, which emphasized her long, dark lashes. "I don't think I can help you." Her delivery was clipped but polite. "You need to contact the Media Relations department. Let me get you their direct line."

She reached for her computer keyboard, but Edward held up his hand.

"That won't be necessary. I already have Professor Taylor's basic information, but I wanted to expand it into an article focused on his life. His contributions. The people he touched. Something tasteful, you understand."

She lost her professional edge by snorting. "No one would believe it."

Edward's eyebrows shot up. "Sorry?"

She looked over her shoulder toward the inner office

where a gray-haired woman wearing a bulky cardigan sat at a desk and flipped through a stack of papers. Satisfied she wouldn't be overheard, she rested her forearms on the counter and lowered her voice. "Professor Taylor and taste aren't—weren't—usually found in the same sentence." She pointed at Edward with her pencil. "Unless you meant bad taste."

"Could you explain yourself?"

"I'm not sure I should say—I mean, it's not exactly private information, he had a certain reputation and, well, everyone knew what he was like, but it wouldn't be nice especially now he's dead."

Edward lowered his voice to match hers and it came out a soft rumble. "Was he unethical? Immoral? Was he a cad?"

"A cad?" She bit her lip as if trying to hold back a laugh. "I suppose so. Yes. He wasn't a nice man." Her eyes opened wide. "But don't quote me on that."

Edward sighed. "I'm not surprised he wasn't well-liked. He wasn't a pleasant man when I studied under him."

One finely plucked eyebrow went up. "You're an alumnus?"

"Many years ago." He gave a self-depreciating chuckle. "Long before your time, young lady."

She blushed with pleasure and giggled. He was laying it on pretty thick. I would have put her in her late twenties. Old enough to see through his tactics.

Her chocolate-brown eyes made a slow survey of my brother, as if she hadn't given him proper notice before. She liked what she saw—the tall, muscular form of a former college linebacker that no suit could hide, not even the very expensive and finely tailored suit he wore; the penetrating gray eyes; the short, black hair struggling not to curl and the trim Van Dyke beard. It must have been the suit because I'm almost as tall, have the same gray eyes and dark hair sans beard, and I was a running back, yet she ignored me.

After another glance toward the back room, she leaned forward, making it a cozy, confidential conversation.

"It's not just the staff and students who didn't like him. Supposedly, his wife left him years ago after he got involved with a student. Or maybe it was several students."

"Really?" he said, slapping one large paw on the counter so his thumb brushed the skin of her forearm. I suspect he thought it was a flirtatious move, but it looked more as if his intent was to extinguish the life of a large spider.

"So, he betrayed his marriage vows and took advantage of the naïveté and generous nature of a young woman. Deplorable. Definitely a cad."

"I like the way you say that. Cad. Makes it sound…naughty."

They shared a chuckle.

"Save it for the movie," I snapped, getting bored. "Look, sister, did anyone on the staff know him better than most?"

She straightened up and lost the friendly expression. I might have been too abrupt, so before Edward could chastise me, I said, "I apologize." I glared at Edward. "I'm nervous about my probation. This story is my last shot at proving myself. I'd appreciate any help you can give me."

While she didn't cozy up to me like she did to Edward, she decided not to hold a grudge. She tapped the tip of her pencil against her straight, white teeth. "Does it have to be someone who liked him?"

When I told her it would give us a more objective background if the person weren't best friends with Professor Taylor, she directed us to the English Department.

"You could ask around there. Since that's where his classes were held, someone should be able to help you. As for a particular name…" She looked sideways and squinted, as if she were going over a list of names in her head. "Maybe Professor Kanchalian. He's at the end of the first hall to your left. I've seen the two of them talking out in the parking lot, so they might be friends."

We exited the office, and after a lecture from Edward on controlling my tongue, we headed back across the campus to the Arts and Letters building. When I caught him checking his watch, I asked if he had an appointment.

"I have work to do."

"Sure, you do," I agreed with complete understanding. "You're a busy guy. It helps to set priorities. Only, I would think staying out of jail trumps making up with your girlfriend."

"You're wrong. I haven't thought about Claudia once this morning."

"Not once?"

"No. You and I are out to discover if Professor Taylor had enemies. I was just thinking we might be wasting our time, since I'm sure Detective Sykes is following the same line."

"You mean time better spent mooning away at home on the chance your girlfriend will call. Say you're right and Detective Sykes has already visited this campus. We have one advantage he doesn't have."

"And what would that be?"

"We know you're innocent."

After delivering my zinger, I opened the door and let Edward into the Arts and Letters building. We walked right into a wall of students trying to escape. Or maybe they were late for class. Since I had been a student once, I doubted they were committing that much energy to getting to class, so I went with the escape theory. This was confirmed when we found a tall, middle-aged man in a brown sports jacket—a few years older than us—in the second to last classroom. He stood at the front of a room filled with empty chairs and was packing his books into a briefcase.

"Pardon us," Edward said.

The man looked up with intelligent brown eyes shielded by rimless glasses. When he realized we weren't students, he frowned. "Can I help you?"

"I hope so," Edward said, stepping into the room. "Professor Kanchalian?"

"That's me. Ken Kanchalian."

"Excellent. Just the man we were looking for. Were you acquainted with the late Professor Taylor?"

Either the man had a sudden attack of indigestion, or he knew the least-liked teacher on campus. His face muscles seized up along with his shoulders, and his glasses slipped down his nose. He pushed them back in place before answering.

"Why?"

"We would like to ask you a few questions."

"Why?" he repeated.

"For background information. For an obituary."

His facial muscles relaxed, and he adjusted his glasses, this time from habit. "Oh. Of course. But shouldn't you be speaking with his family members?"

I grinned. "You mean the wife that left him after he messed around with a student?"

"Yes. I see what you mean. She might not be amenable to talking about him. I don't think I can offer you any information that would help. I don't know where or when he was born or what he did outside of class."

"What was he like?" Edward asked. "I'm sure you formed an opinion of him. That's as good a place to start as any."

The indigestion was back.

"I don't think it's my place to talk about another member

of the staff. Why don't you ask in personnel? After his untimely death, they probably have a biography ready for the press."

"Which will not give us anything except a list of facts." Edward gestured to a chair. When Kanchalian nodded, reluctantly, he took a seat. "We'd like something more personal. The real Professor Taylor as told by the people who knew him best. His colleagues. His friends."

Kanchalian held out his hand, palm upturned. "Look. Can I be honest with you? Off the record?"

Edward stroked his beard and made a show of considering the request and then nodded yes.

"I'm not the best person to ask. I thought Taylor was a horse's ass."

Edward feigned surprise. "I see. Did you base your feelings on anything in particular?"

"This is still off the record, right? He had a swelled head with little to back it up, the morals of a Tom-cat, and lacked basic manners." Kanchalian let out a breath as if he had been dying to shout out those exact words for years.

"Sounds as if it's not a surprise someone murdered him," I said.

Kanchalian eased back from me. "You never think a person, even an unlikable person, will really get killed."

"Even if you didn't like him, it sounds as if you knew the man well," Edward said.

"Not really." The teacher motioned toward the hallway. "His classroom is next door. I couldn't help but run into him. And he didn't have an *inside voice*, always speaking in that same, booming tone, so I couldn't help but overhear conversations."

I was all for Taylor being a pain in someone's side— someone other than Edward—but we needed examples that would give the police somewhere else to look for the murderer. "You said he was unlikeable. Did he neglect to say please and thank you or was he an actual menace?"

"I don't know about menace, but he was pathologically inconsiderate." Like a good teacher, he gave us examples. "Our parking spaces have our names on them, but on several occasions, I arrived at work to find his car parked in my space. I had to track him down and ask him to remove his vehicle. I think he took pleasure from making me ask." His hands balled up into fists. "Dammit! It was my space." He took a deep breath and apologized.

Edward nodded. "Your frustration is understandable. Did he focus his harassment on you? Or were there other victims?"

"He—he behaved lewdly with some of the more attractive female students. I know we're all supposed to be sexually liberated, whatever the hell that means, but it was not appropriate behavior for a teacher."

Edward let out a low growl. "Were there complaints?"

Kanchalian frowned. "Women are a mystery. There are lots of nice boys in my class. Respectful. Funny. Smart. Yet some female students preferred to go out with Taylor, who could have been their father, or even their grandfather." He sighed. "*Fifty Shades of Gray* is starting to make sense."

"Fifty what?" Edward demanded. I should mention he considers Dorothy Sayers contemporary reading.

"It's a book, Edward. A—"

As up to date as I am, I couldn't bring myself to call it a romance. "The gist is women find it exciting to be physically and mentally dominated and abused."

He stared. "That's absurd."

I knew exactly what he meant. We were raised by the same mother. I shrugged my shoulders. "Or at least they like to read about it. The book is a bestseller."

He sent a sharp glance toward Kanchalian, who also shrugged. Another low growl started at the back of Edward's throat. "The cad."

The English professor broke into a smile. "Cad. I like it. Good word choice."

"Thank you."

"Does he have a, um, relationship with any particular student right now?"

Kanchalian shrugged. "I wouldn't know. I think you could better describe his experiences with students as one-night stands. I don't think he stuck with anyone long enough to call it a relationship."

We were getting too focused on one aspect of Taylor. "What about outside his love life?"

Since Professor Kanchalian now believed Edward's ridiculous assurance that everything he said was off the record, or possibly because he found it impossible to feel threatened by a man who used the word cad, he rested his rump on the edge of the closest desk and became gossipy.

"Taylor couldn't stand it if any of his students stood out. Maybe had an article published. What kind of attitude is that for an educator? He'd tell me he would take them down a notch, and the next thing, some straight-A student would be stuck taking makeup exams over summer."

"That's unethical."

"He always had some excuse to back up his decision." He lowered his voice. "There were rumors he sabotaged one student who had a promising career ahead of him."

"Do you have a name?" I asked. Finally, we had a lead.

"Sorry. It was a long time ago, but it's an example of the kind of thing he would do."

"Too bad," I said, prompting the man to protest. "What I mean is the former student probably would have gotten revenge by now. We need something more recent. Were there any other rumors?" I asked, hopeful.

"Other than his wife assaulted him with an iron when she found out about his liaisons, no. Nothing specific. And that was over ten years ago."

I gave a mental salute of respect to Mrs. Taylor. "A tire iron?"

He shook his head. "Clothing."

Edward cleared his throat. "You based much of what you said on hearsay or rumor. Other than the parking space incident, though I agree that would annoy one, is there anything else you know about him through personal experience?"

Ken folded his arms across his chest. "I teach Popular Fiction." He waited for a reaction, so I gave him one.

"That's nice."

Apparently, I passed, because he went on.

"Taylor said the subject didn't belong on a college campus, and he made his feelings known to the board. I, of course, disagree. Students who take my class should get a psychology credit, too. Popular fiction is an important reflection of a society's values. I mentioned the way women seem to enjoy being dominated, or at least treated poorly, a la *Fifty Shades*. Or they at least enjoy fantasizing about it. Then there is what I call the Harry Potter syndrome. A nod to the entitlement age. People want to have things without working for them. Just wave a wand and say a few words and presto."

From the way he frowned, I guessed he was thinking about some of his students.

Edward rested his hands on his thighs and exhaled. "Everything you've said makes Professor Taylor sound like a horror. It's too one-sided. The man couldn't be all bad. Was there anything to recommend him?"

Kanchalian thought about it. "He's dead."

"At Babbitt and Brown Bookstore," I murmured. "Thirty-seven miles door-to-door. That's not another country, but it's not local. No one would just stumble across the event on their way to pick up their takeout." A point struck me. "Would anyone here have known he would be at the Citrus Grove event?"

Professor Popular Fiction gave a loud snort. "It was probably on his Facebook page."

Edward gave an even louder snort. "I told you social media was a menace."

I ignored him. "Did the professor have a lot of friends?" For Edward's benefit, I added, "Facebook friends."

"Hundreds."

My surprise must have made it to my face because he explained.

"Many of his students followed him. They did so to make fun of him." His face turned red. "Not that I followed him myself or took part in anything so juvenile. I've overheard them laughing about him between classes."

Edward was so disgusted that, once he had thanked the professor for his time, he headed straight for the parking lot and stood next to the car while I fished the keys out of my pocket.

"If we were looking for an enemy," I said, keeping my tone optimistic, "Professor Kanchalian fits the bill."

"Seducing students. Sabotaging careers. Stealing parking spaces. Remind me again why we're searching for his killer?"

"To keep you from being arrested."

"Bah!"

Yes, Edward said bah, right before he got in the car and slammed his door. I followed suit, but like an adult. Calm.

"I don't think Sykes will let it go, Edward. He sounded like a detective who is certain a murder had been committed."

"Nonsense. That's what he's supposed to sound like. I'm

sure they will—er—test Professor Taylor and discover he had a heart condition. This is the end of our investigation."

My instincts told me Edward was wrong, but he's the boss.

CHAPTER 5

I 'd like to say the next eight days were free from any thoughts of murder, but that wasn't the case. Edward had a few talks lined up, and they went without a hitch. We even sold a few dozen books. But every time one of Edward's lectures wrapped up and the guests were invited to graze at the dessert table, my brother would pale and find something to do in the farthest corner of the room. Offering him a cherry tart or a glass of lemonade would bring on claims of allergies or indigestion.

This afternoon's event took place at a home and garden show. He managed to insult the organizer who had innocently—and proudly—offered him a taste of her prize-winning rhubarb crunch. We wouldn't be invited back.

As we arrived home, Mrs. Abernathy met us inside the connecting door that led from the garage to the kitchen. Edward's housekeeper and cook stood around five-feet-five, had smooth gray hair she wore in a bun, and always wore a skirt and cardigan in neutral colors to work. Her clothing labels were from quality stores, and since I wrote out the check for her salary, I knew she could afford them.

"Any messages for me?" Edward said even as she held them out with a tolerant smile. Since he flipped through them with a sour expression, I knew there weren't any from Claudia, which meant I had to listen to Edward slam drawers and stomp around the house until we were called to lunch.

We ate our meals at a glass table in a nook just past the kitchen next to a wall of windows that looked out over a ravine. Though Edward blew into the room in a huff, once he took his seat at the table, he became a pussycat. That's because Mrs. Abernathy was worth her weight in Amazon stock.

"Did you boys have a good morning?" she asked as she set a plate in front of each of us, her face softly wrinkling into a smile. She always addressed us as "you boys."

Edward picked up a thick ham sandwich on homemade bread and paused before taking a bite. "Yes, ma'am. We couldn't have asked for finer weather." Before he took a bite, he asked again. "Did anyone call and not leave a message?"

She tilted her head and gave him an admonishing yet not unkind look. "You know I would have told you. Maybe not the first time you asked, but certainly by the third time."

"Of course. I didn't mean to imply—"

"Are you having words with Miss Claudia?"

While Edward made a choking sound, I held back a laugh. Mrs. Abernathy chuckled.

"It wasn't hard to figure out. I haven't answered a call from her in over a week." She gave a sweet sigh. "Young love." And shaking her head as she walked away, she added, "Turns the brightest people into morons."

"Did she just call you young?" I snickered. When he chomped away at his sandwich rather than reply, I added, "I'm *certain* she just called you a moron."

He set his sandwich on his plate and sighed like a depressed bear. "Maybe I should call her."

I gaped. "And do what? Apologize?"

He stuck out his jaw. "It would be the manly thing to do."

"Yeah. Sure. For what exactly are you apologizing?"

"For getting involved in another mess. Although it appears I was right and Detective Sykes is no longer interested in us."

Don't get me wrong. I enjoy seeing Edward eat dirt occasionally. It keeps him tolerable. However, I don't like to see him emotionally bullied by anyone but me.

"Could you explain how you caused the mess? Did you kill Professor Taylor?"

"Don't be ridiculous."

"Did you text his killer and let him know the professor would be at the bookstore?"

"I didn't know he would be there."

"Do you even know how to text?"

"Don't be an ass."

Leaning back in my chair, I clasped my hands behind my head and proceeded to dole out advice. "Your girlfriend has accused you of something ridiculous."

"It was an unfounded accusation," he agreed.

"That's putting it mildly. She's holding you responsible for acts outside of your control. Now she wants to rub your nose in it." I shook my head sadly. "I think that's pretty low."

After thinking about it for ten seconds, he picked his sandwich back up, tore off a bite with his teeth and put Claudia on the back burner where she belonged.

It was seven o'clock that evening, hours after Mrs. Abernathy had gone home for the day, when the doorbell rang. I pulled open the front door, and Detective Sykes filled the frame.

"May I come in?"

I didn't think slamming the door and screaming Run,

Edward! was an option, so I held the door open and invited him inside.

"Is this a social visit?" I asked.

He smiled. "I'd like to speak with your brother, please."

Now I had a dilemma. Was a policeman a guest and entitled to be invited to take a seat on the couch in the living room? Or was he more of a tradesman, someone who should cool his heels in the foyer?

I asked him to remain where he was while I looked for Edward and I found my brother in his office staring at a blank computer screen.

"Detective Sykes stopped by to say hello."

He continued staring for a moment and then roused himself and stood.

"I left him in the foyer. You could make it out the back door and he wouldn't suspect a thing until he heard the car start."

"Invite him into the living room. Never mind. I'll do that. You make coffee and see if we have any of Mrs. Abernathy's cream cakes left."

I nodded. "You're going to off him by poisoning the cream cakes. Good plan, though you might want to consider changing methods if you don't want to go to the electric chair."

Since a low growl had started at the back of Edward's throat, I skedaddled into the kitchen to prepare the goodies. By the time I made it to the living room, Edward and the detective were both seated on the couch, although they didn't look cozy. I arrived just in time to hear Sykes say in his baritone:

"You're making this more difficult than it needs to be."

I set the serving tray down on the coffee table.

"That's my brother's specialty. What's the problem?"

Sykes, with the willful focus of a pointer, held Edward with his gaze. "Do you or do you not write the Aunt Civility books?"

On the outside, Edward's jaw was set, his posture straight, and his gaze steady. Inside, I knew he was quailing at the thought of not answering a direct question with complete honesty. He hadn't thought of answering a question with a question, so I did.

"Did you contact Classical Reads?"

Sykes finally honored me with his attention. "I did."

"And what did they say?"

"That I need a warrant if I want the information, which I am ready to do if I don't get a straight answer from your brother. Or from you."

Edward, more relaxed now that Classical Reads had his back, served the coffee. "We will have to defer to the publisher. After all, I depend upon them for my living, as does Nicholas." He nodded in my direction and I caught the veiled threat.

The detective surprised us both when he leaned back in the deep, white couch and put on a pleasant smile. "Perhaps you don't understand how serious your position is. Let me share something with you."

He pressed a few buttons on his cell phone and then held it out. I was closest, so I took it from him and glanced at the screen.

A smiling Professor Taylor stared back at me. It was a post on his Facebook page dated the day he died. I held the phone out for Edward to see.

"It appears to be one of those social media sites. I don't go in for that myself."

"That's funny. You have a page of your own for the Aunt Civility books."

55

I raised my hand. "That would be my doing."

Edward glared at me. "Remind me to thank you later."

"If you would spend five minutes learning how to promote yourself—"

"I do several appearances a month."

"But not *public* appearances. There are a limited number of people in those societies you like so well. Eventually, they're going to die of old age. Half of them are in rigor mortis now. Who will buy your books then if you don't have a following?"

Sykes held up a hand. "Enough. Please."

It was the please that made Edward shut up. He responds well to good manners.

The detective gestured at me. "Would you care to read it out loud?"

Having scanned the post, I did not care to read it out loud, but I didn't have a choice. I cleared my throat twice.

"Groupies, you have a chance to hang with me outside of class this Tue. night at the Babbitt and Brown Bookstore, Citrus Grove. It's at 7. That's p.m. for you late risers. (HA!) I plan to—"

My voice cracked, so I cleared my throat again before I continued.

"I plan to drop a bomb. I've recently uncovered a—do I call it a charade? No. That's too nice a word. It's a LIE. A FALSITY, and I won't allow it to continue. Be there to watch me ruffle some feathers. BIGTIME!

Sykes held out a hand, and I loosened my grip a finger at a time and returned the phone.

"Sounds like he intended to call you out in public," Sykes said after he tucked the phone back into his pocket.

Edward sat ramrod straight. "Not necessarily."

"Do you have another interpretation?"

He pointed the finger of shame at Sykes, or rather at the

phone, which showed he was panicked, since he normally reserves that finger for me. "That poorly written, egotistical...the man didn't explain in detail. He could have meant anything."

Sykes nodded. "It's possible. However, you must admit it sounds as if Professor Taylor was talking about you. Then, he approached you at the event and threatened to reveal your secret, which seems to confirm it."

I hurried to cut off Edward before he could make it worse. "Seems. That's all you have. We think the professor was talking about someone else, though we don't know who. But we don't have to know. You do. As for his stunt with Edward, maybe the professor was just that kind of guy. Someone who looked for opportunities to throw mud just to see if it stuck. Well, he was wasting his time with Edward. Now, if he had called Classical Reads and made the threat to them, then you might have a suspect, if a company can be a suspect. They're the ones with a vested interest in the series. And why are we talking about suspects, anyway? You still don't know what killed the man, but you're treating my brother as if he were a criminal. Taylor probably had a bad ticker and it caught up with him. Or maybe he liked fried food and had a stroke, or he inherited an aneurysm from his grandma."

Often, when I'm dealing with Edward, I'll blather on, annoying him until he gets exasperated and blurts out valuable information. I admit that wasn't my intention with Sykes, but it worked, only his information wasn't something I wanted to hear.

"The pathologist ordered a toxicology report."

Edward rubbed his knuckles against his beard.

"Then he—"

"She," Sykes corrected.

"She has definite suspicions."

"She doesn't order tests for the fun of it," Sykes agreed. He pulled his notebook from his jacket pocket, opened it, and set it on his knee. "In fact, we got the results. The cause of Jonathan Taylor's collapse and subsequent death was—" he peered down at the notebook, "—*Nerium Oleander.*"

The detective had succeeded in stunning Edward, though that didn't mean my brother was speechless. "A Jericho Rose?"

"Indeed." Sykes said it just like my brother would, with the silky purr of a big cat who had found something interesting to play with. "The pathologist recognized the symptoms from a mild case of poisoning she'd seen last year. She has a good memory."

I showed them both my hands. "I've got brown thumbs, so you're going to have to explain it to me. Are you saying he was killed by a flower? Hold on." I slumped back in my chair. "That means it wasn't murder."

No matter how much my brother protested later when I confronted him about his big mouth, I'm positive he spoke up in order to show off.

"Any part of the plant would have killed him. It's highly toxic. All one would need to do would be to introduce it into something the professor ate or drank." Edward crossed his arms. "Maybe boil the leaves in some hot water and introduce it into a beverage. I'm not sure if the taste is bitter, but a little sugar might cover that. In fact, I don't see any difference between killing a man with oleander or killing him with arsenic other than the logistics of obtaining the poison of choice."

Sykes listened with an expressionless face, so I couldn't gage how he was taking Edward's words.

"Where would you find this Jericho Rose?" I raised my brows. "Since it's so poisonous, I don't imagine it's easy to get hold of."

Sykes took over my education. "It's a decorative shrub found all over Southern California."

Edward leaned his head back. "There weren't any floral decorations at the event, nor were any salads served, so there isn't a chance the leaves were mixed in accidentally. I've heard of people innocently serving poisonous greens and mushrooms to unsuspecting guests. Maybe he had dinner with an adventurous cook before the event."

The detective nodded as if Edward had confirmed his own thoughts. "We can't trace where he was between five o'clock when he left the college and a quarter to seven, when he arrived at Babbitt and Brown's. As you know he broadcast on social media that he was coming to the event. He even talked about the evening with his colleagues over lunch. They said he didn't mention any other engagement. But I do agree with you, Mr. Harlow, as far as the method, especially the part about adding it to someone's food or drink. I do not think Jonathan Taylor accidentally ate a poisonous plant."

Edward's face turned red. "I was simply offering theories."

I clasped my hands on my knee because I noticed I'd been swinging my foot in a nervous tempo. "So, you tested the leftover lemon-barley water. Did you find anything?"

"No," Sykes answered pleasantly. "But it could have been in the first pitcher, the one that conveniently broke while you were standing next to it."

The detective stood. "Now do you understand how serious it is?"

Before Sykes left, he asked for a tour of our backyard. I switched on the outdoor lights and showed him our landscaping, but the only roses we had were *floribunda*.

"Well, that was fun," I said when I returned from locking up after the detective.

Edward was stroking his chin. He paused and looked up. "How would you like a vacation?"

I nodded. "I'll get the bags packed. Are we just crossing the border, or will we become residents of Mexico and let the courts fight for extradition?"

"We're headed to Citrus Grove."

Didn't sound like much of a vacation to me.

CHAPTER 6

"**Y**ou've come back?"

It wasn't the most welcoming of greetings, said as it was with a marked incredulity and none of the *warm, family feeling* promised by the cross-stitched sign behind the front desk of Robbins' B&B. Yes, Mrs. Regina Robbins, the woman who supervised the snack tables at Edward's failed book event, ran her own bed-and-breakfast. And the front desk was just that. A desk. Don't get me wrong. It was a nice desk made of a syrup-brown wood that curled in spirals at the feet, but the informal setup reminded me of my grandma's house rather than a professional establishment. I wondered if the living room furniture would be covered in plastic.

"We couldn't resist," Edward said in a voice I've heard women refer to as suave. Those would be repressed women fascinated by gems such as creative ways to fold their napkins for company. "Once I saw your charming establishment on the Internet, I told Nicholas we must visit Citrus Grove in pleasanter circumstances. Didn't I, Nicholas?"

"Why?"

From the way she was looking up at him from her chair behind the desk, staring at him through narrowed eyes, it was clear Regina Robbins didn't give a damn about her napkins.

Unused to such abruptness from a person Edward would have called a lady, he made a blustering noise. "We didn't see your city in its most favorable light."

She wasn't biting.

He raised his eyebrows. "Because of the, er, tragedy."

"You mean your lecture?"

I barked out a laugh, but at Edward's glare, I cleared my throat and said, "The murder of Professor Taylor."

"Oh. That." She touched a finger to her bottom lip. "I lost one of my favorite pitchers that night. It broke."

The lady had her priorities. Then it occurred to me this was the perfect opportunity to find out what happened to the first pitcher of barley water.

"What happened?" I asked.

She transferred her attention to me. "Someone bumped the table. I didn't see who. People were crowding around and pushing to get at the baked goods. Why?"

Her attachment to the word why was reminding me of a four-year-old.

Edward used his soothing voice. "We just wondered because you would have been in an excellent position to see if anyone tampered with the replacement pitcher."

"Tampered with it? What are you hinting at? The man had a heart attack. Or maybe it was a stroke. The only reason the police showed up was because of the circumstances. It happening in a public place."

Sykes must have been keeping the poisoning quiet. After I exchanged a glance with Edward, he proceeded with caution.

"The police have to look into every possibility when a man in his prime of life dies suddenly and unexpectedly."

"He looked past his prime to me. Anyway, if anyone did any fiddling, it was after I set the pitcher out."

"Of course," Edward repeated. "Did you know the professor well?"

"Why would I? And why so many questions?"

She was on to us, and Edward didn't have the subtlety to divert her attention. Taking over, I leaned my hands on the desk and looked down on her with a self-conscious grin.

"Edward is just making small talk to cover our real purpose. There was someone we met during our brief visit. Someone I wanted to get to know better. My brother came along to chaperon."

"Who?"

I thought of the first and only young female I could remember.

"Hattie Channing."

At least I thought she was young. It was hard to tell behind the pink polyester suit and horned-rimmed glasses. When Regina Robbins' eyebrows shot up, I feared my estimate of Miss Channing's age had been off by a decade or two, but the proprietress of Robbins' B&B broke into a warm smile. She slid the registration book over and murmured something about arranging a luncheon so Miss Channing and I could get acquainted.

I didn't want to get backed into a corner, so I said, "I'd rather feel her out first."

"Excuse me?" She pulled back the book as Edward was signing and he left a long scrawl down the page.

"You know. Test the waters. Chat with her first to find out if she's interested."

She tittered, shook her head, and returned the book. "I'm afraid I'm not up to date with the slang. I thought you meant —" When she blushed, I knew just what she meant.

63

I held up my hands, showing her they were innocent. "No, no, no. Not what I meant. At all."

I shuddered at the thought of getting physical with the repressed Miss Channing, though Mrs. Robbins took my response as an aversion to seducing youngish maidens and nodded several times with approval.

When Edward handed back the registration along with his credit card, Mrs. Robbins explained the rules as the charges went through.

"No company, smoking or alcohol in the rooms. I lock the front door at eleven, so if you'll be out later than that, let me know and I'll give you a key. I don't see why you'd be out late though, since hardly anything stays open past ten. Would you like meals?"

Edward replied we would. Once he signed the receipt, she scampered to the kitchen to make sure she had enough dinner for two more mouths. As soon as she disappeared behind the swinging door that led out of the room, I grabbed my brother's arm.

"You got us separate rooms, right?"

Last winter at Inglenook Resort, we had been forced to share a room. During our stay, Edward had complained about the shortage of towels, set his alarm for six a.m. every morning and taken advantage of our proximity to start me working before breakfast. I wasn't strong enough to go through that again.

"Naturally." He handed me my key and headed for the stairway, leaving me with the luggage.

The bed-and-breakfast was an old house. Citrus Grove had been incorporated in the early seventies, so most of the homes we had seen from the road were ranches. Single-story and boring. Mrs. Robbins had managed to snag an old farm-house that dated back to the days of chicken farms and orange groves. The wood floors creaked under a thin carpeting with a faded print, and on the walls, spots of lime green paint peeked out from behind a more recent layer of peach.

My room was eight-by-eight with a narrow closet, a child's dresser, and a single bed. A circular area rug braided from fabric strips covered most of the wooden floor and matched the pink-and-green paisley print wallpaper. Through the window, I could see the neighbor's lilac bushes and the edge of the B&B's garage. Mrs. Robbins had informed us there wasn't room in it for us to park, so I had to leave the Caddy on the street.

I set my suitcase on the bed and unpacked. Edward hadn't told me how long he planned to stay here, so I'd brought one brown suit in addition to the navy-blue suit I was wearing, two dress shirts, a pair of jeans, slacks, and a few casual shirts. Once I got them hung up, I took an assortment of sweatpants, sweatshirts, t-shirts, and personal items to the dresser. The paint had worn around the knobs from use, and there were only three small drawers, but I made it all fit.

After placing my suitcase on the floor under a cross-stitched wall hanging of a cat, I evaluated the sleeping arrangements. The single bed, covered in a quilt composed of fabric scraps, sagged in the middle, but everything looked clean. That's all I cared about.

I carried Edward's luggage across the hall, knocked, and got the okay to enter. His room was the same size as mine, as was his bed, which was bearing his weight under protest as he sat on the edge, though his paisley-print wallpaper consisted of blues and greens. He glanced up at me with his eyebrows joined in one dark line.

"I can't sleep on this bed. My feet will hang over the edge."

"Not if you curl up."

"I have to sleep on my back." As his gaze wandered the

room, he blinked. Or maybe it was a twitch. "Where's the bathroom?"

"I'm sure it's a communal bathroom."

He frowned. "You mean we have to share? With strangers?"

"You managed just fine in the college dorms, where it wasn't unusual for someone to use the shower as a toilet or vomit in the sink. I doubt if any of our fellow guests will ever be that drunk, so it should be a step up." And then, because I didn't want to listen to him whine, I said, "I'll go check out how many strangers there are."

Unable to hide my disgust, I left him and patrolled the short hallway. In the years since his Aunt Civility books had taken off, my brother had spent too many nights in first-rate accommodations. There was a time when he would have flopped down on the bed without a care for comfort, but he had turned into a snob. It would serve him right if a rat gnawed on his toes while he slept.

Every step brought creaks and pops from the old wooden floor. There were two more bedrooms on this level, but when I leaned in and put my ear against each door in turn, I didn't hear movement. Of course, it was the middle of the day and the guests might have been out enjoying the mild weather.

The hallway ended in a large sitting room with a love seat and an armchair. There was a bathroom on one side and glass double doors covered on the inside by curtains directly across the room. The bookshelf against the wall to the left was more for holding knick-knacks than books, like the vase of fake, orange flowers, although there were a few paperbacks on the bottom shelf. A striped area rug in neutral colors covered most of the floor.

The bathroom had a claw-footed tub large enough to

hold Edward. There was a sink and a toilet and nothing else. When I described it to Edward, he refused to believe me.

"You're mistaken. There must be a shower."

"I'd hardly miss an entire shower. Besides, it's a nice, old-fashioned bathtub. You'll love it."

He stood. "I need to breathe. Let's go check out downtown. Then, after dinner, we can get some work done."

I knew the latter was coming, since he had insisted I pack his laptop.

Before we made it out the front door, Mrs. Robbins suggested we stop by the Happy Chicken Cafe so I could introduce myself to Hattie Channing.

CHAPTER 7

W hen I suggested we change out of our suits and into casual clothes before we left, Edward balked. After all, I pointed out, this was a vacation. If we ran into any suspects, we didn't want to come across as stodgy or intimidating. He replied that, although he didn't agree with my assessment, if our style of clothing happened to intimidate people into answering our questions, it would be a good thing. To make him pay, I bypassed the car and said I needed to stretch my legs.

As we passed the neighbor to the left of the house, a dog barked. Across a patchy lawn, seated on a set of rickety wooden steps in need of new paint, an overweight Labrador with a brown coat had his butt on the bottom step and his front legs on the cement walkway. He didn't seem inclined to chase us.

His laid-back attitude reflected the tone of the neighborhood. Nobody had a fence, and I could see into backyards that had clotheslines, picnic tables, and vegetable gardens. Most of the front porches had swings to encourage friendly chats with the neighbors. Even though we didn t run into anyone, I had a prickly feeling we were being watched as we made our way down Lemon Lane.

After a brisk five-minute walk, we knew we had reached the edge of downtown Citrus Grove because a small metal sign told us so in bright, orange letters. I probably would have missed it except Edward grabbed hold of the pole for balance as he removed a pebble from his shoe.

"Well, genius," I said. "What now?"

He leered at me. "If you're going to court Miss Channing, you should meet her first."

"I have no intention of giving the poor woman false hopes. It would be cruel."

Since Edward disapproves of cruelty, that shut him up.

The street we were on, Lemon Lane, seemed to be the main thoroughfare through a business district that stretched out for six blocks, maximum. The original lane— I imagine it started out as a dirt road separating the orange groves—had been widened into a two-lane street with angled parking in front of the businesses.

Since it was late morning, the sidewalks were fairly crowded with residents going about their routines and a few people who, from their down-turned mouths, looked like disappointed tourists who had missed the exit for Knotts Berry Farm.

I grinned at Edward. "We could skip down the lane, stop everyone we meet, and ask them if they knew Professor Taylor."

Edward dislodged the stone, flicked it onto the ground, and straightened his sock. "We'd almost have to. There isn't a hope either of us could recognize anyone from the audience other than the council members. I was focused on my lecture, and you were catching up on your beauty sleep." He stood, hands on hips, and studied the landscape. "We should begin with the known factors, and maybe they'll have leads we can follow up on."

"The council members. Okay. Where do we find them?"

"The old women are probably home during the day."

"You mean Dora and Flora."

"And the one with the knitting bag. The General is retired military, and I don't suppose Ted—"

"Ned. His name is Ned."

"Right. They all looked like retirees to me. Perhaps Jeffrey Babbitt would give us their home addresses."

"That leaves Hattie Channing and Mort."

Edward stroked his chin. "That Morton fellow was a businessman."

"A banker."

We both turned our heads and looked down the street. Even though it was across the street and two blocks away, I spotted it first.

"Home Field Credit Union."

Edward led the way. Since he thought he was in charge, I decided to let him do the talking. He didn't have any authority except that implied by his physical presence and attitude. No one had to answer his questions. I knew I wouldn't.

We passed Mimi's Boutique, which boasted an assort-ment of citrus-themed doodads in the shop window. I shook my head. "Does anyone but us even know Citrus Grove exists? I can't see tourists flocking here to see the last resting place of the oranges, and I don't think the locals need to be reminded of where they live with lemon charms on their key chains."

"Don't be so quick to knock them. These people are proud of their history, and they have reason. At one time,

Citrus Grove produced a sizable portion of the state's lemons and oranges. We weren't always bringing fruit in from other countries. People had to wait for the appropriate season to eat grapes, or oranges, or lemons, and they appreciated them when they got them."

"You're preaching to the kid who grew up in the same house with you." Apart from Edward's long-winded and annoying lecture, I'm an admirer of civic pride, so I adjusted my attitude and tried to view my surroundings through the eyes of the town's citizens. Funny, but I hadn't noticed all the little nods to their culture. The lettering in the window of Brisbey Accounting Services had a tiny orange dotting the *i* in Brisbey, and the awning over the drugstore was made up of stripes resembling sherbet. Even the name of the street we were on, Lemon Lane. I was starting to crave something sweet and tart.

We reached the credit union. Though the building front didn't have a fruit theme, the savings and loan was, after all, named after fields. I imagined the clientele were probably dungaree-clad folks who came by to exchange gossip, like their latest purchase of farm equipment. Once we stepped inside, I changed my mind. Instead, I expected a gang of outlaws to follow us in and tell us to *reach for the sky*.

A row of desks in some kind of light-colored wood—pine or oak—took up the center of the room. The teller windows, fronted by a polished wooden counter, were encased in wood and looked exactly like the setup from an old western except they had windows instead of iron bars to protect them from the customers. The place even had a brass spittoon next to the service counter for looks. I hoped it was for looks. Funny, but when I thought of sauntering, spitting men, I thought of ranchers and cowboys, not citrus farmers.

The man who approached us wouldn't have qualified for

either profession. He wore his receding, brown hair clipped short. His rimless glasses were not from a discount store, nor was his suit. When he shook hands with me, I could have named seven women with tougher skin than his.

"Welcome to Home Field Credit Union," he said in the slick, oily voice a politician might use to explain the only reason he's running for office is because he cares a damn about your life.

"I'd like to speak with Mr.—er—Morton." Edward might have had a point about wearing our suits because in his exquisitely tailored gray pinstripe, he looked like a man who could promise a healthy deposit.

"Mort?" Oily Guy glanced over his shoulder toward an office at the back of the room. The closed door had a panel of frosted glass with Morton Spunkmeyer, President, written in gold lettering. He decided to show us he wasn't impressed. "Do you have an appointment?"

I glanced around the empty room. "Do we need one?"

Allowing a thin smile to creep across his lips, he said he would see if Mr. Spunkmeyer was available. As soon as Oily Guy oozed away, I asked Edward, "What are you going to ask Spunky?"

"If he knows who murdered Professor Taylor."

Since Edward likes to yank my chain, and I couldn't tell if he was kidding or not, I nodded. "That's good. Be direct. I'm sure he'll tell you everything he forgot to tell the police."

"And what would you ask him?"

Since Mort stepped out of the office and waved us back, I didn't have a chance to make something up.

The banker's office was outfitted for the current century, with a light cherry executive desk, a matching credenza with four doors, and a bookshelf peppered with stacks of folders and books on high finance. There were also two cushy, beige armchairs in front of the desk. After shaking our hands, Mort motioned for us to take a seat.

"I hope you're not here to pitch another lecture for the council," he began with a chuckle.

At the thought of Edward voluntarily pursuing public engagements, I joined in with a full belly laugh. I should have known better than to taunt the bull. He kept his eyes on Mort and said, "Nicholas has something to ask you."

The gaze Mort turned on me was still pleasant, but until then, behind his joshing, there had been a glimmer in his eyes suggesting the possibility of doing business with the famous man. The glimmer receded.

"Yeah." I nodded. "The evening didn't turn out as expected. Did you know Professor Taylor before that night?"

"Me? Never heard of him. His obit says he worked at some puny college in San Diego. I went to Penn State."

I ignored his criticism of my alma mater. "He wasn't a client of yours?"

Mort folded his hands on his desk and put on his professional face.

"I'm afraid that would be confidential information."

Edward put in. "But if he wasn't a client, what confidential information would you be releasing?"

The corners of the banker's mouth twitched. I thought I interpreted his expression correctly and explained it to my brother.

"Taylor's death was probably big news around here."

Mort nodded. "Front page of *The Citrus Grove Courier*."

I turned to Edward. "If he says the famous man didn't bank here—definitively—then he loses the possible advantage notoriety brings. People might want to sock their money away the same place Taylor did. It doesn't make sense, but that's human nature for you."

Mort grinned at me. "Want a job? Neumann doesn't get it.

He wants to vet my calls and turn away the curiosity seekers. Being one of the council members, I've become pretty popular. Most of the folks want to hear about what happened. Still, I tell Neumann any one of those people could become a customer."

I assumed Neumann was Oily Guy's real name. "Thanks for the compliment. Do you know if the professor had any contacts in Citrus Grove? Any connection to the place?"

"Like I said. Never saw him before that night."

"What about *during* that night?" Edward leaned forward and rested one forearm across his knees and put the fist of his other hand at his waist, so his elbow stuck out. I'd seen a male model in Edward's *Elegant Man* catalog strike the same pose. "Did you see him talking to anyone in particular?"

"He was mingling, like everyone else. I wasn't keeping track of him. I was more interested in if we'd pick up some new members. No offense to Dora and Flora, but I can only listen to so many stories about making my own butter."

"You were watching the registration table?"

"All night. Well, on and off. I mingled, too."

"Was Professor Taylor ever in the vicinity? You couldn't help but notice."

Mort settled back in his chair and folded his hands over his paunch. "Not that I'm not happy to see you again, but what's the point of all these questions? The deputies haven't been around since the day after it happened. I assume they're satisfied. Why aren't you?"

I looked at Edward, and he looked back. We were thinking the same thing. Sykes just got back the results of the toxicology report, so the calm experienced by the citizen's of Citrus Grove was at an end. However, if we mentioned it to a possible suspect before the questioning began in earnest, would the detective lose the advantage of surprise? Would we jeopardize his investigation? More important, would we make him mad?

Edward solved the problem. "We just happened to run into Detective Sykes yesterday. It sounds as if the police have not closed their investigation. Naturally, since it happened at my event, I feel a responsibility."

That made no sense, but Mort didn't notice. Instead, he put on a serious expression, probably the one he used when he foreclosed on a farm. He leaned forward, folded his hands on his desk, and nodded.

"So that's how it is." He nodded again and answered our question. "Professor Taylor wandered to the back of the room and looked at the sign-up sheet, but he didn't commit. He stood there, checking out the other guests. I remember it irritated me because he was blocking the table. I *did* see him talking to Charlie Grant. That's our local reporter.'

Edward nodded. "We've met."

"Charlie looked annoyed. From the bits I overheard, I think Taylor was trying to drum up publicity for a book. I understand he was an author."

My brother grimaced. "So he said."

"That's all I can remember. He seemed to watch people more than talk to them."

"Was he watching anyone in particular?"

"Not that I noticed. He just hung around the sign-up table. Although…" He shifted in his chair. After a quick glance past my shoulder to assure himself the door was closed, he lowered his voice. "He must have known someone local. Let's say the professor didn't come here just to enjoy your lecture."

Edward nodded to show he got it. Boy did he get it. We both knew what was coming, but my brother managed to control both his voice and his expression. "Do you know who he came to see? Or what he came for?"

Mort pointed at Edward. I stopped breathing, but it turned out he was only making an emphatic gesture.

"In my business, I like to know about people. It helps when someone hits us up for a loan. Not just what they tell you because, of course, they will put themselves in the best light. It's only natural. Social media has been a godsend. People confess all sorts of things online they wouldn't dream of telling anyone face-to-face. Not even their priest."

He leaned back, one hand still on his desk, and chuckled. "I'm not sure who they think is reading it, or why they don't think future employers or loan officers or mothers-in-law will ever get on the Internet. Kind of stupid of them, really."

Edward nodded.

"Well, after the man died under such public circumstances, I looked him up. This Taylor guy said he was coming to your lecture so he could spill someone's secret. Again, not very bright of him. If the person whose secret he knew read the page, of course they had warning. I wouldn't be surprised if they headed him off. Got to him first. That could be why he's dead, don't you think?"

"It could be," Edward murmured. "Possibly."

The banker narrowed his eyes, disappointed in our reaction.

I raised my hand. "Do you know anyone with a secret worth killing for?"

Mort grinned. "If I did and told you, it wouldn't be a secret anymore, would it?"

"One man has already died," Edward protested. "If you know something—"

"I'm joking. Citrus Grove isn't exactly a hub of excitement and passion. I can't imagine anyone here getting worked up enough to kill someone."

He refused to give us the contact information for the rest of the council members, though he was polite about it.

Privacy issues. Before we left, he invited Edward to open a savings account.

"We have great rates."

"Isn't this credit union for farmers?"

Mort shrugged. "Hardly anyone farms around here anymore. We've relaxed the qualifications. Do you have a garden?"

Edward declined his offer.

CHAPTER 8

W e waited until we got a few buildings down from the savings and loan before we stopped to consider our next move.

"One down, six to go," I said brightly. "I haven't decided if our first council member was a waste of time or not. Although, I thought Mort should have looked more surprised at the suggestion of murder."

"He might have suspected something already," Edward replied. "After all, Taylor's death was unexpected and, with him shouting at me before he died, sensational. Perhaps Mort subconsciously thought there was more to it."

"What do you think about our banker's little joke? *It wouldn't be a secret anymore if I told you.* Do you think he knows something he's holding back? It could be to protect someone."

"Small communities like Citrus Grove have closed ranks before when something disagreeable happened, but that doesn't mean they have something to hide. On the other hand..."

"Tell you what. If Mort knows anything, I say he's dead

before the end of the week. If he's still around by then, he's clear. So, do we wait it out?"

Edward ignored me. "Finding him was pure luck, but we can't count on the same luck to locate the other council members."

"Mrs. Robbins served the event. She might give us the members' surnames if I promise to date them all and we can search the telephone directory."

Edward made a quick turn into an entrance, and I glanced up to see a smiling poultry over the Happy Chicken Cafe sign. I hooked my arm through his and jerked him back.

"I thought we decided not to play with Miss Channing's feelings.

He pulled away. "It's eleven-thirty. I'm hungry."

Inside, waitresses scurried around a typical 1970s diner holding coffee urns and plastic trays laden with plates. The customers were an even mix of denim overalls and business suits, a few groups of women, two couples and one family with small children. I didn't see an empty table or Hattie Channing.

"Looks like the lunch rush beat us." I inched back toward the door. "Too bad. I looked forward to meeting Miss Channing, but I bet Mrs. Robbins could rustle us up something to eat."

Edward grimaced. "Don't be absurd. Our hostess might be a poisoner."

Just then, a couple at the back corner of the room left. Once the busboy wiped the table down, the hostess, a blond Amazon, invited us to make ourselves comfortable in the bright yellow booth. Edward asked if we could wait to be seated in Hattie Channing's section. As luck would have it, this was it.

As we checked out the menu, I could feel the eyes of our fellow diners upon us. When I stared back, I noted the expressions were open and friendly, just interested in the newcomers. If they had identified Edward as the featured speaker at the Babbitt and Brown debacle, I'm sure there would have been a few frowns, or at least an amused smirk.

"How are you gentlemen doing? Are you ready to order?"

In my defense, the clear alto addressing us sounded nothing like the breathy squeak I heard the night of Edward's talk, so when I looked up to respond, my mouth dropped open and I missed a breath.

Miss Hattie Channing had lost the neck ruffles, the horned-rimmed glasses, and the yogurt-pink suit. She filled out her knee-length, sky-blue uniform in a way that let a man know she would be soft to snuggle with, and she wore her long, chestnut-brown hair pulled back into a high pony-tail. From this angle, I could see her eyes were hazel, more browns and golds than greens. In a unique twist, her irises were encircled by a black ring. I'd only known one other woman with eyes like that, and I still dreamed about her.

"Hi." To my ears, my voice sounded like it belonged to a hormonal teenager, so I cleared my throat and tried it again. After seeing this new version of Hattie Channing, I was more than willing to allow Mrs. Robbins to arrange that luncheon.

She glanced from me to my brother, and her eyes opened wide as she made the connection. Her freckled skin paled and she swayed, but before she went into a full swoon, Edward put in his order.

"I'll have the BLT, but instead of fries, I'll have a side salad with the light vinaigrette dressing, please." He flipped the menu over. "And a mango iced tea to drink."

Now that he had prepared the way to a satisfied stomach, Edward gave his attention to our waitress.

"Ah. Miss Channing. It's a pleasure to see you again. I hate to bring up a distressing topic—"

I interrupted him before he could further traumatize her

with talk about the murder. And I deny my primary influence was Hattie Channing's improved looks. Asking questions of a person who looks ready to run screaming from the room is not productive.

"I'm ready to order."

It wouldn't hurt to clarify that I was all man, so I made sure my order didn't include leafy vegetables or tropical fruit.

"The patty-melt for me, with fries and a cup of coffee, black." I handed her the menu with a smile and a thank you. Her lips trembled on the returning smile. She snatched up our menus and left us in a hurry.

"You interrupted me."

I met Edward's gaze head-on and lied. "I'm hungry, too."

"You wanted to stop me from asking her about the murder. And for the record, you take cream in your coffee."

"Okay, smart guy. Maybe I headed you off."

"Why?"

"Because I saw the look on her face when she recognized us from the other night." Since there is nothing that can make Edward balk like a public scene, I added, "Because I didn't want her to pass out right here in the middle of the restaurant.

"I see." Edward picked up his fork and rubbed it with his napkin. "As long as you are aware we can't avoid asking her about the subject forever."

"Agreed."

He set his fork back down in its proper position. "Maybe she was feeling ill because she murdered the man and thought we might be onto her. Did you think of that?"

I hadn't thought of that, and I said so. "She doesn't strike me as the murdering type."

"Nicholas, Nicholas, Nicholas." He heaved a loud sigh. "Your track record with the opposite sex is questionable.

Margarita? Murdered. Bethany? Murdered. Amanda?" He tilted his head. "Murderer."

Those were women I had met at Inglenook Manor. One I had liked. The others didn't count, as I only got close to them because they had information about the murder, especially one. Still, he had a point.

"If you think I'm being too protective of Miss Channing, then by all means question her when she brings our order. Don't blame me if she lands face-down in your side salad with a light vinaigrette."

He never got the chance to speak with her again. The waitress who returned with our lunch was a stranger. She informed us Hattie Channing had to leave abruptly, which did not bode well for me and my instincts about women.

CHAPTER 9

Right inside the front door of Robbins' B&B was an octagon-shaped foyer. A large, round rug with a rose print took up the center of the room, and a few chairs lined the edges, making it a sort of waiting room. In one of those chairs sat Detective Jonah Sykes. He stood when we entered, but before he could speak, Regina Robbins hustled into the room and stated the obvious.

"The *police* are here to speak with you."

She held her hands clasped in front of her apron, waiting for an explanation.

"Do you have somewhere private where I can speak to these gentlemen?" Detective Sykes asked her.

Pride of house took over.

"Of course I do."

She led us past the den, through a swinging door and into a room crowded with furniture and brick-a-brack. It was nice furniture, solid mahogany and oak that dated back to the turn of the century. Apparently, Mrs. Robbins believed in both quality and quantity. A butler's buffet with a recessed wine rack stood next to a china cabinet filled with a collection of teapots. The opposite wall was home to a solidly built sideboard and a petite serving table. Lest the far corner of the room feel neglected, it held a hutch covered with useless but pretty knick-knacks, mostly statues of birds and dogs.

"I don't really use this room except for parties." She sent a guilty glance around. "It's a little crowded right now."

"It will do fine, thank you."

The detective dismissed her nicely, and she took the hint with reluctance. I scooted past the china cabinet and took a seat next to Edward at a dining table that filled the center of the room. Sykes chose a chair across from us.

He smiled. "Taking a vacation?"

Edward launched into the same explanation he had prepared for Mrs. Robbins, but Sykes held up a hand to stop him.

"It's not necessary. Our suspects don't usually go out of their way to make themselves available. It's a new experience. That's all."

Edward blustered. "How did you know we were here? Are you having us followed?"

"Your housekeeper told me where to find you."

"Have there been any developments?" I asked.

"I just have a few questions." Sykes gave me one of those smiles of his. Not showing teeth and nowhere near his eyes. "We're always clarifying points. I know, it's a bore, but it has to be done."

"Ask away. We have nothing to hide."

"Except the authorship of the Aunt Civility series." Still smiling. "I want to walk through the moment you gave Professor Taylor the cup of lemon-barley water. Did he ask for it?"

"You mean specifically say *Pass me a glass*? No. I told you already. He was coughing."

"And you picked up the closest cup. Did you smell anything sweet?"

I raised my brows. "Sweet? If I did, it didn't make an impression."

He leaned back in his chair, though his burly form didn't relax. "I've been doing some research. Oleander is bitter. One article compared the taste to rotten lemons. Since it was lemon-barley water, the victim might have thought the lemons used weren't fresh. He did make a face after drinking it."

I tried to relax my face muscles. "That was taking a chance. What if he didn't want it? Anyway, whether the poison was in the first pitcher or in a pre-poured glass, Edward and I didn't set out the food and drink. I grabbed a cup someone else had already poured. We're not the ones you should be asking."

Completely without my say-so, my gaze drifted to the swinging door where Mrs. Robbins was most likely hovering to eavesdrop. Sykes followed my gaze.

"Don't worry. I plan on speaking with your hostess as well as the other servers."

Edward folded his hands and rested them on the table. "Then you've eliminated even the remotest possibility he ingested the plant by accident? You definitely believe it's a case of murder?"

"Until I discover something—something definitive—that points to an accident, it's a homicide." He studied Edward. "It's interesting that you mentioned poisons in your talk, Mr. Harlow."

"Arsenic. As a method of coloring desserts long ago." Edward clenched his teeth together. I could hear the grinding from where I sat. "It was an amusing tidbit."

"Not for Professor Taylor."

"He didn't die of arsenic poisoning," I snapped. "You're just harassing Edward for fun."

Sykes stood and fastened the button on his suit jacket. "It's not as amusing as you would think. So, do you write the Aunt Civility books?"

Edward looked up. "How is that relevant to your investigation?"

"It gives you a motive."

"Have the people at Classical Reads changed their minds?" When Sykes didn't answer, Edward couldn't disguise his pleasure. "Then I'm afraid we can't help you."

After a brief nod, the detective left.

Sykes wasn't our only visitor that day. We were upstairs in our rooms, having retired immediately after a dinner of pot roast, mashed potatoes and green beans, which Mrs. Robbins had served at a wooden table in the more spacious kitchen. The pot roast was a little tough and the beans a little mushy, but everything went down okay. We were the only guests at dinner and, to my surprise and relief, Regina Robbins ate with us. She wouldn't be likely to poison herself.

After assuring our hostess we were not in imminent danger of arrest, conversation dried up, so Edward didn't feel bad about taking Mrs. Robbins' *Courier* up to his room with his coffee. He asked permission first.

She made a dismissive gesture. "Take it. I only get the paper for my guests. I never read the news. Everything I need to know gets talked about at my gardening group."

Since there wasn't anything to do, and Mrs. Robbins didn't seem to feel like conversation, I followed Edward up five minutes later—just in time to hear the roar coming from his bedroom.

He couldn't be angry at me, so I opened the door without knocking and stuck my head in. He was sitting on the edge of his bed, and he held up the newspaper and shook it at me.

"Have you read this?"

"Obviously not, since you're hogging it."

He shoved the front page at me. I read the headline. "It's Murder!" I looked up. "Catchy title."

"Keep going," Edward growled.

"Detective Jonah Sykes of the San Diego County Sheriff's Department confirmed today the death of Professor Jonathan Taylor at Babbitt and Brown Bookstore on Monday, March twelve, is officially a homicide investigation. Taylor died after ingesting *Nerium Oleander*, the infamous Jericho Rose. Readers will remember how the college professor from G.W. Marston College dropped dead in front of a horrified audience after a lecture by Edward Harlow, representative and relative of author Aunt Civility."

I looked up again. "You got a mention."

"Keep going."

"One of Professor Taylor's last acts before he died was to invite his social media followers to attend the event. The professor intended to expose a lie, but he never got the chance. Did that lie cost the professor his life? What secret could so threaten an individual that he or she would take a life to protect it? *The Courier* wants to know."

And then the article listed Charlie Grant's contact information for anyone who had information. The following article talked about oleanders and had plenty of photos to help homeowners identify any Jericho Roses lurking on their property.

I folded the paper and returned it to him.

Edward tossed it aside. "It's a witch hunt! Irresponsible journalism at its worst."

"Actually, it's a clever idea. It's just too bad you're involved. And you'll notice he referred to the killer as he or she. Equality for all."

"How long do you think it will take the citizens of Citrus

Grove to make the same connection Detective Sykes made? What if someone overheard Taylor suggesting I'm the author of the Aunt Civility books? Classical Reads won't stand for it. It will ruin me." Edward glared at me. "It's in my contract."

"Okay, but what's the worst that could happen if people found out you wrote the darn books?"

"I'd be terminated. Unemployed."

"What good would that do? It's not like the publisher could just assign another writer to take your place. People would know. I think both you and Classical Reads are making a big deal about nothing."

My brother looked like his head might explode, so I left him with that thought and went back to my room.

I had counted on the B&B having Wi-Fi available. It did not, and I was playing solitaire on my phone, using up gigabytes from our network plan, when I heard a knock on Edward's door. I peeked into the hallway and saw Regina Robbins staring up at him with her fists on her hips. He had exchanged his shoes for slippers and removed his tie.

"You have a guest," she accused.

My brother had a copy of *More Great News for America* by Gerard Lameiro in his hand with his index finger marking his spot.

"Is it Detective Sykes again?"

"It's a young woman."

I stepped into the hallway. "Hattie Channing?"

"It's nobody I know." Regina Robbins sniffed. "She looks respectable enough, but I remind you I do not allow women in your room."

After he put his shoes on, I followed him downstairs to the foyer, but it was empty, so he opened the front door and made a sound like gack. Claudia Inglenook looked up at him, anger and concern struggling to dominate her expression.

"What are you doing here?" he demanded.

Anger won. "I'm happy to see you, too." She set her jaw. "You never called me back."

His chest puffed out, and he rose to his full six-foot-two. "You refused to take my calls."

She couldn't say that if he cared he would have just kept trying to reach her until she felt like accepting the call, but I could tell she was thinking it.

A round face under a jaunty hat with gray feathers peeked around her shoulder. My stomach muscles tightened, and I took an instinctive step backward. It was Claudia's crazy Aunt Zali. The only thing I knew about the woman is she had attacked a man with gardening shears shortly before we met her last winter at Inglenook, where she was *taking a rest*. She held on to reality by her fingernails, and her child-like enthusiasm gave me chills.

She gave us a huge smile and said, "Surprise!"

It was clear from Claudia's expression she had just lost the upper hand in the argument and might try tears next, but she made a strategic decision, firmed up her features, and delivered her next lines as an accusation.

"I couldn't leave her alone—I mean behind. Robert is handling Inglenook by himself. He doesn't have time to—to keep Aunt Zali entertained. And I wouldn't have had to drag her to Orange Grove—"

"Citrus Grove," Edward said, always a stickler for accuracy.

She gritted her teeth. "The point is, I'm here because I couldn't get hold of you."

Other than my natural and intelligent fear of Aunt Zali, I was enjoying this moment immensely. Not only was my brother on the spot, a position he rarely occupies, but Claudia, with all her feminine wiles, which I admit she has, was about to get a dose of reality.

I didn't approve of her influence over my brother, and I

definitely didn't enjoy seeing him led around by a ring in his nose. Since I had pointed out her game to him back in San Diego, Edward was prepared for her tricks.

I crossed my arms over my chest in a sign of solidarity and waited for him to let her have it, but then Edward's expression softened—a sure sign of weakness in the face of the enemy.

"You called me?" he said.

Claudia averted her gaze to the doorknob.

I elbowed his ribs to get his attention. "That means no, Edward."

Claudia shot me a glare and then remembered Edward was watching her. She pursed her lips and batted her eyelashes. "I was worried."

Like a sap, he fell for it. He took her hand in his big paw. "I'm sorry I worried you."

She murmured something about it being okay, which made me want to slap them both. The clever minx had just gotten him to apologize, which was exactly what she'd been after. I took out my frustration on my brother.

"Edward, are you going to leave the ladies standing outside all night? Why don't you invite them in? We can all get a cup of hot cocoa and snuggle up in the cozy den while you describe your role as a murder suspect."

He flushed, stepped aside and invited them in.

"I'm sure you're exaggerating, Nicholas." Claudia's haughty stare as she passed me confirmed our feelings about each other were mutual.

I clapped Edward on the back. "Don't be modest."

"I think you underestimate the detective," Edward said. "I had no hand in the professor's death, and I'm certain Detective Sykes will soon discover the fiend that gave him the poison."

Zali shoved her hand out toward my brother. "I'm Zali."

That was only the tenth or eleventh time she'd introduced herself to Edward. He accepted her hand and expressed his delight at meeting her. She squinted at him.

"I know that voice." She grinned as if she'd just opened the best present ever. "I remember! You were one of the judges."

Zali had been under the delusion that the very real murders that took place last January at Inglenook were part of the entertainment package. A murder-hunt. A game. Her smile melted into a frown.

"I never heard who won. There wasn't an announcement. Should have been a public announcement." She sighed. "I know it wasn't me. I never got a prize. What was the prize?"

I informed Edward I had an appointment and left him to deal with his visitors. He insisted we had work to do, but I told him not to be rude to his guests. When I finally maneuvered past him, which was difficult because he placed his bulk in the center of the door frame to block my exit, I headed back downtown.

CHAPTER 10

Maybe the arrival of Claudia and her sidekick was a good thing. She might haul Edward back to San Diego where we could watch the investigation from the sidelines. It really burned me how Edward couldn't resist stirring things up. The way he impressed us with his knowledge about the oleander plant would have made me suspicious if I'd been the lead detective on the case. My brother feels the truth is his best friend, but it's uncanny how his virtue always winds up giving me a pain in the side.

That social media post was the sticking point that might land Edward in jail. Yes, it was vaguely worded, but what else could Taylor have been talking about other than my brother's subterfuge?

Regina Robbins was in a position to administer the poison. So were her volunteers. Jeffrey Babbitt might have known Taylor would be there, since the event was at his place of business. Any one of the Citrus Grove Culinary Arts Council members could have sent an invite to Taylor.

I'd made it downtown without paying attention to my

surroundings. There were flashing lights up ahead. Not the kind that come with sirens but the florescent kind with a dancing cocktail glass under the name Bill's.

Once I stepped through the heavy wooden door under the sign, I let my eyes adjust to the dim lighting. The theme was dark wood and burgundy, with benches separated by high partitions lining the walls. The only decoration was an American flag behind the bar.

Most of the clientele, which consisted of men in the last chapter of life, skipped the scattering of round tables in the center of the room and opted for stools at the bar.

The chatter stopped while the locals assessed the newcomer. There was an empty stool at the far end of the room by the washrooms, but that didn't suit my purposes, so I leaned against the bar between two old men who, from the way they were dressed, were probably the last of the citrus farmers.

"Nice night," I said, pointing at a local beer on tap and giving the bartender a nod.

"That's original," sneered the guy to my left. He looked familiar. Wispy, white hair. Big nose. It was Ned, the grumpy old man.

"You're on the Culinary Arts Council," I observed, hoping to establish a bond.

He ducked his head as the rest of the men guffawed.

"Are you an artist too, Mr. Fancy Pants?" someone called out to me.

"Look," I said, taking in the rest of the old geezers with a sweeping gaze. "I'm in a suit, you're in dungarees, but we're all men created equal on the inside. That's what makes this America."

A cackle came from an old crone with uncombed white curls seated in a booth in the corner of the room. She wore her plaid shirt open over a baggy, red t-shirt, and the half of her that was under the table had on jeans and low-top, white sneakers.

"And ladies," I added.

That set off the guy to my right in a fit of giggles. "Ain't nobody accused Bill of being a lady in fifty years. He got knifed for his trouble."

I nodded at her and said, "No offense intended," and took the lopsided grin she shot back as apology accepted. I loosened my tie to show I was just one of the guys here to relax after a long day. "If I interrupted you, pick up where you left off while I think of something clever to say."

Ned turned away from me, but he wasn't snubbing me. He was taking me at my word and continuing the conversation.

"So, the calf was breached. Thought I was going to lose them both. Doc Jensen, he weren't no help. Delivering puppies at Markham's place. If a bitch can't whelp her own puppies, she's a poor specimen of a dog."

A skinny guy with buck teeth registered his protest. "You can't blame the dog. Jane Markham would lose thousands if one of those pups died. She's the one who called Jensen in."

Discussion followed over whether this request had been reasonable and if any dog was worth that much money. I'm not sure it ever got decided. Ned, getting irritated by his audience's lack of focus, yelled out the rest of his story.

"I had to get in there—I mean reach a-l-l the way up there." He looked over his audience to see if they appreciated how far he had ventured into the cow. "With both hands." He held his hands up for inspection the way a surgeon would hold his hands up after washing them. "Had to turn the thing. A few minutes later, he dropped."

"Was he okay?" I asked to be polite.

"He looked glad to be out of there." He picked up his beer bottle. "Named him Pretzel."

The bartender handed me my glass, and I slid some bills over the counter and ordered a round for everyone present. Then I raised my beer and said, "To Pretzel."

Once everyone got their refills, I said, "I'm surprised to hear you talking about cattle. I thought Citrus Grove would be all fruit trees."

Bucktooth said, "Haven't seen a locally grown piece of citrus in twenty years. Not for sale, anyway."

"I bet you haven't seen a murder in that long either."

I had fumbled. The room went silent.

Ned took off his cap and scratched his head. "A man died, but what makes you say he was murdered?"

"Don't you read the paper?" Bucktooth shouted.

"It's just an assumption on my part. Maybe I'm wrong. Maybe *The Courier* is wrong. Does anyone know different? Were any of you at Babbitt's that night?" I nodded at Ned. "Other than the council member?"

They scoffed at the idea of hanging around a bookstore to listen to a lecture on etiquette, but I could sense an underlying regret that they hadn't witnessed the main event—Professor Jonathan Taylor's demise.

"Seems silly to drive all the way from San Diego to get yourself killed," someone said.

I grinned. "It does, doesn't it? Unless Taylor knew someone who lived here. Any of you seen him before?"

That got me a chorus of *No siree, bub*, and *Nope*.

I looked down at Ned. "I heard he spent a lot of time by the sign-up table. Any reason?"

Ned grimaced at the memory. "Just standing there taking up space. Told him he should put up the membership fee or move along. He wasn't inclined to listen, so I sicked Georgie on him. You want a man to jump, get a woman on his case, especially one with no sense of humor."

The majority agreed with him. Even Bill raised her cup of coffee in a toast.

"That's right," I said. "The mad knitter was back there with you."

That made him chuckle. It gave him an alibi of sorts.

"Says working the needles soothes her nerves. I told her a beer was less work, but she enjoys it."

"How long has Babbitt and Brown's been open?"

Ned scratched his ear. "Ten years, mebbe. Before that, Jeff Babbitt worked at the library."

I thought I had an idea. "Where's Brown?" Maybe the partner deserved a closer look.

"Cecil Brown is at the corner of Haymaker and Fifth," Bucktooth said. He kept his face straight when he offered this information, but the rest of the men chuckled. I was about to write the information in my notebook, when Bill called out from her corner.

"That's the cemetery."

Her voice was loud and sharp, like a drill sergeant's. I closed my notebook and returned it to my pocket, while she got up and came over. She ambled as if one of her hips pained her, but her shoulders were straight and she held her chin hairs high. She may or may not have knifed a man for calling her a lady, but it took some effort to stand my ground while she squinted up at me.

"You're not a reporter, are you?"

I shook my head. "You've already got one of those. Charlie Grant."

She nodded. "Charlie's a good kid."

Charlie was around my age.

"All your questions have been about that man's death. How come?"

The eyes she directed at my face were chocolate brown and intelligent. I abandoned any idea about handing her a story.

"My brother was the one giving the talk the night Professor Taylor died. I don't like the way Detective Sykes looks at him."

She stared for a few minutes as if those eyes were performing a personal MRI on me that would show her any rotten spots. Apparently, she didn't find any because she invited me to follow her down the hallway past the restrooms.

Mother always told me not to make judgments about people based on what little I thought I knew about them. There was always a part of them they shared only with their nearest and dearest. She usually made this point when I tried to understand the relationship between her and my father, so I thought it was her way of saying it was none of my business. As I stepped across the threshold of Bill's office, I gave Mother a mental salute.

The walls were painted dusty rose, and the curtains on the window looking into the alley used enough lace to make an Irish-woman proud. There were flowery cross-stitched sayings about Home Sweet Home and America the Beautiful decorating the walls, and a doll with blond, curly hair wearing an antebellum dress, rested on a chair in the corner.

"Close the door behind you," she said. "I don't want to ruin my reputation."

As she sat behind a large desk, she was framed by an American flag on her right and a picture frame holding various medals on her left. I recognized the Purple Heart.

She followed my gaze. "Vietnam. I was a nurse. Most of those men out there are veterans."

I cleared my throat. "I can't claim flat feet, but I never served."

JACQUELINE VICK

She jerked her chin in the direction of the bar. "The way the government treats them, I wouldn't recommend it. Now, what's this about your brother? Why is that detective interested in him? Did he do it?"

I grinned. "The only reason you can ask that is because you don't know Edward. He did not do it, but Taylor put up an interesting post on his social media site that said he was going to reveal somebody's secret. Edward has a secret."

"Ha! Everybody has a secret. Is his worth killing for?"

I shook my head. "No, ma'am. However, it doesn't seem Taylor knew anyone else in Citrus Grove."

She toyed with a pencil. "I wouldn't say that."

My eyebrows went up, but she held up a hand to stay my excitement.

"As soon as I saw his picture in the paper, I knew he looked familiar. He'd been sniffing around here last month. Trouble is, I don't know who he was interested in."

"Was he ever with anyone?"

"Not that I saw."

"Was he hanging around a particular part of town? A specific business? Maybe the savings and loan?"

She pursed her lips. "I noticed him because he was a new face, but he could have been passing through, so I didn't pay much attention."

"If you saw him, maybe someone else did. Do you mind if I ask your customers?"

She was going to get stubborn, but after I promised to make it an adventure for them and nothing else, she agreed. Besides, I could have waited outside the bar until closing time and caught them as they left. However, she was adamant about my final request.

"Would you tell what you know to Detective Sykes?"

"There's no point. I don't know any more than I told you,

98

but I give you permission to repeat what I said. Just keep me out of it."

It didn't seem in character—her wanting to stay out of it —but I had to take it or leave it on her terms, so I took it.

It wasn't worth much. Half of the guys couldn't remember Taylor's picture from the newspaper and didn't know what he looked like. The other half said they would remember if they had seen him in person and they hadn't. They all agreed Taylor hadn't come into the bar.

CHAPTER 11

When I got back that night, I knocked on Edward's door but got no response. I knocked louder, since he was the one who said he wanted to get some work done, but still, there was no answer. While unlocking my door, I heard low rumbling murmurs and a woman's soft laughter. It's not that I was a stickler for Mrs. Robbins' rules, but if he was ignoring me because he had Claudia in his room, there would be a reckoning. I crossed the hall and pressed my ear against his door and listened for a full five minutes. Nothing.

It wasn't until the next morning I found out what happened between him and Claudia.

I took a quick bath and dressed for the day. Since Edward had referred to this as a vacation, I slipped on my jeans and a green, long-sleeved sweater and brown loafers. When I reached the kitchen, I stopped short.

Claudia looked up from her conversation with Edward and gave me a broad smile that showed teeth, part angel for my brother's benefit and part vindictive witch-woman just for me.

"Good morning, Nicholas."

My smile strained at the edges, but I got it on and answered her appropriately.

Mrs. Robbins joined us again, so that made five at the table, including Zali.

"I missed you last night when I got back," I said as I pulled out my chair and sat down. "Did you find a hotel?" I asked, my tone pointed.

"Miss Inglenook and her aunt will be staying here," Mrs. Robbins announced. "In the back room." That seemed to fix it for her, as if the back room came with armed guards and a chastity belt.

I raised one brow. "Is that...wise? Miss Inglenook and Edward are dating. It seems cruel to place temptation so near." I ignored the growl coming from the back of Edward's throat. "Of course, I *might* be wrong."

"Of course you're wrong," Claudia snapped. "We are grown adults, not hormonal teenagers. We are perfectly capable of self-restraint."

"Not according to what I heard last night."

Edward set down his fork. "I hope you're not suggesting what I think you are."

"I'm not *suggesting* anything. I'm saying it in plain English."

Edward's nostrils flared, and he tightened his hands into fists, but then he darted a glance at Mrs. Robbins and decided against violence.

Our hostess was blushing bright red, so I turned to face her and pressed my point. "Of course, you might be interested in attracting a different type of clientele Romantic getaways for unmarried couples. In that case, you don't need to worry about your B&B's reputation." I leered.

"Oh!" Mrs. Robbins took her bottom lip in her fingers, but then Zali spoiled the effect when she raised her hand.

"I'm the chaperon!"

Zali wasn't capable of chaperoning two rocks, but Mrs. Robbins didn't know that.

The aged relative squished up her face. "Though they don't appear to need one."

The proprietress of Robbins' B&B gave a sigh of relief.

"All Eddie and Claudia did all night was talk. *Bo*ring! He didn't even try to grab her knee." She shot Edward a look that expressed her low estimation of men who ignore knees. "If I wanted a man, I'd find one with more spirit."

I wondered how much spirit Norbert had shone before she stabbed him with the gardening shears. As I was imagining the terrifying scenarios any man who dated Zali might face, I noticed Claudia Inglenook was staring at her plate with the corners of her mouth turned down, as if she, too, was wondering why Edward hadn't made a pass at her knees. Sexual Frustration. I admit pure vindictiveness motivated my next move.

"I'm relieved," I said, turning my chair to face Zali. "In fact, I'd be happy to help you out, should the need arise."

She narrowed her eyes in thought. "It would be a good idea if there were two of us keeping an eye on them. I can't watch 'em myself every minute." She grinned. "And that way I could take a break and enjoy my vacation."

"Everyone needs time off," I agreed.

"That's very kind of you, Nicholas," Edward said in a silky voice that let me know hanky-panky wasn't the only thing I would have to watch out for.

After breakfast, my brother found the daily newspaper in the den, the sections separated and tossed on the couch by the last reader. He methodically put them back into their proper order, sat down with his coffee, and proceeded to ignore me.

"Good as new," I said. "You can hardly tell it's used."

Without looking up, he said, "I'm taking Claudia around Citrus Grove to show her the sites. We will not require your presence."

Or want, he implied. So, he was taking a day off. That explained his casual wear, which for him meant a white long-sleeved shirt, red sweater vest and slacks.

Zali entered the room as Edward was telling me his plans. She did an about-face.

"I'll get my hat."

As she scurried back to her room to retrieve it, Edward tossed the paper aside and stood.

"Aren't we supposed to be clearing your name?" I asked politely. "Isn't that why you dragged me down here? Or maybe Claudia would find it exciting to visit you in prison. Do they still have conjugal visits for married couples? You could put a rush on the license."

He thumped me on the chest with his knuckles. I had to dig in my heels to keep from tipping back.

"If you must know, Claudia shared some thoughts about the murder. We discussed it at length last night. I think she's onto something. And another thing. I resent your insinuations. You need to apologize to Claudia."

"Apologize my eye. I know what I heard."

"Whatever you think you heard, you're wrong. I was alone and asleep by the time you returned."

I waved off his explanation. "Have it your way, but I'm not apologizing."

Claudia was interfering again. Not that Edward and I were a crime-solving team, but we had done all right at Inglenook. I had assumed we would work together to find the solution to Professor Taylor's death. The two of us.

"It's just as well she's going to keep you busy because I planned to spend the day following my own hunch."

Not that I had a hunch, but I couldn't let Edward think

his lady love had one up on me. I moved to leave because I didn't think I could be polite if I ran into Claudia, but Mrs. Robbins had other ideas. She planted herself in front of me and glared up with slits for eyes and lips that trembled with emotion.

"I understand it was you who told the detective he should interrogate me. I can understand wanting to deflect attention from your brother, but really!"

Technically, that wasn't true. When speaking with Sykes, I only referenced the kitchen volunteers. My glance at the dining room's swinging door was involuntary, so it didn't count.

"Me? I didn't even mention your name."

"Hmph." She crossed her arms across her sturdy bosom. "That's not what Detective Sykes said."

I rested a hand on her shoulder but pulled it back when she bared her teeth. "The police have to check out anyone associated with the murder. As for giving me credit, he probably didn't want you getting hostile with *him*, so he laid the blame at my feet." I shook my head. "Pretty inconsiderate of my feelings, don't you think?"

She lowered her arms and called a truce but added a sniff to show I wasn't the only injured party.

On my way back to downtown Citrus Grove, I put order to the facts I'd gathered since we arrived. First, Taylor had been in town before Edward's talk, which meant he had a reason for being here other than to see my brother. If I could figure out who he had been in town to see before, and if that person had been at the book event the night Taylor died…I wasn't looking for a murderer. Just another suspect for Sykes to consider. But not any suspect would do.

I didn't agree with Edward's assumption that Hattie Channing's quick departure from the diner once she recognized us was a sign of a guilty conscience. Maybe the sight of us brought up emotions she couldn't handle. After all, that night must have been her first contact with a corpse. At least, I assumed it was.

I got an uncomfortable sensation in my stomach brought on by the memory of the *poor innocent woman* who nearly brained me after drugging my drink at Inglenook. What did I really know about Miss Channing? Maybe Edward was right and I was letting my hormones cloud my judgment.

I had tried to protect her from his questions. I decided it was a reaction, or call it an impulse, based on my surprise at seeing the woman behind the polyester outfit. It would be interesting to find out if I could be objective with Hattie, and I was curious if she could affect me the same way on a second viewing.

It seemed efficient to resolve this question as soon as possible, so I headed straight for the diner and waited until the hostess approached me with a menu.

"Thanks anyway, but I'm looking for someone. Is Miss Channing here today?"

It was the same big, sturdy blond hostess as yesterday. She held the menu close with both hands over her chest. "No, she isn't. Can I help you?"

To help sell my story, I rubbed the back of my neck, something I do when I'm stressed. "The thing is, I'm only in town for a few days and thought I'd say hello." I held up my cell phone. "When I upgraded, I lost all my contacts."

She relaxed and set the menus on the back of the closest booth. "Oh, I hate it when that happens." She gave me a steady look and decided I wasn't a serial stalker. "I'm a little worried about her. Not seriously, but it's not like her to call in sick at the last minute."

"I could check on her. Let her know to call you."

"Have you been to her house?"

How far to push it? I said it had been a long time ago. If

she could just tell me the street, I'm sure it would come back to me.

Apple Street. Apart from the oddity of the name, since as far as I know apples are not citrus, it was a nice street lined with old trees. All the houses were ranches that came with yards on the large side for California. A few of the home-owners had erected white picket fences. It was behind one of these fences I caught sight of a young girl, about ten, with long brown hair and square-cut bangs.

"Can you tell me which of these houses belongs to Miss Hattie Channing?"

She eyed me for seven seconds, interested, and then turned her head toward the door and shouted. "Mom!"

At first, I mistook her response as a case of the young calling out for mother's protection, and I started to move before a momma bear arrived, but when Hattie Channing appeared behind the screen door, I halted.

"Miss Channing?"

If she were happy to see me, she did a good job of hiding it. She clutched the handle to hold the door shut, but then, perhaps realizing the child was on the wrong side of safety, she pushed the screen door open and told me I might as well come inside.

CHAPTER 12

I don't dislike children. I'm just not ready to have one running around that I can't send home, especially one that will be a teenager in a couple of years. I looked at Hattie Channing through a different lens once I had taken a seat at her kitchen table and accepted the offer of a glass of water. She was still easy on the eyes, but now an aura of don't touch surrounded her.

Sunlight poured into the kitchen through the window above the sink and the glass panels on the back door. I approved. After losing everything to an unethical business partner, before Edward had offered me a job as his secretary, I had scraped out an existence in a basement apartment. It felt like a cave, and the lack of sunlight added to my depression. I couldn't imagine ever feeling depressed in Hattie's kitchen.

"I'm sorry I took off, but when I saw you and your brother at the diner, I assumed you had come to talk to me about Professor Taylor's death."

When the little girl, Laurie, came into the room, Hattie

got an apple from the refrigerator and asked her to eat it at the picnic table in the backyard.

"You're talking about adult stuff," Laurie said with an eye roll.

"Just eat it outside, okay?"

As soon as the kid left, Hattie gave me a smile that was a half-hearted attempt at a flirt. The woman needed practice.

"You must think I'm awfully silly for acting like I did. Your brother would naturally have concerns about—the man's death, since it happened at his event. My only excuse is I was so upset about that night I wasn't up to answering questions."

I grinned. "I could avoid asking you the questions you don't want to answer if you tell me what they are."

She didn't return the smile. She seemed tense, but I brushed it off. Anyone who had experienced death in close-up might feel that way.

Since Edward considered her a suspect, he would have warned me to be on my guard and treat her as the enemy, but my instincts argued my best move would be to put her at ease. I leaned my forearms on the table and clasped my hands.

"I'm going to be completely open with you, Miss Channing. Sykes, that's the detective, suspects my brother might have had a motive to kill the professor from something he saw on Taylor's Facebook page."

She didn't cover her gasp in time.

I leaned back, unconsciously distancing myself from her, and nodded. "You've seen it. But why would you follow Taylor's page? What's he to you?"

Her natural alto shot up to a soprano accompanied by a forced laugh. "Nothing. Nothing at all. I attended G.W. Marston College years ago. He was simply one of my many professors."

I kept my expression neutral as I considered the beautiful woman in front of me.

"That's quite a coincidence. I went there myself. What year did you graduate?"

"I-I didn't. Not from there. I only attended one year."

"And yet you still keep up with the news. Especially Taylor's news. You're not one of his groupies. You look too intelligent to be fawning over an old fool like the professor."

Her cheeks flushed. "I most certainly am not. Not a groupie, I mean."

"Okay. I'm glad to check off that possibility. Have you written any articles lately? Submitted a story to the *San Diego Courier*?"

"Are you joking with me?"

"Then he's not a networking contact. You might be the nostalgic type, but if you really wanted to keep in touch with your past, you'd join an alumni group. But you're not an alumnus, and Taylor didn't attend Marston."

She tapped nervously on the tabletop with her fingernails. I don't think she knew she was doing it, but then she noticed me noticing the nervous habit and pressed her palms flat.

"You were young and dopey once, just like the rest of us. Taylor had a certain reputation with the ladies. Did you have a relationship with him when you were at Marston? Or after?"

Her eyes made a quick move toward the screen door, which gave us a view of Laurie munching away at her apple. My eyebrows shot up.

"A relationship with ties?"

She stood, crossed to the sink, and rinsed out her cup. Since she didn't seem to like the question, I answered it for her.

"Laurie is Taylor's child."

She lowered her head and nodded. I didn't really want to know the answer to the next logical question, but I asked it anyway.

"Did the two of you keep in contact?"

Naturally, I thought she would spill a sob story to get my sympathy, so I flinched in surprise when she spun and took a step forward with her fists balled up.

"Not on your life."

Hoping to make up for the flinch, I kept my gaze steady and my expression neutral. "His post could have been referring to you. He said he had a secret to reveal. He came to Citrus Grove to do it. I admit I wouldn't send him a Father's Day card, but what's the big deal? He wasn't fighting for custody, was he?"

When she didn't answer, I blew out a slow breath. "A mother would do a lot to protect her child."

She dropped into her chair and folded her arms across her chest. "I didn't have to protect Laurie from that creep because he didn't know he was her father."

"So you say."

The story came out then. She was a naïve freshman and Taylor was a big-wig, or at least he thought he was, and you couldn't expect an eighteen-year-old woman from a small town out on her first adventure to know better. When he paid attention to her, it went to her head, at least until the real Taylor came through.

"I discovered he was a married man. It was awful! I ended it right away but discovered I was pregnant. Naturally I couldn't stay there, but I just didn't have the energy to start over somewhere else. Then Laurie was born. Taking care of a child is a full-time job."

"Are you the one who broke up Taylor's marriage?"

"Jonathan Taylor broke up his own marriage."

I nodded. "Point taken. Did you ever meet his wife?"

"There wasn't an opportunity for introductions." She pressed her lips together. "You're going to tell the police, aren't you?"

Her motive was better than Edward's. One word in Sykes' ear and he would set my brother aside and go after her. She had been there that night, which gave her opportunity. She had a reason to want Taylor dead. A good reason. As for means, how difficult would it be to get hold of a flower?

On the other hand, here was a beautiful woman and dedicated mother. My instincts, which admittedly have been wrong before, told me she wasn't capable of murder.

I gave her a friendly smile and stood. "Let them do their own investigating."

She followed me to the door and watched me leave. When I reached the picket fence, I glanced back. Hattie stood in the doorway with her arm around Laurie's shoulders. She might not have told the truth when she said the professor didn't know about his child, but I wasn't going to sacrifice a single mother and her offspring for a man like Taylor. I'd have to find another way to clear Edward's name.

"Goodbye, Mister."

The kid waved, and I waved back. When her mother added her own weak goodbye, I got a pang in my chest thinking about a man like Taylor using such a nice, beautiful woman. She deserved better.

That was my objective opinion.

CHAPTER 13

Hattie Channing had a fine motive for murder, but I didn't let that weigh heavy on my mind. There were still four other council members I hadn't talked to, and I might find at least two other motives better than hers.

Edward and I had located Mort through a lucky guess. I had stumbled across Ned at Bill's bar. We couldn't count on luck to find the rest.

Jeffrey Babbitt might be shy about violating their privacy by giving us their contact information, but if I had just hosted a spectacularly failed event that ended with a guest clawing at his throat and expiring on the floor, I would be happy to do anything to deflect attention from my place of business. Maybe I could sell him on my point of view.

Turning left when I got to Lemon Lane and then right on Sprout Street took me to the front doors of the Babbitt and Brown Bookstore.

The owner slumped over the shiny, dark-wood sales counter, his head resting on his palm and his eyes closed. A little bell jangled on my entrance, and he jerked awake and came out from behind the counter to greet me.

"How may I assist—"

The words dropped off when he recognized me, but instead of ordering me out of his place of business or hiding from me, he broke into a toothy smile and spread his arms in welcome.

"Business has been *booming* since your brother's lecture."

My gaze scanned the store. In front of the far wall, a woman was standing on tiptoe to read the spine of a cookbook. Another lady squatted in the mystery aisle, searching the bottom shelf. The third customer, a man, looked like he belonged to one of the two ladies and was killing time next to a display of knick-knacks.

Jeffrey caught my glance, giggled, and motioned toward the back of the store. "They're all in the community room, where we held the talk that fateful night. They want to see the place where *it* happened. Most of them will be back for the signing tonight."

"I'm surprised you're ready to face another event so soon, although I can see how it would be rough on the author if you canceled last minute."

Jeffrey made a scoffing noise. "I wouldn't waste my time on a phone call to schedule an event while the murder is still front-page news. Although, if *I* were an author, I'd grab the chance for free publicity." He shook his head. "Anyway, it's not a real event with a professional author. The Citrus Grove Culinary Arts Council put out their own cookbook a few years ago. Well, more than a few. Over a decade ago." He waggled his hand. "Didn't do so well, but, by popular demand, they hauled old copies out of storage. Everybody wants one."

"Congratulations. Maybe murder could be a new marketing strategy."

He let loose another giggle. Most men can't get away with giggling, but it fit Jeffrey. He reminded me of an imp. "Could be." He waggled his brows. "Who should be the next victim?"

I waved my hand. "Forget it. A bad joke, although the joke was on the professor. Did you invite him to come to Edward's talk? Not that you expected him to be a victim."

"*Invite* him? I'd never *met* him before that night." He leaned in and lowered his voice. "Truthfully? If *I* were one of his students, I would have been happy to bump him off." Here came another giggle. "Or, at the very least, I'd reconsider my major." He raised one arm and waved his hand around mimicking those personalities who ride floats in parades. "So full of his own self-importance, which is fine if you have something to be proud of, but," he pointed a finger at me, "he broke the cardinal rule." Now he waggled the finger. "Never bore your audience." He sucked in a breath and squeezed his eyes shut in a pained expression. "The man was a bore."

It was like watching a one-man play.

He grabbed my arm and led me to the counter where a stack of books was on display. "Speaking of boredom, did you know he wrote a book? I put a rush order on a few copies after his spectacular demise. People are snatching them up. Can you believe it?"

I extracted my arm, politely. "Hard to fathom."

"Since I have you and your brother to thank for the increase to my bottom line—in a manner of speaking, not that you actually killed the man—I could let you have one at a discount. As a souvenir?"

"I'll pass."

He grabbed the top book from the pile and thrust it at me. "Go on. It's on the house."

The muddy beige cover with thick, black lettering in some grand serif font looked like it had something important to say. The title didn't live up to the expectations. *The Language of the Contemporary Sexual Revolution.* I flipped it open to the copyright page and noted the book had come out back in 1997. The publisher was Cannonball Publishers, located in Utah.

I tucked the book under my arm. "I'll save it for the next revolution. Are any of the council members here now?"

"Thirty-five new members signed up Monday night after the professor's death. It looks like they might break one hundred if the pace keeps up."

"I mean of the original seven."

"Dora and Flora will be here for the signing tonight. I don't know about the rest."

"I've been meaning to ask. Is there any way you could give me the addresses of the council members?"

"I could, but I won't. It doesn't seem right."

I cocked my head. "You don't feel any responsibility for finding out who killed him?"

His cheeks turned a mottled red, and his typically twinkling eyes took on a different kind of light. "Why should I? I had nothing to do with his death. The person who poisoned him is solely responsible." He shook his head repeatedly, shocked by such a monstrous suggestion. "It's incredible to think anything I said or did had a bearing on what happened. Ridiculous!"

Making a shushing motion with my hands, I added some soothing noises. "Okay, okay. You're as innocent as an angel. No one is saying otherwise."

That calmed him down. With his cooperative mood gone, I figured it might be worthwhile to leave now and come back when the council members were here. I told Jeffrey I would see him later.

As soon as I mentioned leaving, his good humor was restored. "I heard your brother is in town with you. I ran out of signed copies of Aunt Civility's books, and I wondered if he could lay his hands on more. Maybe run some copies down to her and bring them back signed."

I never went anywhere without signed copies of Edward's books in the trunk of the car. It looked as if my foresight would pay off.

"This is your lucky day. I just happen to have a couple of boxes back at Mrs. Robbin's B&B." I checked my watch. It was going on lunchtime. "I'll drop them off tonight."

He winked at me. "Got to ride the wave."

I left Babbitt and Brown's thinking this visit to Citrus Grove might turn out to be a good thing after all.

CHAPTER 14

I f I had wanted my good mood to last, I should have stayed away from the B&B. There was a strange blue sedan parked out front, which wouldn't have raised a question except it was book-ended by two black-and-whites. I hurried up the front steps and into the foyer where I ran into Sykes with his hand grasping Edward's upper arm.

Claudia stood at her man's side, her lower lip trembling, while Zali sat at attention in one of the chairs, a delighted smile stretching across her round face. I didn't see any deputies.

"Where's your posse?" I asked as I set down Tyler's book on one of the chairs.

Sykes' looked even more grim than Edward. "They're in the kitchen, and I didn't bring them with me. They were driving past and saw my car."

"Good thing they're here. You might need backup." I ran my gaze over Edward. "He looks like a hardened criminal to me, especially in that red sweater vest. And the khakis? A dead giveaway. Aren't you going to cuff him?"

"Nicholas!" Claudia's eyes were moist and her face red. "This isn't funny."

Zali clapped. "No. It's exciting!"

"I'm being sarcastic because the situation is so ridiculous I can't take it seriously. Are you actually arresting my brother?"

"I'm taking him in for questioning."

"You've already questioned him. You might not like the answers, but they're the truth. And who else have you questioned, besides Mrs. Robbins? And many thanks for telling her I sicked you on her."

"Your brother is the only link to Professor Taylor in Citrus Grove."

This is where I could have told him about Hattie and Laurie. Should have told him, and it was almost out when something inside of me balked. What came out instead was, "Taylor was seen in town several times in the past month. That means he knew somebody here, somebody other than my brother."

Sykes dismantled my pronouncement with one word. "Who?"

I dropped my arms to my sides. "I don't know who, but if you ask around, you can probably find out."

He pulled a small notebook and pen from his pocket. "Give me the name of your witness and I'll check it out."

That was a reasonable request. It was also a problem. I had given my word to Bill. "The witness prefers to remain anonymous."

"Convenient." He put the pen and notebook away.

Edward cleared his throat. "You don't need to lie for me, Nicholas. The truth will prevail."

He obviously didn't read the newspapers.

"I'm not lying."

"Come on," Sykes said with a jerk of his head, and he led my brother out to the sedan. I kept pace with them.

"What's the name of your lawyer?"

"I don't have one," Edward replied. "At least not a criminal attorney."

Sykes opened the back door of the sedan and Edward started in.

"I'll call Classical Reads and get you one."

When Edward jerked upright, he hit his head on the door frame. With one hand rubbing his scalp, he said, "Don't you dare." I stared at him with my lips pressed together and my arms crossed, and he took a step in my direction. "Nicholas! I don't want anyone to know about this. Do you understand me?"

"Loud and clear," I snapped back, but it was too late to keep it quiet. Charlie Grant, rumpled slob and news hound, was taking it all in from his position on the sidewalk in front of Robbins' B&B. I stuck my hands in my back pockets, strolled over to him, and then turned around so we could both watch the back of Edward's head as the sedan drove away.

"My brother is helping the police with their inquiries into the death of Professor Taylor."

"Inquiries, huh?"

The reporter shot a glance at the front porch where Claudia stood alone wringing her hands together. The pose was that of a damsel watching her convicted love being led to the noose. A woman without hope.

I dismissed her with a manly snort. "That's his girlfriend. She was at Inglenook Resort last year when a crazed killer was running around knocking off guests and employees. Edward, who was helping the police, almost got it himself. She's worried about his safety."

I was the one who came close to dying, but I was happy to

revise the story with Edward in the role of naïve nincompoop who almost got his skull bashed in.

"Inglenook Resort?" Charlie's eyes lit up. "That was a bloodbath, from what I remember. Six people dead, wasn't it?"

If Charlie was any kind of reporter, he would have a natural desire to leave his competition in the dust. I couldn't keep Edward out of the papers, but I might be able to steer the angle. I reached my hand out to tap him on the chest, but there was an unidentifiable stain on his shirt, so I pretended to swat away a fly instead.

"It was three, actually, but the details are extra gruesome. Edward captured the killer single-handed." I yawned to show this was all in a day's work for Aunt Civility's official representative.

Some of Charlie's natural suspicion surfaced. "Funny. The police didn't mention that in any story I read."

The hook was baited. I only had to reel him in. I nodded, solemn. "Edward didn't want the credit. He's devoted to Aunt Civility and only wants his name associated with her books. He's like a public servant that way. His only interest is the welfare of society."

The reporter guffawed. "That's stretching it. He's the official rep of a famous author who writes about manners. That doesn't seem altruistic to me."

"Really? Etiquette is all about civil behavior. Treating your fellow citizens with respect. What's more uncivil than taking a life?" I waved my hand. "It all ties in."

He scratched the stubble on his cheek. "I suppose you're right."

The conversation had wandered into broad concepts which can bore anybody, and what could a reporter do with high ideals and genteel behavior? That didn't sell papers. I cocked my head and shot him a sideways glance. "You seem like a nice guy."

"That's what my wife tells me."

I hid my surprise at the news of his marriage. I had assumed he was a widowed dad. I couldn't believe any self-respecting woman would allow her husband out the door looking like that.

"What if I got you an interview with Edward's girlfriend, who just happens to be Claudia Inglenook, half-owner of Inglenook Resort? We'll give you the whole story, bloody details and all. The stuff that didn't make it into the papers."

"What's in it for you?"

"Well, and it's just a suggestion, how about a headline that reads, *Local Author Rep Risks Life to Find Killer.* It would be filler information, giving your readers the background on Edward's experience and qualifications, and then you could launch into the current investigation. Did I mention the amount of blood at Inglenook? They may never get the carpets clean."

One victim had died on the bathroom tile floor, the second, an employee, had been stabbed while cleaning the tub, and the third had been strangled, which doesn't generate a lot of blood, but it's called literary license.

He nodded. "I think it could work."

I clapped him on the shoulder. "In your capable hands? Of course it will work. Just let me talk to her first."

He double-checked the battery life on his digital camera. "Why don't I come with you?"

"You could, but then she might jump to conclusions. I need to explain how involving the public will make Edward safer, since that's her worry."

"Why don't you explain it to me?"

"It's obvious. Your readers will be on his side, watching it all play out through your stories. With alert citizens looking out for the killer, he—or she—won't be able to make a move against Edward. You've already asked for the public's help. Maybe you could run a contest or have a giveaway for anyone who supplies information leading to the arrest of the murderer."

"I'd have to clear that with the boss first."

The front door swung open and Mrs. Robbins escorted four deputies off the porch.

"Thanks for the pie, ma'am. It hit the spot." This came from a deputy who looked as if hers wasn't the first pie he'd eaten that day. He hoisted up his belt, but his belly pushed it back down.

She tittered with pleasure. "You men can't do your best on empty stomachs."

Charlie looked me in the eye. "That's a lot of cops for someone who's not considered a suspect."

"Weren't you listening? They didn't come for Edward. They came for pie."

Claudia, leaning on the railing for support, got a jolt of energy and swooped in front of the men. "Where have they taken him?" she demanded.

As the smallest of the deputies answered her, Charlie moved to join the fun, his reporter instincts operating on high. I pulled him back. "Once she's done talking things over with the deputies, I might be able to swing that interview for today."

His gaze remained on Claudia, who was waving her hands around more than a flight attendant giving safety instructions. "She looks angry."

"Fear does that to people. We'll just give her a couple of minutes to cool off—"

Her voice rose in both pitch and volume—I distinctly heard the word bullies—and Charlie raised his camera to eye level. I slipped in front of him.

"You're blocking my shot."

"I'm trying to keep you from making a fool of yourself. Look, did Detective Sykes walk my brother out in cuffs? No, because he wasn't under arrest." I pointed at Claudia. "There's his girlfriend, worried to death about him and, I admit, not behaving rationally, and you want to jump in there and antagonize her. She'll never talk to you then." I shook my head. "Maybe you're not the right guy for this story. You're too fast with the conclusions."

He kept his eyes fixed on Claudia.

"Did I mention the details, never released, about how Edward discovered the Inglenook emeralds?"

That got his eyes off Claudia and back on me. "Today."

I grinned. "Today."

Claudia stormed back into the house, and I hoped to Heaven she would be amenable to my suggestion. After all, by holding back the information about Hattie and Laurie, it was my fault Edward had been carted away.

CHAPTER 15

I t wasn't easy to convince Claudia that opening up to a reporter was the best thing she could do for Edward right now. We stood in the parlor. I had both hands on her shoulders to keep her from zipping off and carrying through with her plan to call a taxi and keep vigil at the sheriff's station.

"We have a chance to preserve Edward's dignity." I was using my rational voice.

"And how will a tell-all about Inglenook accomplish that? And what will it do to the resort's reputation?"

I let my hands drop. "So that's it. You're worried about business. Good to see you're just as mercenary as the rest of us."

"That's not fair."

"Okay. Maybe not. But right now, there is a reporter on the front porch who is itching to write about what he sees as Edward's arrest. Once that story hits the newsstands, bye-bye to his job. More than that, he could lose his identity, which is closely tied to his job."

She brushed her hair behind her ear. "It's just a job."

I stepped back. "It could be you're right. Maybe this Aunt Civility stuff is just a phase and he would be better off returning to his ways before all this manners and etiquette nonsense filled his head. He wanted to be a sports reporter. Of course, he wouldn't allow you in the booth because those guys can get pretty crass."

She gave me a haughty smile. "Edward hardly ever uses rude language. Even then, it's mild."

"Now, maybe, but once he's hanging around with the guys again, going out for beers after the game to brush up on the players and statistics, who knows? And he'll have to keep up with sporting events. Have you ever seen him slumped in front of the television, shoving a bag of chips into his pie-hole? I kind of miss that Edward. That guy didn't make me wear a suit to work."

"What would I have to say?" she mumbled.

"Not much. Just tell the reporter—his name is Charlie—what happened. Maybe embellish it a little. Amp up the scares and suspense. And the blood. Make sure there's plenty of blood."

"I suppose I could do that."

"And make Edward the hero of it all. That's important."

"Naturally."

Zali came barreling around the corner with Charlie on her heels. "Guess what I found?"

It was decided without words that I would get Zali out of the house to avoid any embarrassing incidents. Or violence. I didn't know if Mrs. Robbins had a garden out back and the tools to tend it, but I wasn't taking any chances. Zali put on her jaunty hat and we headed to downtown Citrus Grove.

"Eddie didn't look happy when he left with that policeman."

She was panting, her thick, little legs scurrying to keep up with me, so I shortened my stride and slowed down.

"Eddie wasn't happy."

"He probably hated being parted from Claudia." She snickered. "Not that I let them have any fun. The ticklish kind of fun, I mean."

Ticklish fun. I refused to go there with her and changed the subject. "We need to make a stop at a bar. Are you okay with that?"

She squealed. "I've never been in a bar other than at Inglenook."

I stopped walking. "You're not serious."

She nodded solemnly. "Came close once, but my father headed me off before I could slip inside. Said they weren't nice places, which made me want to go even more. After that, I just never got around to it. Inglenook's okay, but it's a bore, and Claudia and Robert don't like it when I mingle with the guests. They look scared when I suggest it."

If the prospect of combining Zali with alcohol frightened Claudia and Robert, who knew their aunt well, maybe it was a mistake to bring her to Bill's, but here we were. I was about to put down some ground rules but decided it was wrong for a man my age to lecture a woman in her sixties on how to behave. I met her grin, took a deep breath, and opened the door.

"It's dark! Like a spook house." Zali raised her voice. "Nobody better jump out at me or you'll be sorry."

The same regulars were on the barstools. They halted in mid-conversation and turned their heads as one. Ned had foam on his upper lip.

I headed directly to Bill's corner, steering Zali along with me. As soon as she spotted the proprietor, the aged aunt waved and said, "I'm Zali!"

Bill leaned forward and shook hands with her. "I'm Bill."

"No offense, but that's not a great name. I hate getting bills in the mail."

Bill smiled. "Me too."

"We need to talk," I said over Zali's head, brushing the feather from her hat away from my nose. "Privately."

She nodded and led the way. At the bar, I put Zali on a stool, ordered her a ginger ale, and asked the guys to look after her. Once she got settled, I stepped into Bill's office and skipped the preamble.

"They've arrested Edward. They say they've just taken him in for questioning, but it won't be long."

"I'm sorry to hear that."

She looked sorry, too, but that wouldn't help Edward.

"Detective Sykes dismissed the information you gave me because I couldn't give him the name of the witness. I should say wouldn't. I need to give him your name."

"I don't want the cops poking around here."

She didn't invite me to sit, but I pulled a chair over and used it. "Then I'll send him around to see you at your house."

"When I saw the dead man, I was here."

"Did Taylor come into the bar?"

"No. I was out front, but the detective might get the idea to question my men, and I don't want that." Her expression softened and, for a moment, I got a look at the pretty young nurse who soothed wounded soldiers in Vietnam. "They've got enough troubles of their own. They don't need to take on someone else's." Amend that. Pretty and fiercely protective.

"Why couldn't you have been taking a stroll when you saw him?"

She stared down at the blotter on her desk and absently picked at the corner. "I understand your predicament, but I can't risk this bar getting into the news."

"Risk? That sounds serious."

She leaned back and transferred her gaze to me. "I have my reasons and that's all I'll say."

She set her jaw. I wasn't going to alter her decision, so I

put my mind on what I really needed from her. "Okay. The end goal is to find out who Taylor was in town to see. If you show me where you saw him, I'll take it from there."

She agreed that was fair.

Back in the bar, Zali had moved—or been moved—to a stool in the center of the customers. They surrounded her and gazed at her face with something close to awe. She, in turn, wore a pleased grin. There were ten empty glasses in front of her. I swiped one off the counter and sniffed. Ginger ale.

"What's going on?" I asked, keeping my voice steady.

Bucktooth turned, looking like he wanted to witness to me about a holy apparition. "Miss Zali has been telling us about Norbert."

The man she attacked with a pair of gardening shears. Curiosity overtook horror. I'd never heard the whole story. I slipped my fanny onto a bar stool.

"What about Norbert?"

"It would be a bore to tell it all over again," Zali said. "Besides. It wouldn't sound as good the second time."

Ned hissed out, "What a woman."

The raconteur threw back the remains of ginger ale in the closest glass and then popped off her stool. She handed out waves to everyone present and said, "Bye-bye, fellas."

I stood aside and let her lead the way out of the bar.

CHAPTER 16

While Zali made faces at the puppies in the window of the pet rescue adoption agency next door, Bill pointed out Taylor's whereabouts on the two times she had spotted him. Once, he was turning into a doorway down the block—she thought it might have been the Happy Chicken Cafe. The second time, he had been about to turn off Lemon Lane onto Grove Street. Maybe. She hadn't seen him make the turn, but there was something about the way he approached the corner that made her think he was headed in that direction.

Taking Zali along to investigate was out of the question. I never knew what she might blurt out, so we returned to Robbins' in time to see Charlie get into his car. He shot me a grin and winked before he drove away.

Claudia was in the den staring thoughtfully at nothing. The television, tuned to some talk show, played without the sound, which is the only way to watch those shows. Two empty teacups and saucers were on the coffee table in front of her along with a serving plate with a single shortbread cookie remaining.

"How'd it go?"

She held out a hand to Zali and invited her to sit next to her on the couch. "How was your walk, Aunt Zali?"

Zali grabbed the cookie and bounced up and down on the cushion. "Loads of fun. Nicky took me to a bar. I made all sorts of new friends."

Claudia shot me a glare that would have frozen me if I hadn't been burning with impatience. "Isn't that nice, sweetheart? Do you need a rest?"

"I suppose I should." Zali looked up at me. "You'll keep an eye on them for me if Eddie returns, okay?"

She made me cross my heart before she agreed to leave us. Once she left, I took her place on the couch.

"How'd it go?" I repeated with emphasis.

"I heard you the first time. And what possessed you to take Aunt Zali to a bar?"

"She was perfectly safe. You'll notice she reeked of ginger ale. I was working a lead and, while I was out of the room, she entertained the troops like a pro. Now what happened with Charlie?"

"Charles is a nice man. An *intelligent* man," she added, implying the adjective didn't apply to the present company.

"You better hope not, or that story you were selling him won't stick. Did you get the impression he believed you?"

The corners of her mouth lifted in a private smile. "I think it went well."

Since she was a woman, I resisted the urge to wipe the smirk off her face with a friendly tap. "And? What did you tell him? Did he buy that Edward was working for the police instead of being their prime suspect? Did you follow my advice and add extra gore to the Inglenook murders?"

She stood. "It went well. You can read about it tomorrow morning with the rest of Citrus Grove." When she strolled off, humming in a self-satisfied way, I had to tell my foot, which was itching to kick her backside, about the rules concerning women. Maybe, when this was all over, I could convince Bill to take a shot at her.

Mrs. Robbins swept into the room and turned the television set off, moved a magazine, and then strolled back out with her chin held high. Apparently, she still hadn't forgiven me for sicking Detective Sykes on her. I was now invisible, which suited me just fine. I headed back downtown to go over Taylor's tracks and see where they led.

The first place Bill had seen Taylor go was the Happy Chicken Cafe. The same blond Amazon stood behind the glass counter next to the cash register. After giving me the expected customer greeting, she asked if I had found Hattie.

"It was a happy reunion. We caught up on the news, both the old and the more recent. Which reminds me. I have a quick question for you. You've heard about the man who died at the bookstore a couple of weeks ago? Professor Jonathan Taylor?"

She leaned her elbows on the counter. "Who hasn't? Someone said he had been working undercover for the police and a gang got him, but I also heard he had been part of a gang and wanted to give it up. One of the other gang members got to him before he could turn traitor. That option makes more sense to me."

"Perfect sense. Were you at Babbitt and Brown's the night he died?"

She wrinkled her nose. "I had to work. A shame. Usually I work days, but that night I had to cover for Angela. Her kid gave her the flu." She sighed. "It's the most exciting thing to happen around here in years."

"So, you never saw him."

She shook her head. "Not in person, but his picture was in the paper. Kind of old." She squinted as she thought back.

"He was smiling, and I think he was missing a tooth, though it could have been a shadow on the picture."

"Good girl. You have an excellent memory. I understand he used to come here to eat."

She glanced around the room as if making sure we were talking about the same place. "Here?"

"It would have been over the last few months. Let's say two. Do you remember seeing him hanging around?"

"No. I—wait a minute. I think he did stop by, but only once, and he left right away. That's why I remember. It was odd. I started walking him to a table. One minute he was there, the next he wasn't. If he was sick, he would have been smarter to keep going right to the washrooms."

She pointed to a hallway off the corner of the main dining area, and it gave me an idea.

"Do the waitresses always serve the same section?"

"Sure. It's easier for them and for me."

The section right before the hallway was the same cluster of tables and booths Edward and I had sat in yesterday. Hattie Channing's section. I thanked her and headed toward the location of the second Taylor sighting.

Assuming the professor had intended to turn off Lemon Lane and onto Grove Street, I walked up that side street. When I came to the intersection of Grove and Apple, an uncomfortable weight settled in my chest. Hattie Channing lived on Apple Street. Hattie Channing also said she hadn't seen the professor in years and he wasn't aware he was Laurie's father. I had sacrificed my brother for a liar.

No one answered Hattie's door when I knocked, so I walked along the side easement until I came to a large, tidy backyard. A hedge of shrubs separated the back border of the property from the neighbors. In the far corner, a low, white fence marked off a square garden. A clothesline cut diagonally across the corner nearest to me.

There were signs of Laurie. A bicycle rested against the house, next to a pair of rollerblades. Past a round, wooden picnic table, two reclining lawn chairs sat side-by-side. I imagined Hattie and Laurie spending evenings looking up at the stars, while Hattie pointed out the constellations. Sappy, but possible.

I returned to the front porch and waited fifteen minutes for Hattie to show before I gave up.

Since I had skipped lunch, I arrived at our home-away-from-home hungry for dinner. Fortunately, Mrs. Robbins' good manners wouldn't allow me to be invisible at the table. I got served along with the rest of the gang.

Zali led the conversation with a detailed reflection on her exciting exploits at Bill's, which seemed to consist of swapping war stories, with Zali's own personal war being the attack on Norbert. Once again, I was destined for disappointment because Claudia stopped her aunt from sharing the gory details, saying that kind of talk shouldn't take place while people were eating.

Even without the blood and horror to jazz things up, Zali turned out to be a good storyteller with an ear for comic timing. I'd lay odds she wasn't aware of her natural gift. She seemed surprised whenever any of us cracked a grin or laughed out loud. It touched me when she finished up by thanking me for providing her with one of her more memorable experiences.

"I've put it in my diary. Don't often do that, since my life at Inglenook is pretty boring."

Claudia stopped mid-chew and swallowed hard. "Aunt Zali! I thought you enjoyed living with Robert and me."

Zali squished up her nose. "S'all right, I suppose. It's better than that place I lived before I moved in with you. All those nurses and doctors asking me about my feelings, as if my feelings were any of their business." She made eye contact with each of us. "My feelings are my own, don't you think?"

"I know I'm for keeping them private," I said.

"After today, I knew you'd agree, Nicky. It's been a long time since anyone treated me like a grownup."

"That's not true," Claudia said with a quick glance at Mrs. Robbins.

Our hostess sat up straight in her chair with her lips pursed in disapproval, but her eyes gave her away. They shone bright with an eager interest in the dirty details.

Claudia wiped her mouth and set down her napkin in a slow and deliberate move. Her voice got tight like she might cry. "I'm sorry you feel that way, Aunt Zali."

"Oh, Claudia." Zali rolled her eyes. "You're doing that weepy thing again and it drives me bonkers." She put her finger on her lips. "Don't know why I call it that because you never actually cry."

I could have kissed her, but since I was still scared stiff of the woman, I offered her my cherry pie instead, which she picked up and ate like a sandwich.

"This is awfully good. You're a natural, Mrs. Robbins. Almost as good as Mrs. Beckwith."

Claudia explained to our hostess that Mrs. Beckwith was the cook at Inglenook and stressed it was a huge compliment. Regina Robbins blushed and looked at Zali fondly, as if her dream was to fill her to the brim with pastries.

"I won a blue ribbon at the county fair with that pie recipe. There's more if you're still hungry, or if you want a snack later."

But the pie wasn't destined for Zali's stomach. We heard the front door open and, a few seconds later, Edward stepped into the room. I almost jumped up with relief. Fortunately, I controlled it. Edward would have known something was wrong. Instead, I barely glanced at him and said, "You're late."

His bangs, hanging over his eyes, had curled. There were creases in his khakis, and not the kind that ran straight up the front of his pant leg, the ones he has Mrs. Abernathy iron in. He looked okay. That's not what gave me a punch in the stomach. It was the way he stepped into the room, giving me, his brother and secretary, the one who had weathered the Inglenook murders with him and been his right hand for ten months, the one who had been there for him his entire, arrogant life, a brief glance before seeking out Claudia. They locked eyes, and after he stared at her long enough to perform a Vulcan mind-meld, he took the chair closest to her and patted her knee. Zali would be proud.

Once he got settled, he spared me a nod, and after finishing the four remaining pieces of fried chicken, all the leftover mashed potatoes and carrots, three rolls with butter, and the leftover pie, which Zali graciously handed over, he sat back and closed his eyes. We waited in silence for the fugitive to speak, something he didn't do until Mrs. Robbins had placed a fresh cup of decaf in front of him.

"Thank you." He inclined his head at her.

"I take it they didn't feed you," I said.

Claudia countered with, "You don't have to talk about it now if you don't want to," causing our hostess to eye her with disfavor.

Zali poked his ribs. "Did they give you a ride back, Eddie? Oh! Did they let you run the siren?"

"I didn't ask them to, no," he said, his voice weary.

"I would have. You've got to grab your opportunities when they come. Who knows how long it will be before you get to ride in another police car?"

He grimaced. "Never, I hope."

Zali looked at his empty plate. "Was that one of their

135

tactics? Starve the prisoner? Or did they use the hoses on you?"

I watched my brother for *the signs*. A twitch in his left eye. A pulsing jaw muscle as he gritted his teeth. Already his delivery bordered on deadly calm. He had been through an ordeal, and I was confident his temper was boiling beneath his cool exterior. I just hoped his anger had a source other than me.

"I wasn't a prisoner. They were very kind to me."

Mrs. Robbins, who hours before had been complaining about Sykes' mistreatment of her, gave a brief nod. "That detective has manners."

"Maybe he's read your books, Eddie." Zali picked up Edward's fork and concentrated on shredding his paper napkin with it. I scooted my chair away from the table in case I should have to make a dive and take her weapon away, but she only set the fork down and added, "They're very interesting."

Well, look at that. Our little Zali, all grown up and lying like an adult. She'd have to work on her technique. A good lie takes practice. One rule is to not fidget while you're talking.

"Did he ask you about anything in particular?" I tried to make the question casual. "You were gone a long time."

Instead of answering, he put his palms on the table and pushed himself to standing. "I need a bath."

Okay. Maybe he wanted to talk about his experience in private. "I'll be up soon."

He shook his head. "That won't be necessary."

Claudia's expression didn't change except for a small twitch at the corners of her mouth. She obviously thought his need for solitude didn't apply to her. After a decent interval and an offer to help Mrs. Robbins clear the table, she followed him upstairs. I wasn't worried, though, because Zali blew out a breath that scattered her straight-cut bangs and said, "Looks like I'm back on duty." She trotted after them.

With just me and our hostess in the room, I stood and cleared the rest of the dishes and then waited armed with a dish towel as she swished them around in a sink full of sudsy water. Mrs. Robbins didn't seem inclined to start a conversation, so I did.

"Are your guests usually this exciting?"

She ignored me and glanced up at the clock on the wall, so I changed my approach to one guaranteed to generate goodwill. Sympathy.

"It must be hard on you, having the police hanging around."

"I still think it was a heart attack that killed the man. Maybe a stroke."

"Detective Sykes seems pretty sure he died from poison."

"He's covering his bases. Can't blame him, but I think it's a lot of hoopla over nothing. Never thought I'd see the day when a guest of mine was hauled out of here by the law."

"You're holding up well."

I meant it sarcastically, since she wasn't the one who spent hours being interrogated at the sheriff's station, but she grunted in agreement.

"My first husband was full of inconvenient surprises. I should be used to it by now."

"You mean Mr. Robbins?"

"Harold was my second husband. He was an angel.'

"Is that why you started the bed-and-breakfast? Funerals are expensive."

"Harold left me well provided for. We married later in life, so we didn't have children." She paused. Whether she was remembering Harold or regretting her lack of children, she shook it off and went back to scrubbing a serving spoon.

"I guess I was lonely. You meet the most interesting people when you take in guests."

"I imagine you got more excitement than you bargained for with us."

"Yes."

"I suppose that's also why you joined the Culinary Arts Council. To meet people."

She handed me the spoon. "I'm not a member. I only helped with the serving because Hattie asked."

"She has her hands full with a youngster running around the house."

"You've met Laurie?"

"Sure. Nice kid."

I wouldn't say the room got colder, but her chatty manner dried up and she went back to scrubbing and handing off without comment.

CHAPTER 17

I gave Edward enough time to relax in a bath and change before I sought him out. I rapped a few times with my knuckles on his door and waited ten seconds. When he didn't respond I banged with the side of my fist.

"I know you're in there and I know you're awake, so you might as well open the door because I'm not going away."

"What do you want?" he snapped.

I jiggled the knob.

"Let me in. We have a double date."

He muttered, "What nonsense is this?" but he was interested enough that he unlocked the door and opened it. My brother had changed into red silk pajamas, and he had an open copy of *Discrimination and Disparities* by Thomas Sowell in his hand.

"Catching up on your light reading?"

I pushed past him and dropped onto his bed, which was still made but carried his imprint on the covers. Since there wasn't a headboard available, he had been propped against the wall with his legs stretched out in front of him. The fact he hadn't pulled down the covers meant he was too keyed up to sleep, which was good news for me and my plans.

"Dora and Flora are at Babbitt's tonight." I glanced at my watch. "At least I assume they're still there. Country girls go to bed early, so you better get a move on it if we're going to talk to them."

He tossed his book onto his pillow, shoved me to make room and sat beside me. "I'm not going anywhere." He clasped his hands between his knees and let his shoulders slump. "I've had a distressing day."

"Look, I know it's been tough on you, but we have the perfect opportunity to talk to two more members of the council. More, if they show up. We couldn't ask for a better chance to find out what Ned and Mort and The General and the old dolls, including Knitting Woman, saw or overheard that night."

"You forgot Miss Channing."

"And Miss Channing." If the opportunity to question her would get him there tonight, so be it. "Think about it, Edward. That night, they were working the crowd, trying to drum up new members. It's as if we had Babbitt's community room wired. We can walk in tonight and look over the information gathered."

"We're probably wasting time with the old ladies," he grumbled. "Neither of them wears glasses. At their age, they probably couldn't distinguish between you and Mrs. Robbins from more than three feet. And they're probably hard of hearing as well," he added, just to be churlish.

"You may have a point. I haven't tested their eyesight or their hearing, so I don't know." I stood. "In fact, it probably would have been a waste of time."

He reached for his book.

"Oh." I snapped my fingers. "I almost forgot. Jeffrey Babbitt ran out of your books. I told him I'd bring by a couple dozen copies, but I can do that tomorrow morning. The crowds will be gone, but—"

"Give me five minutes. And make yourself presentable."

That meant putting on my brown suit, cream dress shirt, and mauve tie and ditching my tennis shoes for leather loafers, but it was a small price to pay.

When he met me in the foyer seven minutes later, he had on a dark-navy suit, white shirt, and yellow tie. He'd combed the curl out of his hair, and I could smell the mint from his toothpaste. We had to take the two stragglers with us and, since we were bringing the books, we drove. That is, I drove while the three of them crammed into the back seat with Zali in the middle, chaperoning.

"Are you taking us to the murder scene?" The aged aunt leaned forward and hooked her elbows over the front seat.

"Yes, ma'am."

"I suppose they've taken the body away by now, eh, Eddie?"

Edward sighed. "I certainly hope so."

"Too bad. It'll still be creepy. I like creepy, but I don't like shocks. Nobody better jump out at me."

I glanced in the rearview mirror. She was chewing her lower lip. "I'll warn Jeffrey Babbitt to control himself." She blew out a breath and wiggled back into the space in-between Edward and Claudia.

After the short drive, I turned onto Sprout Street, and as I pulled up to the curb one shop down from the bookstore, I had a dilemma. One of my duties as secretary is to open the car door for the author when we arrive at any kind of public event. It gives the impression Edward is important. This wasn't a scheduled appearance, but there were plenty of people wandering on the sidewalk and entering the book-store. My problem was that good manners dictated I open the door for the lady.

Edward provided the solution by getting out and going around to tend to Claudia, leaving me to help Zali out of the car. She scooted over and I took both her hands in mine, leaned back on my heels, and hauled her out.

The gang went ahead while I got the boxes out of the trunk. There were three, but I could only balance two if I wanted to close the trunk, so I left the last one for later. Jeffrey Babbitt scurried up as I pushed through the doors.

"My dear boy! You've come through and then some. I didn't expect you to bring your brother along. He's already in the community room and making quite a stir." He eyed the boxes. "I'm sure there's room on the table for the books, and if I bring another chair—"

"If you're going to suggest Edward horn in on the council members' event, save it. My brother wouldn't intentionally offend a person, let alone an entire council full of them."

Besides, I wanted to keep the members in a friendly frame of mind, which would not happen if we stole their spotlight. Instead, I convinced him to let me place the Aunt Civility books in stacks on the front counter next to the register.

"I'd go in with you," Jeffrey said, "but I have to stand guard and make certain nobody leaves without paying for their cookbook after they get their signed copy."

"Wouldn't it have been easier to have them pay first and then show their receipt at the signing table?"

He didn't miss a beat. "But not as profitable. Now, when they approach the counter, they will have the opportunity to buy your aunt's book."

I almost stumbled and asked him what Aunt Mary Dell had to do with the price of eggs, but then I realized if Edward were Aunt Civility's nephew and I was his brother, she'd be my aunt, too. It made me feel kind of important knowing I was related to a celebrity and not just the celebrity's official representative. I left him arranging the book display and joined the rest of the crowd.

The little gnome wasn't kidding about the local interest in the murder. The room was packed elbow-to-elbow with men and women soaking up the atmosphere. Some of them had dusted off their Sunday best, and with the high-spirited chatter and bursts of laughter filling the room the scene reminded me of a cocktail party, without the drinks. All those bodies generating heat made the room stuffy. The air reeked with the scent of perfume and Old Spice.

Quite a few folks were vying to get a signed copy of the council's cookbook. I wondered what they would request for an inscription. Probably something tasteful that just hinted at murder, like *Best wishes from Dora and Flora, who were in at the death.*

A group of spectators—I call them that because they didn't look like they were here to buy anything—had ganged up on Edward, pushing Zali and Claudia to the edge of the room. My brother's eyes met mine and, having known him for a lifetime, I interpreted the gaze as one of *Unhappy Surprise.* He thought we could simply drop off the books and exchange a few pleasantries with Dora and Flora while a trickle of their public passed through. Then he could say he'd given me my chance to question them and we could all go home. Instead, he had to talk to people. A lot of people.

I let the two Inglenook ladies fend for themselves and fought my way through to reach the two signing tables at the front of the room. They had been pushed together to form one long table. Edward was right. In this atmosphere, there wasn't much chance of having a private conversation, but, by gum, I had gotten us here, and I planned to go ahead with the program. And we had hit the jackpot as far as available council members were concerned.

Mort and The General shared the table on the right.

While the banker scribbled his signature like a man used to signing off on loan documents, The General took his time, forming his John Hancock in neat, square letters. Both wore suits. Mort's mid-weight heather-gray was obviously bespoke and made to deemphasize his slight belly, but The General's navy-blue pinstripe looked like it had come off the rack a few decades ago. I will admit that, with his ramrod straight posture, it hung on him nicely. Dora and Flora, who occupied the table closest to me, had donned their best poly-ester pantsuits, Dora's in lime green and Flora's in canary yellow.

Their system for handling the books didn't make sense to me. A single line formed in front of each table. One member would grab from the pile and sign it before passing it around to the other members. I don't know how they kept track of which book belonged to which person, but if they didn't offer personalized inscriptions, I guess it didn't matter.

The fifth member of the council present that night sat a short distance from Flora, maybe two or three feet, in a pair of black slacks and a floral-print silk blouse. She might have spruced up for the event, but she found it a bore. At least that's what it looked like. She focused her attention on her knitting needles and ignored the customers.

I had yet to hear Knitting Woman speak. Hoping she had something interesting to say about Taylor's demise, I held out my hand.

"I'm Nick Harlow, the famous rep's brother." She didn't take my hand, so I added with a touch of pride, "And nephew to Aunt Civility. Pleased to meet you, Mrs.—"

"Georgie will do." She employed a no-nonsense tone used by all the best schoolteachers. Still, she ignored my proffered hand and kept her needles clicking.

"Interesting name," I said to keep the conversation going. "What's it short for?"

"Georgette."

"Like the flaky blond woman on *The Mary Tyler Moore Show*?"

She narrowed one eye. "You can see why I prefer Georgie."

I picked up a book and looked at the cover. *Eat Up!* was written by the Cooking Club of Citrus Grove. "If you don't mind me asking, why aren't you signing books with your fellow council members? Or are they club members?"

Flipping the book open, I noted the members who contributed to the book included Dora, Flora, Ned, The General—whose full name was Terrance Henderson III—Mort, and Regina Robbins. I raised a brow over the last name.

"I hadn't joined yet when the Cooking Club—what a tedious name—came out with the book. I'm only here to offer my support." She sent her light gray eyes over the crowd. "If I had known so many people would show up, I would have stayed home. They don't need me."

The sisters broke in with protests and assurances as to Georgie's worth as a support team of one, which answered any questions about their ability to pass a hearing test. Georgie and I hadn't been speaking loudly, and the crowd was providing plenty of background noise.

A familiar voice broke through the chatter. It was raised and headed toward the danger zone. I swiveled my head and spotted Edward several feet behind me facing off with a tall, skinny man wearing a cardigan over a striped shirt and jeans. I moved closer.

"Which is it?" the guy demanded. "I think it's very clear."

The guy was trying to convince my brother that the Continental style of dining reigned supreme over American style. Diners of both species held the fork in the left hand and the knife in the right while cutting their meat. His

145

complaint seemed to be over the time lost while Americans moved the fork to their right hand before they lifted dinner to their mouth. Since both ways were acceptable to manners-minded folk, Edward declined to take sides, but the guy wanted a ruling.

"Time is a valuable commodity," the man said in a high, thin whine.

"Yes, it is," Edward snapped. "And you're wasting mine."

I stepped between them, laughing as if I'd heard a good joke, put my hand on Edward's shoulder, and squeezed. "My brother means because the answer is so obvious."

Everything about the guy was thin, including the smile he gave me. "You mean European-style, obviously."

A debate wasn't on my agenda. "To each his own. If you like European, there's your answer. The same if you prefer American."

"That's not an answer."

I looked over my shoulder and moved closer. "That's the politically correct answer. Of course, you're right, but we wouldn't want to start an international incident, so we'll keep it between ourselves." I winked.

He nodded, his eyes bright with victory, and headed for a couple of equally repressed-looking individuals across the room, probably to inform them his opinion had been confirmed.

"Maybe you should run for office," Edward growled in my ear.

"I got rid of him, didn't I?"

"Oh, Mr. Harlow!"

A large woman in a white sundress and sandals wiggled her fingers at him. He gave me a pained expression. I left Edward with his latest fan and returned to the tables. While I was performing my intervention, the ladies had continued their conversation. Dora was in the middle of a surprising statement that she made as she handed a signed copy of a cookbook to her sister.

"Who knew we could find so much excitement by joining a group of fuddy-duddies who like to cook? Romance, death. All we need are babies!"

"Don't be foolish," Georgie said, though she blushed like a maiden.

I arched one eyebrow. "I'm sorry. Did you say babies?"

"Georgie won't be thinking about babies for another month," Flora offered as she waited for Dora to finish signing the book of a teenage boy. "That's when she and Mort walk down the aisle."

I thought it highly unlikely the subject would come up even then, considering Georgie was around seventy years old. And then it sunk in and my other eyebrow joined its neighbor.

"Mort the banker?" I said. Hearing his name, the banker glanced over. When he spotted me, he grinned.

"Not bad, for amateurs," he called out, nodding in the direction of the fans.

"All it took was a sudden death," I mumbled, ignoring the gasp of the woman next in line as I cut between her and the teenager to get to the edge of Mort's table. That put me right in between the two lines. I stuck my hands in my trouser pockets and looked down at him. "So, you're the lucky guy who snagged Georgie."

He chortled in the overly hearty way men do when they're talking about relationships. "She finally said yes."

"Congratulations. You'll never run out of scarves."

He gave a short speech about how lucky he was to find love later in life. I gave him the appropriate response, and a few people within earshot cooed and congratulated him. After a brief pause, I introduced a subject that interested me.

"Any thoughts since we last spoke in your office?"

147

"You mean have I remembered any lurking killers and suspicious characters?"

The General jerked his head to stare at Mort, his eyes boggling. "Who's a killer?"

"There's a murderer loose in Citrus Grove," I said. "Haven't you read *The Courier*?"

The ex-soldier relaxed. "Newspapers. Ha! Bunch of nonsense. Like to get people worked up over nothing."

"Detective Sykes doesn't think it's nothing." My pleasant gaze moved from one man to the other. "Has he paid a call on either of you?"

Next in line was an older woman who looked like she'd lose the tryout for America's favorite grandma only because her bony angles might put a kid's eye out if he came in for a hug. She peered over half-moon glasses at the two men and waited for their answer as if she had asked the question.

Mort leaned back his head to meet my interested gaze and smirked. "The detective came to my office this morning. I didn't have anything to tell him either, though his questions were more interesting than your brother's. Much more interesting."

His smirk begged me to ask what additional ground Sykes had covered during their meeting. I didn't want to disappoint him, so I asked.

"For example?"

The smirk broadened into a grin. "He asked if I saw you do anything to the barley water."

The second-rate grandma hugged her book and stared at me. I growled at her, and she let loose a squeak. Feeling better, I turned back to Mort.

"What for? He already tested the pitcher for poison." I made a noise like t'cha. "He's grasping at straws."

"No one came to see me." The offense in The General's tone made it clear the person responsible for this omission would have to drop and give him twenty. "Though I was out much of the morning." His gaze slid up to meet the woman's eyes. "Had my daily walk. Important to stay fit."

She tugged the hem of her blue cardigan down over her skinny bottom and nodded once. "It's obvious you do."

The General sat even more erect, which didn't seem possible. I interrupted them before he strained his neck.

"But if Sykes did come and see you, what would you have told him about that night?"

The General considered. "Depends on what questions he asked."

He glanced at the lady and got an approving nod.

"Let's pretend I'm him." I held up my hand. "I'll set the scene first. Edward has just given his talk to a packed room. The attendees, parched and hungry after a half hour of hearing about food, move to the dessert tables. Did you notice anyone hanging around the snacks who wasn't interested in eating? Or overhear somebody make a snide comment about Professor Taylor, or even college professors in general?"

"Difficult to say."

"Where were you standing after the lecture?"

His expression brightened as the light bulb went on. "I came over with the rest of the council to congratulate your brother. Georgie and Ned went to the back of the room to sign up new members. They didn't need me, so I stayed put. Then I took a meringue kiss from the table." He ducked his head, embarrassed. "I took two because they were damn good."

The woman lowered her gaze, and he blustered out an apology for his language.

"Oh, it's not that," she said in a voice that threatened to break out in a giggle. "I grew up with seven brothers. It's just that, well, I made the meringue kisses for the event."

The General sucked in his breath. "Best I've ever had. Partial to them. Mother used to make 'em."

I pushed down my exasperation. "I had one too, ma'am, and they were tasty. While you were enjoying your meringues, General, did you wander the room?"

But he only had eyes for her. "Don't remember seeing you here Monday night. Would've remembered."

Rather than fight a losing battle, I drew her into the conversation. "Did either of you notice Professor Taylor before he was taken ill?"

"I saw him over by the dessert table," he said. "He was standing next to you, and you handed him something to drink."

My jaw clenched. "Before then."

The woman came out with a surprising observation. "Why did it have to happen after the lecture?"

She was exactly right. Edward, Sykes, and I had even discussed how Taylor could have been poisoned before he got to the event. I switched gears.

"Did any of you see the professor arrive?" I included Mort in the question, as well as the people standing in line. "He was wearing a blue linen suit and tennis shoes and carrying a water bottle."

"Sounds pretty cheesy," a middle-aged man mumbled.

I nodded. "So, he'd be hard to miss."

The grandma raised her hand. "I might have seen him walk in."

"Was he with anyone?"

"I don't think so."

"Did anyone walk in at the same time?"

"Not noticeably. I mean, a couple walked in right before him, and a few people who didn't look like they were together entered afterward, but nobody was with him. The only reason I saw is because I was waiting for my friend." She turned to The General and her cheeks flushed pink. "Only a lady friend of mine."

Before his pleased expression could turn into a declaration of love, I said, "Are any of the people you saw then here tonight?"

She turned around and scanned the room The people surrounding her turned and peered at faces along with her, which was silly, since she hadn't provided descriptions. Then she pointed.

"Him."

The General guffawed. "Why, that's our own Ned. Don't think he's a killer."

"He's the only one?"

"I'm afraid so. I wish I could be more helpful."

I patted her shoulder. "No worries. Thanks for trying. Did any of the rest of you notice Taylor?"

That got me a wealth of nothing. One woman had him stumbling around as if he were drunk. The middle-aged man said he hadn't seen Taylor and was glad he hadn't. The rest came somewhere in-between, with Taylor either acting odd or doing a good imitation of the Invisible Man.

Killers were supposed to enjoy returning to the scene of their crime. I considered the possibility that the person who offed Taylor had nothing to do with the council and scanned the crowd. Most of them were over fifty. My glance stopped on a woman dressed in slacks and a jacket. There were plenty of dressed-up people hanging around the community room. What made her unusual is she hadn't hit the forty-year mark yet. She wasn't wearing the uniform of her contemporaries—clinging knit leggings or painted-on jeans. It made a nice change, and I took a moment to appreciate her.

She was talking to some guy wearing a man-bun. Not all men look ridiculous with a top knot. Sumo wrestlers and samurai, for instance. I wouldn't laugh at *them*. But your average Joe getting in touch with his feminine side by wearing sandals, wrinkled pants made from hemp, and a bun…Those men are fair game. She looked too good for him.

My gaze followed her as she crossed the room to exchange words with one of a trio of women gathered close to the wall where the snack tables had stood on that fateful night. I recognized two of them as volunteers from the event. Unless the murder had been a group effort and they were holding a reunion, they were probably complaining about the sour fruit born of their volunteer labors. The one with graying brown curls turned her head, locked eyes with me, and pinched her lips together. Taking it as a challenge, I made my way across the room.

"I remember you," I said to the frowner. Turning to include them all, I added, "You were the ladies who did such a great job at the Culinary Arts Council's last event. I didn't get a chance to thank you for your efforts."

I gave a broad smile to the younger woman. "Although I don't remember you."

She smiled back. I would have rated her smile as above average, but then she snapped her gum, going at it like it was a contest to see how loud she could make it smack. I changed my mind. She deserved the guy with the bun.

"See you later, Mom," she said, kissing the frowning woman on the cheek before joining her boyfriend at the doorway that led into the bookstore proper.

"As I was saying, you ladies deserve a gold star. I hadn't properly thanked you, what with the excitement of Professor Taylor's death."

They exchanged wary glances, which guaranteed Taylor had been the topic before I arrived.

"It must have been horrible for you, especially as it happened so close to where you were working."

A short woman with curly hair raised her hand. "I was in

the kitchen. Missed the whole thing, except for when they took him away."

"You were lucky." The frowning woman shuddered and jabbed her finger at the ground a few feet away. "I was standing right there when he fell. Might have landed on my feet, he was that close. His expression was horrible. I've never seen anything like it. It's as if he knew."

"Knew what?" I asked.

"Well, that he was going to die and somebody in the room was responsible."

Without pausing to consider the possible ramifications, I said, "Did he mention a name?" And before you think unkind thoughts about me, please remember I was focused on the killer being someone other than Edward.

She squished up her face in thought. "He pointed, and he accused someone across the room. I couldn't see who. There were people in my way." She turned to the woman next to her. "Did you see who it was?"

I held my breath.

"Sorry. I was collecting empty cups and paper plates. People are slobs. I didn't even know someone had died until the paramedics showed up."

I could have kissed her until she added:

"If the man accused his killer in front of everyone, you would think the police would have made an arrest by now."

"Did Taylor say this person is my killer?" I demanded.

Frowning Woman put her fingers to her bottom lip. "Well, no. Not in those words."

"Then we have no idea what he was trying to communicate. Maybe he was pointing at someone because he thought that person could help him. Or maybe he was trying to say something completely unrelated to his death."

"Like what?" Frowning Woman said. "He was dying."

"It's not a good idea to jump to conclusions. That's all I'm saying. A person could get sued for slander."

The one who had been busy cleaning during Taylor's death scene put her hand on Frowning Woman's shoulder. "He's right. We don't really know what Professor Taylor was thinking."

Now that I had regained control of the conversation, I decided to add some butter before asking the most important question.

"You ladies are so good at your jobs because you are observant. You keep an eye on everything so you can anticipate everyone's needs."

They stood taller and nodded their agreement.

"And while working the room, you were in the perfect position to have heard or seen something that might help catch the killer. The police probably consider you star witnesses."

Frowning Woman didn't look like she appreciated that role. The one from the kitchen giggled, and the cup-collector sighed.

"That detective already asked us for our statements," the frowner said, "but I will tell you, they didn't get much information from me. I was too busy to pay attention."

"Me too." At least the cup-collector sounded sorry.

"I wish I had seen something," the woman from the kitchen said with regret. "You should ask Regina Robbins. She was overseeing the service. That woman doesn't miss anything. Old Eagle Eye."

Mrs. Robbins hadn't had much to say to Edward and me, but now that the police were calling it murder, she might open up.

"You're certain you didn't see the dead man before, well, before he was dead?"

Frowning Woman folded her hands over her middle. "I

didn't say that. He was over by the signing table when I went to see if Georgie and Ned needed anything. He also stopped by the table to look over the snacks before they were made available."

"Did he eat anything?"

"I think I said they weren't available yet."

"Was anyone with him?"

"Not any of the times I saw him."

I thanked them for their time and turned my attention to the other occupants of the community room.

Human beings are fascinated by any hint of fame or notoriety. Tonight's lookie-loos were no different. They glommed onto the bit players in Taylor's death with giddy enthusiasm. People shoved books in front of the old ladies, who were signing as fast as their arthritic knuckles would allow. There were regular bursts of laughter and joking, and cliques had formed to share gossip. All we needed was a snack table.

I wandered back up front to where Edward had been pushed by the crowd. A head of white hair caught my eye. Ned was neglecting his signing duties in favor of conversation with a couple of men in overalls, which I thought would make it perfectly natural for me to ask the whereabouts of the final council member. Positioning myself between Flora and Georgie, facing the crowd, I said, "Someone seems to be missing, unless I've forgotten how to count. Aren't there seven of you?"

Flora put her hand on her cheek. "I can't think who you mean."

Dora joined in the fun, pointing with her bony finger to count the members out loud. "One. Two. Three. Four. Five, and six. I suppose there must be someone missing, but I can't think who. Maybe that young, good-looking gal. What was her name?"

Georgie didn't know how to play. "Hattie couldn't find a sitter for Laurie. That's what Regina said."

"Where is Mrs. Robbins tonight?"

"Working, I assume. She's got guests to take care of at the B&B."

The next woman in line asked Dora a question about how best to steam milk, and the two sisters started an argument over whether it was better to use a thermometer or watch the edges of the pot.

Since the members were otherwise occupied with fans, and the one who wasn't didn't seem big on conversation, I found a spot in the corner and watched while Edward reluctantly posed for photographs with his fans, many of whom had grabbed copies of his book from the front counter. He was a regular celebrity tonight, although he didn't seem to be enjoying his fame. He was used to hiding behind the alleged author of the Aunt Civility books and had gotten too comfortable and too damn lazy as far as I was concerned. No risk of writer's cramp from signing books. No audience members asking where he got the ideas for his book's themes. No grammar experts telling him he should have used a colon instead of a semi-colon. I was enjoying his discomfort. However, when one portly man tried to get my brother to put his hands around his own throat in an imitation of Taylor's last moments, I stepped in between them, held up my hands and raised my voice.

"People. Have a little respect. We are shocked and saddened by Professor Taylor's passing, and since we're standing ten feet from where he expired, we'd like to comport ourselves with dignity."

The crowd fixed their gazes on the random spot I pointed to as if hoping Taylor would pop out of the kitchen and reenact the scene for their benefit. The portly guy sneered at me.

"Who are you? Spokesman for the spokesman?"

I leaned in so my mouth was about an inch from his ear. "I'm the guy that's going to haul you out of here by your pants if you don't behave yourself."

He took a startled step back.

The crowd did calm down after that, though it wasn't out of any respect for the deceased. They gathered around the spot of Taylor's demise, pointing and clucking, my brother forgotten for the moment. Before he could relax, a woman in a forest-green, flowing dress tugged on Edward's sleeve and asked him to sign her book. He opened it to the title page and pointed.

"The author has already signed it."

Her heavily mascaraed eyes opened wide. "But you were there! Actually there!" She placed her fingertips against her lower lip and the numerous bracelets around her wrist clanked. "Just a few feet away as the life force left the man's earthly body and joined the cosmos." She moved her fingertips to Edward's arm. "Did you sense anything...otherworldly? A hint of aura? The shadow of his spirit?" She lowered her eyes to his sleeve and ran her fingers up and down the fabric. "There could be residue of the event on your clothing."

Claudia pushed herself forward and pried the woman's fingers off my brother's arm.

"His suit is fresh from the cleaners."

Now that the line for signatures had petered out, Mort left his spot at the table to join Ned. The General was doing likewise. However, the sisters had been paying attention to the nut-job hassling Edward, and they leaned their heads together and snickered. I saw an opening.

"People can get nutty over a thing like sudden death."

"Oh, we know," they answered in unison.

"The two of you handled the unpleasantness like a couple

of pros." My attention that night had been on Taylor, then Edward. I hadn't seen the sisters' reaction, but I thought they might take my observation as a compliment.

Flora giggled. Dora smiled at me and said, "You naughty boy. But you are correct. Flora and I have seen many deaths in our time. Family members used to die at home."

Flora nodded. "And then there was that silly farmhand who taunted Tiny."

Dora gave me another sweet smile and clarified. "Our bull. And the man's name was Hank Roper. He made a good run for it, but Tiny was faster."

"Daddy always warned us not to taunt Tiny, but Hank wouldn't listen. Made an awful mess," Flora said, relishing the memory. "Bulls are very curious creatures. It took us forever to get Tiny to stop playing with the body."

Zali bounded up to the table during the latter part of the conversation and offered her two cents. "Flip, flop. Flip, flop. Served him right. Men never listen to warnings."

I wondered how many warnings she had given Norbert.

"Professor Taylor didn't make a mess, but he did cause a scene. Did you notice how people reacted?"

Dora nodded. "They freaked out, but quietly, since they were in a bookstore."

Zali nudged my ribs. "And Eddie is always talking about how people don't have manners."

"Did anyone react oddly?" I persisted.

They shook their heads no.

"This Professor Taylor sounds as if he wasn't a nice man, but I wouldn't wish murder on anyone."

Dora and Flora, who moments before had been relishing the details of a goring, looked uncomfortable at this pronouncement.

"That detective is foolishly optimistic if he thinks he'll

ever catch the killer," Georgie continued. "There must be thousands of oleander bushes in Southern California."

"Do you have one?"

She finally lowered her knitting and looked me in the eye. "No, but I wouldn't be surprised to find it growing on Dora and Flora's property."

Dora pressed a finger to her bottom lip. "I do seem to remember one of the cows getting out of the pen and being poisoned by a plant, but I'm not sure if it was oleander. Anyway, the cow didn't die, and daddy burned the plant to be safe. But oleander can grow wild, so who's to know where the killer got the plant?"

"You don't know anyone else who grows it?"

They said no.

Another customer walked up to the table just then. The sisters glommed onto the opportunity to end the conversation and twittered over him like robins surrounding a big, fat worm.

The crowd had thinned out into groups of three or four people chatting among themselves, probably digesting any new items of interest they had picked up tonight. If gossipers were the rodents of the human hierarchy, these were the chipmunks, with bright, wide-open eyes and twitching noses. When Edward declared he was leaving, I didn't argue, but I asked if he might have a question or two for the ladies.

He glared at them and shuddered. "I think I've suffered enough today. Besides, I'm sure you've already gathered any information they have to offer. You can tell me later."

Since I was left to escort Zali to the car, I first had a short chat with the ladies. After getting what I wanted from them and saying goodnight, I crooked my elbow out for the aged aunt, and she took it.

"They were lying, you know." She rubbed the side of her

nose. "About not knowing if anyone had oleander bushes. Obvious."

I grinned at her. "I had my suspicions."

When we passed through the main store, Jeffrey Babbitt was behind the counter with a long line of customers waiting their turn. I waved to let him know we were going, but he was so involved managing his booming trade that I don't think he noticed.

"Good thing the professor died here," Zali said. "Otherwise someone else would be getting all the business."

I glanced back at Jeffrey. She had a point. At least one person was benefiting from Taylor's death.

CHAPTER 18

Since Edward marched straight up to his room and locked the door behind him when we got back to the B&B—like a big baby—I had to wait until morning to talk to him. Even then, the third wheel was at his side as if the FBI had ordered her to keep tabs on his every move. Call me petty, but I wasn't about to share any information about the murder with Claudia around. Still, it would have been nice if he had asked me to share. Then I could have turned him down politely and explained why, but since he didn't give me that opportunity, I figured he could go lick green wallpaper and went downstairs to breakfast.

We were seated at the kitchen table eating scones and honey with a side of fruit while Mrs. Robbins refilled coffee cups and wiped crumbs from Zali's side of the table. Edward's mood had improved with breakfast. In fact, he was as close to chipper as he gets.

"Take a note, Nicholas. I might want to approach Classical Reads with a book on etiquette for prisoners."

"I thought you weren't under arrest."

"I wasn't, but when we arrived, before Detective Sykes

took me to an interview room, he left me alone while he conferred with a colleague. That gave me a chance to observe my surroundings. I sensed there was a protocol at work in the prison. A hierarchy. It could be interesting and save someone an uncomfortable learning curve if he—or she— ever found himself—or herself—in the unthinkable position of having to spend the night in a cell."

I crumpled up my napkin and tossed it on my plate. "Give me a break. Sykes took you to the city jail, not to prison, and you didn't spend one minute behind bars. You're talking out of your—" I glanced at the women and amended the part of anatomy to which I was about to refer. "Out of your nose."

Not that I spent a lot of time hanging around prisons, or even jails, but men trapped together in rooms with strangers and a very public toilet probably weren't minding their manners and couldn't care less about breaking an etiquette rule.

Besides. Jailbirds weren't Edward's audience. I wondered about this sudden interest in what he would normally consider lower life forms until, while drinking my after-breakfast coffee, I reached for the morning edition of *The Citrus Grove Courier*, a small paper consisting of twenty pages.

The first thing that caught my eye was the caption under the front-page picture of Edward standing next to Sykes' car yelling at me. *Edward Harlow expresses rage over senseless killing.* My gaze moved to the headline.

Edward Harlow Investigates. Charlie hadn't used my suggestion, which I thought had more potential to promise excitement to the average person. However, I conceded that the reporter must know his readers.

Edward Harlow, the distinguished official representative of the esteemed author and world-famous columnist, Aunt Civility, has

162

encountered death, but it will take more than murder to intimidate
this fine example of American masculinity.

I gagged and set my coffee cup down. Edward's column based on the Aunt Civility books was syndicated in about a hundred small papers, none of them reaching beyond the borders of the USA. I admit the Internet might make them accessible to foreign powers.

As I scanned the rest of the article, I questioned my decision to let Claudia open her mouth without me around to supervise. When it came to the subject of Edward, that woman needed a muzzle.

After reading another paragraph, I relented. Claudia had done what I'd asked her to do. I couldn't hold it against her if she thought of Edward in the role of hero. I was more surprised a reporter would write and an editor approve this tripe. The next three paragraphs covered how my brother, without the aid of those lesser mortals known as the police, had apprehended the notorious Inglenook Killer, saving the life of an intended fourth victim. While I appreciated his saving my life, I was doubly thankful Charlie had decided against naming me. He probably thought it might stink of nepotism.

Then he gave a few details about the murder of Professor Taylor. The article's assessment of the victim made me wonder if his death had been a crime. He was lecherous, vindictive, and an all-around poop. Charlie must have made a trip to San Diego and talked to Professor Kanchaliar.

It pleased me to see Edward's books get a plug along with the Babbitt and Brown Bookstore. As I re-folded the paper, I decided to let go of the parts I didn't like and be grateful I'd accomplished my goal—to pull Edward out of the role of suspect and place him side-by-side with the police.

"Nicholas. Could you come into the den?"

I got to my feet and followed my brother, expecting a thank you for saving his reputation. That would put us on equal footing, and then I would tell him all about Hattie Channing and the information I'd wrangled from the old women last night.

Instead, as I entered the den, I got a poke in the chest.

"Taking Zali to a bar? What were you thinking?"

"I was thinking about how to get you out of this mess." I kept my voice polite. "She did fine. The guys loved her, and she had a good time. What's the problem?"

"The problem is—" He adjusted his volume from booming to a loud whisper. "The problem is you've upset Claudia."

"Oh, boo-hoo. Tell her to put on her big girl panties and toughen up."

He got distracted when I mentioned panties, which only increased my irritation.

"I think it would be a miracle to find Claudia not upset. She's got a chip on her shoulder so large she's in danger of losing an arm."

"She does have a lot on her mind. You should cut her some slack."

I gaped. "Her? What about me? I'm running around thinking of ways to keep you out of jail."

"So is Claudia. I think her idea to get the press behind me was ingenious."

I wasn't about to lower myself to set him straight on where the idea originated. Instead, I turned on my heels and left the house to attend to unfinished business.

Hattie Channing had lied to me about not seeing Taylor since she left Marston, and I had believed that lie and allowed my brother to suffer for it. Edward was right. I was a sap.

My next move should have been to call Sykes and tell him

everything I'd learned about the relationship between Taylor and his former student including the child produced by the union, but I convinced myself I wanted the satisfaction of watching her squirm when I explained I wasn't as stupid as she thought.

Laurie wasn't in the front yard when I arrived, and Hattie was alone when she answered the door. My insides flinched when she looked at me as if one of her nightmares had followed her into the daylight, but that was no way for a man on the offensive to behave. I firmed up my features.

"Do you want to do this outside?"

She sighed and held the door open. When she offered me a seat on the couch, I declined and remained standing. With what I had to say, I didn't feel entitled to her hospitality. She remained standing, too.

"I don't like this any better than you do, but there's something that isn't fitting together. You said you hadn't seen Taylor since you left school as a pregnant teen."

"That's right."

"And yet he was seen in Citrus Grove at least two times before he died. Who had he come to see if not you?"

She paled and dropped to sitting on the couch. Steeling my resolve, I brushed aside my concern for her and tried to enjoy not being a sap.

"First, he went into the Happy Chicken, which would make it seem as if he was looking for you."

"You're lying."

I shook my head. "He was remembered. The second time, he was turning onto Grove Street, which as you know leads to Apple Street."

After clearing her throat a few times, she said, "I didn't see him." She repeated it, louder. "I didn't see him. He never came here, or if he did, I wasn't home."

"But he was looking for you."

With a return of her former spark, she lifted her chin. "Really? Now you want me to guess what he was thinking?"

"No, but if he had been asking around, I'm sure your neighbors or coworkers would have mentioned it."

"Oh. I see what you mean. Nobody mentioned it to me."

A little twinge of doubt niggled at me. The Amazon at the Happy Chicken said Taylor had fled before being seated. Since he was being led to Hattie's section, it was possible his quick departure came after spotting his former love. Not the actions of a man who had found what he was looking for. She could be telling the truth.

"You're sure he didn't know about Laurie?"

"Positive. I dropped out of Marston as soon as I found out I was pregnant. We had already broken up."

Maybe. Maybe not. Taylor struck me as someone who would revel in notoriety. However, his bosses might not find his behavior with the female students amusing. That led me to another point. If his job was in danger, it would make him a candidate for blackmail. Since half the women I'd met at Inglenook last winter considered extortion a legitimate career, I had to ask the question.

Glancing around the pleasant room, I noted the solid furniture, which doesn't come cheap. Assuming there were at least two bedrooms, there had to be sixteen hundred square feet to this house, which takes money in California, especially with a good-size yard like the one out back.

"If you don't mind my asking, how do you afford this very nice home on a waitress's income?"

She looked me straight in the eyes, and I noticed again how her irises were lined with black, like a cat's. "I do mind, but it's not a secret. This is my parent's house. They retired to Florida and let Laurie and me live here for a small amount of rent. I have my waitress job, and I take on some bookkeeping for one or two businesses in town. That was my major. Accounting." Her lips twisted into something I wouldn't call a smile. "I took Jonathan's English class to meet the required courses."

Jonathan. Not Professor Taylor. It gave my stomach a jolt, but I should have expected it. People who produce a child together wouldn't stick to a formal address.

"You mean to tell me you never took advantage of child support?" I gave a harsh laugh. "I'm not sure how much a college professor makes, but surely enough to go around. But you're telling me you didn't hit him up for what was only your due. I don't believe you."

"You have a lot of nerve. I've only shared the story behind Laurie's birth with a few people. None of them have rubbed my face in my mistake except you."

It wasn't like me to take a conversation with a stranger personally. I made Edward my excuse. I had guilty feelings over allowing Sykes to haul him to the station.

"You're right. I apologize." I searched for a neutral topic. "Accounting, huh? It surprises me you abandoned your education. I mean, you could have picked it up at a different school or taken online classes."

"I had morning sickness throughout my entire pregnancy. It would have been too difficult."

"There are plenty of women who would have handled the problem differently."

"Problem?"

When she moved, it was such a surprise I didn't react in time. She covered the six steps between us and slapped my face. I grabbed her wrist to discourage a repeat, but I needn't have worried. She was breathing fast, and her lower lip trembled. She looked like she might be sick.

"It was just an observation," I said, leading her back to the couch and taking a seat next to her.

She wiped her face with trembling hands. "You have no

idea how many people tried to pressure me into—that. My friends. Former friends. Even my own doctor, for God's sake. He referred to my baby as an inconvenience. Doesn't a doctor take an oath to protect life? That's when I knew I had to get out of the college environment. It's so promiscuous and casual—" She blushed in acknowledgment of her own experience with the first half of the statement. "I moved back here to be with my parents. I could never—" She gulped down some air.

This woman valued life, even an inconvenient life. She might be faking it. If so, she was a first-class actress.

I had a new problem. The part of my brain that demanded I remain objective was losing the fight with the part that insisted I pull her close and comfort her, so I stood and walked out the front door without risking a goodbye.

I dropped by Bill's next, purely as a social exercise. The owner wasn't in her usual spot, but I got plenty of updates on Pretzel. While at the bar, I took a sheet of paper from my pocket and unfolded it.

Last night, before taking my leave of Dora and Flora, I got them to share the addresses of the other council members by telling them I wanted to send a personal thank you for Edward's invitation to each one. They approved. Unfortunately, neither woman carried an address book. Their memories of a killer bull named Tiny were sharper than their memories for house numbers. At least I got the street names.

Dora and Flora lived together in a retirement community on the edge of town where they moved after they sold the farm they inherited from their parents. Georgie lived alone on Scott Street, but not for long. Her intended, Mort, lived on Kennedy Circle in a newer neighborhood of large, two-story houses, which I assumed she would move into after the nuptials.

The General lived in a one-bedroom apartment on

Dorothy—either street or lane. By the time the sisters finished telling me the life history of the original Dorothy, the one they named the street after, I had forgotten and didn't care to ask them to repeat it. When they gave me Hattie's address, I wrote it down to avoid any gossip. That left Ned, who lived in a bedsit on Peachland Drive.

Upon request, the bartender fished out an old phone book from Bill's office, and I was able to get the numbers to go with each address.

I finished my beer, made a suitable parting crack to the gang, and headed to Grove Street, the street Taylor might have turned down. The way I saw it, if any of the streets inhabited by council members crossed Grove, I would have something to consider.

Naturally, I could have pulled up a map on my phone and found the answer in a few minutes, but as long as I was avoiding Claudia and Edward, I needed to kill time before returning to the B&B. Besides, the day was perfect for walking. The temperature hovered just below short-sleeve weather. My gray sweater was comfortable without being warm. The recent dry spell had brought out the blooms on the bougainvillea bushes, and a breeze tickled the blossoms on the many trees, encouraging them to open up into leaves. During the summer months, Grove Street would resemble a shady lane more than a street.

The first few houses were interesting. I amused myself making guesses about the occupants based on the way they enhanced their yards and front porches. It wasn't hard to guess that the yellow house with smudged front windows lined with artwork made from cereal probably contained a young family. The hedge of blossoming rose bushes next door had to belong to an elderly spinster or widower. No one else would have had enough time to tend to such a vivid display, and the choice of house colors was traditional blue with white trim. Hippies, I thought, as I passed the porch with a swing covered in tie-dyed fabric.

By the fourth house, I had lost interest. After a few blocks, I decided the builders had limited themselves to two plans—those with porches and those without. Otherwise, the houses themselves were identical except for the color schemes. They all had driveways leading to detached garages and bay windows on the opposite side of the house from the driveway.

When I came to Apple Street, I ignored it, since Hattie wasn't on my list of suspects, nor would she be in the future. Two blocks farther down, I hit Scott. By turning right and passing three houses, I came to Georgie's home.

It was painted cornflower-blue with white trim and was one of the porchless models. The garage door stood open. As I got closer to the short man in a fisherman's jacket, work gloves, and straw hat who was rummaging through the piles of junk inside, I recognized Georgie.

She took off the hat and wiped her brow with a sleeve.

"What brings you here? Have you come to thank me in person?" She cackled at her reference to the excuse I had offered Dora and Flora for wanting the addresses.

"Just stretching my legs. You look like you're getting a workout. Preparing for the move to Mort's?"

She nodded. "This is the home I grew up in. I moved back in to help my mother when she started to have trouble getting around."

"It must be hard to leave all those memories behind."

"I'm not sentimental. I would have moved out long ago, but I couldn't be bothered to find a smaller place after Mom passed. And why would I? Before my father died, he paid off the mortgage." Her gaze wandered over the piles. "My word, that woman saved everything."

I lifted the lid on the closest box and peered down at an

assortment of hats, some covered in big, colorful flowers, some with veils, and a few with both. They brought back vague memories of my grandmother.

"Vintage nineteen fifties." She pointed to the back of the garage. "There are dresses to match and a few jackets, if the moths haven't gotten to them."

"Speaking of old things," I said in a lame segue, "had you ever met Jonathan Taylor before the night of the book event?"

Georgie barked out a laugh. "You mean the night he died. If you're going to question me, you are required to work for the answers."

By the time I left an hour and a half later, I was glad I had worn jeans today but not so glad I had worn the sweater. Cobwebs and dirt covered my knees from crawling under a workbench to retrieve an old hammer. My sweater was soaked with sweat and grime from moving heavy boxes that had accumulated decades of dust and, in the case of an old suitcase, mold.

All I had gotten in return for my trouble was that Georgie had never laid eyes on Taylor before that night. She wasn't sure she could pick him out of a lineup, even now. She got along well with the other council members, though she would prefer it if Ned wouldn't whine like a little girl over every darn thing—her words, not mine.

She based her remembrances of Taylor's death on commentary offered by Dora and Flora because she thought it was crass to crowd in to peek at a tragedy, especially as she had no personal feelings for the victim.

Just for laughs, I went back to Grove Street and continued with my experiment. My clothes weren't in any condition to allow me to make social calls, but at least I would be able to find the council members if I wanted them. However, a few blocks later the street ended at an empty field that hadn't been used in years for anything other than a dump. People had dropped off threadbare tires, dried up cans of paint, and even an older model refrigerator with rusty hinges.

I backtracked and turned right on Apple just for the pleasure of passing Hattie's residence. If Laurie was home, she must have been playing in the backyard because the front yard and windows didn't show any signs of life. I couldn't imagine life as an only child. Lucky kid.

Before I hit the end of Apple Street at Mercer and had a choice of turning left or right, I learned Dorothy wasn't a street or a lane. It was a short drive lined with five or six small apartment complexes. I still hadn't come across Peachland.

By the time I returned to my home away from home, I'd missed lunch, so I got cleaned up and then went back to my room to have a think.

Edward's bellow woke me two hours later. When he burst into my room, I jerked up into a sitting position and ran my hands over my face.

"Jeez," I grumbled. "Who died?"

"Jeffrey Babbitt of Babbitt and Brown Bookstore."

CHAPTER 19

Babbitt and Brown Bookstore had attracted an even larger crowd than the one on the night Professor Taylor died, only this time everyone was standing on the outside and shoving to get close to the windows, both the ones on Lemon Lane and the ones on Sprout Street. They all wanted details to share with friends and family. The lone patrolman guarding the door had given up bringing order and concentrated on keeping them from gaining entry to the crime scene.

A familiar sedan pulled up to the curb. Detective Sykes stepped out and surveyed the crowd. When he caught sight of me and Edward, he motioned for us to follow him inside.

As soon as we were through the doors, he ordered us to stay put as he walked back to the community room, leaving Edward and me with several uniformed officers and official-looking people who were keeping busy around the sales counter.

"I hope you have an alibi," I said.

"Nonsense. I was with Claudia all afternoon."

"Better marry her quick so they can't put her on the stand."

"Nonsense," he repeated, but with less enthusiasm. I stared at his face. He wasn't making eye contact.

I poked him in the shoulder. "Spill."

"I didn't know I'd need an alibi," he snapped. "Claudia wanted to purchase some—er—personal things, so we parted ways for approximately a half-hour."

"And how did you spend that time?" I asked the question, but from the way he was fidgeting, I would have been happy to skip the answer. As it was, he didn't have a chance to respond because Detective Sykes hailed us from the entryway of the community room, and we moved to join him.

On my way there, I made a detour that took me close to the activity. As I passed the sales counter, I craned my neck to see behind it. There wasn't a lot of room back there, so Jeffrey Babbitt had fallen into a slumped position, with his bottom against the back wall and his forehead leaning forward to rest against some boxes under the counter. The collar of his light coral sweater was soaked with blood.

One officer who wasn't directly involved with the body looked over his shoulder at me. "Did you get a good look, buddy?"

"I don't suppose you'd let me take a closer look."

He got angry and told me to beat it.

"I was leaving anyway. I have an appointment with the lead detective."

His frown wavered when he saw Sykes and Edward waiting for me.

When I caught up to them, the detective led us through the community room where Professor Taylor had died and through the swinging door into the kitchen. White counter-tops stretched out on either side of a double sink under metal cabinets. A large island in the middle of the room provided plenty of workspace on top and storage room underneath for bowls and pans. A wastebasket with a lid stood next to the wall inside the doorway.

There was a door on the opposite side of where we entered, and we passed through this and into a hallway. The first door we came to was a unisex restroom. The hall was short and made a sharp left at the end. Right before the bend leading back to the main store, we stopped at the open door of the most crowded office I'd ever seen. I assumed it was an office because it had a desk with a computer on it. The rest of the room was filled with boxes. Boxes on the floor. Open boxes on metal shelves. Boxes stacked on the chair in front of the desk.

Before we could step inside, Sykes held out an arm. "That's far enough."

A skinny guy just out of his teens dressed in jeans and a black t-shirt with a picture of Shakespeare on it sat on a box in the middle of the room. He looked up as we approached. When he saw Edward, he jumped to his feet.

"That's the guy! I'll swear to it."

He talked in a tight-mouthed way caused by the rubber-bands hooked to his braces to help correct his overbite.

My brother maintained a cool, polite expression. "Do I know you?"

"This is Aloysius Kensington," Sykes said.

"Everybody calls me Cooter," the kid volunteered. I didn't blame him.

"At approximately two o'clock this afternoon, Cooter stepped out for a break and saw you skulking around in front of the store, peering into the windows along Lemon Lane."

After delivering Cooter a look of distaste, Edward said, "I wasn't skulking. I was looking."

"At what?"

"Into the store, obviously. I wanted to observe the customers to see if anyone was showing an interest in my—my employer's books."

"And were they?"

He cleared his throat. "There weren't any customers that I could see. It must have been a slow period. People might still have been at lunch."

"He was making sure the coast was clear so he could kill Jeff," Cooter said.

Sykes glared at the kid. "Thank you, Mr. Kensington. I can take it from here."

Cooter sat back down.

"Did you eventually come into the store, Mr. Harlow?"

"Yes. I wanted to ask Mr. Babbitt how the sales were doing. When Nicholas spoke to him yesterday, Mr. Babbitt indicated they were doing well. I wanted actual data to take back to my aunt."

"That's good news." Even though he said it with a congratulatory smile, I didn't feel Sykes gave a fig about Edward's sales.

"It is." My brother didn't sound happy.

"Just to satisfy my curiosity, what were the final sales numbers?"

Edward hesitated. "I don't know. I couldn't find Mr. Babbitt."

Cooter lacked self-control. "How hard did you look, man? He's lying on the floor right behind the sales counter."

Since Edward couldn't shoot his cuffs in a red sweater vest, he toyed with the top button on the white cotton shirt he wore underneath. "It is not my habit to hang over counters and snoop. I called out for him a few times—without shouting, of course—and then I left."

Sykes grunted. "Didn't you think it was strange Mr.

Babbitt would leave his store unattended in the middle of the day?"

"As he didn't have anyone else to manage the store in his absence," Edward gave Cooter a nod of acknowledgment, "that I knew of, I assumed he had run into an urgent situation that necessitated his leaving the front counter unattended."

"Such as?"

"For Heaven's sake. The call of nature."

I grinned and put my hand on my brother's shoulder. "What you two gentlemen don't understand is that my brother is the farthest thing from a busybody. He would as soon address Pope Francis as Frank as he would stick his nose in someone's private business. He thought Jeffrey Babbitt was attending to private business."

Edward shot me a look of gratitude, but it came too soon.

Sykes took hold of my brother's arm. "You're coming with me."

"Is that really necessary?" I snapped. "He hasn't been trying to run. He's been right here where you can find him, which would be a bad strategy if he was guilty. Nuts. If you want to take him in for questioning, go ahead, but you could probably ask those same questions right now."

"Your brother was present for both murders—"

"Correction. He was present for the murder of Professor Taylor, along with about two hundred other people. As for Jeffrey Babbitt, I'm not sure when he died, are you?" I motioned in the direction of the stock boy. "For all you know, this guy killed him, and Edward inconveniently arrived before he had a chance to hide the body."

"I haven't missed that possibility." Sykes turned to Cooter, and the kid gulped loud enough that I heard him. "Were you at the book signing?"

The kid's cocky body language melted into the hunched

shoulders and glaring eyes of a trapped rat. "I was helping out. We expected a lot of sales. I had to be here. And why would I kill my boss? He paid my salary. And why would I kill this professor guy? I never even heard of him before he died."

I raised a finger. "It's just a suggestion, but maybe you should ask my brother if he saw anyone familiar hanging around when he entered or left the bookstore."

The detective sighed. "Well? Did you?"

Edward frowned. "Not if you mean standing around the entrance. No."

"You don't know what I mean. Did you see anyone you recognized from your event on the sidewalk before you came in here?"

"It would be a surprise if I hadn't. It's such a small town."

"Then surprise me."

Edward put his hands on his hips, for him a sign of protest. "I saw Miss Channing entering the Happy Chicken. Since she works there, that's not a surprise. There was a minor collision at the intersection at the far end of the block. That reporter was taking pictures and talking to people. That's his job. I even saw Mrs. Robbins coming out of the post office, a very normal action. None of it means anything."

"Everyone seemed natural?"

My brother spread his hands in a gesture of exasperation. "How the devil would I know? I hadn't met these people before the book event."

Sykes turned his head toward the still cowering Cooter and then looked back at my brother. He jabbed a thumb over his shoulder. "I'm going to have a talk with this guy now, but I want you to be available at a moment's notice. That means remain in Citrus Grove until I give you the okay to go home."

"I wouldn't dream of leaving," Edward said, heavy on the sarcasm.

An older woman in black slacks and a gray sweater approached us. I should say I thought she was older because of the long, silver hair she wore pulled back into a ponytail and the intelligent green eyes that reflected a calm that only comes to people in later years. Her face lacked wrinkles. Maybe she moisturized.

"He's ready to go when you are."

"You never told us how he died," Edward said.

Sykes indulged him. He gave the lady a slight nod.

"Stabbed in the neck. Something with a pointed tip. I'll know more after I've had him on the table."

The detective's gaze moved to the bulge under Edward's vest. "What's that?"

Edward and his damn fountain pens. He reached through the neck of his sweater vest and pulled a silver one out of his shirt pocket.

Sykes studied the pointy nib and exchanged a glance with the woman.

"Could be," she said. "I need to get a better look at the wound under some decent lighting."

Sykes pulled out a baggie and held it open. "I'll take that, please." When my brother sputtered about how it was his favorite, Sykes added, "Once we've tested it, you can have it back. If it's not the murder weapon."

When I snorted and turned my head away in disgust, my gaze landed on something in the far corner of the room. Cooter objected when I crossed the floor to a cardboard box overflowing with objects.

"What's this?" I demanded.

Cooter said, "Lost and found." Then he pulled back his upper lip in a sneer. "Why? Did you lose something?"

I crouched down and gingerly moved a child's backpack. "No, but Jonathan Taylor did."

Sykes was at my side in an instant. I looked up. "That's his blue water bottle. If you turn it over, there's a book etched on it along with the initials JT. He was carrying it around the night he died."

The M.E. handed Sykes a pair of gloves, and he pulled the bottle out from under a spiral notebook and held it up. There were the engravings, just as I'd described.

"Why didn't you mention the water bottle before, Mr. Harlow?"

"I just didn't think of it."

"You simply forgot."

"Give me a break. Did any other witness mention it?"

He unscrewed the lid and looked inside. From his grim smile, I assumed it wasn't empty. "That's all for now, Mr. Harlow." He stood and nodded at Edward. "And Mr. Harlow."

After Sykes shooed us out, as we were walking back up Lemon Lane, I said, "You said you saw Mrs. Robbins, Charlie, and Hattie."

"I did see Mrs. Robbins, Mr. Grant, and Miss Channing." Edward nodded. "Any one of them could have nipped into the bookstore for a little murder and then gone about their business."

"Just because you didn't see Jeffrey doesn't mean he was already dead. He might have been taking care of business, just like you supposed."

"And they entered the bookstore after I left."

I tried not to crow too loudly. "Hattie couldn't have. You saw her going to work. She would have been waiting tables when Jeffrey was killed."

He spun on his heels and headed back over our tracks. "Let's clear up that point right now, shall we?"

"Why?" I said, scurrying to catch up. "You said you saw her enter the restaurant. What more do you need to know?"

"Nicholas, you can't eliminate a person unless you've verified their alibi. You should know better."

I followed him to the Happy Chicken and waited for him outside. When he returned, he avoided making eye contact.

"Well?" I demanded. "Did you embarrass her? It s going to get so they won't let us in the place."

"I didn't embarrass her."

"That's something, anyway." We turned back the way we came.

"Because she wasn't there. She only stopped by to pick up her check."

I stopped walking. "Maybe she went directly to the bank. It's Friday, so the line would be long. It would take time. We can straighten it out right now by asking the tellers." I couldn't decide if the urgency to clear Hattie's name came from my firm belief in her innocence or a desire to make certain I wasn't being taken for a patsy.

He grabbed my arm and pulled me in the opposite direction. "Let's not worry about it until we find out Jeffrey Babbitt's time of death. Okay?"

We walked in silence until Edward suggested it might be time for Claudia to go home. I concurred with enthusiasm.

"You don't want her calling you a murder magnet again."

"I don't want to expose her to more chaos. And death." He ran his fingers through his hair, leaving it curly and disheveled. "Maybe she's right. Maybe I am a murder magnet." He lifted his chin. "Death certainly seems to be my companion wherever I go."

My brother's overactive imagination had kicked in. He's a romantic. I'm sure he was picturing himself astride a black stallion and sporting a matching cloak, facing an ugly world alone. Never to rest. Never to love. Blah-blah-blah. Me? I'm a realist.

"You travel in your job. Say twenty percent of the population is capable of murder, and they act on it fifty percent of the time. You're bound to run into one of them sooner or later."

"What about Inglenook?"

"You've had more than your share, but maybe you're getting them out of the way all at once. And multiple murders by the same person only count as one. Anyway, the point is Claudia should pack up and leave."

Claudia didn't agree. When we returned, she met us in the foyer, her arms folded and eyes blazing with fury.

"Another murder?"

Zali slipped into one of the chairs and sat at attention.

"Jeffrey Babbitt. The owner—former owner of Babbitt and Brown Bookstore. He was murdered this afternoon. And that's why I'm sending you home."

Her eyes narrowed. "Sending me home. Sending me home? I'll have you know I paid for my own room, and I got here without your help. You don't get to send me anywhere. And why would you want to?"

I could have told him before he answered that he was fighting an unwinnable war. That no female likes to be told what to do, even if it makes perfect sense. In fact, the more sense it makes, the more she'll fight it until you both wind up miserable. Her because you were right and now she's suffering, and you because she'll make sure you know she's suffering. And she will apply a convoluted logic to make sure it's all your fault.

"Because you want to run around with your brother and turn this—" she sputtered. "This *thing* into an adventure, like you did at Inglenook?"

I didn't remember an atmosphere of swashbuckling adventure as I was discovering corpses and trying to avoid getting killed.

"Because you think I'll get in the way? That I'm a weak, fumbling female who you'll have to rescue?"

Silently, I willed Edward to say yes. I might even have mouthed it, and I knew damn well I was going to shout it if she kept it up.

He stepped closer to her. If he had bent his head toward her upturned face, he could have kissed her. Thankfully, he did not.

"Because I think you're too kind and good and beautiful to expose to the uglier side of life. Because, dammit, I want to protect you. If that makes me a chauvinist, then I'm a chauvinist."

Of course he was a chauvinist, but I would argue against his reasons for wanting to protect her. They stood there, staring into each other's eyes. The air cracked with electricity. I wondered how awkward it would be if I chose this moment to mention I was hungry.

Zali broke into applause. "Bravo! When is the second act? Will there be popcorn? And how long is the break because I have to tinkle."

Claudia left the room with Zali to take care of business, so the question of Claudia's departure remained unanswered, but the scene had served one good purpose. Edward had a determined set to his jaw and a fire in his eyes. He would solve this murder and protect his woman, and that meant he needed my help. Finally.

CHAPTER 20

E dward was determined all right. Determined to make me miserable. Here we were with my brother suspected of two murders, one that had happened right in front of us. Were we going out to search for clues that might clear his name? No. Instead, we spent the next hour answering Aunt Civility's fan mail, which Mrs. Abernathy had forwarded to Edward. The bedrooms didn't have desks or writing tables, and the kitchen was too public, so Mrs. Robbins had graciously allowed us to set up on the dining room table.

I had the laptop in front of me. Edward was across the table in the same chair Sykes' fanny had warmed two days ago. In front of him were a stack of handwritten letters and printed emails. I know you're thinking nobody writes letters anymore, and you'd be mostly right. No one does except grannies and people who read books that tell them how to respond to strangers who ask them the baby's due date when they aren't pregnant.

"Read it back to me."

I scrolled back up the screen.

"You are under no obligation to tell your nosy friend how much money you spent on your discount rug, yet you do not want to hurt her feelings or start an argument over such a trivial matter. Tell her in a jocular manner you spent more than you should have and then change the subject." I looked up. "What if the friend keeps pushing? Some people won't stop shoving unless you shove back. This woman needs to set boundaries."

"You don't think that's clear in my response?"

"No."

"And how would you phrase it?"

"For starters, how about it's none of your damn business?"

Edward smirked. "You're just sulking because you have to work. You thought this was a paid vacation. Change nosy to inquisitive and then add the usual signature."

I did as instructed and saved the document under today's date and called it nosyrug. Usually Edward went through the letters on his own and made notes, and I worked directly from them. The fact that we were doing this as a group project meant he was using it as a distraction. I didn't know if it was a distraction from the murders or from the presence of his girlfriend upstairs. If it was the former, he needed a push.

"I wonder what the connection is between Jeffrey Babbitt and the professor?" I asked, my tone casual.

He ignored me and picked up the next letter.

I moved my wrist in a circular motion and the joint cracked. "Because I won't buy it's a coincidence. That someone has been planning to kill Jeffrey Babbitt for years but lacked confidence. Then, when Taylor gasped his last breath in a packed room, they thought, by gum, it's easier than I thought."

My brother snorted. "Now you're being deliberately obtuse. Of course there's a connection."

"Oh, yeah? What?"

He responded by reading the next letter aloud. "Aunt Civility, my sister used my toothbrush last week, so I called her a pig. My mother didn't do anything to my sister, but I've been grounded for a week. It's not fair. Which one's worse? Her using my toothbrush or me calling my sister a pig? My mom told me to ask you."

He closed his eyes, squeezed the bridge of his nose between his index finger and thumb, and set down the letter. I'd seen him like this before. My brother preferred more dignified problems, like how to address royalty in conversation. It would pass. I just had to wait it out. When he opened his eyes ninety seconds later, he said, "Jeffrey Babbitt was too old to be one of Professor Taylor's students. Was he a colleague?"

I kept my fingers on the keyboard to assure him this conversation wouldn't interrupt our work. "According to local gossip, he worked at the library before opening the bookstore. His partner is dead. Not murdered, I assume."

He picked up the letter, glanced at it, and set it back down. "It wouldn't be unusual for an English major to wind up at a library. Where did he go to school? What year did he graduate? Did he ever live in San Diego?"

"Good questions, and I know why you asked them. Taylor went to school in San Antonio, Texas, and graduated with a Masters in English, without honors, in nineteen eighty. He didn't move to California until nineteen eighty-four, when he took a position at a community college. He went on to earn his doctorate, published a few uninspired articles, and then, through his connections, worked his way up to his current position as Professor of English at G.W. Marston College. He married young, at twenty-six, and his wife was the daughter of a colleague. Gina Hendricks. No little Taylors running around seducing the female population, at least none that he's claimed. That's all according to *The Citrus Grove Courier.* I read the paper, too."

Since his memory is as good as mine, my brother wasn't impressed. "The article didn't mention any awards or papers published in respectable journals, but he did write a controversial book called, *The Language of the Contemporary Sexual Revolution.*"

I snorted. "The article said controversial, but I'm skeptical. A controversy requires more than one person, but I doubt if anyone but Taylor ever bought a copy."

"I bought one last night."

I leaned back and stretched my arms. "I have a free copy from Jeffrey Babbitt."

"Maybe I can get a refund."

"And? I never got around to reading it."

Edward grimaced. "It was an exercise in obscenity, thinly disguised as a study of the effects of words on human sexuality. An opportunity to use obscene language under the guise of scholarship. It doesn't sound like the kind of book Babbitt and Brown's would normally carry. I suppose Jeffrey Babbitt could have put a rush order on copies after the professor's death. He came across as a man who wouldn't miss an opportunity."

He pushed the letter aside, giving up any pretense of getting work done. "What exactly did Professor Taylor say to you before he died?"

"Just what I told Sykes. It sounded like mwif and ack. That's not really saying anything."

"Was he looking at you?"

My forehead wrinkled. "He was, and he wasn't. His eyes weren't focused on anything. Sort of at the wall behind me.

About your questions. The ones about Babbitt. Who would have the answers?"

I knew very well who would have the answers, but I didn't want to be the one to suggest we leave the discomforts of Mrs. Robbins' dining room, so I let Edward think the idea was his.

"I suppose we could talk to Charlie Grant."

I firmed up my lips. "Who does *we* include?"

He glanced upward in the direction of Claudia and Zali's bedroom. "I don't think we need to bother the ladies with this."

And so, we were able to talk to Charlie Grant in an estrogen-free environment, which suited me fine.

CHAPTER 21

Edward made me change into something less sloppy before we left for our interview. I talked him out of a suit and put on brown slacks, a blue-and-white striped shirt, and a light tan sports jacket. Once we left the house and there wasn't a chance Claudia could overhear, I told Edward about my talk with Bill—without naming her, of course. His response?

"So, you weren't lying."

It took me a few seconds, but I finally got it. "When I told Sykes that Taylor had been seen around town?" I made a face. "You flatter yourself. It was the whole truth and nothing but the truth."

"But you won't tell even me who your source is."

"No can do. I made a promise."

"Did you learn anything last night?" Edward said this with a smirk.

"Fine. You were right. It was a waste of time. The General didn't see anything except me handing the barley water to Taylor, Dora, and Flora's bull ate something, maybe oleander, but it was years ago. The cow didn't even die. One of the volunteers noticed Taylor a few times throughout the night and said he was always alone. So, it looks like nobody killed the professor, unless it was Ned, who walked in at the same time as Taylor."

"So, you did learn something of value."

"What?"

He ignored the question. "You were right. It was a good idea to talk to those people. You were looking out for me." He chuckled. "That job usually falls to me."

"I suppose so." My hand went automatically to the back of my neck to massage the muscles.

My brother's eyes narrowed. "You're fidgeting, Nicholas. What haven't you told me?"

I dropped my hand, ticked I had given myself away. "There is something else, but I don't want you to get excited because it's a dead-end." I reached up to rub the back of my neck again but nixed it in time. "You remember how Taylor's wife left him over his affair with a student? There were probably several students."

"More than likely."

"I found one of them."

"Did you really? I'm impressed."

"This student didn't know he was married. When she found out, she ended things right away."

"Admirable."

"But not soon enough."

"What—" He paused to consider. "Oh. A baby. That's unfortunate."

I grinned. "Don't tell her that."

Instead of smiling with me, Edward looked grim. "And Taylor might have been ready to surprise her secret."

"She says Taylor didn't know about the child."

He turned those steady, gray eyes on me and asked, "Do you believe Miss Channing?"

My face grew warm. "I don't remember mentioning a name."

"Nonsense. I don't imagine you ran around questioning every woman with a child in Citrus Grove, and Miss Channing is one of the council members. I repeat. Do you believe her?"

"I think so."

"But you're not sure."

"You keep reminding me I'm an idiot when it comes to women. I'm being cautious."

He stepped aside to give way to a woman pushing a stroller. "The most concrete connection to Professor Taylor we have is Hattie Channing. Tell me again. Why haven't we handed her over to Detective Sykes?"

I shook my head. "No dice. That woman isn't capable of murder."

"They share a history. And a child. Women are unreasonable at the best of times, but when their young are threatened…"

"It's not her."

"Your witness said the professor turned up Grove Street. Which street does Miss Channing live on?"

I hesitated, but it would be easy enough for Edward to find out. "Apple."

"I could get a map, or you could just tell me if Grove Street leads to Apple."

"It does. But it also leads to other streets where other people live, such as The General and Georgie. And it might lead to Ned, too. I haven't found Peachland yet."

"As a member of the Culinary Arts Council, Miss Channing would have known Jeffrey Babbitt."

"As would the others I just mentioned."

"Maye he also discovered her secret."

"Maybe Jeffrey Babbitt discovered somebody's secret, but

it wasn't hers." I realized my voice had gotten louder when a group of men standing outside a pawn shop looked at me, so I lowered the volume to a reasonable level and went for his soft spot. Edward was a romantic. He probably thought he was the king of chivalry. "If you want to give up a defenseless woman and her child to hours of grilling—"

"I hardly think Detective Sykes would grill a child."

"Hattie Channing made a mistake a long time ago. She bypassed the easy route and chose life, and she has been working hard to give her daughter a home. I'm not going to add to her troubles by handing her over for hours of questioning and possible embarrassment when it all becomes public. It would not be the gentlemanly thing to do. It would be throwing her under the bus to keep from getting hit yourself. And it would be pointless hours of questioning because she doesn't know anything about the murder because she didn't do it. Them. Either murder."

My brother stroked his chin. "A fine speech. I'll defer to your judgment for the time being, unless other facts come to light." He heaved a big sigh, and I felt my shoulders relax. Now that I wasn't on the defensive, I steered the conversation toward a point that was bugging me.

"Jeffrey Babbitt got hold of Taylor's books awfully fast. The publisher was some small shop located in Utah. Hold on."

I pulled out my phone, went online, and looked up *The Language of the Contemporary Sexual Revolution*. A few bloggers had reviewed it, I assumed for laughs, but I clicked on a website bearing the same name as the book. A headshot of Taylor popped up, and scrolling down led me to a 3-D picture of the cover. I pressed on the "Buy Here" button and came to a page asking for my credit card information and mailing address. Estimated shipping time was two weeks. I suspected if I had filled out the information and paid for a copy, my order would have been filled in Taylor's garage, if he had been alive.

When I moved on to Amazon and entered the title into the search bar, the only options to buy were from used booksellers, which confirmed my first opinion. Jeffrey Babbitt hadn't ordered Taylor's books and waited for delivery. He had gotten hold of copies directly from Taylor. I told Edward my idea.

"It's possible the professor brought them to the event with hopes of making a sale." Edward nodded in agreement. "But when did he have a chance to give them to Jeffrey?"

My brother stopped walking. "Jeffrey Babbitt was at the book table until I began my talk and immediately afterward. He might have gone with Taylor to retrieve the books while I was at the podium. I didn't notice."

"That's more than I know. I had my eyes on you the entire time."

"When you weren't sleeping."

"Think about it, Edward. Jeffrey has a packed book event. He stands to make money on your books. Would he abandon the table to retrieve unknown books from a strange man?"

"We haven't investigated whether he knew Professor Taylor."

"If so, he'd have a good idea about the book's content and would know it wouldn't be a bestseller. Also, he said he had gotten the books after Taylor's death."

Edward looked over my shoulder and I turned. We were at *The Citrus Grove Courier* building. The receptionist was away from the desk, but a skinny kid with black spiked hair led us past a row of offices and dropped us off at our destination. Charlie's office was smaller than my bedroom at the B&B. He only had one chair available, the rolling variety with rips in the pleather, so while Edward took a seat, I stood against the wall next to a pile of precariously stacked reference books that reached from the floor to my elbow.

Charlie still hadn't found an ironing board. His flannel shirt, open at the front to reveal a San Diego Chargers t-shirt, looked as if it came out of a laundry basket after a few days on the bottom of the pile. He had on a surprisingly stylish pair of black glasses. With them on, he almost looked handsome. With his facial stubble and the glasses, he resembled a slightly pudgy version of one of those mussed up yuppie models for an overpriced clothing store, but only from the neck up.

"I hear you discovered the latest body," he said in greeting. "Maybe I should just follow you around and let the stories come to me."

"You're mistaken. I heard about Jeffrey Babbitt after he had been discovered by his stock boy, Cooter."

"Then Sykes is holding out on me. No surprise. You say Cooter found the body?" Charlie grimaced. "Poor kid. How's he taking it? The cops let him go, but his mother swears he's not at home. Of course, she might mean it the way maids used to say not at home when their mistresses didn't want to receive visitors."

Edward nodded, apparently not finding it odd that a reporter and confirmed slob would know about this nicety. "I don't know how the young man behaves in normal circumstances, but I suspect the ordeal may have affected his brain. He accused me of murdering his boss."

"Did he really?" Charlie chewed on the tip of his pen. "Did he have a reason?"

"He saw me looking for Mr. Babbitt earlier in the day."

Charlie perked up at this piece of news. Recognizing the gleam in his eyes, I put on a pleasant expression and said, "Looking for someone and talking to someone are different from killing someone. For instance, I bet you exchanged words with Professor Taylor the night he died, but nobody has accused you of killing him."

He lost the gleam and slumped back in his chair. "Couldn't avoid it."

"Did he have anything interesting to say?"

He shrugged. "The guy blathered a lot, mostly about his book. He told me it would be a good career move to interview him before he became a bestseller. Get in on the ground floor, so to speak. He said he had copies with him and would be happy to give me a discount, but I declined."

Edward gave me a glance filled with significance. "He had copies with him. Did he show you a copy?"

"He wasn't carrying it around with him, but if I know authors, he would have produced one quick enough if I had shown any interest."

"Why didn't you? It might have had potential. I would have thought the chance to make national news would have been appealing to an ambitious man. Potentially, that is. If he became a bestseller, you could have resold the article, or at least used the interview material to write another for a more lucrative market. Maybe even catch the attention of a prestigious newspaper."

Charlie gave my brother a thin smile. "The less prestigious *Citrus Grove Courier* has been very good to me. I'm not looking to move from here." He leaned back and tapped his pen on his desk. "He did mention you. Said if I knew the truth about Aunt Civility, I would have a good laugh."

I thought Edward was going to swallow his tongue. I made a noise of disapproval. "Laughing at an elderly woman? Not very nice."

"What do you expect from old nee—an old Neanderthal like that?"

Edward nodded. "The man was a menace. I heard he'd seduced a college student."

"Probably several." The reporter shuddered. "I don't even want to imagine that."

"And sabotaged a student's career."

"Wouldn't surprise me."

"Do you have any idea what happened to Professor Taylor's car?"

Charlie chewed on his pen, thoughtful. "Why?"

"Call it curiosity. The man had to get here somehow."

Charlie added suspicion to his tone. "Why don't you ask Sykes? You are working with the police."

"Detective Sykes is very busy right now with this new murder and not likely to welcome questions. I would like to remain on friendly terms with him."

The reporter cracked a smile. "Been there myself." He leaned back and tented his fingers. "The cops towed it. An older model Toyota. Silver. Early turn-of-the-century, if I know my cars. One of the first Prius models, which would have been a big deal back in 2001 or 2002, but not anymore. Taylor obviously didn't spend his cash on cars or clothes. I think that suit he wore was from the eighties."

"What can you tell us about Jeffrey Babbitt?"

Charlie grinned at Edward, ready for a game of information exchange. "Such as?"

"What kind of person was he? Was he from Citrus Grove? Did he go to college around here?"

"That's a lot of questions."

Edward spread his hands. "We're at a disadvantage in that we're not from the area."

The reporter reached for a folder on his desk and flipped it open.

"Jeffrey lived here his entire life, the younger of two brothers born to Jedidiah and Maureen Babbitt. He was a good student and liked by his teachers. He went to Santa Ana College and left it with a Certificate Degree in Library

Science." He tossed the folder down. "As for my personal impression of him, Jeffrey was a nice guy with a sharp sense of humor, especially for those he didn't like. He kept Babbitt and Brown's in the black after the death of Cecil Brown, which surprises me. I assumed Brown had the business smarts, but I guess they both did. He volunteered at the animal shelter, visited his mom at the retirement center every day until she passed away three years ago, and had dozens of friendly acquaintances, but no real friends. And he was a philatelist which may explain the lack of friends."

I frowned. "He was a pervert?"

Edward had a hearty laugh, but Charlie only smiled.

"A stamp collector."

My brother stood and thanked Charlie for his time, but the reporter wasn't ready to let him go.

"We've had a nice talk. Were any of the answers of special interest? Didn't seem like much to me, but did it give you any ideas? Any new angles? Why did you want to know about the car?"

Edward smiled. "That's a lot of questions." He sighed. "Nothing valuable, but you did your best. By the way, where were you when Professor Taylor died? You might have gotten some good photographs for your paper."

Charlie flushed. "Are you kidding? That's not *The Courier's* style. More important, I had to get Zack out of there. The deputy let me wait with him by the door until his mother picked him up, which I thought was pretty decent of him."

"I'm sorry. I'd forgotten about your son. He's not upset by the murder? No bad dreams?"

"I don't think he understands what happened, and we're not giving him details."

As soon as we were outside, I said, "Give. You practically kissed him goodbye, at least before you asked him about his son. You heard something in there, something I missed."

It looked like he might keep it to himself, but I wasn't worried. This was the brother who couldn't make it past December 1st without telling me what he got me for Christmas. I just kept pace in silence and let the pressure build. To kill time, I pulled my phone out of my back pocket and typed in a word. "Philatelist. One who collects and studies stamps. I thought maybe you were pulling my leg."

Tired of waiting for me to nag him about his secret, Edward finally burst.

"Didn't you notice Charlie's slip?"

I returned the phone to my pocket. "No."

"He said, 'What did you expect from Old Ne—?' He changed it at the last minute to Neanderthal. Very clever, but not clever enough. He meant to say Old Needles."

"So? Taylor was unlikeable. Prickly."

"I'm not sure where the nickname originated. When I was a student at Marston, it had been in place for a long time. All the students called him Needles."

"All the—You're kidding me. Charlie Grant was Taylor's student?"

"Exactly."

"You mean to tell me there are currently four former students from G.W. Marston College in this tiny rural town? This is starting to feel like a bizarre reunion."

Edward nodded. "A reunion for death. The point is Charlie Grant knew the professor before he visited Babbitt and Brown bookstore."

"And what was the point in asking for a description of Taylor's car?"

Edward smirked. Did I mention I hate smirks? "What do you always carry in the trunk of my car?"

"Your books. That would explain how Jeffrey Babbitt got copies of Taylor's books so fast."

"But how did he get into the car?"

I snorted. "That's easy. He was helping me do CPR. When Taylor croaked, he must have frisked him for his keys. Jeffrey was a businessman to the core."

"He was indeed. And now, back to Charlie."

Edward gave me instructions and told me to act on them right after dinner.

CHAPTER 22

I would have started on my research as soon as I finished dinner, which ended with an above average peach pie, except for two things: Claudia was on the warpath and the B&B didn't have a Wi-Fi connection. The first was Edward's problem. As for the second, I still had my cell phone. However, as soon as I tried to connect, I got a warning that the monthly allotment of data for our account had been depleted. The service provider warned me data would now cost me by the megabyte. Since this was a company phone and my brother pays the bills, I had to ask permission to move forward, so I tracked him down to the den. He was alone, but the miasma of an argument still clung to him.

I held out my phone. "It's going to cost you if I proceed. Do I?"

He made a face. "Our phone plan should have plenty of data, unless you're squandering it for personal use?"

I shook my head. "Nice try, but the blame is yours. I keep telling you when ideas pop into that big skull of yours when you're out of the house to jot notes and do the actual research on the computer when you get home."

"I only use the Internet from my phone in pressing circumstances."

"You don't have pressing circumstances."

Mrs. Robbins came in just as Edward said he shouldn't have to mortgage the house to access the Internet.

"The library has free online services," Mrs. Robbins suggested. "They're open until eight tonight."

Edward gave me a smug look, and I knew I was stuck. Then Claudia came in and told Edward she needed to speak with him privately. I left my brother to deal with one of the original Harpies and returned downtown. Fortunately, Citrus Grove only covered three- or four-square miles, so everything was walking distance, including the public library.

If I hadn't written down the Pine Street address, I would have passed it. The major source of reading material for the citizens of Citrus Grove was housed in a two-story residential building one block south of Lemon Lane and identified by a small wooden sign that hung over the front porch. The front door was open, so I stepped into a square foyer and looked around. There was an octangular room to my left, which had probably been the sitting room in the house's former life. The room to my right looked much larger, like a living room and dining room combination. Straight ahead, a stairway climbed to the upstairs rooms. No sign of a librarian.

I headed right and found long metal bookshelves lined with fiction that had been divided into topics that read more like warning signs. Cozy Mysteries were separated from Violent Mysteries and Mysteries with Explicit Sex. There were too many divisions in the Romance section to list. Not even mainstream fiction escaped segregation. Pet Fiction.

Family Friendly Fiction. Local Fiction. Exotic Fiction. I wondered what they meant by exotic. Was it the setting, or did the story include veiled women doing the Kuchi dance?

There wasn't time to investigate, as a middle-aged woman with a pleasant face and dressed in a beige pantsuit offered me her assistance. When I asked to use one of her computers, she responded to my request with a disappointed sigh.

"If it's not convenient, I could come back later." Let Edward wait.

"Oh, it's available." The way she said it, I waited for the but. It never came.

"Oh. That's great. Just point me in the right direction."

It wasn't going to be that simple.

"I just wish someone would come in who wanted to read." She gently rubbed the spine of the closest novel. "All these wonderful stories, just longing to fill the imagination of a lucky reader." She realized she was molesting the cover of *Lady Chatterley's Lover* and pulled her hand back, but she met my gaze without any sign of embarrassment. "A book can be more than entertainment. It can be like having a special friend."

"I'm sorry." I meant it sincerely. She really seemed heartbroken for the books, and I felt I should explain my rejection of her best friends wasn't personal. "I'm only in town for a short while. The place I'm staying doesn't have Internet access. I really need to do some research as soon as possible."

She perked up. "Research? For a term paper? Or an article?"

"Something like that."

"This way."

She led me up the staircase. Once we reached the landing, I paused to soak it in. This had once been someone's home, but where there should have been a hallway lined with bedrooms, the walls had been removed, leaving one large space. Magazines in clear, plastic sleeves faced forward on shelves, with a few selections displayed on coffee tables surrounded by couches and armchairs. Farther back, hefty reference books filled the shelves. At the end of the room sat a single desk, the kind of bulky garage sale find a teenager might use to do their homework on.

An old man occupied the swivel chair in front of the desk. As we got closer, I recognized the proud papa of Pretzel the calf. The way he was leaning in and leering at the screen suggested Ned was ogling girly pictures, but when I saw what he was looking at with such intensity, I gaped.

"That Holstein has great udders," the librarian said. "Tight."

"Calf would have no problem with those teats," he agreed with a reverence that should be reserved for church.

I folded my arms across my chest and glared down at him. "Shame on you."

Ned swiveled his head up at me, startled.

"Are you thinking of replacing Pretzel's mother? After all she's been through for you?"

I regretted the joke as soon as it was out. He sucked in his lower lip so fast I thought he was going to swallow it.

"Never," he whispered. "I just—I—" He drew himself up. "Well, a feller can look, can't he?"

"Your time was up ten minutes ago," the librarian said, gently nudging him out of the chair.

He closed the site as if to say I wasn't worthy to rest my eyes on those voluptuous udders, heaved himself out of the chair, and promptly took a seat on one of the couches nearby to wait until I was finished.

"Don't worry," I said to him. "I memorized the website address. I'll bring it up for you when I'm done."

The librarian tittered. "Ned's one of the few users who is

polite enough to close the screen when they're done." She shook her head in wonder. "It's amazing how much insight into the town I get just by cleaning up after people. You would be shocked at some of their favorite movies. Those searches come up often in February before the Academy Awards. Then there are the recipes. Someone had left up a search for homemade granola bars right before the church bake sale. I looked for them, but apparently it was for personal use. Then there are the gardeners. Why, back in January, someone was researching shrubs for their backyard, though I have to say you shouldn't plant oleander until spring. Just a wealth of information."

I remained calm. "Do you remember who was researching gardens?"

She put her fingers on her bottom lip. "It was so long ago. However, I do get the impression it was a woman. But don't go by me."

"Do you keep a record of who uses the computer?"

She pulled herself up, displaying the pride of all librarians in their record-keeping skills. "I have a book. You'll have to sign it before you leave."

I told her I would check in with her on my way out and settled down at the desk. The monitor was on the small side, and the letters had been worn off the keyboard, but what worried me most was the prehistoric tower sitting on the floor next to the desk.

"It's not dial up, is it?"

"Oh, no. We have DSL. Oh. You don't have a library card. Let me enter the password."

She did so and left. And she was right. The browsing speed was just fine. The alumni section on the Marston site required a password. Edward had given me his, and as soon as I was logged on, I typed in a search for Charles Grant. I figured he hadn't registered at the college as Charlie. After a brief wait, his picture loaded on the screen. He had managed to comb his hair and put on a fresh shirt for the photo, but his face was pudgy even back then.

I scrolled through his particulars. Journalism major. Graduated in 2005. He had an impressive list of awards under his name. Too impressive for *The Citrus Grove Courier*, no offense to them.

The information available on his alumnus page was kind of skimpy, so I expanded my search outside of Marston's website. I did a Boolean search for Charles Grant and journalism, not that I was expecting much. I didn't think Charlie had made it into Who's Who. However, when I saw the results reported by a local rag, I felt confident both Edward and Hattie Channing could relax. We had another suspect.

As soon as I got up, Ned took my chair.

"Say, Ned, when you came to Edward's talk, you arrived the same time as Professor Taylor."

"I did?" he said, distracted by entering his library card number as required.

"You did. Did the professor come in with anyone?"

"How would I know? I didn't know him then, did I?"

Before I left, I found the librarian behind the checkout desk, which looked like an old portable bar, the kind they use for parties. I didn't like the expression she wore. Her lips were pressed tightly together in a quiet anger that left me wanting to confess to the library fine I'd never paid.

"Did you have a chance to check last January?" I asked cautiously.

Her lower lip trembled. "It must be someone's idea of a joke because it makes no sense."

She turned a large, hardbound ledger to face me.

"Someone tore out January."

CHAPTER 23

Back in 2003, Jayson Blair was a young reporter for *The New York Times*. His career ended when it was discovered he had made stuff up. Quotes. Dates. Sources. For a while after that, newspapers were sensitive about any whiff of impropriety surrounding their employees. Things have changed a lot since then.

Unfortunately for Charlie Grant, things hadn't changed enough by the time he approached graduation and received several offers of employment from prestigious papers. I'll admit I made some assumptions based on the impressions I had of the late Professor Jonathan Taylor. Here's how I think it went down.

Charlie's stellar success irked one of his thesis committee members. I can't imagine any student would keep offers from the cream of the crop to himself. Taylor must have heard about them. The envious old coot wrote discreet notes to the papers interested in young Charlie alluding to possible plagiarism in his term paper. Since the reporter managed to graduate, I assumed no concrete charges materialized, but just the hit of scandal caused the steadfast sources of news to skitter away like bunny rabbits faced by a starving coyote. News traveled fast, and after he lost his initial offers, Charlie found the only paper that would have anything to do with him was *The Citrus Grove Courier*. No wonder he was loyal to them.

"It's what you suspected, isn't it?" I said after I had laid it all out for my brother.

He put on an expression he thought displayed modesty. "I thought it was a possibility."

"So, you're saying Charlie Grant may have wanted revenge on the professor and invited him up to the book event in order to kill him." I shook my head. "I don't know why the professor would accept an invitation from someone whose career he had sabotaged. The guy couldn't have been that dumb."

Edward, seated on the most comfortable chair in Mrs. Robbins' den, crossed his arms over his chest and narrowed his eyes thoughtfully. "Taylor was arrogant. He might have been fooled by Mr. Grant if the latter applied a generous layer of rump-kissing to the invitation." He waved away the importance of how the professor had come to Citrus Grove. "It could have been mere chance. Professor Taylor shows up. Mr. Grant might not have had murder in mind at first, but the professor's suggestion that he promote the book written by the man who had stolen his good prospects away from him may have moved him to violence. Can you imagine anyone so self-centered, so absorbed in his own success he would treat another man with such cavalier condescension? The mind reels."

My brother had just described his relationship with me. "Shocking."

Edward ran his fingers over his beard and then, since there weren't any witnesses around, scratched his chin. Scratching in front of strangers is verboten. "It still doesn't explain why the professor came to Citrus Grove before that. If your source is to be believed."

I shook my head. "Not a chance. My source is rock solid." I told him about getting the addresses of the council members and walking down Grove Street to see if any of them were possibilities. "His destination could have been Georgie's house or the General's apartment. Another possibility. Mrs. Robbins rents rooms. She doesn't have a monopoly. Why couldn't someone else who happened to live off Grove do the same? I assume Taylor had a car with him on both of his visits. He could have been taking his morning constitutional, picked up his car outside the place he was staying, and driven out to see Dora and Flora in their retirement community, or even dropped by Mort's mansion."

My brother toyed with the button on his shirt cuff. "Well then, who did he intend to expose that night?"

"We've got three solid possibilities so far." I held up three fingers. "You, Hattie Channing, and Charlie Grant. I can't say I like any of those options. We should take a closer look at the other council members."

Mrs. Robbins put her head around the corner. "Dinner is ready."

I looked to Edward. "How many will there be at table?"

His lips twitched. "Claudia checked out this afternoon. She finally listened to reason. It's for her own good."

"And you believe her?"

"Claudia is not a liar."

"Did she say she was heading back to Inglenook?"

"Well, no, not in those exact words, but I trust her. Unlike you, when I say something to Claudia, she doesn't search my words for wiggle room. We understand each other, and we respect each other."

"Says you." I stood and stretched. "I almost forgot. Someone was looking up oleanders on the library computer.

They covered their tracks by tearing out the sign-in list for January. The librarian couldn't recall if it was a man, woman, or child. Apparently, there's quite a rush for the online services in the Citrus Grove Library. And that gives us proof Taylor's death wasn't an accident."

Edward raised one brow at me. "Did you ever think it was?"

My brother didn't talk much during dinner. Mrs. Robbins also seemed preoccupied. While celebrating Claudia's departure, I hadn't thought how the loss of two guests would affect our hostess's pocketbook. She told me her late husband had left her well off, but she might have been bragging to a stranger. I hadn't run into any other guests since our arrival on Wednesday, so this place wasn't in demand. Guilt made me ask her if she had any other bookings this week. The old gal blushed.

"A gentleman checked in last night."

I'm a light sleeper. It seemed unlikely a man could have navigated those creaking floors without waking me up, but maybe the stress of two murders had taken its toll on me.

"And he skipped your delicious dinner?"

By Mrs. Abernathy's standards, the stew served tonight would have been slopped out to the dogs, and the homemade bread sat in my stomach like a lead weight. But I was curious. Citrus Grove wasn't a hub of tourist activity. The businesses were the kind that closed for the dinner hour except for places like Bill's or the diner.

"He made arrangements for a late supper."

"Maybe we'll meet him then."

She pressed her lips in a tight line. "He's very busy. I'm sure it will be long after you've retired for the night."

She made it sound like an order, so we went back to our rooms after drinking coffee served with butter cake topped with whipped cream out of a can.

I dropped Edward off at his doorway. Once I had changed into flannel pajamas, I flopped down on the bed with my notebook.

When we were at Inglenook last year, Edward had pulled out a piece of paper and written down the names of our suspects and their motives. I repeated the process now, except I didn't bother with neat columns and labeled subsections.

Edward. My brother would not have killed the professor; he would have bored him to death with a lecture. I crossed him off.

Hattie Channing. Edward was right. She had several great reasons for wanting Taylor dead. At first sight of him at the Babbitt and Brown Bookstore, she might have felt a wave of revulsion that set her on a murderous path to exact revenge for the way he'd treated her. Or she might have subconsciously wanted to bury Taylor along with her shame over her youthful indiscretion. I'm sure there was a psychological term for it. Or her protective mother instinct could have kicked into overdrive. It didn't matter. No motive in the world was going to make me consider her a serious suspect, so I crossed her off as well and wrote Charlie Grant.

Charlie's motive? Revenge for a despicable act. Considering the circumstances that would have moved him to murder, if he had killed the professor, I wasn't going to lift a finger to catch him. I crossed him off.

Then I flipped to a clean page and wrote Jeffrey Babbitt across the top. The council members met at Babbitt and Brown's each month, which made them Jeffrey's acquaintances. If Taylor knew a secret about one of them, Jeffrey might have discovered it. After the murder, the bookseller might have put two and two together and blackmailed the killer. I was getting obsessive about blackmail. Maybe Jeffrey, in all innocence, let something slip about the secret and the killer thought it would be a good idea to silence the bookstore owner before he mentioned it to someone else. I wrote down the council members' names minus Hattie Channing.

Mrs. Robbins knew Jeffrey. She helped out at events at his bookstore. It didn't mean she liked him. I wrote her name down, but then I realized she didn't know Taylor and crossed her off. The same person most likely committed both crimes.

I tossed my book on the bed. We were going to need more suspects.

Edward must have been thinking the same thing because he walked into my room, fully dressed.

"It's still early."

"Not in the boonies. Why? You want a night on the town? Maybe we could find a Moose lodge and play cards. I think that's as exciting as it gets in Citrus Grove."

He jangled the change in his pocket. "We could visit Mort at his house. Maybe he'd be more relaxed outside his office."

"And admit that he knew the victim? Not likely." But I got changed and met him at the front door anyway. What else did I have to do?

CHAPTER 24

Mort's house had a name. Grove Manor. Not very original, but to be fair, I wouldn't have expected a banker to score high in creativity.

The place didn't look like a manor, but it was big. A large box painted white with green trim. There wasn't a grove, either, though the quarter-acre yard was separated from the neighbors by a row of shrubs.

When Mort answered the door, he was still talking to someone in another room. He took a step back once he saw the two of us looking at him. Edward had insisted we wear suits, so we had the advantage over Mort. He was dressed in a navy-blue tracksuit with a white stripe down the leg of the pants, something no respectable man over fifty should wear. Not even in his own home.

"I wish you had called first," he said, feigning regret. "I have company."

Someone called out, "Who is it?"

I recognized the voice and grinned. "Acting like an old married couple already?"

Mort blushed.

Georgie came up behind him. She wore clive-green slacks and a white sweater set with a string of pearls and matching earrings. Her only concession to casual were the house slippers on her feet, but even they were leather.

Edward smiled. "Ah, Miss—"

"Everyone calls me Georgie."

Edward gave a slight bow. "We're so sorry to intrude, but we hoped you might be able to help us."

He was treating her like the lady of the manor, she liked it. She invited us in, first telling us to remove our shoes. A row of house slippers in various sizes—not leather—were lined up next to the door, something she obviously expected her guests to use.

We complied. At least we tried. The couple didn't appear to know anyone who wore size eleven, or, in Edward's case, size thirteen. I understood the necessity when we stepped into the living room. Thick white carpeting covered the floor and the oak stairs leading to the second floor. Not pet friendly or child friendly or shoe friendly.

After an offer was made, Edward and I settled onto the burgundy leather couch. Our choice of seating was the only offer made. No tea. No whisky. Not even water. Georgie needed to brush up on her hostess skills.

Mort and Georgie sat in the two chairs on either side of us, and the banker asked, "How can we help you?"

Edward beamed. "I haven't had a chance to offer my congratulations on your upcoming nuptials."

Clasping his fiancée's hand in his, Mort thawed.

"Thanks. Thanks a lot."

Still beaming, Edward said, "You both waited a long time to find the right person. People our age used to marry in their twenties at the latest."

This was nonsense, as Edward and I were the generation after Georgie and Mort, but vanity works.

Mort's face fell into a solemn frown. "We both survived our first spouses. I can only speak for myself, but when Mary died, I thought that was it for me. We didn't have children, so I figured between the bank and the council, that would be my life." He gazed fondly at his beloved. "And then Georgie showed up."

"Ah. Love the second time around can be sweeter because it's unexpected." Edward nodded as if he weren't talking out his butt. His first love had been a crush in grade school. I doubt if he remembered the girl's name.

"That's it exactly," Mort agreed.

Georgie remained silent on the subject, but I didn't have her pegged as the gushy type.

"How long did you know each other before you discovered you were more than friends?"

I'd never known Edward to be interested in other people's private business, so I kept my ears open, searching for a clue as to why he was interested now.

Mort put his elbows on his knees and clasped his hands. "Well, I first saw her at a Culinary Arts Council meeting."

"You mean Cooking Club of Citrus Grove." Georgie nodded at us. "That's what it was called when I joined."

He went on without noticing the interruption. In my opinion, Georgie was probably a major interrupter and corrector. His ability to blot it out was the secret to their happy relationship.

"Ten years ago, wasn't it?"

She nodded. "More like nine."

Mort winked at us. "I'll let you in on a secret. I was interested right away, but Georgie seemed shy, so I took my time."

Georgie puckered her lips. "You didn't ask me out for another six years."

Then she turned her pale gray eyes on Edward. "I'm sure you didn't come here to hear about our courtship."

"You're right. That was a benefit. I'd like to ask you about the professor. Specifically, when he was standing around the sign-up table."

Mort gave us a curt nod. "Like I said. He was blocking the table half the night."

He turned to Georgie for confirmation. Optimist.

"I didn't notice. If someone wanted to sign up they only had to walk around him. I was working on a complicated stitch that took all my concentration."

"Did either of you notice if anyone approached Professor Taylor or talked to him while he was back there?" Edward straightened up as if he had a new idea. "Or did it look like he was waiting for someone?"

"Now that you mention it," Mort said, "he did have the look of someone who was waiting. For who or what, I don't know. Maybe he got stood up."

Edward rose. "That's all I wanted to know. You've both been very helpful."

Mort and Georgie looked at him, surprised, as did I. The rest of us stood, and the couple walked us to the door.

"This is a lovely home," Edward said as he discarded the slippers and slipped on his shoes. "I hope you have many happy years here."

I waited until we got into the car before I asked him to explain. "You got me out of bed to drive here and ask them one question? One you already asked, though I like the twist when you mentioned the professor might be waiting for someone. Shows imagination."

My brother gave me a self-satisfied smirk. "I got exactly what I came for."

"That the professor was waiting for someone?"

After pulling away from the curb, I did a U-turn and headed back for the B&B.

"How does that help us? If the person was a no-show, he or she couldn't have killed him."

"Thank you."

I narrowed my eyes. "For what?"

"I had hoped to be subtle, and you've confirmed I was."

And that's all he would say about it.

CHAPTER 25

Mrs. Robbins overslept the next morning. When I ran into Edward in the hallway, he sent me back to my room to put on my suit, insisting I was still on the clock. It was my fault. I shouldn't have tried to get away with jeans and a sweatshirt. By the time we made it downstairs at eight a.m., she was in the kitchen wearing a blue, terrycloth bathrobe and mule slippers and fluttering through the cupboards.

"I'm so sorry. I must have forgotten to set the alarm."

"I heard it beeping for five minutes," Edward said as nicely as he could and still growl.

"Oh, dear. I must have been very tired. I didn't hear it."

She pulled down two bowls, grabbed a glass bottle of milk from the refrigerator, and set these on the table. Lifting her chin to get some dignity going, she said, "This will have to do."

Edward's gaze left her face long enough to glance at the table setting. "We are not cats."

She scanned his face to see if he was serious, transferred her gaze to the table, and let out a shriek, followed by a nervous laugh. "So stupid of me." She added a box of cereal and, at the last minute, went back for spoons. Then she stood behind a chair with her hands gripping the top of the backrest and waited for approval.

Edward likes to stock up on calories in the morning, and the B&B brochure did promise three home-cooked meals upon request and payment. I could tell he'd like to demand his money's worth, but that wouldn't have fallen in with the number one rule of civil behavior—always make the other person comfortable. He courteously thanked her.

"If you'll excuse me." She scurried off to get dressed.

He proceeded to eat three bowls of grainy rings that promised to make him as regular as the old British train system. I skipped it in favor of a piece of toast I made myself.

With just the two of us at the kitchen table, things seemed almost back to normal, although Mrs. Abernathy wouldn't dream of serving us cereal for breakfast. However, there was a downside. Once we finished, Edward asked me if I had any plans for the day. Without Claudia around to massage my brother's ego, he insisted on following me downtown. Not eager to bring him with me to Bill's, I suggested we stop by the bookstore to see if we could learn anything new.

"And who will we talk to?" he demanded. "That nincompoop, Cooter? He'll probably accuse me of stealing the toilet paper from the washrooms."

The police had finished with the site. Babbitt and Brown's was closed until further notice, but when we both leaned against the window to peer in like children gaping into a candy store, we saw someone move around inside the shop. Lest you think we had lost our sense of dignity, there were six other looky-loos already lined up at the glass windows and doing the same thing.

A man stood behind the counter right where Jeffrey Babbitt's corpse had been. He had thick silver hair and a stocky build. I placed him somewhere between sixty and seventy. He sorted through books, separating them into piles on the counter. He glanced up, made an annoyed expression and looked back down at the book in his hand. Then his eyes opened in surprise, he made eye contact with Edward, and he came out from behind the counter and crossed the room at a lumbering gait.

Two of our fellow peepers fled when he approached, but when he unlocked the door and motioned Edward and me to enter, the remaining four tried to push their way inside with us. He blocked their way.

"We're not open for business yet," he said in a raspy baritone. He closed the door on them and locked it.

"Well, well, well," he said, looking us over with a critical eye.

While his tone wasn't warm and welcoming, neither did he sound like a bookie who'd just caught up with a customer in arrears. He still held the book, and he turned it to the picture on the inside back cover. Edward's latest masterpiece. I knew the back cover had a picture of Aunt Civility, or at least of the model Classical Reads had hired to look the part. The inside bottom of the back dust jacket flap had a picture of Edward and a brief bio as well as contact information to set up events.

"My brother sold a lot of these babies this past week.'

Edward, so easily distracted by his own concerns, said, "How many?" the same time I, who has my head on straight, said, "Brother?"

The man studied us, trying to decide whose question to answer. "I'm Joe. Jeffrey was my twin brother."

I squinted, thinking a different perspective might bring out the similarities, and he flashed back a quick smile.

"Fraternal twin, obviously."

"I thought Jeffrey had an older brother?" Edward said.

Joe Babbitt grinned. "By three minutes."

He turned and headed back to the counter. Since the front entrance was still locked, we took it as an invitation to follow. Once back behind the counter, he pushed a pile of books aside to make room to rest his crossed arms.

"Cooter mentioned you." When Edward sputtered, he held up a hand. "He's an excitable kid and not used to dead bodies. I know it's just talk."

"I'm afraid I didn't know your brother was dead at the time I was in here. I assumed he was away on an errand, so I left."

Joe nodded and wiped his hand across his mouth. "An ugly business. Jeffrey was harmless. Can't think who would want him dead, or why. I heard from Cooter that business had picked up after the man's death, but most people pay with credit cards. Not much cash in the till."

From the way Edward's eyes opened in surprise, I could tell he hadn't considered a simple motive. Greed.

"Was anything taken?" I asked.

Joe sent a sweeping glance around the surrounding shelves, filled with stock. "I wouldn't have a clue. Of course, I'll be taking an inventory, but that's closing the barn door after the horse is gone."

"Are you the executor of his will?" Edward asked. "I mean, is that why you're here?"

Joe nodded. "He left everything neat and clean. Just some outstanding bills and small bequests. Jeffrey left the shop to me."

"Congratulations," I said, meaning it.

Edward glared at me, but I didn't see why I shouldn't acknowledge good things just because they came on the heels of a tragedy.

Joe shrugged off his good fortune.

"I'm not a great reader. Never cared for books. Prefer to

get my hands dirty, unlike Jeffrey." He made clean hands sound like a deficiency. "Don't know if I should have a sale and close the place up or try to run it with help in honor of his memory."

"I'm sure that will be a difficult decision," Edward murmured. "One you should make when the mourning period is past."

"Mourning period?" Joe reacted as if Edward had just suggested he wear a dress. "Don't have time to get weepy. The government and the landlord won't care if my brother is dead. They'll still want their rent and taxes." He hauled an unopened box from the floor without exerting much effort and set it on the counter. Then he flicked out the sharp end of a utility knife and paused before slicing through the tape. "Was there anything particular you wanted? You don't seem the type to gape through windows for the excitement."

Edward's face turned a nice shade of red. I stifled a laugh just in time.

"We thought the cops might be here. Edward is helping them out on the quiet, and he wondered if they'd come up with new questions to consult him on."

"Helping them out, huh?" With one eyebrow raised and the corners of his mouth threatening to break out in a grin, he didn't appear to believe us. Then he got serious. "I'd appreciate anything you can do to find my brother's killer."

When we were back on the sidewalk, Edward waited until we had moved past the remaining gawkers to chastise me. "You didn't need to make it sound like I was working with the police. What if Joseph Babbitt asks them about me? I'll look foolish."

"You don't need my help with that. Besides, I said on the quiet. He'll just think the police are being reticent about your role."

He let out a sigh. "Where to next?"

I looked around, pretending to think. I didn't want an audience when I talked to Bill.

"Are you hungry? Cereal isn't much of a breakfast."

"No."

I stared. Edward's stomach is the original bottomless pit.

"Should I call a medic?"

"We need to solve this riddle as soon as possible. My books don't write themselves, you know. I miss my routine. Now, where to next?"

"Maybe we should talk to Charlie Grant again," I suggested, knowing he wouldn't go for it.

"Not yet. His credentials suggest the man is not a moron. I need time to consider the right approach. The man won't be eager to talk about his humiliating experience."

"We've talked to Mort. I took on Ned at the—" I'd almost mentioned Bill's. "I saw him at the library, The General, Dora, and Flora at the cookbook signing, and Georgie on my walk."

"I haven't spoken with Miss Channing."

"And you won't. She's not on the suspect list." I rubbed the back of my neck and started to wish Claudia hadn't taken his advice. At least she would have kept him occupied. "I know. Why don't you go back and ask Mrs. Robbins who went into the bookstore's kitchen that night? Someone who wasn't a volunteer and didn't belong there. From what the volunteers said the other night, it's possible she's holding out on us."

"Why don't we both go?"

I shook my head, emphasizing my regret. "You'll have to tackle her on your own. I don't think she likes me."

Edward briefly considered the option. "That may be true, but I have a better idea. Why don't you stop trying to get rid of me and take me where you were planning to go without me?"

That's the problem with my brother being related to me.

He's had plenty of time to learn to read me. I scowled and headed for the bar. Once inside, I stopped to let my eyes adjust, but Edward pushed forward and, after a quick glance to size up the occupants, headed straight to the back booth where Bill sat. As before, her gray curls stood on end, and she still wore a flannel shirt, but Edward treated her as if she were royalty, which is how he treats all women.

"Ma'am, my name is Edward Harlow. I wonder if I could have a word with you."

The regulars turned to watch. Pretzel's dad looked away when he caught my eye. Probably still feeling guilty over the bovine-pornography incident.

Bill stood and gripped his hand. "Pleased to meet you. I'm Bill." She glanced at the gapers at the bar. "Let's go somewhere more private."

I'd already seen the office and so was immune to surprise, but Edward's reaction disappointed me. He didn't have one, though I knew he had taken in every detail and probably approved. Once she was seated behind her desk, he sat in one chair, while I took the other. She didn't wait for us to start.

"I know about your difficulty."

"Ah." Edward gave her a brief nod. "Then I'll be brief. What can you tell us about Joe Babbitt?"

My head jerked in his direction, but Bill didn't find the question surprising.

"He used to live here, but Joe's not the kind to stay in one place too long. He takes odd jobs where he finds them. He likes the outdoors. I assume he's been working on farms. Not the actual labor, but management. He learned the ropes from their father, Ben, who owned an orange grove. Lost it during the Savings and Loan crisis. He eventually recouped some of his losses, but not enough to start again. When Ben died, he left what he had to the boys. Jeffrey went into the bookselling business with a partner who has since died. Joe took off. I haven't seen much of him. The brothers didn't seem to be that close, but maybe Jeffrey kept in contact with him. Will that do?"

"What kind of man is Joe Babbitt?"

Her brows went up. "That's not the kind of question I—or anybody—can answer."

"I'm asking for your impression."

Her chair squeaked as she shifted her position. "I don't like it. I wouldn't want to hear someone describe what kind of woman I am. No one but me really knows."

He nodded toward the bar. "I'm sure those have formed an impression of you."

She smirked. "I'm sure they have, but they also know me a lot better than I know Joe Babbitt."

"Fair enough. From your own observations, did Joe Babbitt have a close relationship with anyone in Citrus Grove?"

She grinned. "Are you asking me if he was sweet on anyone?"

He bowed his head. "Or good friends. Does he have a reason to settle in Citrus Grove?"

Bill barked out a laugh. "I'm sure he wasn't a choir boy, but nothing serious. The one person he might have married already had a husband."

"May I ask who that was?"

"You may. Mrs. Regina Robbins."

CHAPTER 26

After Bill dropped the bomb about our hostess, she decided to ask some questions of her own. She leaned forward and clasped her hands on her desk. Though her countenance was still friendly, her eyes had the somber strength of judge, jury, and executioner.

"Did your brother tell you I don't want my men both-ered?" She nodded toward the bar to show who her men were.

He scrunched up his eyebrows. "You've spoken to Nicholas before today?" His brow cleared. "Ah. You must be the witness who saw Professor Taylor in town several times before the evening of his death."

She looked at me with surprise and a little respect. "You kept your mouth shut."

"He allowed the police to detain me rather than give them your name." His expression was one hundred percent devoid of respect.

"My instincts about people are still sound." She directed her gaze to Edward. "I'll repeat it for your benefit. I won't have my bar or my men involved."

Edward stood. "We will proceed using the information you've given us." He raised his eyes to the plaques on the wall behind her. "And I thank you for your sacrifice and service to our country."

She cackled. When someone knocked on the door, she said, "Come in." It was the postman. With me standing next to the wall and Edward standing on the far side of his chair, we had unintentionally blocked his access to Bill's desk. He reached over the chair and tossed a bunch of envelopes on her desk, only his aim wasn't so good. A few fell to the floor.

I bent down and retrieved them for her. I didn't intend to be nosy, but my eyes naturally scanned the addressees. One, a check, was made out to Cecil Brown at this address. Cecil Brown, the former partner in the Babbitt and Brown Bookstore. Cecil Brown who now resided at the corner of Haymaker and Fifth, the cemetery. Several other envelopes also looked like checks. I kept my face neutral as I handed them over, which was difficult with the way Bill was staring at me with her intense brown eyes.

"An admirable woman," Edward said as we left. He turned in the direction of Robbins' Bed & Breakfast.

I matched his long stride. "First of all, how did you know which one was Bill? Scratch that. You probably checked out the bar before we went there."

"Did not. She was sitting alone, overlooking the patrons. And she was drinking coffee. Do you know anyone who goes to a bar to drink coffee?"

"It's thin, but I'll give it to you. Second. What's the deal with Joe Babbitt?"

"I was curious, that's all."

"I'll believe that right after I start leaving my stocking out for Santa Claus."

"You should be flattered. Once I found out she was the source of your information about Professor Taylor, I assumed you had learned everything she knew regarding the murdered man."

"Okay. If you mean that as a compliment, I'll accept it. I suppose the next step is to ask Mrs. Robbins about her relationship with Joe Babbitt."

"Why would we do that?"

I stepped in front of him, so he had to stop walking. "What do you mean, why? Because she used to date the dead guy's brother."

"Clean out your ears. Joe Babbitt was interested in her, but she was married. Now that she is a widow, why shouldn't they court? And why shouldn't he come to Citrus Grove to take care of funeral arrangements for his brother? Although, I would like to know if Joe Babbitt knew he would inherit the bookstore."

I snorted. "It's a lousy motive. You heard him. The bookstore is an albatross, not a welcome surprise."

"Nicholas, you need to learn not to trust everything you're told."

I was half-listening. Since I was facing Edward, I had a view of the scenery over his shoulder, which allowed me to see a jaunty feather pop out from behind the corner building and then disappear again. I recognized that feather. It belonged on the hat of a crazy lady.

I sighed with gusto. "You're probably right. If we question Mrs. Robbins, who knows what she'd cook for dinner."

"Something terrifying, like haggis," Edward agreed.

My mouth opened in a wide yawn I didn't bother to cover. "I think I'll stretch my legs. Check out what little there is of downtown Citrus Grove." I grinned. "You never know. I might get inspired and solve both murders."

Fortunately, my brother was too arrogant to consider that possibility and, with a chuckle, he told me he would see me at dinner. I strolled to the corner, stopping to look in shop windows in case Edward turned back. He didn't.

When I got to the corner building, I leaned against the cool stone wall to wait. It took about two minutes before Zali peeked her head around the corner. When she saw me looking down at her, she straightened up.

"It's only you. That's a relief. I was afraid Eddie would spot me."

She headed past me on the pavement, and I adjusted my pace to one that wouldn't put stress on her short, thick legs.

"Did you ditch Claudia? Or is she lurking around here somewhere?"

"I wasn't lurking," she said in her typically cheerful way. "I was hiding. First from Claudia, then from you and Eddie."

I searched the sidewalks. "Where is Miss Grumpy-Two-Shoes?"

Zali chortled herself silly over that one. "Fits her perfect because she's a bit of a nag, but she's also a goody-two-shoes, at least most of the time. She'd have two fits if she knew I was out on my own."

She looked up at me, her expression serious. "Nicky, I'd like to visit my friends alone." She shrugged one shoulder and fidgeted with her hands. "It feels as if I've always got a bodyguard. A little humiliating. After all, I'm old enough to be a mom to all of you." By all of you, I assumed she meant Edward, me, and Claudia.

I returned her serious gaze and conceded the point. Granted, none of us had stabbed a man with gardening shears... I grinned. "Knock yourself out."

She clasped her hands together at her bosom. "Thanks, Nicky. It means a lot that you trust me."

I never said I trusted her, but I thought she deserved the chance to screw up her own life, just like the rest of us.

Besides. The people at Bill's were ex-soldiers and able to defend themselves.

"Hey," I called after her. "Where are you staying?"

"I'm not supposed to tell you we booked a room at the Best Western."

"Which room?

She held up seven fingers, gave me a wave, and headed into Bill's.

CHAPTER 27

Zali had flashed me seven fingers to identify her room number at the Best Western. Following Zali logic, that meant Room 107. If it had been Room 207, she would have just shouted the number.

The hotel was located right off the five freeway, about a mile and a half outside of town. It took me twenty minutes to walk it using the shoulder of the road. By the time I arrived at the nearly empty parking lot, I was sweating and had gravel in my shoes.

A sweet-looking brunette not much over drinking age looked up from behind the front desk when I entered the lobby. I waved at her and kept walking until I reached an indoor swimming pool. I could have found it with my eyes closed by the strong smell of chlorine. A plaque on the wall pointed which direction to take down the carpeted hallway to reach Room 107, and when I got there, I knocked without hesitating.

I admit I made a mistake. It wasn't a big deal to me Claudia had defied Edward's suggestion and stayed in town. Until a man and woman stand up before God and family and make promises, they are under no obligation to each other. My mistake was spending the walk to the hotel reveling in the look on her face when I surprised her secret rather than thinking through what I was going to say to her. I wasn't prepared for the curve ball.

She flung open the door, and I took a step back. Her hair was wet and tangled and she'd thrown a bathrobe over her—well, whatever she had on under it. Her eyes were wide and frantic, and I noticed that, even without makeup, her dark lashes framed her green eyes nicely. She pushed past me and looked both ways up and down the hallway.

"Where is she? Where's my aunt?"

She was missing the point. This was my moment of victory. Catching her in the act, in a manner of speaking. She needed a reminder of how things stood.

"Fancy meeting you here, Claudia. I heard you left town. At least that's what you told Edward."

I didn't get to the part about how she had violated Edward's unwavering trust in her because she grabbed my arms and shook me.

"Where is Aunt Zali?"

I shrugged her off. No wonder Zali wanted to get away. Claudia had control issues. I suddenly felt sorry for the aged relative, and that made me want to keep her secret. "Probably strolling down the streets of Citrus Grove looking for a cinema to help while away the hours."

She clapped her hands over her eyes. "I just wanted a lousy shower. Ten minutes. That's all the time it took."

Since she was obviously unbalanced, and there was a family with small children headed our way, I took a firm grip on her elbow and steered her out of the hallway. Then I had to decide whether to behave like a gentleman and keep the door open or close it to spare the bathrobe-clad Claudia embarrassment should that family pass by. I closed it.

The room was a typical hotel room of neutral colors with two beds, a small desk, a television, and a mini bar. If they had drawn a chalk line down the middle of the carpet, it couldn't have been clearer which bed belonged to Claudia and which one to Zali. The pillows on the closer bed were piled against the headboard, the covers and sheets were tangled together, and chip bags and candy wrappers spilled onto the floor.

Proving me right, Claudia sat on the edge of the neatly made bed closer to the sliding glass doors and gathered the covers in her clenched fists. She pulled in a deep breath and spoke slowly. "Nicholas, I need to find Zali. Will you help?"

She had to choke out the request. I appreciated the effort, but I waved it aside and sat down on Zali's bed. As I took my shoes off and shook the gravel from them, I asked, "Does Edward know you're here?"

Prim rebuke overtook her panic. "I don't need his permission to—to take a vacation."

"Of course you don't. But three pairs of eyes are better than two." I reached for the phone on the nightstand, looking forward to exposing his lady love as a liar. "Why don't I ask him to join us?"

She covered the space between us with a lunge and held the receiver down with both hands. Her robe fell open to reveal a lacy bra and matching panties. I averted my gaze.

Gathering the robe together in front, she gave me a loud, emphatic, "No."

I raised one brow. "No?" I let it hang in the air.

She sunk back down onto her bed. "I want to prove I can help him solve this case by solving it myself."

The logic of women. "But then you wouldn't be helping him, you'd be competing with him."

She glared. "You wouldn't understand what it's like. I'm on a need-to-know basis, only being told what Edward thinks I'm capable of handling, as if I'll melt into a puddle of tears if something distasteful happens. I'm tired of being on the outside. Being taken for granted. His assumption I'll just do what I'm told."

I cocked my head at her. "You just described my life."

She snorted. "Oh, please. You and Edward are as thick as thieves and—I'm jealous. There. I said it."

Either this was an expert manipulation by a twisted mind, or she meant it. I didn't have time to consider the point because we heard the click of the lock and Edward strolled into the room escorting Zali. Both Claudia and I shot up from our respective beds, and her robe fell open again. She quickly pulled it closed, and when I saw who it was, I fervently wished I had kept the door open.

My brother took in the scene, Claudia closing her robe and me holding my shoes. He had Zali by the arm. Or maybe he was holding her up because when he maneuvered her to the foot of her bed and let go, she oozed away from him and fell back, flat.

"Aunt Zali!" Claudia knelt at her side and tapped her hand. I leaned over her shoulder for a closer look. The Inglenook relic had dirt on her face and one jacket sleeve had come loose at the seam. Edward dropped her hat on the bed. The feather wasn't so jaunty anymore.

"What happened?" Claudia demanded, rising to her feet. "Who did this to her?"

"I received a phone call from Bill's."

I looked over when he spoke. He had used that silky growl that meant he was holding it together with an effort. It didn't help that he kept staring at my stocking feet.

"Bill's? Who is Bill?"

"It's a bar."

"Damn fine bar!" Zali's eruption dwindled into a snore.

Claudia gasped in horror. "Has she been drinking?"

We all looked down at the prone figure on the bed, lips flapping with each exhale and a line of drool coming out of the left side of her mouth.

"I would say that's accurate."

"B-But look at her!" Claudia lifted one of Zali's limp arms. "She's been manhandled. Who tore her jacket?"

"According to the seven witnesses including the owner of the bar who I would say is reliable, the man who did that was acting in self-defense after she tried to stab him with a mixing spoon."

Claudia closed her eyes and swayed. "Stab him? But she was doing so much better."

Edward caught hold of her, and I stepped aside so he could lead her back to her bed. While I sat down in the one chair and put my shoes back on, he forced her to sit. That damn robe slipped open again. Edward tugged it closed and gently tied it shut. She didn't even notice what he was doing, and when he finished, he patted her shoulder. "She'll be fine once she sleeps it off."

She ran a hand over her face and pushed her hair back. Then, as if coming to, she blinked up at Edward. "Thank you for taking care of her."

My brother put his hands on his hips in a pose of a man who knows he's in the right. "It surprised me to find her there. I thought you had left town. In fact, you gave me your word."

She raised her chin and responded with her snooty voice. "I never said I was leaving Citrus Grove. And I'm not going to talk about that right now."

My lips pressed firmly together to hold back an *I told you so* for Edward. When she didn't elaborate or retract, he said, "Fine." He turned on his heels and left, calling out, "Come along if you want a ride back, Nicholas."

With my dogs tired and sore from the walk, I accepted his

invitation and followed my ride out the door. Edward was taking advantage of his long stride. Though I'm only a few inches shorter than his six-feet-two, I had to push it to keep up. Between that dangerous, low tone he used back in the room and his determined pace, my brother was teetering on the edge of an explosion. That made me nervous, so I kept the chatter up to distract him from the source of his anger, especially if it was me.

"Women are born unreasonable. Wouldn't you say so? You just rescued her aunt, and yet she won't give an inch and tell you why she's in town. You know why? Because she's embarrassed. She got caught in a lie."

Edward pushed open the front doors. I slipped through before they closed. He stopped walking, so I moved to stand next to him, but then he rounded on me. I scrambled backward to dodge him, stepping into the landscaping alongside the front entrance. He slammed me against the cement wall, his forearm pressed against my collarbone and his face inches from mine. When he exhaled, his breath warmed my face.

Without raising his voice, he said, "Would you like to tell me what you were doing in a hotel room with Claudia?" He shoved harder. "While she was in a state of undress? While you both were in a state of undress?"

I let my body go limp, making me a dead weight, and I jerked my head sideways to avoid his breath. "I'll confess all if you'll answer one question."

He tensed. "All right."

I looked him straight in the eye. "Are you out of your ever-lovin' mind?"

The corner of his left eye twitched while he reasoned it out. He let me go and stepped back. "Probably."

I jerked my shoulders and straightened my jacket. "I'll let you have that one because an infatuated man, especially when the object of affection is a temperamental dingbat like Claudia Inglenook, is wallowing in a whole lot of stupid. Just to be clear, the infatuated man is you. And for your information, I had to make a call, and I chose to close the door to preserve your girlfriend's dignity. I imagine she didn't want everyone who passed by to check out her bathrobe. And I took my shoes off to shake the rocks out of them."

His car was in one of the spaces lining the front of the building. To my surprise, he unlocked the driver side door and got in without insisting I chauffeur him.

"And what, pray tell, were you doing here?"

He had moved on to sarcasm, which meant his temperature was inching back to normal. I had to decide whether to tell him the truth or make up something that would reflect well on me. I picked truth because keeping the lies straight takes too much effort.

"When I ran into Zali—"

"You knew she was in town and you left her unaccompanied?"

"She said it was humiliating to have a guard."

He looked over his shoulder and backed the car out of the space. "I suppose it would be, but it's necessary."

Exasperated, I threw up my hands. "For crying out loud! She had ginger ale last time we were in Bill's. She seemed to enjoy it, so I thought she'd stick to it."

"She likes whiskey-and-soda even better."

"Now I know. Anyway, she told me where they were staying and—"

Before turning onto Lemon Lane, he took time to smirk at me. "You thought you had leverage against Claudia." He laughed as if the idea delighted him, but I didn't laugh along. "How exactly did you envision benefitting from this knowledge?"

"I hadn't looked that far ahead," I muttered, since I would

have come across as childish if I had explained the point was to catch her in a lie and rub his nose in it.

"You wanted to pick her brains. After all, she has come up with some clever ideas, such as turning the media coverage in our favor."

"Yeah. That was a doozy."

He missed the sarcasm.

"I can appreciate that you wanted to impress me."

I unclenched my teeth. "It's my fondest wish."

"And, after all, no man wants to be bested by a member of the gentler sex."

"I can't come up with a worse fate."

My twenty-minute walk took less than five minutes by car. After he parked on the street, I told Edward I was going to sit on the porch steps and enjoy the fresh air.

It had been hard, but I had refrained from responding to his ludicrous suggestions that Claudia was smarter than I was or that I had even the remotest wish to impress him. I kept my mouth shut because I had come up with a much better way of making him pay for those comments.

As soon as I was sure he wouldn't pop back outside, I pulled out my cell phone and dialed.

The receptionist transferred me to Room 107. Claudia answered with a hopeful yet slightly miffed tone that told me she expected to hear Edward's voice.

"I have a proposal. Hear me out before you get snippy. You and I will work together to solve this murder and then rub Edward's face in it."

She greeted the idea with silence. After a brief pause, she said, "I gave you the wrong impression. I don't want to humiliate Edward."

"He said the most demeaning thing he could think of was to be bested by a mere woman."

More silence. "He didn't."

"He's sure we're both out to impress him."

"He what?"

"Maybe I've misjudged you. Seeing as how you care about him and all, it's possible impressing my brother might be your fondest desire. It's not mine. I'll see you when I see you."

"Wait!"

I grinned.

"Meet me at the hotel restaurant at nine tomorrow morning."

"Hold it. First, it needs to be early, like seven a.m. Second, it can't be at your hotel. What if Edward decides to drop by to see how Zali is doing? And before you get all dreamy about that possibility, remember your dignity."

There was another brief silence. She was probably playing out the entire scene, with Edward contrite and begging forgiveness. "We could have breakfast in my room."

I didn't want to tell her about Edward's reaction to seeing me in her room because I didn't want her to feel flattered. Still, I didn't want to press my luck with him.

"I'll call you right back."

I made another phone call, got the okay, and then called Claudia back with directions. She balked at first, but I talked her into it.

After I hung up, I stood, stretched, and went back to my room. I didn't need Claudia to help me solve the murder. She might even be a hindrance, especially since Zali would have to tag along, but the satisfaction of presenting Edward with the solution with his lady love at my side would be worth the trouble.

CHAPTER 28

I t took some doing to get to Bill's by seven a.m. without running into Edward. He likes to rise with the roosters, and there hadn't been an opportunity to switch off his alarm clock before he went to bed.

I buried my travel alarm under the covers to muffle the noise and I slapped it off the minute it rang. Then I slipped out of bed, cracked my door, and listened. The grunts and heavy breathing coming from his room meant he was doing his morning exercises on the floor of his room, so I skipped my bath, put on the jeans and flannel shirt I had laid out last night, and waited to put on my tennis shoes until I had tiptoed to the front door. I didn't risk breakfast.

It took me ten minutes to get to the bar. Bill was waiting for me. She lived above her place of business, so I didn't feel I was putting her out by requesting to hold an early morning meeting in her establishment.

"You're lucky I'm an early riser."

I grinned. "I figured you would be and that you wouldn't be able to resist helping us bring a murderer to justice."

Claudia drove her rental car up and parked in front of the

bar. Before she had turned off the engine, Zali came bounding out the passenger door. Bill kept her face straight when she saw her, though she slipped me a glance.

I held up my hands. "We'll stick to coffee."

"Unless you have hot chocolate," Zali chirped. "I love hot chocolate." She showed no embarrassment about the scene she had caused yesterday, and the bar owner seemed willing to let it slide.

"I think I can rustle some up."

I introduced Claudia, and Bill led us inside. In the early hours with the lights on, the decor seemed more faded and the dark wood bar patchy and scratched in spots. It had that lonely feeling of an abandoned home. It took us a minute to get settled in a booth because we had to talk Zali out of a game of darts. The thought of her wielding sharp pointy objects made all three of us nervous.

Bill must have put the coffee on before we arrived because a few minutes after stepping through a door behind the end of the bar, she reappeared with three mismatched mugs, two with coffee and one a hot chocolate topped with an enormous mound of whipped cream.

"You're the best," Zali sighed, accepting her treat.

"I'm going to work in my office. Cream is in the mini fridge behind the bar. Just holler if you need anything else." And with one last glance filled with curiosity, Bill left us.

I stared at Claudia and she stared back, neither of us trusting the other enough to speak our mind first. Finally, she pointed out that, since I had suggested the partnership, I should go first.

"I don't know what you know," I said reasonably. "I would hate to bore you."

"Assume I don't know anything."

I held back a wise comment and started at the beginning. I got out three words before she interrupted.

"Whose idea was it for Edward to speak in Citrus Grove?"

"As his secretary, I arrange all of his functions. If he had any say about it, Edward would be a recluse."

"But why Citrus Grove?"

"It's kind of a dump." Zali licked whipped cream off her spoon. "A nice dump, but a dump."

"Well, he had just come out with a book about eating, so I looked for food venues."

"You mean you searched for culinary councils and cookbook reading groups?"

An uncomfortable sensation wormed its way into my belly. "Reading groups, sure. I didn't even know there were culinary councils. They contacted me."

She frowned. "That makes it even odder."

"Not necessarily," I said, refusing to give her an inch. "That's why we have Edward's contact information on the inside flap of the Aunt Civility books."

Risking Edward's wrath for additional data charges, I pulled out my cell phone and searched my emails for the original request. It came from a general email address for the Citrus Grove Culinary Arts Council and was signed with a list of the council members' names.

Zali snorted. "Sounds like you were lured here. Poor Nicky."

"Okay. Let's say we were lured here, and the same person invited Professor Taylor. Why?" I narrowed my eyes. "Do you know about the message Taylor posted on social media right before the event? The one about exposing someone's secret?"

"Of course." She answered with satisfaction. "Edward told me all about it."

"Even so, it's not as if—"

I had been about to say nobody knew about Edward's secret—that he was the author of the Aunt Civility books—when I realized I didn't know if Claudia knew Certainly,

Zali was in the dark. But why would Edward tell her about the post unless he explained why it was a problem?

"As if what?" she asked.

"Nothing. A sudden thought turned into a dead end."

Zali raised her hand. "I think I know why you were invited. Eddie was a former student, and the killer knew the professor wouldn't be able to resist showing up to hassle Eddie or take credit for his success. The guy was a cretin."

Claudia and I stared at her.

"That's what Eddie says. I looked it up. It's an abusive term used to say a person is stupid. I don't think Eddie is using it right most of the time. He probably means barbarians or philistines. But don't tell him. I wouldn't want to hurt his feelings. Anyway, in this case, cretin is the right word. Professor Taylor was stupid."

It was like watching an idiot savant blossom.

"I like it." Claudia nodded. "The killer used Edward as bait to lure the professor here."

"If you're right, we need to find out who suggested that Edward come speak."

Claudia gasped. "What if it was Jeffrey Babbitt?"

Zali chuckled. "You won't get an answer out of him."

"You mean someone suggested it to Jeffrey and then killed him in case he put it together with the murder? The killer wouldn't want to wait for that. From what I saw of him, Jeffrey wasn't shy. He probably blabbed it out to dozens of people before the event." I leaned back and reconsidered what I'd just said. It was possible Jeffrey had been a pawn, and the killer decided to get rid of any loose ends. Still, the invitation came from the council, not from the bookstore. We had to find out who suggested Edward's event, and only by questioning the council members would we find the answer.

"We need to question the council members to make certain," Claudia said.

"I was just about to suggest that. If we know who planted the idea, we could wrap this investigation up toot-sweet." I looked around the empty bar. "I suppose we could ask them to meet us here one at a time. I don't think we should take them together. If the killer is one of them and even slightly clever, he or she might try to guide the rest of the member's responses."

"I don't think we can put Bill out like that. We could ask them to come to my hotel." She lowered her eyes and smiled the smile of a woman who knew she had her man right where she wanted him. Under her thumb. "I'll just keep fighting with Edward to keep him away. I'll tell him I need space."

"What if he gives you a lot of space and returns to San Diego? What will I do then? I work for him."

"Don't you get a vacation?" Zali asked. "If you don't, you could sue Eddy."

"No." I made my voice firm. "I'm not spending my vacation time in Citrus Grove."

"Come on, Nicky!" Zali smacked her hand on the table and her spoon flipped out of her mug, spraying hot chocolate on the table. "Take one for the team."

"While I appreciate your enthusiasm, drastic measures aren't necessary. Yet. I have an idea, but I'll have to get permission first and let you know. It will give us a private place to meet, and it will guarantee Edward won't come looking for me."

And with that, I adjourned our first meeting.

CHAPTER 29

While Claudia and Zali went shopping for whatever women shop for in a Podunk town, I headed to Apple Street. It was just after nine, so I assumed Hattie would be awake.

She answered the door without enthusiasm, but at least she invited me inside and allowed me to take a seat next to her on the couch.

"Are you and Laurie doing well?" I asked to be polite.

"Cut to the chase. I'm doing laundry. And if you're here to ask me where I was when Jeffrey was killed, you can leave right now."

The new, tough Hattie. I liked it. "Okay. I need a favor."

That stumped her because people suspected of murder aren't usually asked for favors, and she probably assumed I still suspected her. She lowered her defenses a notch.

"What kind of favor?"

"I need to use your house."

I hoped she wouldn't ask me why because it made for such a long, boring story with me looking like a baby trying to score one off his big brother, which I was.

Her brows furrowed into a cute line. "You want to live here?"

I disapproved of the little jump my stomach did imagining Hattie waiting for me at the end of the day, so I may have vetoed the idea with too much enthusiasm. "No. Never in a million years would I ask—. Uh-uh."

My response seemed to amuse her. "What then?" She laughed, as if something had just occurred to her. "I'm not renting the place out. I don't need money that badly."

I explained I needed a private place to conduct interviews.

"What kind of interviews?"

"General interviews."

"With whom?"

"Well, for starters, with you."

All friendliness skittered away. "I warned you—you can leave now."

I held up my hands in surrender. "All I want to ask you is who came up with the idea to invite Edward to speak at Babbitt and Brown's. That's a harmless question."

Her eyes opened in surprise. "I wrote the email. I handle all the council's correspondence, what little there is of it."

"But who asked you to write it?"

She placed a finger over her lips, which drew my attention to what nice lips they were. "Why do you want to know?"

"I want to add him—or her—to my contact list so I can send notices of future releases." I grinned. "I may look like I'm relaxing with a pretty woman, but a secretary's job is never done."

It sounded lame even to my ears. I'd just asked her if I could meet with people, strangers for all she knew, in her living room. My last two visits concerned the murder of Professor Taylor. Now Jeffrey Babbitt was dead, and

245

suddenly I was interested in increasing Edward's subscriber list.

"Technically, the entire council invited him."

"But someone put the idea forward."

"Well, I did."

I pinched the bridge of my nose, grateful Claudia wasn't here. Like cleaning a windshield, I wiped away any memory of the conversation that said the person who invited Edward was the murderer.

"What put the idea into your head?"

She shrugged, and I noticed she directed her gaze toward the floor when she said, "I must have seen the release announcement in a catalog."

Classical Reads, though a perfect fit for the type of books Edward writes, is not a giant in the publishing world. I doubted they could afford a mass mailing, let alone a catalog.

"You're sure the idea was all yours."

Her eyes met mine, and she said it was. As distracted as I was by those cat eyes, I still noticed the rest of the picture. Lips pressed into a firm line. Hands clasped in her lap. She didn't even blink. A nearly perfect lie. I would have admired her if she hadn't been lying to me.

I pretended to accept her answer. "Well, I'd still like to use your place for private talks, if you don't object."

"Why here? Why not use the diner? Or the bed-and-breakfast? Regina would let you use her parlor."

I cleared my throat. "I asked you because you're an attractive woman. It would be convenient if Edward thought I was interested in you and that's why I was over here. Then he wouldn't interfere."

"Oh!" She shook her head. "I don't like that at all."

I counted to three. "Is the idea repulsive?"

She flushed. "I—it's—"

It came to me she might think I was some kind of creep

who might take advantage of her, so I clarified. "We won't be alone. I'll be bringing my brother's girlfriend with me."

She stopped struggling to be polite and her expression rearranged itself into a prim scowl. "I see. Well, my home isn't the right place for you." She stood.

I caught the implication and jumped to my feet. "No, no, no. Not that kind of meeting. Did I mention her aunt would be with us, too?" I reached for her hand but changed my mind. Two rejections in a row could damage my self-esteem. "Seriously. We three want to have some conversations without Edward knowing. We want to surprise him." Which was true. It wasn't my fault she didn't consider that not all surprises involve cupcakes and balloons.

"Oh." She laughed. "Oh! In that case, my living room is yours. Tell me when, and I'll be here to let you in." A wave of pink ran over her cheeks. "About using me as an excuse. I'm still not comfortable giving the impression—with you and I being—"

"I promise you only Edward will think there's something between us, and my brother never tells tales. It will only be for a day. Maybe two. After that, I'll tell him you dumped me so you can keep your dignity intact."

"I suppose that's all right. A little weird, but okay."

After lining up our interviewees—which took some wrangling on my part since it was last minute—confirming with Hattie, and passing the news to Claudia, my next move was to convince Edward. Before I entered the B&B, I tousled my bangs so they hung over one eye in a manner a woman friend once described as boyishly vulnerable. I hooked my fingers through the belt loops of my jeans and tried to find a balance between looking like a man in love and looking like a sap, though they might be the same look. He was seated on the plaid love seat in the den, and he spared me a glare before returning his gaze to the newspaper in his hands. He snapped the pages straight.

"How unusual for you to rise before me. What was so important that you couldn't tell me where you were going or leave a note?"

I shrugged. "I just felt like a walk." I kept my voice low and thoughtful as I plopped onto the cushion next to him.

He glanced up. "What's the matter with you?" He lowered the paper. "You sound weak."

My laugh was hollow. "I guess I forgot to eat today."

He folded the paper and set it on the coffee table. "You forgot to eat?" Before I could dodge it, he pressed the back of his hand against my forehead. "You don't have a temperature."

I jerked my head away and snarled, "I'm fine."

"You're not fine, Nicholas." His eyes and voice held real concern. I felt my resolve weaken. "Why don't you tell me where you went?"

Growing up, Edward was a pain in the backside, but anyone else who gave me trouble had my brother to deal with. He was protective until I had my growth spurt and caught up with him, almost, and he continued to be there for me whenever trouble came my way. The thought of handing over our suspicions about the invitation to Citrus Grove and letting big brother take care of it sounded more appealing than working with Claudia and her mood swings. I almost relented and spilled all, but then he added, "You're obviously in over your head somewhere and need me to bail you out. So, what is it?"

I stood and gave him my best sneer. "Can you bail me out of love?"

His eyebrows shot up, and then he roared with laughter. He held up a hand to stop my sputtering. "I'm sorry. I had an image of you wooing Mrs. Robbins. You haven't had time to develop a relationship, and as for eligible women…" He stopped laughing. "Are you seeing Miss Hattie Channing?" Before I could answer, he swore. "She is a suspect in a murder investigation. Need I remind you what happened at Inglenook when you played around with a murderess? If it happens again, I may not make it there in time to save your life."

He was talking about Amanda. She thought I suspected her, which I didn't, and so she drugged me and was just about to bash my head in with a heavy walking stick when Edward, who had figured out she was the killer, found me in time.

"Miss Channing is not Amanda."

"Thank the heavens for that."

"Nor is she a murderer."

Edward heaved a sigh. "Nicholas, don't you remember what happened to the other two ladies you showed interest in at Inglenook?"

A chill ran up my spine and I had to tense my muscles to hold back the shiver. The other two ladies were dead, though that wasn't my fault. They had tried to blackmail the killer, who wasn't amenable to parting with her money. It occurred to me I should hang out with a better class of women, and that brought Hattie Channing's face to mind.

"I will be seeing Miss Channing this afternoon. I'll bring my cell phone so I can call you if she takes a whack at me."

CHAPTER 30

The interviews didn't go so badly if you ignore the fire.

I arrived at Hattie's fifteen minutes before the time I told Claudia to be there so I could prep our hostess. She had changed into a pleated green skirt and a fitted, matching turtleneck and had swept her bangs back in a clip at the back of her head. She looked nice, and I flattered myself that she had dressed up for her role as my girlfriend. With her feminine outfit and the dark brown suit I wore to encourage the old folks to take me seriously, we made a nice contrast. I steered my thoughts back to the conversation.

"I don't think she's dangerous, but keep your liquor locked up and put any sharp instruments away." I thought I might be exaggerating, but better to be safe. I couldn't see the council members bringing up topics hot enough to set Zali off, especially if she didn't have access to alcohol or gardening shears.

Hattie leaned against the kitchen sink with her arms crossed over her chest. "You didn't mention you were inviting a mentally ill woman into my home. What if Laurie gets home before you're finished? I won't allow—"

The doorbell cut her off. She glared at me and moved to answer it. We had agreed I would hang back until I was certain it was one of our guests. Hattie didn't want any rumors started about her love life.

"Hi! I'm Zali!"

I entered the living room and made introductions. It was interesting to watch as Claudia and Hattie sized each other up. When women meet for the first time, they subtly check out everything from face wrinkles to bust size as if they were in competition for a job as a floor model. I can't say I understand it. Men like women in all shapes and sizes, and it's not as if there was a man around in this instance who either of them wanted to impress. In this contest, Claudia would have lost because she was wearing brown slacks and a floral-print blouse, her auburn hair hung loose, and she couldn't claim to have a black ring around her irises. A close second, but a loser.

They must have found each other acceptable because they shook hands and took the cushions at opposite ends of the couch, which sat three comfortably. Since Zali grabbed the recliner, I could either take the middle spot on the couch or take the rocking chair. I took the rocking chair.

"We need to go over our game plan," I said to Claudia, but Hattie made no move to leave. "The game plan for our secret surprise."

Hattie pretended not to get my hint. "So, the surprise is for Edward? Is it his birthday?"

Since Hattie was looking at me, only I caught Claudia's narrowed eyes. By the time Hattie turned her head, the competition's expression had smoothed into sweetness and light.

"How well do you know Mr. Harlow?" Claudia, irked by our hostess's friendly tone, stressed the formal address.

"Know?" Hattie spread her hands. "I met him at the book event. He seemed like a very nice man."

"He is. Did you just happen to be there, or did you go specifically to meet Mr. Harlow?"

Hattie laughed. "I definitely wanted to meet Edward." Hattie wasn't good at taking hints. "After all, I had to introduce him."

"You're a member of the council?" Claudia gave me a pointed look. "Nicholas didn't mention that."

My eyes opened wide. The picture of innocence. "Didn't I?"

"Definitely not."

"Do you have any cookies?" Zali beamed at our hostess. "I'm feeling a little peckish."

Hattie stood. "How silly. I forgot to put them out. Would anyone like coffee as well?"

I smiled up at her. "I would love some." Claudia accepted, and Zali asked about the availability of hot chocolate. After Hattie gave her assurances that she had cocoa on hand and might even scrounge up a marshmallow or two, she left the room to take care of our orders.

"Why didn't you mention she was on the council?" Claudia hissed. "Is it a good idea to have these meetings in the enemy's camp?"

"She's not the enemy, so get that idea out of your head."

"Just because she's attractive—" she rubbed her forehead. "Okay. She's beautiful, but that doesn't make her innocent."

"There are other factors."

"I'm sure there are. I, on the other hand, have only one consideration. Getting Edward out of this mess. Are we together on this or not?"

I didn't have to declare a position because the doorbell

rang, and Hattie came out of the kitchen to answer it. I had spaced the interviews twenty minutes apart. Since we really only had one question to ask them, I figured we could move them in and out quickly enough to avoid the council members running into each other. Our first victim stepped inside. It was difficult to decide who was more surprised, The General or Hattie.

His trim mustache twitched. "So, this is your home, Hattie? Charming." He took her hand in both of his. "The surprise of seeing you makes the invitation even more intriguing."

"Not my invitation." Hattie pointed at me.

I stood and shook his hand. "Thanks for coming. I hope I didn't make it sound too exciting. We have a situation that needs straightening out, and we thought you were the man for the job."

"Of course. I'll be glad to help if I can." He looked to Hattie, and she invited him to sit, but first I had to introduce him to Claudia and Zali. He seemed charmed to meet up with his second beautiful woman in under five minutes, but then he got to the crazy lady. She clapped onto his hand and gave it a hearty shake.

"Have you ever shot anyone?"

He hesitated. "Only myself, to my knowledge. When I was a cadet, cleaning my gun."

"Bet that taught you a lesson."

"It did." His face wrinkled in a broad smile. "It surely did."

"So, were you a real general?"

"I have the stars to prove it."

His fanny had just made contact with the couch when the doorbell sounded again. We heard Hattie answer, and then Dora and Flora popped into the room dressed in matching yellow tracksuits, the latter carrying a Bundt cake with white frosting. She held it up so we could admire it.

"Lemon. My grandmother's recipe, except she grew her own lemons, of course."

The General rose, said, "Allow me," and took the plate from the old lady's hands. When he looked a question at Hattie, she instructed him to set the cake on the coffee table while she retrieved plates and utensils. When he turned back to the couch, his spot was gone.

"I believe I told you ladies four-twenty." I kept my tone polite with effort.

Dora nodded. "Always arrive early. That's what mother always said."

I headed to the kitchen to retrieve another chair but did a U-turn at the knock on the front door. Flora called out, "That will be Georgie."

It was Georgie, the knitting fiend, armed with her bag of creative implements.

"Let me guess. Your mother told you a person should always arrive early."

"Don't be dense," she said, nodding at the twins. "They're my ride."

I returned with more chairs. Dora scooted over and made room for Georgie to join them, so Claudia was crammed into the corner. She got up and took one chair, leaving the other for The General. Hattie could sit in the rocker. As I went to retrieve another chair for me, the damned doorbell rang again. It was Mort. He brushed past me.

"My business meeting got rescheduled. I hope you can talk now. I only have fifteen minutes."

Hattie was handing out plates of cake, and the gang called out greetings as if this were a social event. Mort eyed the spot next to Georgie, but it wasn't available. When he moved to take the rocking chair, I asked him couldn't he see the reserved sign? I went for two more chairs and returned to find grumpy old Ned had slipped in to round out the group. I was out of chairs, so I remained standing and sent a disgusted glance over them all.

"I suppose it will be easier with all of you here."

"I like easy," Flora said. She blushed and Dora giggled.

But we weren't all here. The front door opened and Laurie barreled in, tossed her backpack on the floor and shouted, "I'm home!"

She took in the gathering and broke into a grin. "I smell cake."

Hattie cut her a piece. "Eat this in the kitchen."

I raised a finger. "There aren't any chairs left."

Laurie shrugged off her mom's hug. "John showed us how to make a paper airplane that really zips. Can I take the plate outside with me and eat on the picnic table? That way I can eat while I work."

"Paper airplanes?" Zali sat up straight. "It's been ages, but I used to make mine do wonderful loop de loops. Sounds lots more interesting than what's going on here." She slipped Claudia a pleading glance.

Laurie acknowledged her mental equal by taking her hand. "Would you like to help me?" Once Claudia and Hattie had given their approval, Hattie with a worried look in my direction, the two of them marched through the kitchen doors. I took Zali's spot.

Mort checked his watch. "What did you want to ask us?"

"It's simple, really. We would like to know who came up with the idea to invite Edward to speak at the Babbitt and Brown bookstore."

Hattie's fork clattered on her plate. "But I already told you. I invited him."

"We want to know where the idea originated."

She set her plate on the coffee table. "And I told you, with me. Are you saying I lied?"

"Your lips told me you were the one, but the rest of your

body language was saying the opposite. I figured you, out of sheer good manners, didn't want to speak for someone else."

"I'm sorry, young man," Dora said, "but before we voted, I'd never heard of your brother. I'm sure he's a talented writer, but manners manuals are not something I would spend any time reading."

Flora glanced at her sister and turned to face me. "I think I may have heard of him. He's very famous in certain circles."

"No, you haven't," Dora said. "You're just trying to be nice. This young man wants the truth."

"I would appreciate it," I said sincerely. "But thank you for considering my feelings." Flora told me it was no problem.

The General seemed like a methodical man, and he didn't disappoint. "Once the meeting came to order, we established all members were present by roll call. Next, we addressed old business, which as I recall was whether to hold the Christmas party at a restaurant or in a private home, with everyone bringing a dish to pass. We hadn't yet decided."

"We had decided all right," Mort said, "if you call a majority vote a decision, but Ned was still complaining."

The accused lifted his chin. "I saw no reason to spend good money. Not all of us are rich."

Georgie glanced up from her knitting. "I didn't hear you volunteer your home."

"My place isn't big enough."

She snorted. "Convenient. It would have been up to one of us to clean the house and decorate. You'd only have to show up with a bag of chips and a bowl, if you even bothered to bring the bowl."

I raised my hand. "Could we get to the new business?"

The General cleared his throat. "Once we had settled the old business, we moved on to new business. Since it was our December meeting, we had to vote on whether we would continue to meet at the bookstore."

"Where else would we meet?" Dora asked. It sounded as if she really wanted to hear the other options.

"We weren't planning to move the meetings, dear." Flora patted her hand. "We just have to make it official every year."

"What will we do now?" Dora touched her fingers to her chin. "We can't discuss it at the next meeting because we don't know where or if the next meeting will take place. What if Joseph refuses to let us use the community room? Or what if he sells the bookstore?"

The members exchanged glances, and I saw the warning signs of a long conversation coming. "Mort has to leave, so why don't you table that topic until later?"

"Very good." The General jerked his head in agreement. "Then we looked in the Tribunal."

"The Tribunal?" Claudia wrinkled her brow.

"Stupid idea," Ned grumbled. "If people want to make suggestions, they should have to join and pay dues. Then maybe the rest of us would get a reduction. The dues used to be five dollars. I haven't seen any additional benefits after the increase."

Georgie didn't bother to look up this time. "Are you still crying poor mouth? Get over it. Ten dollars a year isn't going to kill you."

"Says the woman who is marrying a banker."

She shook her head. "It's the gambling that's leaving you short of cash."

"Now, now," The General said. "Let's not air our dirty underwear in front of these folks."

"It's my money and I can do what I like with it," Ned snapped. He leered at The General. "Better than spending it on girly magazines."

Mort stood. "This is a waste of time. I gotta go."

I put my thumb and index finger to my lips and let loose a

shrill whistle that got their attention. "Pardon me, but what exactly is the Tribunal?"

Georgie looked at me like I should go outside and play with airplanes. "It's a suggestion box. We call it the Tribunal because people who submit ideas are usually complaining about something. Passing judgment on the council."

"Are these suggestions signed?"

"Anonymous," Georgie said. "Keeps them honest."

"You're saying the suggestion to have Edward speak came from the Tribunal?"

The General said, "Obviously."

I nodded. "Stupid of me. Is that where you get the idea for all your speakers?"

The General cleared his throat. "This was the first time. Odd, now you mention it. Usually the suggestions are just trivial stuff like changing the time of the events to early afternoon and suggestions for what refreshments we should serve."

"That's not even our department," Dora said. "The Sweet and Sour Book Club is responsible for refreshments."

"If the handwriting is distinct, someone might be able to identify it. Where is this suggestion?"

They turned as one to Hattie, and her shoulders went up.

"I threw it away. I mean, once we acted on it, there didn't seem to be any point in keeping it."

I was going to try another approach, but Laurie ran in. "Mom, it's not my fault, but the backyard's on fire."

Hattie cried out and jumped up, but I got there first. Laurie had employed childish exaggeration. Only the clothesline was on fire, along with one white polyester blouse. By the time we arrived, it was only smoldering. I slapped away the sparks and then grabbed a garden hose and doused it. The lawn was littered with the bodies of paper airplanes, and Zali was stomping on the smoking remains of one. She looked up and gave me a sheepish grin.

"We were having a battle, and I thought, to make it realistic, some planes should go down in flames. One got away from me."

Laurie took her mom's hand. "I know you don't want me to play with matches, but I thought it would be okay, since there was adult supervision."

CHAPTER 31

"Adult supervision."

"It's not her fault," Claudia said. "The plane got away from her, and it didn't do much damage. For Pete's sake, buy the woman a new clothesline. And while you're at it, ask her who the suggestion really came from."

We were standing on the sidewalk in front of Hattie's home and, though the door was closed, I told her to lower her voice.

"You do realize she's lying."

I sighed. "Of course, I do. What I can't figure out is who she's covering for. It's not one of the other council members. I don't believe in mass conspiracies."

"Does she have a boyfriend?"

The unpleasant idea had never occurred to me. "I don't think so."

"A woman that beautiful probably has at least one."

"When I told Miss Channing part of our subterfuge was to make Edward think I was interested in her, she didn't say my boyfriend wouldn't like it. That would be the natural response, wouldn't it?"

Claudia reluctantly agreed.

"Her parents don't live in town, so she's not protecting them. Laurie's a bright child, but I don't think she's up to planning and executing a murder."

"Of course not." Claudia fiddled with the clasp on her purse. "You know, Nicholas. There is another possibility."

"Don't say it," I warned.

"She did have a reason to want Professor Taylor dead."

"Edward." I said his name with all the ice I could muster. He had betrayed my secret. The secret belonged to Hattie, but I felt some ownership, since I had appointed myself to guard it.

"Of course, Edward. He tells me everything. Well, most things." She narrowed her eyes as if contemplating ways to get him to spill any remaining secrets. "The point is Hattie has the best reason of all. A mother's love for her child."

"I told you not to say it."

I squared my shoulders and took a step forward. My next move would have been a warning shove, a growl, or both, but that was because my antagonist was usually Edward. Since I was facing a woman, I had to hold myself in check and settle for a manly snort. Claudia was so caught up airing her thoughts she didn't even notice.

"If Hattie did do it to protect Laurie, I won't lift a finger to help the police. We'll have to find another way to get Edward off the hook."

Zali blasted the car horn and leaned her head out the window.

"Don't stand there jabbering!"

Claudia had promised her ice cream.

I declined the offer of a lift.

"I need to think," I said without mentioning it was now necessary to walk off the increased adrenaline, since I hadn't been able to resort to my usual outlet. "I'll call you later, probably after Edward's gone to sleep."

I took my time walking home. It wasn't pleasant to believe Hattie Channing would murder someone even with the best of motives, but that's not what was haunting me. Two women at Inglenook Resort held back information from me. They were both dead now because they kept their secrets. Hattie wasn't a good liar. Even Claudia could tell she was sitting on something, and that made me worry for her safety.

My feet trudged up the steps to the B&B, intending to bypass the kitchen and go straight to my room, the only place I could be alone, but Edward appeared at the kitchen doorway. He let it swing shut behind him. "If you skip another meal, I'm hauling you to the doctor."

"Edward, I'm just not hungry." This time, I meant it.

He threw his arm around my shoulder and steered me toward the kitchen. "I think you'll enjoy what's on the menu tonight." I slipped a glance at his face. He seemed pleased with himself.

I was still protesting when he pushed me through the door, but then I shut my trap and stared. The newest guest of the B&B, the one who Mrs. Robbins seemed reticent for us to meet, sat at the head of the table and looked up at my entrance. Joe Babbitt.

"We've been holding off dinner for you," he said. "I was going to lead a search party if you didn't get home soon. I'm starved."

Mrs. Robbins stirred the contents of a gigantic pot on the stove. When she giggled, she reminded me of Macbeth's witches. "There's plenty of my chicken and dumplings to go around." And eye of newt and toe of frog.

She served us up bowls of her brew along with hot rolls and butter. When Edward started to say grace, Joe paused, mid-chew, and bowed his head. With the final Amen, he started chewing again.

"Spend a lot of time on my own. Not used to the niceties."

Mrs. Robbins pulled out a chair and joined us. "Speaking of niceties, Joe Babbitt, I made an apple pie for dessert."

He beamed at her. "My favorite. You remembered."

It wasn't my idea of steamy conversation, but there were underlying sparks, albeit the restrained flashes that came with an attraction in the later seasons of life.

"How are you coming along with the bookstore?" Edward asked as he speared a dumpling with his fork. "Have you decided whether you're going to sell?"

Joe sent a covert glance in Mrs. Robbins' direction. "I may stick around and take a shot at owning my own business."

"Ah. I wish you good fortune."

"I don't know about a fortune," Joe said, "but maybe it's time for me to settle down. Stop wandering and put down stakes."

"A fine idea."

Mrs. Robbins concurred. "It's not good for a man to be without a home." Joe gave her a long, serious look and darned if she didn't blush.

The conversation continued along those lines until after Mrs. Robbins served us coffee. Then Edward stood, thanked our hostess for the meal, and said, "Come along, Nicholas," as he exited.

Never a moment's peace. He skipped the den and headed straight for his bedroom, which piqued my interest. What he had to tell me must be too sensitive to risk being overheard. That suited me because I had questions of my own that I preferred to ask in private. He hadn't behaved naturally— naturally for him—during dinner, and that meant he was either preoccupied or up to something. I wasn't about to stay in the dark and then scramble to keep up with him when he decided to act. That had almost cost me my life at Inglenook. I dropped onto the foot of his bed.

"Why were you so pleasant to Joe Babbitt?" I demanded. "The man slurped when he ate, used a fork to eat out of a bowl—a fork he pointed at you at least three times—and he took a piece of chicken bone out of his mouth with his fingers. That's four strikes. I didn't expect you to lecture him on dining etiquette, but you didn't even flinch. What gives?"

His grin broadened into a toothy smile. He couldn't hold in his elation. "What did you learn from the council today?"

"Not much." My head snapped up. "What did you say?"

He clasped his hands behind his back and strolled to look out the window with the arrogance of a member of the landed gentry peeking at his vast holdings. "Claudia telephoned me after the meeting." He rocked on his heels, barely able to contain himself. "It seems she doesn't have confidence in your ability to be objective."

I narrowed my eyes, rethinking my position about shoving women. "Why that dirty double-crosser. I'd like to tell her a thing or two about objectivity."

He looked over his shoulder at me. "You can have that conversation when the ladies arrive."

I gaped. "They're coming back? Whatever happened to Claudia, you're so good and pure and I want to protect you."

He nodded. "At least this way I'll be able to keep an eye on her. On them. Mrs. Robbins agreed they could have the two beds in the back room again. They should arrive any moment."

Either he was excited his lady love would be within kissing distance, or he was enjoying the failure of our attempt to best him. The point was, he was happy, so naturally, I wasn't. I stood.

"Well, my room only has one bed, and I'm going to it right now."

His shout of laughter followed me into the hall.

CHAPTER 32

I came down to breakfast at 6:30 the next morning hoping to avoid Edward and his double-crossing lackey. I had nothing against Zali. She wouldn't have betrayed me.

When I got to the kitchen doorway, I had to stop to gather my thoughts. Mrs. Robbins wasn't alone. Seated at the table and sharing a pot of coffee with our hostess, Hattie Channing was dressed for a day at the diner. They both looked up on my entrance.

"Good morning, ladies," I said in a cool voice that I hoped betrayed none of my pleasure at seeing Hattie. I crossed the room to the breadbox on the counter. "I just want a piece of toast. No need to get up."

"Young man," Mrs. Robbins said, her voice firm with disapproval. "You've been pestering Hattie. Doesn't the poor girl have enough on her mind? I want you to leave her alone."

The younger woman flushed. "You don't have to stick up for me, Regina. I planned to speak to Mr. Harlow after work."

I leaned back on the counter. "I'm here now, and I'm all ears."

Hattie had both hands wrapped around her coffee cup, and she ran her thumbs over the handle. "You seem to have gotten it into your head that whoever put your brother's name in the suggestion box must be the one who killed Professor Taylor."

"I didn't say that. My goal is to trace how Edward wound up here so I can talk to the person, that's all."

"Then talk." Mrs. Robbins raised her chin in defiance. "I put his name in the suggestion box. I wish to Heaven I hadn't. Two men are dead. I've known Jeffrey Babbitt for years."

"And you suggested Edward on a whim?"

She marched over to the counter next to the stove and gestured with her hand at a small rack of cookbooks. I recognized the spines of Edward's works of art mingled in with the rest of the books.

"You're a fan?" As his secretary and brother, both positions that require loyalty, I shouldn't have let my surprise show.

"Now that I'm running a business, I like to make sure the details are right when I serve a large party. Growing up, my family wasn't so formal, so I needed a reference. Your brother's books were as good as any, and I liked the covers."

"I'll be sure to pass on your compliment to the artist."

"There's nothing more to it."

"Why didn't you just tell the council about Edward? Why an anonymous suggestion?"

She sat back down. "I didn't want them bothering me with questions, that's all. I wanted to put in my suggestion and be done with it. You get a committee talking and trying to make a decision, it can go on for hours."

I saw her point. I thanked them both for their honesty

and left the room without my toast. In my experience with murder so far, eliminating a theory was part of the process. I should have been happy to cross off this lead as a waste of time and turn my attention to one that might bear fruit. But I couldn't do that, and I had to lay the blame at the feet of my keen observation skills. One of those ladies was lying.

Edward's books had not been in the kitchen before this morning. I would swear to it.

I wasn't the only one up early this morning. The happy threesome was in the den. Edward called out to me as I passed. Zali, on duty as chaperon, sat between the couple. Neither of the lovebirds looked pleased.

Edward struggled to get up when I walked in, but his hips were wedged between the couch arm and Zali's generous proportions, made wider by the horizontal stripes of a dress in red and light gray. Claudia, who wore a yellow turtleneck with the same brown slacks she had on yesterday, crossed her legs and smiled up at me, defiant.

"Good morning, Nicholas. Did you sleep well?"

"So-so. It was a little awkward with a knife between my shoulder blades."

"She took the only practical course of action," Edward said with a grunt as he popped out of his cramped position and stood. "Very practical."

"Is that what they call it now?" I waved a hand. "Forget it. It's over."

"That's very sporting of you."

My brother did not understand how unsporting it was because he wasn't privy to my brain. While he and Claudia, with Zali along to chaperon, went in search of new leads—I figured Mrs. Robbins would enlighten them about her role as the source of his invitation—I would continue to dig for the real source because I knew she was lying.

After chatting about nothing important for ten minutes, I

said I'd leave them to pursue whatever agenda they had planned and excused myself. My brother called after me.

"You could come with us."

When my eyes met his, I saw a desperation that matched the pleading he tried to hide under hearty tones. If he was sick of Claudia after less than twelve hours of her company, most of them spent sleeping, then maybe I didn't have to worry about him making the relationship permanent. I ran a cool gaze over the Jezebel and the crazy lady on the couch. "Thanks, anyway."

"Or…" He took a step forward. "I know. Why don't we come with you?"

Claudia cracked the whip. "We have our own plans, Edward."

He didn't look at her. "Plans can change. What about it, Nicholas?"

It pained me to see him wallowing in the mess he had made, but it was his mess. All I had to do to strengthen my resolve was remember his smirking face as he crowed about how Claudia had sold me out.

"I'm meeting someone. Maybe I'll catch you later."

I didn't have a destination in mind, so I set my pace to stroll and enjoyed the fresh air. When I hit the downtown, my first stop was the Happy Chicken to make up for my missed breakfast. When the Amazon led me to my usual spot, the waitress who came to take my order was a short, stocky brunette.

"I'm not criticizing your service, since you've never waited on me before, and I'm sure you're a wonderful waitress, but isn't this Hattie Channing's section?"

She inspected me, like she was trying to decide if she had seen me before. "She's not here today."

"But I just saw her at Robbins' B&B an hour ago, and she was dressed for work."

"She called in at the last minute and said something important came up."

"Did she sound upset?"

"I didn't talk to her." My server glanced at another table in her section where two old men were being seated. They grinned at her, so I assumed they were regulars. She tapped her notepad with her pen. "Did you need more time?"

I asked for two eggs over easy, ham, sausage, toast, hash browns, and coffee with cream. As I ate, I played a game with myself. I would guess what Hattie's problem was. If I was right, it meant I should ask her on a date because it showed I was in tune with her. If I was wrong, I'd ask her on a date. It meant I needed to get to know her better.

Important. Did she mean it was important to her? Like she had a dentist appointment she forgot about? What if she had been so upset by my talk with Mrs. Robbins that she needed time to cool off? She didn't look mad. Mrs. Robbins looked mad. Or did the emergency involve someone else, such as Laurie getting called to the principal's office for showing her classmates how to set paper airplanes on fire? Or maybe the school called because Laurie was sick. I had to dismiss that theory when I checked my watch. It was only just past seven-thirty.

I hoped it wasn't something bad. Her parents must have been in their sixties, which is young these days, but still. Accidents happen. By the time I cleaned my plate, I decided to let it be a surprise, since I was planning to ask her out on a date either way as soon as this murder business was over.

I tipped the waitress five dollars to make up for treating her like second best when she showed up to take my order and set out to kill time. Hattie had to deal with her problem before I could show up at her house to ask about how it went. Since it was before nine, most businesses weren't open.

I decided I owed it to Citrus Grove to admire her downtown area and headed east on Lemon Lane.

It took five minutes to confirm that Citrus Grove had no highlights, not even stimulating scenery. There were the usual suspects: a post office, a drug store, insurance offices, a travel agency, and the savings and loan. A traditional red, white and blue barber pole marked the barber shop, while the beauty shop lined the front window with mannequin heads wearing wigs to model the latest coifs.

I crossed the street and doubled back, beginning with the Navy recruiting station on the corner. They called it a Navy Career Center, but I assumed it was the same thing. Next door, a middle-aged man rolled a seven-foot tall clown outside and parked it in front of a sweet shop. I thought the decoration was a poor business decision, since so many members of the target market—kids—are afraid of clowns.

By the time I made it to Babbitt and Brown Bookstore, Joe Babbitt had opened for business with the aid of his multi-talented stock boy, Cooter, who also knew how to run the register. Already they had a line. I told him I was just browsing and started in the front corner with the biographies, slogging my way to the self-help section.

There they were prominently displayed face forward. Two copies of each of Edward's books leftover from our visit to the cookbook signing the other night as well as the rest of his books. Here they were, ready for Mrs. Robbins to purchase, or, since she held Joe Babbitt's fancy, she could have asked him to bring them home last night. Unless. If Hattie Channing first told our hostess about the meeting over coffee this morning, then the books had already been there and I should get my eyes checked. I refused to consider that option seriously, but the thought of talking to Hattie Channing again appealed to me. Hopefully, the important issue that made her cancel her shift at the Happy Chicken had been dealt with. I made my way to Apple Street.

My mind wasn't solely on the question of when Hattie had reported on our meeting to Mrs. Robbins. It was thinking of topics that might jumpstart a personal conversation. Likes and dislikes. The things you talk about on a first date. I wasn't paying attention to my surroundings, but when I got within three houses of Hattie's residence, something caught my eye and stopped me in my tracks.

A familiar blue sedan was parked at the curb.

"I'll kill him," I muttered under my breath. While I was deciding on my next move, the front door opened and Sykes stepped outside, turned back for a goodbye, and then descended the steps. He must have been busy with his own thoughts because he didn't notice me. I waited until he pulled away and turned at the corner before I jogged to Hattie's house and up her front steps.

I rapped lightly, and when she answered, her eyes looked puffy and there were tear stains on her cheeks. The changes in her expression went by in quick succession. At first, her eyes opened wide, she gave a little gasp, and she swayed forward, happy to see me. She caught herself in time and pulled back. Her face flushed red and her full lips pressed tightly together as she decided I was the enemy.

"You just missed him."

I held up my hands. "I know what you're thinking—"

Her voice turned cold. "You have no idea what I'm thinking. You don't know me at all."

"You're right. I don't. All I have are my impressions."

"And is it your impression I'm still a naïve college girl? Ready to believe whatever a handsome man tells me?" She looked down at her hands. "You may be right. I thought you meant it when you said you wouldn't expose me."

Before she could slam the door, I slipped my foot onto the jamb and said, "It wasn't me."

"Then how did the police find out?" She twisted her hands together. "I know what you're thinking." She said this without irony. "That I'm a coward. But you're wrong. I don't care what anyone thinks of me, but I don't want the ugliness to touch Laurie. Thank God she wasn't home. How would I explain a visit from the police to her? And she would have heard the whole, sordid story as I told it to the detective. Sure, I could have sent her out of the room, even outside, but children her age have a gift for hearing things they shouldn't. Even now, people might talk. Who am I kidding? They will talk."

She seemed to realize she was dangerously close to getting hysterical because she inhaled, straightened her shoulders, and let out a sigh. "It doesn't matter who told him. The damage is done. It would have come out, eventually. There are others who know. It was foolish of me, but I was hoping to put off explaining—what happened—to her." She clenched her hands into fists. "She's still a child, and she shouldn't have to deal with things like dirty, old married men."

"I believe we call them cads."

She glared at me. "Cads? That's a much nicer word than the one I was thinking. And it's much, much nicer than the word I have for you. Please leave."

"I already told you I'm not responsible. I told Sykes nothing."

"Good for you. Now, go."

"Hattie, I want to help you."

"Just leave me alone."

Her voice sounded so cold, so final, I took a step back. She took advantage and slammed the door.

CHAPTER 33

I headed straight to the B&B to have it out with Edward, but when I got there, Mrs. Robbins informed me he was still painting the town with Claudia and Zali. The big buffoon. *Why don't you come with us? No? Then why don't we come with you?* One big happy family.

I had mistaken the desperation in his eyes for that of a man trapped by female company, but the only thing he was anxious about was me learning he had blabbed Hattie's secret to the police. He must have known Sykes would be paying her a visit today. He thought he could steer me away and find ways to occupy me, and then I would never know he had betrayed me. That made it worse, that he had conspired with others behind my back. It showed a lack of respect. Hell, I would have settled for him asking my opinion before he decided. He probably thought I would warn her. He was right.

In my bedroom, I jerked my suitcase onto the bed and threw my clothes inside. I stuck my tongue out at my suits, the ones Edward demanded I bring along, and left them in the closet along with my dress shirts and good shoes. Once I had everything else packed up, I opened the drawers and looked under the bed to make certain I hadn't missed anything. I took the computer to Edward's bedroom and left it in the middle of his bed where he wouldn't miss it and then returned to my room. The thoughts racing through my head, thoughts of what I would tell Edward next time I saw him, made me less aware of my surroundings than usual. I was locking my suitcase before I heard heavy footsteps right outside my door. Edward pushed his way inside and looked from my suitcase to me.

"Don't you knock?" I snarled.

"Nicholas, calm down. Let's discuss this like gentlemen."

"A gentleman wouldn't sneak behind his brother's back. A gentleman wouldn't throw a lady to the wolves."

"You're angry."

"Damn right I am."

"It's your own fault."

I gawked. "You sold her to the police. You felt the heat and tossed her to Sykes."

"If you had retained one ounce of objectivity, I wouldn't have felt the need to alert Sykes. She has a motive for wanting Taylor dead. A very good motive. Instead of considering that possibility and working to eliminate her, you kept her completely out of the investigation."

"You're just mad I didn't let you talk to her."

"Your actions have been unreasonable. You've lost your head over this woman, and your good sense. Claudia and I discussed it—"

"Don't ever discuss me with that she-devil again."

He raised his brows in surprise. "We were concerned about you. Both of us were."

"Is this the part where you tell me you did it for my own good?"

He got a martyred look and spread his arms. "If it makes you feel better to hit me, do so. I won't hit you back."

He knew damn well I wouldn't hit a man who wasn't willing to fight back. I balled up my fists and yelled with my mouth closed to keep from alarming the household. I took a step toward him. "Here's what I understand. I told you something in confidence, and you used it for your advantage. You wanted to get yourself out from under with the police and you wanted to bond with your girlfriend."

"You did not tell me in confidence. We were discussing a murder investigation. Hattie Channing is a suspect, something you would see if your emotions hadn't warped your perspective."

"So now I'm warped and emotional. Is that it?"

"As a matter of fact, I think you understand her precarious position, and that's why you're acting so unreasonably. Because it scares you."

Telling me something that was true only made it worse. I grabbed my suitcase off the bed. When Edward stepped in front of the door, I shoved him, hard. I only meant to get him out of my way. Normally a shove from me would make him take a small step back at most, but his foot slipped on the area rug and he went down, bumping the back of his head on the wall. We stared at each other, both of us wearing looks of surprise, and I almost held out a hand to help him up but caught myself in time. Edward slowly got to his feet and dusted off his pants. Once I saw he was all right, I clamped my jaw and jerked the door open. Claudia and Zali stood outside, probably alerted by the loud thump he made when he landed. After one look at my face, Edward's lady love rushed past me to tend to her fallen hero. Zali just said, disappointed, "I missed all the fun. Did you get in a good one?"

"Not as good as you might think."

"You're just trying to make me feel better, Nicky"

Mrs. Robbins stood at the foot of the stairs. As I descended, I asked her to call a taxi. When she hesitated, I assured her I wasn't skipping out on my bill. Edward would take care of my room. I went outside to wait, and when a yellow cab pulled up to the curb, I got in without looking back.

The young receptionist at the Best Western recognized me from my last visit.

"Your friends have already checked out."

"Claudia Inglenook is no friend of mine." I handed her my personal credit card, accepted the room key, took the elevator to the second floor and strode to the last room on the left.

The room came with two double beds. I tossed my suitcase on the closer one and opened the curtains and the sliding glass door to let out the smell of stale cigarettes and disinfectant. Then I sat on the end of the second bed to figure out what to do next.

I put find a new job and a new place to live at the top of the list. There was no way Edward would keep me on after I knocked him down, even if it was an accident, but I couldn't worry about that now. The police were focused on Hattie, so my priority had to be finding the person who killed Taylor and Babbitt. It wasn't that I didn't think it was important when Sykes only suspected Edward, but I always figured my brother could take care of himself. Hattie was different. She wasn't a feather that would blow away with the slightest breeze, but I wanted to spare her the pain of having her embarrassing spots dug through by strangers if I could.

For two straight hours, I sat in that room and went over every detail since last Monday night, trying to think of anything I might have missed. Then I made a list of all the outstanding questions I had.

The first and most obvious question was who invited my brother to the Babbitt and Brown event? I didn't believe that person was Regina Robbins. Otherwise, why all the secrecy? Her claim that she didn't want the council members bothering her with questions sounded like nonsense to me. They didn't seem likely to come up with two good questions between all seven of them, let alone enough to pester her with. In fact, I hadn't heard one member talk about culinary arts with any passion unless I counted the antique methods discussed by Dora and Flora. I suspected they were all there for the gossip and snacks.

So, where did the suggestion come from? Who would the council members have wanted to protect? I had three choices. Regina Robbins had suggested Edward's visit, and they all wanted to protect her; another council member had suggested him and they all wanted to protect him or her; or the suggestion had been anonymous, but Regina Robbins knew who had made it but didn't want us to know.

It didn't take long to eliminate the second option. The council members would have to be united in their subterfuge. Not one of them would have been willing to protect cranky Ned, and I didn't believe *he* would risk his neck for any of them. So, either Regina Robbins was the culprit or knew his or her identity.

Then I got a bright idea. Charlie usually had his camera handy. He might have captured something on film that might point to the killer. Don't ask me what I expected to find. Maybe someone grinning broadly as Taylor took his last breath. Really, it just bothered me that I had been so focused on Taylor while he was dying, which was understandable, I hadn't noticed what anyone else had been doing. I wanted to see for myself.

I called the reception desk and asked for a taxi. The guy who answered said an Uber driver was the cheaper option. Since an unemployed man must watch his pennies, I told him to place the order. Ten minutes later, a rusty, gold pickup truck pulled up to the entrance. I leaned over and peered inside.

"You've got to be kidding me."

Cranky Ned leaned across the seat and pushed open the passenger door, grinning at me the whole while.

"Your chariot is here." The old man cackled at his own joke.

I slipped my fanny onto the seat and pulled the door closed. It needed a second slam before it clicked shut.

"Don't they have standards for Uber drivers?"

"I haven't had a ticket since nineteen seventy-nine. That's when I bought this workhorse."

I leaned in to smell his breath. "You didn't come here from Bill's, did you?"

"Sure, I did. Don't worry. I always stick to soda water when I'm on call." He shifted the truck into first gear. "Where to?"

As soon as Ned dropped me off, Bill's regulars would be gossiping about my new residence. That was okay. Let them guess why I was at the hotel, but I didn't want them to know more than that. I told him to drop me off anywhere downtown. Then I prepared to have my insides jostled.

Ned must have replaced the shocks. The truck turned out to be a surprisingly smooth ride.

"You belong to quite a group."

He grinned. "They're alright. Nobody gets along with everybody all the time."

"You said it, brother," I muttered. "What do you all do when you're not listening to lectures?"

"What most people do, I suppose. We argue."

"About where to have the Christmas party?"

"Nah. That was special. Usually it's over the best way to cook something."

"You and The General don't seem to be best friends."

Ned grinned. "The General is a master at the grill and doesn't think anyone else's advice is worth a listen. That's usually where the arguments start."

My brows went up. "I had him pegged for plain cooking with a cast iron stomach for deposits."

"That's Mort. He can eat anything. So can I, but I don't want to. I like my food to look good. Makes it more appealing. Maybe it's 'cause I'm older. After a lifetime of eating what you can, you decide to eat what you want."

"There wasn't anything behind Georgie's comment about you bringing chips to the Christmas party?"

"She was just mouthing off. Jealous, I suppose, since she's never been able to bake a soufflé without it falling. I've made three, but my specialty is coffee cakes."

I whistled. The things you thought you knew about people but didn't. "I had you pegged wrong. Culinary art doesn't strike me as your line."

He turned his head quick to check if I was making fun and got his eyes back on the road. "I agree the name is artsy-fartsy, but the ladies insisted on it. Made it sound important, I guess. I joined to learn something new. Got to keep your mind fresh by trying new things. That's my motto."

"A good one, too." The truck's cab was full of friendly feelings, so I ventured to ask, "Just between you and me, was the suggestion to get Edward here really anonymous?"

He screwed up his lips. "Well, it was, and it wasn't. The suggestion was anonymous alright, but between you and me, I saw who put it in the box. Didn't want to contradict a lady."

"Regina Robbins?"

"No. Hattie."

He pulled up in front of Bill's just then, so I didn't have to arrange my face to hide the surprise. I handed over ten bucks and got out. He locked up his vehicle, came around the front of the truck, and held open the door to the bar.

"You coming?"

"No thanks. I need to stretch my legs."

CHAPTER 34

The way I felt after the punch in the gut Ned had delivered, my first instinct was to discuss the implications with my brother, since that's what I'd always done. However, any conversation with Edward right now, especially about Hattie, would be unhealthy. If he were to appear in front of me, say through some unknown scientific advancement or a miracle, I might lose my temper and knock him down, fully intending to. If it hadn't been for his constant harping about my lack of sense with the fairer sex, I would have written off Ned's statement as the blathering of an old man trying to make himself important instead of asking myself, yet again, how well did I know Hattie Channing? Then I looked at it from another angle and calmed down.

Regina Robbins might have written the suggestion and asked Hattie to put it in the box. That fitted in with my opinion of Hattie, so I decided that's the way it was. She had innocently acquiesced to a request from her elder.

As usual, my intellect tried to nudge aside my instincts. The latter told me there was something fishy about Mrs.

Robbins' confession that she had been the one to suggest Edward to the Culinary Arts Council, but my brain butted in and said if that were so, it meant she was covering for Hattie. Why had our hostess put out Edward's books? Because Hattie had warned her. Warned her of what? Hattie said she only told Mrs. Robbins I was looking for the person who got Edward down here, but who could confirm that except Hattie and Mrs. Robbins?

Since I wasn't getting the answers I wanted, I decided I was making a big deal out of nothing. Mrs. Robbins might have made the request that resulted in Edward's appearance in complete innocence. Maybe Hattie's warning had made her think she was in trouble. Our hostess, feeling the need to back up her story with proof, pulled books she already owned out of storage and put them on display. Best to eliminate our hostess right now.

Taylor had a reputation for three things. Did any of them give Regina Robbins a motive?

One. He liked to seduce young women, which excluded our hostess. Unfortunately, that scenario included Hattie Channing. I reprimanded myself for straying off the point, which was Mrs. Robbins' motive.

Two. His vindictive nature led him to sabotage careers. Our hostess had expressed no longing to be a writer. I'd seen no signs of a typewriter or an excess of pens and writing tablets. However, my research at the library showed that motive applied to Charlie Grant.

Finally, none of his colleagues liked him because of his disagreeable nature, but since Mrs. Robbins wasn't a colleague, she wasn't exposed to him daily and wouldn't have had a reason to kill him. Maybe we should have gotten an alibi from Professor Kanchalian.

I picked up my pace. From what I had seen of Citrus Grove so far, it didn't seem to be a hotbed of vice if I discounted The General's girly magazines and grumpy Ned's penchant for gambling. A murder would have been big news. Any self-respecting reporter would have gone over Taylor's life with a magnifying glass in search of one salacious detail other papers might have missed. Charlie might not have enough self-esteem to iron his clothes, but I didn't believe he could bury the instincts that had led the former college kid to earn so many offers from prestigious papers. I was counting on it.

Once the rail-thin assistant with spiked hair, which was now purple instead of black, had escorted me back to Charlie's office, the reporter invited me to sit. I put my proposal to him and waited.

He rubbed the stubble on his chin. "You might be interested in my research so you can write up a nice story. Publications would jump on something from the brother of the famous Edward Harlow."

"Forget it. He's not that famous. Besides, I was a business major. Edward's the writer of the family."

Charlie leaned back and tapped his fingertips together. "He's a writer? How interesting. Maybe Professor Taylor was on to something with his hints. You know, it would make a great story if Edward Harlow was Aunt Civility."

The wince didn't make it to my face. I'd stumbled, but not enough to fall. "Sure, he's an author, if you consider penning lectures to etiquette-conscious old ladies—and I include men in that category—a writing career."

He held eye contact with me for a few seconds and then broke into a laugh. "That would be something."

I grinned along and let out the breath I'd been holding.

"Seriously, the only thing I'm interested in is tagging the person who killed Taylor and Babbitt."

"I thought your brother was the one assisting the police with their inquiries."

"Call it sibling rivalry. I wouldn't mind getting to the killer before he does."

He leaned back to reach into a pile of folders on the floor behind his desk, snatched one of medium thickness from the middle and slid it across his desk. "Help yourself. But you can't take it with you."

I looked around at the mess in his office.

"You can use the conference room."

He led me down the carpeted hallway to the last office on the left. Inside, a rectangular wooden table took up the center. Yellow sticky notes covered the upper half of one wall right next to a white board showing the layout for an upcoming edition. Or maybe it was left over from a past edition. I wasn't a subscriber, so I wouldn't know.

After bringing me a cup of coffee, the reporter left me to it.

Most of the notes were in shorthand on pages torn from a spiral-bound notebook. It was Gregg Shorthand and not Charlie's own invention, so I didn't have a problem reading it.

The first page was an interview with Jeffrey Babbitt. To my surprise, the gnome had decided against entertaining the reporter. It read like a press release. He was shocked and saddened over the death of a fellow human being. He hoped it would not cause people to blame the bookstore in any way. They were not liable. As a precaution, they would ban outside food at future events. He managed to plug the upcoming Sweet and Sour Book Club meeting, mentioning he had extra copies available of their selection of the month, *Perfecting Pasta*. That made me feel better because it sounded like the Jeffrey I knew.

Over the next few pages, Charlie talked to the council members. They had presented a unanimous front and, from the amount of ink dedicated to The General, the members had elected him their spokesperson. Continuing Jeffrey's theme, they were saddened and shocked by Taylor's death. They hoped it wouldn't reflect poorly on the Citrus Grove Culinary Arts Council. The General wasn't savvy enough to plug the next council meeting, but that was probably a good thing. It would be hard to impress new members after presenting them with murder at their latest event.

Dora and Flora compared Taylor's demise to the accidental impalement of a farmhand named Tim when he fell from his ladder and landed on his pruning shears, their point being both men had been minding their business when death caught up with them. Except Tim didn't die, although he expressed a preference for a liquid diet after the accident and never climbed a ladder again.

Hattie Channing's contribution was limited to I can't believe it. That didn't help much because I hadn't heard her say it, so I couldn't interpret her tone.

Crusty Ned took Taylor's death with uncharacteristic optimism. I've collected eighty-two dollars in membership fees tonight. It seemed an odd number considering the annual fee was ten dollars, but maybe someone was paying on installments.

Georgie and Mort refused to comment at all, or at least they commented that they had no comment. A purely political move by the banker and the future banker's wife.

I paused over the next page. Charlie Grant had interviewed Regina Robbins, probably because she had been in charge of the kitchen. She stood by her volunteers and dared anyone to find fault with what they had served. As for the food brought to the event by Mr. Edward Harlow, well, she couldn't vouch for that since she hadn't prepared it and didn't know him personally. It made me grin, the thought of Edward, the nefarious poisoner.

When I got to his interviews with witnesses, I took my

time, but the gist of it was nobody had seen anything except an older man having a fit. There were a few mental giants who suspected foul play. I dismissed the woman who swore she saw a man in black who didn't look right waving something at Taylor before he fell. Possibly, he stabbed him. That was followed by some geezer who said he would swear on a stack of Bibles he'd seen something fly through the air in Taylor's direction, again right before he fell. He suspected a Chinese gang, since they were known for subtle ways of killing their rivals. Or maybe that was the Russians.

One witness worried me, but only if the person had given the same statement to the police. Someone named Gladys, most likely someone Charlie knew, since he didn't include a last name, said Taylor had pointed at Edward and accused him, which was accurate, but then she said my brother had sent me to keep watch over Taylor to keep him from talking to anyone before he died. I did order the crowd to stand back but only to give the dying man room to breathe. It surprised me Sykes hadn't asked me about it.

Thinking back, I had been near the tables when the pitcher of barley water fell and broke. I had dismissed it as an accident, but what if it had been a decoy to get the police focused on Edward and me? If so, it had worked, at least until I spotted the water bottle and pointed it out to Sykes. I wondered why the killer hadn't disposed of Taylor's fancy bottle. Maybe he or she didn't want to draw attention to it. Or maybe it had been kicked aside in the commotion and the killer couldn't find it.

I rubbed my eyes to work out the strain from translating shorthand scribbles. After slipping the papers back into the folder, I stood and carried them to Charlie Grant's office.

"Did you find what you were after?"

With a shrug I said, "At least I know who killed Taylor. All I have to look for is a man in black working for a Chinese gang." I let him have a laugh before I brought up my request. "You had your camera with you at the book event."

Charlie looked me over with a wary eye. "Y-e-s."

"I'd like to look at the photos, if I may."

"For what?"

"I'm a visual kind of guy. I hoped looking at photos of the night might inspire me to remember something important."

"Nothing jumped out when I looked over them, but you're welcome to come over tonight." As he wrote down his address, he explained the police had taken his camera, but he had first transferred the pictures onto his computer. We set a time, and I went in search of dinner.

CHAPTER 35

The bookstore was only a block away from the Happy Chicken, so I stopped in on my way to dinner because it occurred to me Edward and I had been remiss. We had been so caught up the other day in answering Sykes' questions about the discovered water bottle we had ignored a possible source of information. I wanted to rectify that omission.

Two murders in one place were too much for the public to resist. Bodies packed the sales floor. A long line had formed in front of the counter, so people were buying, not just browsing. Joe Babbitt might have a goldmine on his hands if the murders kept up.

The new proprietor was behind the counter ringing up sales. He nodded when he saw me, so I wandered over and leaned on the counter next to a woman who should have sued her fashion consultant. Spandex is an unforgiving fabric. Even young women with attractive figures jiggle and bounce enough to make a man pause to consider the jiggles and bounces won't improve with age. The woman had too many bulges to count. I looked away before she moved and set it all in motion. I didn't think I'd recover.

"Hey! Back of the line."

The next customer up was a thin woman with a pinched face and a shrill voice who looked ready to go a round with me if I usurped her rightful place.

"Calm down, lady. I'm not in line." To Joe I remarked, "Business is good."

He handed the bulgy woman her purchases in a bag with handles, but she stayed where she was and gave him a smile that encouraged him to rethink things.

Joe stared, returned the smile with one of his own, and then smacked his forehead. "Oh. Your change. Sorry about that."

She nodded and laughed, relieved he was merely forgetful and not trying to cheat her. He leaned back his head and shouted.

"Cooter!"

The stock boy skittered up. Once the new owner explained the situation, the kid hit a button and the register popped open. When Joe asked him to man the front for a few minutes, he seemed glad to take a breather from unpacking boxes of books.

"I wish it would slow down long enough for me to get the hang of the cash register and get clear on a few other things, like what we have in stock. This was my brother's arena, not mine."

"But you're going to take it on? Maybe settle down, get married—"

I almost said start a family, but Mrs. Robbins was past her expiration date excepting a Biblical miracle. As it was, Joe averted his eyes and shifted his feet.

"Man gets to a certain age it seems like a wise move. Can't spend the rest of my life drifting around."

"That's a point. With you drifting and all, how did they know where to get hold of you when your brother died?"

He chuckled. "You make it sound as if I was a ghost. My brother was a nut for organization. Probably had my cell phone number in his weekly planner's emergency contacts."

Cooter raised a hand to get Joe's attention, and I followed him back to the counter. The stock boy had been my objective anyway, so I hung around until Joe dismissed him. After giving him a head start, I followed him through the hallway to the office.

"You're not allowed back here," Cooter said when he saw me.

"I was looking for the bathroom and got lost."

"I recognize you." He tried sneering at me but it didn't work so well with his braces. "Have you lost something?"

"I assume you're referring to the lost-and-found box. That was a pretty nifty surprise I gave the police." Cooter had to agree. "As long as I'm here, I have a question for you. The day Jeffrey died," I began, but he cut me off.

"The police know everything I saw, and they're the law, not you. I don't have to talk to you."

He bent over a box of books. One friendly tap from the toe of my shoe would have him flat on his face, but I let the opportunity pass because I wanted answers.

"The police are better at gathering information than giving it, but if they had an open and honest conversation with you, they would tell you you're a suspect." I shrugged my shoulders because I knew he was watching me out of the corner of his eye. "Edward and I are working to find the real killer, but if you're confident the police won't take into consideration the fact you're the only one who can vouch you weren't alone with Jeffrey the day he died, it's no skin off my nose."

I made as if to leave. He called after me.

"A lot you know. I wasn't the only one here that day."

Working up my most pitying look, I said, "Of course you'd say that now. Just remember to stick with whatever you said the first time. The police don't like it when you change your story."

"I'm not making it up! Mrs. Robbins came by to return some serving dishes from the event, the ones she took home and cleaned."

"That story won't hold. Why did she take them home? Isn't there a sink in the kitchen?"

"Yeah, but the police wouldn't let anybody in there, so she just took the serving trays home with her after the event."

I leaned against the door frame and crossed my arms, keeping my interest away from my expression. "Okay. That's one."

Cooter held up two fingers. "Charlie."

"Charlie Grant?"

"Yeah. The reporter for *The Courier*."

I cocked my head. "Shopping for grammar books?"

"Not even close. He wanted to take a few pictures of the empty community room. For his article. Said a crime scene after the fact with no people emphasized the emptiness of death, and if he printed it in black-and-white, people would subconsciously think of old-time crime photos. They would feel they were getting a peek inside the police files."

Maybe Charlie Grant had minored in psychology. Or maybe he was looking for the water bottle. "Keep going."

"One of the council members came for the sign-up list."

"Which one?"

"Mort. The police kept it so they could copy it. He wanted it back."

"What time?"

"I don't know." He pointed to a clock on the wall that read

ten minutes after nine. I looked at my watch. It was eighteen minutes after four.

The kid folded his arms across his chest in an unconscious imitation of me. I took that as a signal he had finished.

"How do you know these people stopped by? You work back here." I looked over my shoulder at his view from the room of the hallway wall. "You can't exactly see them come and go."

Cooter curled his lip in disdain, but it caught on his braces and he had to pull it loose with his thumb. "The bell rings when anyone walks in. Mort's list was on the desk in here, so I saw him. I even talked to him. And I ran into Charlie taking pictures when I went on break. I left through the community room so Jeff wouldn't see me and come up with something else for me to do."

"Did you see Mrs. Robbins?"

"No, but the platters are back in the kitchen."

I stood straight. "Wait a minute. You saw Charlie on your break? Would this have been your break at two o'clock, when you saw Edward peering in the window?"

"Nah. The one before that."

"In the morning?"

"After lunch."

I narrowed my eyes. "That's a lot of breaks."

"This job is physical labor, mister. I need to stretch my legs every hour or so. Jeffrey understood that."

"Did you see Charlie and Mort leave out the front door?"

"Well, no, but I didn't see them when I got back."

I let my gaze roam over the room. On impulse, I entered and crossed to the door. Cooter protested, but I ignored him and took hold of the doorknob. It was unlocked, so I swung it open and stuck my head out. The only things back here were a tiny gravel parking lot and a dumpster. A wooden fence stood along the border to separate the lot from the surrounding backyards.

"Is this always unlocked?"

"During business hours."

I shut the door and walked back to the hallway. "Not bad. I'll put in a good word for you with Sykes."

The kid was too young to know if I was full of it or not, so he thanked me, but without enthusiasm.

Joe was still busy at the counter, so I waved as I left and headed for my regular spot at the Happy Chicken.

CHAPTER 36

My purpose in checking the back door to Babbitt and Brown bookstore was to see if Jeffrey Babbitt would have had a nice, quiet entry through which to haul the books from Taylor's trunk, once the man was dead. Of course, he knew about Taylor's books, since the professor had been drumming up publicity, but his mind must have been lightning quick to sense the sales opportunity before the paramedics took over. With everyone's eyes on Taylor, Jeffrey could have slipped out to the car, snatched up Taylor's books, and sneaked them in the back door of Babbitt and Brown's. With a remote, it wouldn't have taken more than a few clicks to discover which car belonged to Taylor. I grinned. What a sneaky, little opportunist.

"Nicholas!" Our Cadillac pulled up to the curb. Edward leaned across the front seat and pushed open the door. "Get in. We can retrieve your bag from the hotel and end this nonsense."

I kept walking, so he put the car in reverse and backed up, talking as he drove.

"This is ridiculous, Nicholas. I've been driving around looking for you all afternoon."

"Why?"

"Dammit! Will you force me to say it? I was wrong. I shouldn't have gone behind your back. I should have discussed it with you first. I thought I was doing what was best for you, but in doing so, I was treating you like a child." He paused, evidently for dramatic purposes. "Whenever danger lurks, I feel I have to assume the role of big brother and protect you." I stopped walking and bent over to look inside. Edward nodded several times, thinking about all the danger lurking. "Even if it's from yourself." He slipped me a glance. "Like I did at Inglenook. You would have died if it hadn't been for me, and the thought of your lifeless body, well, it would have been hard on mother."

I snorted.

"Dammit! It's hard not to think of you as my kid brother. If it makes me a fool, then so be it."

"You're a fool all right, but you're pouring it on a little thick."

He cocked his head at me. "Am I?"

"Let's leave it at you should have discussed it with me, which you should have."

"I apologize. Now, are you coming?"

I glanced behind his car. "I suppose I'll have to. If you back up another three feet, you'll hit that yellow Camry."

He grimaced into the rearview mirror and shifted the car into drive. I slid in and he took off before I had the door closed and headed toward the five freeway.

The young receptionist at the hotel either had good manners or was intimidated by the awkward situation, but she didn't question why I was checking out without having stayed the night. She had to call the manager over to decide how much to charge me. After sending up housekeeping to confirm I hadn't slept in the bed or broken into the mini-bar, he came up with a negligible figure to cover my use of the key.

On the return trip, I opened up about my visit to Babbitt and Brown's.

"He wasn't positive who brought back the trays?" Edward asked, the he being Cooter.

"No. He assumed it was Regina Robbins because she took them home to clean. All he knew was someone had returned them to the kitchen counter."

"And Morton and Charlie Grant were there, too. We should ask Mr. Grant if he saw Jeffrey."

"I can ask him tonight. He has invited me to his house to look over his photographs of the event. I doubt there will be pictures of Regina Robbins lurking in a dark corner with an oleander flower clutched to her bosom."

"I wouldn't be so certain."

I jerked my head to look at him. "Seriously?"

He turned onto Lemon Lane. "I have something to discuss with you, but dinner is waiting."

"Oh. Right." If I didn't sound enthusiastic, it was because I was embarrassed. I didn't exactly cause a scene, but my anger couldn't have escaped Mrs. Robbins' notice.

We rolled up to the curb in front of the B&B and, after Edward turned off the ignition, he said, "I told our hostess you were running an errand for me and weren't sure how long it would take. Hence, the suitcase. She replied it was always best to prepare for the worst, although she commented it must have been a distasteful errand from the look on your face. I assured her it was."

I got out and trailed behind him with my hands stuffed into my pockets and my shoulders slumped. I felt like the kid from that Christmas movie whose mother smooths things over after he gets in a fight so he won't have to bear the consequences, and I was just as grateful.

"It's just a suggestion, but if you look through Charlie's pictures tonight, you might find something that will remove any suspicion from Miss Channing."

"It will take a miracle," I said, feeling the urge to make nice with Edward since he had let me save face with Mrs. Robbins.

"Don't worry, Nicholas. We'll figure something out."

"I hope so."

He hesitated. "And you might apologize to Claudia and Zali. You frightened them."

"Don't push it, big brother. I still haven't decided not to smother you in your sleep."

After carrying my suitcase to my bedroom, I found I was whistling as I descended the stairs. It couldn't have been that I felt better having made up with Edward, so I decided I was happy because I had a plan of action for tonight. But first, I had to make it through dinner.

Edward and Claudia sat next to each other and whispered back and forth, something the big hypocrite condemned in his first book under a chapter about table manners. Regina Robbins and Joe Babbitt attempted to include me in their conversation, but with the way they were playing footsies under the table and expressing an obnoxious level of interest over mundane topics, I felt like a third wheel. In case anyone thinks I'm exaggerating, here's an example:

Joe: Cooter nicked himself with the box cutter today.

Regina: (huge gasp) Was it serious???

Joe: Nah. I found a bandage in the john cupboard and told him to be more careful.

Regina: How lucky he was you were there. You're a rock. A big, handsome rock.

Okay. She didn't say the last part, but it was implied. I

couldn't even count on Zali, who was present in body, but not in spirit. She didn't lift her eyes from the meatloaf, mashed potatoes, and gravy on her plate and methodically shoveled her food into her mouth, both her first and second helpings. When the meal ended, I was happy to make my escape.

Charlie had given me an address on Chicken Hawk Lane. I noted as I pulled up to the curb in front of his house that Chicken Hawk ran parallel to Apple Street on the south side of Lemon Lane and could also be accessed by Grove—if the professor had been turning left instead of right. Bill couldn't say if Taylor had turned right on Grove Street, which meant she couldn't say if he had been about to turn left, either. He might have been headed to a meeting with the reporter. I promised to keep that in mind if my host offered me a bottle of water.

From the lack of respect Charlie showed his appearance, I expected his house to be a shack in need of a paint job centered on a plot of weeds. Not so. On the outside, a cleverly landscaped yard complete with rose bushes and a topiary shaped like a cat invited visitors to stop and admire before climbing the three painted steps to an outside porch. A hanging swing surrounded by pots of greenery looked like a friendly hangout from which to chat with the neighbors. The bright coral door made the surrounding blue-green siding pop, and when I rang the doorbell, the first notes of Mozart's *K545 Sonata in C Major* played out. A woman in her thirties, an attractive blond with no smudges on her face or wrinkles in her clothes, invited me in with a warm smile.

The first thing I noticed as I stepped inside and glanced into the dining room to my right was the floral arrangement of tuberoses and pink lilies that sat in the center of a white, linen tablecloth. A tablecloth that was on intimate terms with an ironing board. Mrs. Grant led me into the living room on the right. The cleanliness theme continued. There wasn't a single pet hair on the black, leather couch. No coffee rings on the large, glass-and-steel coffee table. No stains on the plush, white carpet. No piles of dirty laundry stuffed into the hearth of the stone fireplace or crammed onto the shelves of the expensive entertainment system cabinet against the far wall.

I was about to ask if I had come to the right home when Charlie walked into the room. I did a double take. He wore his dark hair combed back from his forehead, his face was clean-shaven, and his red sweater and black pants were of quality material, sans wrinkles. He grinned.

"When I took the job at *The Courier*, I was just out of college and still kind of a slob. My colleagues, who had heard about the job offers I'd received before graduation, seemed to think my lack of attention to how I dressed or combed my hair showed I didn't care about anything but my career. They came to expect it from me. Naturally, I grew out of that stage, but the one time I came to work in a clean shirt, my boss asked me if I was going undercover on a story." He lifted his shoulders and let them drop. "I give them what they expect."

"Where does the kid live? This place is spotless."

Mrs. Grant gave me a superior smile. "Zachery has a play-room. It's not so neat, but he keeps his messes up there. Mostly."

Charlie gave the missus a quick kiss on the lips and invited me into his office, which was as neat as his living room, though more crowded. There was a light wood file cabinet, shelves lined with research books, and an armchair for guests to use. On his desk, an in-box snuggled up to the base of a desk lamp and held neatly stacked folders. Magazine clippings and sticky notes surrounded his laptop.

I nodded with approval. "So, this is where news stories are born."

Charlie motioned me to sit in the chair in front of the desk. The computer screen was already open to the pictures from that night.

"Help yourself. I'll leave you to it. The printer is ready to go if you want a copy, but I didn't find them interesting."

His generous attitude was unnatural for a single-minded reporter, so I took my time and scrutinized every shot. They were in sequential order and started with what I assumed were some warm-up shots. Jeffrey Babbitt grinning in front of the book table pinching cardboard Edward's flat butt. A startled Mort the banker caught as he entered the community room, probably the first council member to arrive. Grumpy Ned, alias Pretzel's Dad, glaring up from the sign-up table, with Georgie knitting away beside him. There wasn't a signee in sight, so it was probably still early in the night.

Then Charlie moved into the kitchen. The trio of volunteers looked up into the camera, surprised in the act of setting out the desserts. It looked like the desserts donated by the Sweet and Sour Book Club, not Edward's, which was confirmed three shots later by several closeups of the trays.

By the next shot, our dessert trays had arrived. The ladies got playful about Edward's instructions to keep the desserts secreted away until his exciting announcement. The Frowning Woman had peeled back the foil and was holding up a Victorian kiss with one hand and placing her fingers on her lips with the other in a shushing motion, as if she were getting away with something. In the next picture, she held the treat between her index finger and thumb and had opened her mouth wide, while the women in the background had fits of laughter.

Charlie moved on to the community room. First, there

were a few of the council members as they arrived and gathered at the front of the room, then two of Edward and me, arguing, which wasn't a surprise. These were followed by shots of Edward during his talk, and then Charlie returned to the kitchen. The ladies' postures were relaxed and their smiles natural. Even Regina Robbins' lips curved in a tolerant smile. The trays of baked goods were gone.

The reception was next. The line of people ready to buy books. Citizens milling around the dessert tables. The council congratulating Edward on his speech, with The General looking as if he were personally responsible for the night's success.

When I got to a shot that showed the pitcher on the floor, I studied the people present. I was there, with my back to the camera. Regina Robbins crouched down and picked up pieces of broken glass, while Professor Taylor looked down his nose at her. From his expression, he must have made a crack he was proud of. Did he know her well enough to make a wise comment, or was he just rude to everyone? I squinted my eyes and leaned forward, concentrating on Regina Robbins' face. She looked ticked, but that was natural. Someone had just broken her favorite pitcher. There wasn't any indication of murderous rage.

There were several closeups of the council members. Mort beamed, as if he were posing for an ad for the savings and loan. Grumpy Ned seemed ticked about having his picture taken, but there was the hint of a grin starting in the corner of his mouth. The big faker. He sat alone at the signing table. Naturally there weren't any takers.

Charlie caught Flora, Dora, and Georgie gossiping in a corner about something serious, probably tainted butter.

I paused to appreciate a picture of Hattie, though I would have preferred one of her smiling. She had one arm folded over her chest while the fingers of the other hand played with her string of pearls. I would describe her expression as concentrated and serious, and I thought I knew what was on her mind. The sight of Taylor probably brought back all her regrets, and if she were replaying memories of their relationship, I was glad to see they didn't give her any pleasure.

The pictures after the murder were interesting. I looked pretty good, in control and calm, and my suit jacket hadn't bunched up when I knelt on the floor. Edward stood in the background with his mouth hanging open and his eyes popped wide in surprise. I would have laughed aloud if it hadn't been for the dead body in the foreground.

Charlie angled in for some closeups of Jeffrey and me performing CPR. I hadn't noticed him, but he was practically leaning over my shoulder. I paused on a shot that showed Taylor's face. The back of my head was in the foreground. I thought he had been staring at nothing, but his eyes squinted as if he were trying to focus on something in particular.

I thought back. The snack table was behind me. Maybe he had figured out someone had poisoned him, and he was staring at the new pitcher of lemon-barley water as a possible source. Or maybe his eyes were focused on the killer.

The rest of the pictures were of the body, the police in action, and a faraway shot of Sykes interviewing Edward and me. When I got to the final picture, number 248, something niggled at my subconscious. I scanned through the pages, noting the number of each picture. When I got to the pictures of the council members, the count jumped from sixty-two to sixty-six, which were the first shots of the kitchen. Three pictures were missing. The next shots were of the dessert tables. Nothing seemed amiss.

Before I went to find Charlie, I lingered over a few photos of Hattie Channing. I couldn't believe the frumpy old maid looking back at me was the same beautiful woman I'd come to know. Why would any woman play down her looks like that? The more I thought about it, the more it bugged me. Was she trying to look older and more official for the council? No. She had dressed casually the day they met at her house. Of course, she didn't know the council members were the people we invited.

When the obvious answer hit me, a tingle started at the base of my neck and traveled down my spine. I hoped I was wrong.

I found Charlie in the living room drinking tea with his wife. When I asked about the missing pictures, he said the shots had been dark and hard to make out, so he'd deleted them. We engaged in some polite chit-chat, and then I checked my watch and said I had to get back.

It was eight at night. That might be too late to call on a woman with a tween, but I needed an answer now.

CHAPTER 37

I stood outside the front door of Hattie Channing's house for five minutes trying to decide if her kid was asleep. If Laurie was in bed, I should knock lightly. If she was up and doing homework or watching television, I could ring the bell. A sitcom played on the other side of the door, so someone was up, but it wasn't playing loudly. I couldn't decide.

The argument I was having with myself was just an excuse to put off talking to Hattie. I knew that, and I was just about to man up and knock when the door opened. Hattie stood there in a white t-shirt and gray sweatpants looking up at me with those golden eyes ringed in black.

"Well? Are you going to come inside, or would you rather camp out on my front porch all night?"

I had an answer to the child question as soon as I stepped inside.

"Keep your voice down. Laurie is in bed."

I gave myself a mental pat on the back for not ringing the bell.

She sat down on the couch and motioned toward the

armchair, but I took the cushion next to her and turned to look at her. This was no good. The television was the only light in the room. I wanted to see her eyes when she answered me, so I reached over her and switched on the lamp. I should have made her change places with me because the light was behind her, so her eyes were still in shadow.

"Well? What do you want now?"

That was okay. The thought of warming up with meaningless talk didn't appeal to me. I'd rehearsed what I wanted to say on the drive over and launched into my speech.

"The first time I saw you, I didn't look twice."

Her eyes widened in surprise. I held up a hand to stop any comments.

"You looked like a frump, but you intended to give that impression with your polyester suit and the frilly, old-lady ruffles around your neck."

Without my instructing it to, my finger touched the neckline of her t-shirt. "Ruffles that covered your fantastic collarbone." Since she didn't file an objection, that same finger traced her eyebrows. My voice lowered to a murmur. After all, the kid was asleep. "Horn-rimmed glasses to hide those incredible eyes." My other fingers joined the rebellion and brushed her hair behind her ear. "A severe bun to hide your chestnut locks."

While I pointed out her physical traits, she didn't say a word, but her breathing got shallow and her full lips parted. It was only natural my hand would slide to the base of her neck and pull her forward for a kiss.

Her lips were soft, and when she clutched the front of my shirt and kissed me back, I forgot why I came. By the time the fog lifted, she had wrapped her arms around my neck, and I had pulled her in tight against me. This wasn't going as planned. I gathered my willpower, broke away, and said the one thing I knew would cool us both off.

"You knew Taylor was coming to Edward's talk."

She froze.

"Was it a disguise? You're older now. In that getup, you might not remind him of a past romance."

She moved to get up, but I took her hand.

"I'm not your enemy."

Her glare softened, and then her face crumpled. I pulled her against my chest, wrapped my arms around her, and stroked her hair, making shushing noises. She got it out of her system, and when her crying had slowed down to sniffles and hiccups, she snuggled against me.

"It was awful," she whispered. "On the day of the event, a friend let me know he was planning to come."

"Who?"

"Just a friend looking out for me. I was supposed to introduce your brother. It was too late to back out, and I panicked. I didn't want Jonathan to recognize me. I—I was terrified someone would bring up Laurie and he would make the connection. That's all there is to it. I swear."

"Who was the friend?" I repeated.

"Just a friend." She looked up at me, her eyes filled with tears. "Do you believe me?"

A beautiful woman and an uncomfortable lie. I'd been here before, and it hadn't ended well. Maggie at Inglenook, swearing to me she hadn't seen anything the morning of the first murder. I hadn't trusted my instincts, and within twenty-four hours, she was dead, murdered by the killer she thought she could blackmail. She wasn't a bad person. She just sensed an opportunity to make her dream of owning a bed-and-breakfast a reality a few years early. A child provided a much better excuse than a bed-and-breakfast.

I lifted Hattie's chin and stared down at her. "Do you have any idea who killed Taylor and Jeffrey Babbitt?"

"No."

"You saw nothing that might give you a clue? Let me be blunt. You're not blackmailing anyone over this murder, are you?"

"Blackmail? Blackmail!" She giggled. "I was afraid you thought I had murdered them both. It never occurred to me to blackmail anyone, especially the killer. That doesn't sound like a bright thing to do, and I have Laurie to think about."

I held her gaze for another ten seconds, searching for signs of deceit. When I didn't find any, I sighed with relief. "I believe you." I pulled her in for another hug and kissed the top of her head.

"Nicholas?" Her voice was muffled since her face was buried in my shirt.

"Hmmm."

"Turn off the light."

CHAPTER 38

I probably should have driven around the block a few times before I returned to the B&B. Necking with a woman for an extended period was bound to have some effect on my appearance. The downstairs was empty when I got there. I'd just hit the top step without running into anyone when Edward stepped out of his room. He must have been waiting for me.

"Nicholas, we—" He broke off. "You're flushed. What's wrong?" He reached out with the back of his hand. "Do you have a temperature?"

I jerked my head to the side. "It's cold outside."

His eyes narrowed. "Where have you been?"

"I went to Charlie Grant's house."

"After that. It's ten-thirty."

"Taking a walk," I lied.

"In the car?" He ran his gaze over me. I stiffened my spine to keep from fidgeting. "Good gad. You've been with Hattie Channing. I know you believe her to be innocent, and I told you we would think of something to prove it, but it won't help our case if you're playing with the suspects."

"I'm not playing."

He gave me such a look of pity that I turned away to unlock my door.

"Nicholas, Nicholas, Nicholas."

When he clapped a big paw on my shoulder, I jerked away. "I will not listen to any talk about Hattie."

"That's fine. She isn't the topic I wanted to discuss."

"It isn't?" I held open my door. "Then come inside."

After I sat on the bed, Edward paced the room, his hands in his trouser pockets.

"I fear we have a dilemma; one we must handle with the utmost care."

I held up a hand. "You're worried about nothing. Charlie Grant seemed to go for the idea of keeping you in the sleuth role. He was friendly enough tonight, and I think I would have picked up on it if his attitude toward you had changed."

He went to the window and looked out. "I'm not talking about me. I'm talking about the killer."

I swiveled my head. "You say that as if you know who it is."

"I do. Or I think I do." He turned to me. "The first night we were here, we weren't the only guests."

I thought about it. "While I admit I didn't open all the doors for a look, if someone else had been here, wouldn't we have seen them in the hallway or at breakfast? Unless they were invisible. What makes you say so?"

"It's so obvious. Mrs. Robbins doesn't subscribe to the newspaper."

"Shame on her."

"Yet there was a paper here on the day we arrived. I read it after dinner. We didn't make reservations, so she didn't know we were coming."

"I follow. Mrs. Robbins only orders the paper when she

has guests. So, there were other guests. Maybe they checked out that day. Big deal."

"Only one guest."

"What does that have to do with the killer? If I planned to kill Professor Taylor, I would want as few people as possible to know I was in town, and I wouldn't stick around afterward. We didn't arrive here until over a week had passed." I cocked my head. "Or are you saying the killer stuck around specifically to avoid giving that impression? Also, it would be convenient to stay in town if he had plans to kill Jeffrey Babbitt."

"I'm saying the killer stuck around because he didn't have plans to leave Citrus Grove, in particular, Robbins' Bed and Breakfast."

I shook my head. "You're confusing me. The only person with no plans to leave the B&B is Mrs. Robbins, and she wouldn't be hanging around in one of the guest rooms." And then I got it. "Unless she was hanging out with a particular guest, like Joe Babbitt. Huh. You think he doth protest too much about the bookstore? He could have wanted his brother dead so he could have a steady income to make him more attractive to Mrs. Robbins. Even at her age women probably look for stability. The same thing might apply to men. Like Joe Babbitt. But what does that have to do with Taylor?"

"Let me spell it out. In his biography, Professor Jonathan Taylor married. Married a woman named Gina Hendricks."

"Regina," I mumbled.

"Exactly. Through gossip, we learned his wife had left him because of his affair with Hattie Channing."

"Correction. We assume it was Hattie Channing, but the professor had a bad reputation over his female students. It could have been somebody else."

"Fine. Let it be someone else. It doesn't matter who it was, just that his wife left him."

I appreciated his backing off Hattie, so I gave him my full attention and asked him to continue.

"This part is conjecture, but you mentioned Mrs. Robbins' late husband left her well off. That might make marriage more attractive to an itinerant like Joe Babbitt."

"The little mercenary," I muttered. "You think he's making up to Mrs. Robbins for her money?"

"No, no. I think he really cares for her."

"Wait a minute. Why would she care what Taylor thought about her love life? It's not as if she would need Taylor's approval to date, or even to remarry. They're divorced."

My brother smirked. "And where exactly did you read they had divorced? She left him, yes, but I've not found any record of a divorce."

I blew out a breath. "Bigamy." As far as I knew, bigamy was still illegal. For now.

Edward jabbed a finger in the air. "That was the secret Taylor meant to reveal. That Mrs. Robbins was still his wife. She stood to lose everything."

"You lost me. Now she's the killer? And what would she lose? These days, people are perfectly willing to shack up. She and Joe could have come to an arrangement. She'd still have her inheritance. True, he wouldn't inherit automatically should something happen to Mrs. Robbins, but she could make a will and leave everything to him. I don't see a problem."

"It's not Regina Robbins' will that's the problem. Depending on the terms of her late husband's will, the exact wording, she might not have a claim on his money, since she wasn't legally his wife. And if he didn't have a will at all, it becomes even more problematic for her. The State would give the surviving spouse the entire estate."

"And if she wasn't legally his spouse, she wouldn't be entitled to his estate." I scratched my cheek. "She said she ran the B&B because she was lonely. Maybe she found a permanent solution in Joe Babbitt, but she didn't want to choose between love and money. That would be worth killing for, for either Regina Robbins or Joe Babbitt." I shook my head. "You've based your entire premise on the assumption Mrs. Robbins is still Mrs. Taylor. Where did you look for proof of their marriage? They got married in San Diego."

"On the Internet."

"On your phone?" I slapped my hand down, which wasn't very impressive since it landed on the coverlet. "I told you you were the one using up the data."

"We were already over our allotment because of you." He held up a hand. "We're getting away from the point. I couldn't find a record of divorce."

"Maybe you mistyped her name in the search or the divorce records are sealed."

He shook his head. "Even if a divorce is sealed, I should still be able to determine there was a divorce."

Edward liked his theory and wasn't letting go.

"Then why kill Jeffrey Babbitt?"

"Maybe he overheard what his brother was planning, or what Regina Robbins was planning, and had to go. Or maybe he knew the Taylors had never divorced."

Sometimes the facts I gather in my brain need to percolate before something important jumps out at me, like it did now. "When I was going over the statements Charlie collected from witnesses, there were a few theorists with laughable ideas. That's why I missed it when Regina Robbins said something odd. She dared anyone to criticize the food handled by the volunteers, and then she said she couldn't vouch for any food brought by outside sources, meaning you. Everyone I've talked to thought Taylor had had a heart attack or something. Why did she assume it was something he ate?"

"Or drank," Edward growled. "And then she tried to lay the blame at my feet."

"Which, if she suggested you come in order to lure the professor down here, makes sense. She had you set to take the fall for his murder." We looked at each other. "So, that means—"

"Our hostess may be a murderer. Or dating one. It means anyone who knows about Regina Robbins' legal marriage may be in danger. Does Miss Channing know who Regina Robbins is?"

I cleared my throat because my neck muscles were tight. "She said she had never met Taylor's wife. But wouldn't she know if her neighbor had married him? This isn't Chicago. I doubt anything goes on in Citrus Grove without the neighbors knowing. It would have come up in conversation. Did you ever hear what that rat Taylor did to poor Regina?"

Edward stroked his beard. "Taylor married when he was in his twenties. He was in his sixties when he died, so let's say he married thirty-five years ago. That was before Hattie Channing was born. And the couple didn't live in Citrus Grove. He worked in San Diego. She may have moved here with her second husband and no one in Citrus Grove knows of the first marriage except for a few, long-term residents. What reason would she have to talk about him?" He frowned. "How old is the child?"

"Laurie. Her name is Laurie. She's about twelve."

Edward narrowed his eyes. "Then we can assume the separation occurred nearly thirteen years ago."

"But Regina seems to be friends with Hattie. Why would she want to hang around with her husband's girlfriend and child?"

He didn't answer me, which was just as well. I could see

for myself there were several reasons, none of them good. Maybe Regina Robbins felt a sick satisfaction in letting Hattie cry on her shoulder, hating her all the time. Maybe she missed her jerk-of-a-husband and wanted to be close to him vicariously through his child. Maybe she had been all right with the situation until she caught sight of her husband. Then she lost it. But the oleander pointed toward a premeditated murder.

"Miss Channing might be in a state of ignorance. You should warn her to be on her guard."

After he said goodnight and moved to leave, I called out. "I need to apologize.

"For what?"

"That first night after Claudia and Zali arrived, I heard noises. Giggling. I thought—"

"That I was taking advantage of Claudia. You should know me better than that, but since you thought we were the only guests staying here, I can see how you got the idea. Apology accepted."

"You see what that means."

Edward nodded. "That Joe Babbitt was in town before his brother's murder."

"And Regina Robbins tried to hide him."

My brother's eyes narrowed. "The mysterious male guest she didn't want us to meet."

"So, it looks as if they were in on it together."

As soon as Edward closed the door, I tried Hattie Channing's number. The voice mail picked up, so I left a message asking her to call me as soon as possible and stressing the importance. By midnight, I gave up. I had seen Mrs. Robbins retire to her bedroom, so Hattie would be safe in her ignorance for one night. Yes, Mrs. Robbins and Joe Babbitt were both in the house.

I had trouble falling asleep that night, even with my door locked.

CHAPTER 39

Breakfast the next morning was a tricky affair. With Mrs. Robbins high on the suspect list, I wasn't about to eat anything prepared by her. Neither was Edward. We had no proof Regina Robbins had killed her husband or approved of his murder, but Edward had laid out a pretty convincing argument last night.

He tried to talk Claudia into leaving again, but that went over… it didn't. She thought he was out of his mind and ate her full breakfast in front of him, while Edward tried not to gasp every time she lifted her fork to her mouth.

After ten minutes of smelling sausage, eggs, and biscuits with gravy, I decided to use Zali as my gage. She had been shoveling food down her gullet for long enough that even a slow-acting poison would have affected her if it were present. She looked healthy to me, so I requested my own plate and dug in. Edward followed suit, although he sniffed each bite before he sunk his teeth into it.

We helped Mrs. Robbins clean up with a little small talk, and once we washed and put away the dishes, she informed us she had to go out on a social call. As soon as the front door closed behind her, we breathed a sigh of relief and gathered in the den. Since Edward had shared our theory with Claudia, I didn't mince words.

"Well, we all made it through breakfast alive."

"By God's good grace." Edward pressed his lips together and narrowed his eyes, giving Claudia his full disapproval. She ignored him.

"Are you saying Mrs. Robbins is trying to poison us?" Zali picked at her teeth with a toothpick. "She's not as good a cook as old Beckwith, but isn't that a little harsh, Eddie?"

Edward was never sure how much Zali comprehended and, in deference to Claudia's protective stance toward her aunt, he merely said, "You're right. I apologize."

"How are we supposed to get proof either of—" I glanced at Zali, who was still working on her teeth. "That you-know-who killed Taylor?"

"We must set a trap."

"A trap?" Claudia arched her brows. "I don't like that. It doesn't sound fair."

I gaped. "Fair? We're talking about two people who have committed murder."

Edward held up a hand. "She has a point."

"She does?"

He sat on the couch, crossed his legs, and clasped his hands on his knee. "We want to give the killer a sporting chance. There may be future victims who get in the way, but fair is fair."

Claudia flushed and glared, but he wasn't through.

"We need the light touch. Perhaps we should just ask? I'm sure they'd give us an honest answer." Edward's voice carried that special condescending quality he always reserved for me. I grinned. There might be advantages to having his lady love around after all.

When the doorbell rang, he stopped talking. It rang again, but nobody moved.

"Well?" I demanded. "You're the manners expert. Should we answer? It's not our house."

"I'm—it hasn't come up." He stood. "For Heaven's sake, it's just a doorbell."

I followed close behind. I was keyed up and felt the need to move. I wish I'd stayed put because the man on the stoop was Detective Jonah Sykes.

"Mrs. Robbins is not at home right now." Edward said it in a formal manner that would have been the envy of any butler.

Sykes stepped inside. "That's all right. I wanted to talk to you." He glanced at me. "And you." He gestured toward the chairs in the foyer. "This will do."

Once we sat down, Sykes jumped right in. "The oleander was in the water bottle."

After a pause to soak it in, Edward stated the obvious. "Which means you don't know when it was put there, or by whom."

Sykes scratched behind his ear. "We have some ideas."

"You've come to arrest Mrs. Robbins?" It came out before I could think.

He smiled. "Why would I do that?"

"Because my brother—"

"Nicholas."

If my brother had shouted at me, I would have ignored it, but he kept his voice low and controlled.

"Let's hear what Detective Sykes has to say."

"I don't want to." I jumped to my feet and faced the detective. "I know you talked to Hattie Channing about her affair with Jonathan Taylor. It was a long time ago. She's over it."

"That's probably true." Sykes looked like he was trying to be impartial, which made me more nervous. "Did I mention we found out where Professor Taylor's car had been between the time he left Marston College and the time he entered the bookstore? It was parked on Apple Street a few houses down from Miss Channing's house."

"But not in front of it," I pointed out. "Taylor was a dirty old man. He might have been stalking her."

"It's possible," Sykes conceded. "Or maybe he was verifying the existence of his child before he exposed Miss Channing's secret in front of the crowds at the bookstore."

Edward shook his head. "To what purpose?" I shot him a grateful glance. "So, he reveals he has a child with Miss Channing. Everyone knows about Laurie. She's not a secret. What does it matter if Jonathan Taylor was the father? Miss Channing's not a nun. She won't be out of a job. If he wanted to fight for custody—" He turned his hand palm-side up. "I can't imagine a court would order an absentee father joint custody after twelve years."

"It might make a difference if he just found out he had a child."

"Possibly, but hardly a reason to kill the man."

When Sykes smiled, he looked tired. "That's really all I came to tell you. That the poison wasn't in your lemon-barley water. I thought it might relieve your mind."

"Do you know where the oleander came from?" Edward asked the question. I didn't want to know.

"Oleander seems to be a popular shrub in Citrus Grove. It's all over the place." He glanced at me. "Including the house two doors down from Miss Channing's residence."

"And is that bush behind a gate? Or a fence? Or guarded by large dogs with fangs? Or are you just assuming Hattie Channing is the only person in Citrus Grove with garden clippers?"

Sykes stood and angled an unfriendly glare down at me. His jaw pulsed. "It hasn't escaped me that many people have access to these plants. I'm building a case that will lead me to the murderer, Mr. Harlow, not picking someone at random and trying to frame them."

Edward closed the door behind the detective and stood in front of me. "Nicholas, I know it looks bad for Miss Channing, but Detective Sykes is not a fool. Of course, you might have to consider the possibility."

I paced the room. "No. I don't believe it. You said yourself Regina Robbins and Joe Babbitt have just as good a motive. Why isn't Sykes questioning them?"

"Maybe he has. The detective may have shared a piece of information with us, which was kind of him, but he's not going to tell us his plans. And my idea may not be the correct solution. It's just a theory."

"Don't back off now. Your theory is right. It makes sense. The oldest motive in the book. Greed."

"I think that would be jealousy. Cain was jealous of Abel's relationship with God, and so he slew him."

We were saved from a theology argument by a shout of "Yoo-hoo" from the back door. Claudia and Zali joined us as we went to the kitchen to greet the latest invader. In place of her knitting bag, Georgie carried a basket of books, which she deposited on the kitchen table.

"Here is the latest selection of cookbooks for Regina to review."

I raised my hand. "I thought Mrs. Robbins wasn't a member of the council."

"Regina used to belong, but she quit. She's a fair enough cook, and she's got the time to go through them and give us recommendations."

"Is that how you usually choose the authors you invite?" Edward asked. "By her recommendation?"

"We decide. She just slogs through them to help us eliminate the bores. Goodness knows I don't have the time."

"The Aunt Civility books have a few recipes in them, but they're not cookbooks. Edward's not a chef. Why did he get an invite?"

I thought it was a good question, but Georgie gave me a cold stare. "It's a culinary arts council, Mr. Harlow, not a cookbook club. The culinary arts include more than actual cooking. I'll have you know we once had a representative of a cutlery company talk to us about how to choose the best kitchen knives."

Georgie must have been one of the women who voted for the council's fancy name.

"Did you read Edward's book before you invited him?"

"We already explained that." She glanced at Edward. "His name came from the suggestion box."

"And you just trusted some anonymous person? What if the suggestion had been a joke?"

"Someone on the council had read them, or at least looked them over. Does it matter?"

Edward, bored by the conversation, picked up the top book—a spiral-bound Methodist church cookbook—and flipped through the pages. "Mrs. Robbins has a social engagement. I'll make sure she gets these."

"Is it Wednesday already?" Georgie nodded. "She'll be at Hattie's, messing around with the shrubbery. Regina thinks she has a green thumb."

People kept talking, but their voices were muffled. My chest had gone tight, and the blood rushed to my head. To keep from judging me for what I did next, understand my state of mind that morning. Edward had convinced me either Regina Robbins or Joe Babbitt was the person we were looking for, the person who had killed two people so far and gotten away with it.

If Regina Robbins were the Widow Taylor, she would have a low opinion of the object of her husband's fling and the child produced by that union. And if she was the killer and wanted to tie up any loose ends regarding her first marriage, she might suspect the woman who had broken it up of knowing her identity. Killers tend to get paranoid. And she liked plants, so she probably knew an oleander from a rose bush.

My brother called after me as I exited the front door. With the gas pedal to the floor, the drive to Apple Street took less than five minutes. I threw the car in park, jumped out, and ran up the porch steps.

This time I didn't mess around with knocking or ringing. I pounded on the door with my fist and shouted Hattie's name. It didn't bring results, so I vaulted the railing and pushed through the bushes to see inside, past the sheers that covered each front window. Nothing. No signs of movement. I stopped breathing when I thought I saw someone lying prone on the floor behind the coffee table, but after squinting, I realized one of the decorative pillows had fallen off the couch. An accident? Or could it have happened during a struggle?

I went back to Plan A, pounding on the door and shouting, with a vague notion my shout sounded a lot like Edward's bellow. That made me pause and think. Maybe Hattie was at work. If that were the case, she wouldn't answer her door, and that meant I was making a fool of myself. The argument against that possibility was the way Georgie had said "It's Wednesday. She'll be at Hattie's." That suggested a standing appointment, so Hattie should be at home. I pounded again.

Taylor had been poisoned with water. Jeffrey Babbitt had been stabbed through the neck. Regina Robbins had proved to be a resourceful killer. Hattie was strong, but if Mrs. Robbins caught her off guard, she could knock her over the head. Then she'd have time to consider her method. Was Hattie unconscious? Was that why she wasn't answering?

Finally, I stepped back and sized up the door. It took two rushes leading with my shoulder before the frame splintered and the door burst open. My momentum sent me stumbling into the room. I would have landed on my face had Hattie Channing not been there to break my fall. We both went down, and I twisted as we fell to absorb some of the shock. Or, at least keep the brunt of my weight off her.

Our faces were inches apart. She stared up at me, sputtering to get back the wind I had knocked out of her. I was up first, and I helped her to her feet.

"Where is Laurie?" I demanded.

She coughed. "At school, where she belongs in the middle of the day."

It was then I noticed Regina Robbins staring at me with her mouth hanging open.

"I think you should leave," I said. It was rude, but to the point.

Hattie had her wind back, as evidenced by her volume. "You can't come in here and—my door!"

It was still attached to the frame by one hinge, but it had a large crack down the middle.

"What have you done?"

"It stuck when I tried to open it," I snapped.

"Why didn't you just come around to the backyard like a normal person?"

"Backyard?" It's possible she wouldn't have heard me knock from back there.

"Regina was helping me garden. *In the backyard.*"

I took another look at our hostess. She clutched a small bag to her chest, and her shoulders were up around her ears, as if she were stressed. Maybe she was afraid of getting caught in the act. I snatched the bag away from her and dug through it. Gardening gloves. A few packets of seeds. A landscaping magazine. No poison. No gun. Not even a trowel. I handed it back, feeling less certain than I had five minutes ago that Regina Robbins was a menace.

"Maybe I should leave," Mrs. Robbins said. "If you think you'll be all right."

The rest of the sentence—alone with a maniac—was implied.

Hattie passed her hand over her eyes. "Yes. Thank you, Regina. We'll talk later."

The owner of the B&B tiptoed past the hanging door, I felt the need to part on better terms, just in case Edward was wrong about her. "Georgie dropped by with some cookbooks for you."

She looked back and her eyelashes fluttered. "Oh. Thank you."

When it was just the two of us, I took Hattie's face in my hands and kissed her, hard. Then I ran my hands down her arms. "You're sure you're okay? She didn't try to hurt you?"

A new emotion reflected in Hattie's eyes. Fear. "Nicholas, you're shaking. What's going on?"

I took a deep breath to get the adrenaline back where it belonged and squeezed her hand. "I made an assumption. I was wrong. I'm glad I was wrong."

Her gaze roamed over the damage I'd caused. "Would you like to explain?"

I sucked in air between my teeth. "No. But I suppose I'll have to." Putting the words together in my head before I spoke didn't make them sound any better coming out. "I thought you and Laurie were in danger."

"Danger. From Regina?"

"It's Edward's fault. He said—never mind what he said. I might have panicked."

Her gaze wandered over the gaping hole that used to be her front door. "Might have."

"And when you didn't answer the damn door, I kind of lost my head."

"Kind of."

"Look, Hattie, how well do you know Regina Robbins?"

She pressed her lips together. Somehow, I'd made her angry. "Well enough to know I have nothing to fear from her." She poked at my chest. "I can't believe you barged in here. And you insulted my guest."

Hattie apparently didn't take kindly to my coming to her rescue. Never mind that there wasn't anything to rescue her from. I didn't know that. It was the thought that counted.

"I'm calling someone to repair the damage, and you're paying for it."

"Naturally."

She rubbed her forehead. "I don't know how I will explain this to Laurie." She balled up her hands into fists. "First, you set fire to my clothesline. Then you break in my door. You send the police to my house."

"I did not."

"What do you have planned next? A raid?"

I tried to keep my tone reasonable. "Once again, I didn't set fire to your clothesline. I put it out. And the only reason I broke your door is because I thought you were in danger. Some women might thank me for my concern."

"Thank you? You want me to thank you for breaking my door? Get out."

"Shouldn't I stick around until the carpenter gets here?"

"I'll have him call you for your credit card number."

If I wasn't welcome at Hattie Channing's house, I was even less welcome at the B&B. Claudia had to persuade Mrs. Robbins to allow me to cross the threshold, but it was my brother who convinced her to let me stay.

"The man's crazy." Mrs. Robbins trembled with rage. "Certifiable. He's dangerous."

"Insanity is not the problem," Edward said, grim.

"You mean he does this kind of thing regularly for the fun of it?"

"I'm sure if Nicky broke down a door, he had a good reason," my pal Zali put in.

"What possible reason?" Mrs. Robbins objected.

"He thinks he's in love."

Edward said it quietly. Simply. Our hostess's frown faltered. "In love? With Hattie?" She wiped her hands on her apron and let out a sigh. "Oh. Well. Courting used to be more subtle in my time. I suppose things have changed." Then she met my eyes. "If you stay in this house, you will need to control yourself, young man."

"Yes, ma'am." I made sure I looked properly abashed when I answered her.

She harrumphed. "It would have been better if I had invited Hattie over for a simple lunch, like I suggested."

"Yes, ma'am."

"Good thing your brother came along to Citrus Grove to keep an eye on you."

If I looked surprised, it was because it took a minute to remember the story we sold Mrs. Robbins the first day we arrived.

"Go to your room and cool down."

"Yes, ma'am."

Edward followed me up the stairs and into my room. I flung myself on the bed and put my hands behind my head. "I'm not sure I'm allowed to have friends over while I'm grounded."

He shoved his hands in his pockets and poked at the throw rug with the toe of his shoe. "It's my fault. I'm sorry."

I sat up. "You're apologizing? To me? I'm not sure what you're talking about, but I'll take it."

"I didn't realize how serious your feelings were for Miss Channing."

"Neither did I." My voice held a note of wonder.

"I would have done the same thing in your position, if it had been Claudia in danger instead of Miss Channing. Did you—er—hurt yourself? Mrs. Robbins's description of the damage made it sound bad."

"She exaggerated. And I'm fine." I covered my eyes with my hands. "What's happening to me? I'm the reasonable one. You pay me to stop you from doing the kind of stupid thing I just did." I lowered my hands. "Can I have an advance on my salary? I need to pay for a door."

"Use my credit card. We'll discuss it later."

An alien had replaced Edward. That was as good an explanation as any. "Why are you being so nice to me? Not that I don't appreciate it, but I'd like to know the cost up front."

He smiled. "Your behavior has given me the perfect lead-in to a conversation I would like to have at dinner tonight."

He cuffed me on the shoulder—the one I'd used to break down the door—so I didn't ask him to explain. I was too busy gritting my teeth until he left the room. Even then, I covered my face with a pillow before I let out a yell. A man has his pride.

CHAPTER 40

We were all present and accounted for when Mrs. Robbins dished out her chicken pot pie that evening: Joe at the head of the table, Edward across from him, Zali and Claudia in the chairs on one side, and me and an empty chair for Mrs. Robbins on my side.

Edward had already launched into a description of my escapades, something he told me beforehand he needed to do to carry out his plan. He could have skipped the humor, exaggerating my state of mind and Hattie's reaction. If his point was to entertain Joe Babbitt, my brother was doing fine.

"You broke the door off its hinges?" Joe's grin held respect, so I shrugged it off as if it were no big deal.

"It was still attached by one hinge."

He shook his head. "Young love."

Edward thanked Mrs. Robbins for serving him and then said, "I don't know about that. I don't think the emotions are any less powerful later in life, do you?"

Joe's gaze flickered toward the kitchen sink where Mrs.

Robbins was depositing the empty serving plate. "The emotions still feel the same. A little mellower, maybe, and I would hope I'd have more self-control by now." He grinned. "And I don't have the same energy level I used to have. Not so sure I could take on a locked door."

"I'm glad you all think it's funny," Mrs. Robbins said, taking her seat between me and Joe and spreading her napkin across her lap. "This young man scared me out of my wits."

"Well, that's not so nice," Joe agreed.

"What about you, Mrs. Robbins? I believe you mentioned to Nicholas that Mr. Robbins was your second husband. Did you find your emotions had diminished the second time around? I assume the first time you married you were passionately in love."

Claudia looked at Edward in surprise.

"Let's say I was smarter the second time around."

While Claudia had her eyes on my brother, Joe kept a watchful gaze on Mrs. Robbins.

"Ah." Edward made this noise with great significance. "I assumed you had been widowed both times." He sighed. "Divorce can be such an ugly business. Still, you had luck with your second marriage."

"Harold was a good man."

Though Edward seemed ordinary on the outside—confident to the point of arrogance—I knew his insides were suffering. Asking intimate questions about personal relationships that were none of his business...well. My brother would rather have Charlie plaster the front page of *The Courier* with a picture of him in a bathing suit than have any record of this conversation leak out to his fans. It was the height of rudeness. Still, he persisted.

"How many years did you have with him?"

"Nine wonderful years. He's been gone for three."

"Regina." Edward cut his piece of pot pie with a fork. "A nice name. Does anyone ever call you Gina?"

I stopped chewing.

Our hostess laughed with relief at the apparent change of subject. "No, thank goodness. I lucked out by the time my parents got to me. Regina is a good, solid name. No need to hack it to pieces."

Joe bowed his head. "And pretty, too."

She covered her blush by turning her head and dabbing her mouth with her napkin.

"Regina Robbins." Edward nodded. "A bit of alliteration. Was your name before you married Mr. Robbins as lyrical?"

"Definitely not." As she dabbed at her mouth again with the napkin, I noticed the tremor in her hand. "Smith." She let her hand drop. "Not very original, is it?"

Joe took her hand, squeezed it, and held on.

"I apologize. I've distressed you."

She held up her other hand to wave off his apology, but her jaw muscles took a minute to cooperate before she answered him. "It's old news. Water under the bridge."

To change the subject and the mood, Joe grinned at Zali, to his right. "You've got an unusual name. Is Zali short for something?"

Zali talked as she chewed. "Zalinka. Means wondrously beautiful. Arabic, you know. Great-Granddad spent time in Egypt when he served in the British army. That's before he moved to the States and built Inglenook Mansion."

I stared at Edward until he met my gaze. He shook his head slightly and then looked down at his plate and poked at his dinner. He planned to drop the subject just because he made the suspect nervous. A killer would go free because it wouldn't be polite to ask her a direct question. My throat muscles had tightened up along with every other muscle in my body. I set my fork on my plate, rested my elbows on the table, and clasped my hands.

"He's not under the bridge. He's underground."

My brother looked up at me and shook his head again, more definite this time.

"Who's not under the bridge?" Joe asked.

I leaned back in my chair. "Mrs. Robbins told us her first husband was water under the bridge, but Jonathan Taylor is underground, or soon will be."

She froze, her fork halfway to her mouth. "Excuse me?"

The humor left Joe's eyes, and his smile turned mean. I pulled my feet back under my chair and leaned forward in case I had to make a fast move.

"Why don't you just say what you mean?" he said.

"I thought I did. Did you want me to repeat it? Regina Gina Hendricks was Jonathan Taylor's wife."

"Oh, dear." Mrs. Robbins said it softly, more to herself, but I heard it.

Joe set down his fork and, I was glad to see, his knife. "That thing I said about controlling myself. I might not if you continue to harass this lady."

"You mean this wealthy lady."

Regina squeaked. Joe stood. I got to my feet. Zali rested her chin on the back of one hand and continued to eat. I couldn't see Edward's reaction, since he was behind me.

Joe stepped forward. "That's enough out of you."

"Hit him, Nicky!" That came from Zali.

"Nicholas." Edward said it quietly.

"Just a minute. I'm busy explaining to Joe how it would make marriage to his longtime crush more attractive if she could hang on to her inheritance. An inheritance she's not entitled to because she never divorced her first husband."

Regina got up and joined Joe, but she stood between him and me as a buffer. "Calm down, Joe. I'm sure there's a good explanation if we just talk about it like reasonable adults."

But Joe wasn't ready to make peace. He jabbed a finger at me. "I want you and your brother out of here now."

Regina squawked. "You can't order guests out of my place."

"Nicholas," Edward repeated, louder.

Joe looked at Regina like a puppy that had been smacked for returning the ball. "He just accused you of murder. I was standing up for you."

"No. No, he didn't. He accused me of never divorcing a man I never married in the first place." She threw up her hands. "It's too silly to get upset over."

"Nicholas!" Edward set his napkin down and stood. "In the den, now." He nodded to Regina. "Will you please excuse us?"

Since Edward took me by the elbow to usher me out, I didn't have a choice but to accompany him unless I wanted to start a brawl. As the kitchen door swung shut behind us, Zali said, "Is it over? Because that was a dud ending."

Edward didn't let go until we were in the den, and he only removed his hand so he could run all ten fingers through his hair.

"What's the matter with you?" he hissed.

I followed suit and kept my voice to a harsh whisper. "Me? I'm fine. Did you forget our conversation last night? When you told me who the murderer was? At least you narrowed it down to two people, who are both in the kitchen right now."

He slapped the backside of one hand on the palm of the other. "Suspected is not the same as having proof."

"It's good enough for me. I will not stand around while they get rid of Hattie and Laurie. Let Sykes find the proof."

My brother set his big paws on my shoulders and put his

333

big face in front of mine, forcing me to look him in the eye. "Did you even listen to what Mrs. Robbins said in there?"

I strained my memory, trying not to show it, but all that came back was a blank screen.

"We were talking about her name, and she said she was lucky when her parents got to her. That means she has siblings, most likely sisters, since her parents would not be likely to name a son Gina."

"But she didn't deny her last name had been Hendricks. Let's say Gina Hendricks is her sister. She still has a motive. Lots of people have difficulties with the in-laws. Taylor, her brother-in-law, was a jerk to her sister, so she killed him."

Edward closed his eyes, as if he were in pain, then shook his head to get rid of the annoyance. "Will you at least agree the situation needs further investigation?"

"Of course."

He dropped his hands. "It will be more difficult now that you've exposed our position. Mrs. Robbins will most likely alert her sister, if she exists. Now, get back in there and make amends. I don't want to have to move my things to a hotel."

I followed him back into the kitchen, stopped, and squared my shoulders.

"I owe you an apology." I glanced at them with appropriate humility. "Both of you."

Joe stepped forward. "Damn straight you do."

"In my enthusiasm for finding the murderer of Professor Taylor and your brother, I made an assumption." I glanced at Edward, and he gave me a slight nod. I cleared my throat. "My behavior was unforgivable, but I ask you to give me a pass."

Joe's shoulders jerked, as if he was having a hard time controlling an urge to get violent. "You just about accused me of murdering Jeffrey."

"The investigation has been a strain. That's my only

excuse. You know," I added, now that the game plan had changed and we were trying to smooth the way toward harmony, "Edward was taken to the station for questioning. It was a shock to my system."

"He hasn't been the same since," Edward put in. "Sibling relationships are complex, as you would know, Mrs. Robbins."

"They certainly are. I admire your brother's loyalty. My sisters and I were never close. I'm the youngest by a few years. Maybe that makes a difference."

"Well, I suppose seeing my brother taken away by the police might put my nerves on edge, too," Joe admitted. Regina nudged him. He held out his hand and we shook.

Fortunately, the phone rang before it could get too sloppy. Mrs. Robbins answered and passed it on to me. As soon as I had the receiver up to my ear, a snippy female voice said, "Two thousand eight hundred dollars."

"Beg pardon?"

"I went with the fiberglass, since that's supposed to be sturdier. I'm sure you'll agree my decision was wise, and it was on sale. The man is still here. He's waiting for your credit card number. Shall I put him on?"

"For close to three grand, I want to see the work before I pay for it." Before she could protest, I said, 'I'll be right there," and hung up the phone.

CHAPTER 41

I t was a nice door, with the appearance of white, painted wood. I walked up the front steps. Laurie, who was standing in the entrance, closed the door in my face. Before my feelings could get hurt, she opened it wearing a grin.

"I'm testing it."

I nodded. "A good move."

Hattie was in the kitchen with a good-looking, sandy-haired guy in a brown uniform. They sat at the table with cups of coffee in front of them and sharing a laugh.

Hattie ran a quick gaze over me, her lips still curved in an amused smile. "Have you checked out Mike's work? He did a wonderful job, and quick, too. I'll feel safe sleeping here tonight knowing the door is back in place."

They were on a first-name basis.

I nodded. "Laurie has given it her approval."

Mike grinned, showing dimples. "Nice kid. I've got one of my own at home around the same age."

I handed over Edward's credit card. As I waited for my receipt, I wondered if Hattie were pushing my buttons or if she liked this good-looking, hard-working schmuck. He used one of those handheld gizmos to process the payment, so I entered our email address and he forwarded me the receipt.

"I guess I should get going." He got up.

When they shook hands by the front door, he held on longer than necessary. "This has been one of my nicer calls."

After he left, she continued to hold the door open, suggesting I could leave, too. I pushed it closed, gently but firmly.

"Can we talk?"

Laurie was on the couch, mesmerized by the latest offerings of prime-time television.

"You can have five minutes."

Hattie led me back to the kitchen. The chair was still warm from Mike's rump, but at least she pulled down a fresh cup for my coffee.

"Things have worked out okay," I said, casual. "You got a new door."

"Something I've been longing for."

Sarcasm. I could deal with sarcasm.

"I tried to save your life because I thought it needed saving. I admit I was too enthusiastic, and I have apologized. Tell me what more you want from me."

"I think it's sweet you wanted to come to my rescue—"

Sweet. Not good.

"But you should have talked to me about it first instead of charging in here."

"That makes zero sense. How was I supposed to talk to you when you weren't answering?"

"I didn't hear you knock, but I might have heard the telephone."

"Huh. Just so I'm clear, if I think you're in danger, I should take the time to phone first. And if you don't answer because someone has a gun aimed at you, I should wait until you are free, if you're still alive."

"You're exaggerating. People don't run around pointing guns at other people. That only happens in movies." She ran one finger along the rim of her cup. "Or in an overactive imagination."

My saucer clattered when I set my cup down. "You think I have a complex about saving women. That I'm creating scenarios so I can play the hero. Unbelievable."

"Think about it, Nicholas. You broke the door down to get to me because you thought I was in danger. Sounds like something out of a romance novel, doesn't it?" Her face flushed. "I'll admit the thought of a man—doing that—is very, um, romantic, and it's the kind of thing that could take a woman's breath away if she thought about it."

I grinned. "Really?"

She took a long sip of coffee. "The point is it doesn't happen in real life. It's a fantasy. It's unhealthy to think about that kind of behavior because it's not based in reality. So, if you find yourself worried about me, call me so we can discuss it."

I frowned. "You're serious."

"Yes." She nodded several times. "Yes."

She escorted me to the new front door, and we shook hands in deference to the kid's presence.

"Mom."

"Yes, Laurie?"

"You should marry Mike." Ignoring our startled expressions, Laurie added with a grin, "That way the door would be free."

I drove home with unkind thoughts about Mike. Back at the B&B, the atmosphere wasn't any warmer. I glanced into the den as I passed it. Mrs. Robbins and Joe Babbitt were watching television and didn't bother to acknowledge me.

Upstairs, the trio had gathered in the back sitting room. Edward and Claudia were holding hands. When I walked in, they separated like teenagers caught by their parents.

Edward sounded too hearty when he asked, "How did it go?"

"In the future, if I suspect Hattie's in danger, I'm to phone first."

"Sounds reasonable," Claudia murmured.

I glared at her. The workings of the female mind. I'm glad I live in the black-and-white world of men. I'd get vertigo if I had to follow the dizzying, maze-like pattern of a woman's thinking daily.

"What happened after I left?" I sat on the arm of the couch closest to Zali. She was off chaperon duty and sound asleep, slumped into the corner and softly snoring. "I sensed a chill downstairs. Do we still have a place to sleep?"

Edward smirked. "It's amazing how far exercising good manners will go in calming people who have every reason to be upset. I should mention we talked about you after you left. I hope you don't mind if we had a laugh at your expense."

"I seem to remember that gossiping and mocking people behind their backs falls under bad manners."

He ignored me. "They now think you're having an early mid-life crisis."

Claudia patted Edward's hand, which was safely on his own knee. If this went on, she'd be feeding him treats every time she approved of him. She gave me one of her lofty smiles. "Regina explained everything. Her sister was married to Professor Taylor."

I replayed the earlier conversation in my head. "She said she was the youngest by a few years. Let me guess. Was it Dora or Flora?"

"Virginia. Gina for short."

I stood. "Finally, we have our killer. Do we know what

she looks like? Regina wouldn't give you her address. It is, after all, her sister, but we can tell Sykes and he'll have the resources to track her down."

"Her late sister," Edward clarified.

I narrowed my eyes at him. "That makes for a problem. Unless...Any chance Regina Robbins wanted to avenge her poor, dead sister?"

"Quite the contrary. Mrs. Robbins is a practical woman. And, Nicholas, she knows all about Miss Channing." I must have made a noise because Edward held up a hand. "She had a clear view of her brother-in-law's failings and recognized that the young woman was a victim of Taylor's lies. I got the impression that, rather than be angry with Miss Channing, she felt bad about what her brother-in-law had done to her and tried to help when she could. For the record, Miss Channing doesn't know Mrs. Robbins was related to Professor Taylor, so please don't repeat that information. Our hostess thought it would make things awkward, and I agree."

Claudia put in her two cents. "When Regina talked about her sister, she didn't sound emotional. The woman died several years ago. After leaving Professor Taylor, Virginia moved to Citrus Grove to live near Regina. She divorced him. Remarried. Had a nice life." She shrugged. "There's no motive."

I was more interested in how Edward was taking the news. His brows drew together and his mouth pursed. He wasn't satisfied, but he wasn't about to contradict Claudia. He left that to me.

"Mrs. Robbins could be lying. If there's nothing to it, why didn't she just say so when the murder happened?"

"It's possible she didn't want to drag her sister's name into a sordid, murder investigation. The woman is dead and can't defend her reputation. Why bother?"

I looked to my brother to see if he agreed. He shrugged.

"Women," I muttered.

The thump of footsteps coming up the back stairs was too heavy for our hostess, and the person who reached the top of the stairs and headed toward us was much taller than Joe. When he passed the light in the hallway, Detective Jonah Sykes didn't look happy, and he aimed his frown in my direction.

I held up my hands in surrender. "I already paid for the door. It was an accident, of sorts."

He sent a gaze over those present, lingering over snoring Zali. "Where were you tonight between seven-thirty and eight?"

"Tonight? I was with Hattie Channing. Her kid can verify it. So can a workman named Mike. Why?"

"You were at Charlie Grant's home last night, looking through photographs on his laptop. What were you looking for?"

I started to get an uncomfortable feeling in my stomach. "Why don't you ask Charlie?"

"Because he's in the hospital with a concussion. He's under observation and the doctor would only let me have five minutes with him, so he answered what questions he could and told me to talk to you."

"What happened?" Claudia asked.

"He was attacked in his home while his wife was at her monthly Soroptimist meeting. It's a volunteer organization. I have thirty women who will swear Mrs. Grant was there. He was working in his office when he heard someone come in. Thinking it was his wife, he went to greet her. He didn't see who hit him. The only things they took were his laptop and his camera."

Edward stood. "I can assure you my brother had nothing to do with that."

"And neither did Hattie Channing," I added, my voice happier than the occasion called for.

"And where were you?" Sykes asked Edward.

Claudia reached up and took his hand. "Edward was with me all night. If you don't believe me, ask Mrs. Robbins if he left."

"I already did." The detective gave me his attention again. "What were you looking for?"

"He had taken pictures the night of Professor Taylor's murder. I wanted to see them."

He really had the most intimidating glare, probably because he didn't blink. "Were you trying to tamper with evidence?"

"What evidence? The night Taylor died, I was busy trying to save his life. I wanted to see what I missed."

"Did you notice anything out of the ordinary?"

"You've seen the photos." I raised my shoulders and let them drop.

"Just tell me what you saw."

"Nothing."

He held eye contact, just like Edward does when he wants to know if I'm lying. The difference was Edward couldn't throw me in jail if he didn't believe me. I returned Sykes' gaze with one of open honesty and relaxed when the detective looked away.

"Obviously there was something," Edward said. "Why else would someone assault Mr. Grant and steal his laptop and his camera?"

I closed my eyes and imagined I was back in front of Charlie's computer. He'd taken a lot of photos, but I couldn't remember anything unusual about them. Hattie Channing in her pink outfit. Dora, Flora and Georgie gossiping, probably about the advantages of duck eggs over chicken eggs. Grumpy Ned by the sign-up table. The ladies in the kitchen.

"There was one thing. You probably noticed. A small section of photos was missing. Three. Charlie said the images came out fuzzy, so he deleted them."

"I know about those. The technicians are working on recovering and restoring them. You're telling me you weren't looking for anything specific? You were just curious?"

"That's all it was."

He put his hands on his hips. "Why did your hostess say, What's he done now?, when I asked for you?"

"I had a mishap with a door. No big deal, but she might hold a grudge. And, just curious, how does a skilled photographer mess up three photos in a row?"

"He had his son hold his camera while he used the washroom. He told him not to play with it, but you know kids. We've already questioned the boy. He was studying the camera and clicking without trying to take an actual picture. In all likelihood, they're photographs of the hallway rug outside the washroom. So, don't even think about talking to that kid." Sykes pointed his finger at me and then swept it around to include all of us. "Let me make myself clear. If I catch any of you interfering with this investigation, I will arrest you."

After he left us, we listened until his feet hit the floor below before I said, "What now?"

"I have to think," Edward said.

"You mean you haven't been so far?"

"Tell me about the other pictures. Who were the subjects, and what were they doing?"

I gaped. "All of them?"

"If you can remember them all." He said it as a challenge. We both have good memories, and we can get competitive about whose is better. Mine, of course. By the time I finished, I felt confident I had covered every shot. I left out my impressions of Hattie Channing's photos. He only stopped me once, when I described Ned at the sign-up table.

"He was alone?"

"Yeah. I know Georgie started out with him, but she's in a later shot with the old gals. Maybe she got bored."

"Was it a close up?"

"Not really."

"But you didn't see Mort in the background?"

"He might have been out of the shot, or maybe he and Georgie took a moment to canoodle. They are engaged."

"And Taylor wasn't there?"

"The way the shot was framed he could have been standing behind Charlie. Same with Mort and Georgie. Maybe she didn't want her picture taken because she would have been forced to smile."

He thought about it for a minute and then glared at me. "I refuse to allow the death of Old Needles to defeat me."

Zali roused from her slumber. "Needles and pins, needles and pins, when a man marries, his trouble begins." She blinked the sleep out of her eyes. "Pins used to be expensive, you know." She launched into another recital, pointing at each of us in a round. "Tinker, tailor, soldier, sailor, rich man, poor man, beggar man, thief. You're it, Eddie."

Edward was frowning at an invisible spot on the floor.

"Eddie? I said you're it."

He looked up, distracted. "Hmm? Oh. Thank you. What time is it?"

I checked my watch. "Bill's is the only thing open this late."

He announced he was turning in. When Zali had her eyes closed in a gaping yawn, he gave Claudia a kiss on the lips.

Edward was onto something. Since he didn't share, I wasn't about to ask. Instead, I turned in for the night and dreamt about poor sailors dressed as beggars, thanks to Zali.

CHAPTER 42

I ran into Mrs. Robbins at the bottom of the steps the next morning. She dug her keys out of her purse and told me there was juice in the refrigerator and a breakfast casserole in the oven.

"I'm going out." She looked at me with suspicion. "I trust you don't plan to follow me and cause another scene."

"No, ma'am."

"Good. See that you don't."

By the time the other guests came down, I had doled the casserole onto plates. Joe Babbitt took a spot at the table and looked up in surprise when I served him.

"Regina's not here? Did she say when she'd be back?"

"I'm on a need-to-know basis, and she didn't think I needed to know."

He was the first to leave, probably because he was the only one at the table who had to get to work. Those of us who remained had nothing planned.

"So, now that Mrs. Robbins and Joe Babbitt are out of it, as well as Mrs. Robbins' dead sister, do we go back to the beginning? Well, maybe not the beginning. We had a few suspects and motives. I'll eliminate you as a courtesy," I nodded to Edward, "but we still have Charlie. And who knows? Taylor may have fathered other children by other women who weren't as forgiving as Hattie Channing. What we're missing is the connection between Jeffrey Babbitt and Jonathan Taylor."

Edward wrapped the fingers of his right hand around his left wrist and stretched his arms over his head.

Claudia frowned. "Detective Sykes said we should leave the investigation up to the police."

My brother reached out and squeezed her hand. "We're just discussing the matter. No harm in that."

Just to be contrary, I said, "Jeffrey Babbitt might have got killed because he was in the wrong place at the wrong time, but I don't buy it. I think he overheard something. Or saw something. There is no mystery to his death."

"If Jeffrey Babbitt had known something, he would have shared his knowledge with the police," Claudia said, implying Jeffrey Babbitt was a good boy and I wasn't.

I gave her a pitying stare to let her know she suffered from an acute case of naïveté. "If he knew the significance."

"That will be impossible to prove." Edward rubbed his knuckles over his beard.

Claudia pushed back from the table. "Then that's that. I need to phone Robert." She left, with Zali trotting behind her. Robert would probably be devastated by the news his sister was coming home. The past week had been a deliriously happy dream, free from his sister and able to make his own decisions about Inglenook Resort.

"She's right," Edward said louder than necessary. "Our part is over. You might as well get us packed, Nicholas, so we can return home."

"With your name still under a cloud?"

"Taylor's cryptic message about revealing someone's

secret could refer to me, or Charlie Grant, or Virginia Robbins, or Hattie Channing. Sykes has enough suspects. I trust I'm safe."

I could feel my temperature rising. "Did Regina really have a sister? And do we have confirmation Virginia Taylor is dead? Why couldn't you find that divorce decree?"

Footsteps clomped and creaked as Claudia and Zali ascended the stairs. Edward leaned back, listened to the footsteps cross to the back room, and then lunged forward, over the table.

"We need to talk to that child."

"How are we supposed to do that? Sykes will kill us."

"Detective Sykes will thank us. I suppose we could skip getting confirmation from Zachery…"

I narrowed my eyes. "Are you saying you know who did it?"

"I've suspected for some time, but yes. I'm certain." He stood. "Let's go before—"

He glanced upward. "If we leave them to pack, we can have the satisfaction of seeing this case closed."

I followed his gaze to where the ladies' bedroom was above us. "You didn't tell Claudia about your theory, did you?"

"I didn't want to worry her. She might not understand the thrill of closing in for the kill." He said this in a low rumble, like the satisfied purr of a large cat.

"You mean she might find it distasteful that we want to lord it over the killer."

"Exactly."

When we got to Charlie's house, Edward insisted I remain in the car. I'm sure he didn't want me to figure out what he already knew—the name of the killer.

He hopped out of the car as soon as I pulled up to the curb and rang the doorbell. It took some time before Missus Charlie answered the door. Fortunately, Zackary slipped out behind her and stood at her side staring up at Edward.

He gesticulated as he talked. She gesticulated in response. Then he pointed at the kid, and I thought he'd lost her.

She took a step back, pulling the kid with her. He held out his hands, palms up. She shook her head. He pointed at the kid again. Whatever he said, she relented.

Edward crouched down, something he thinks makes it less intimidating for children when he growls at them. I held my breath while the kid stared at him and chewed the fingernail on his thumb. And then I thought the kid would never shut up.

Five minutes later, Edward bounded up to the car and slid inside.

"Any luck?"

"It wasn't luck. I asked the right questions."

"And then you scared the answers out of the kid."

He sat there looking smug, but I finally asked, "So?"

He grinned. "I found the divorce decree. Or rather, I didn't find it because they were never divorced, but I found the marriage license. When Aunt Zali recited her rhyme last night, it gave me an idea."

"Out of the mouths of babes."

"Taylor's nickname was Old Needles. When you're in college, you don't hold common sense in high esteem. It was funny back then, but when I considered it, the nickname didn't make much sense. It would, however, make sense if his name had been Tailer, so I looked for a marriage certificate under that name. The man was arrogant enough to change his name legally to put an end to the needling, if you'll pardon the pun, but obviously, those who knew him as Tailor kept the joke going. Anyway, there it was, Jonathan Tailer, but no divorce decree."

"Virginia Hendricks is dead, Edward. I don't think it matters."

He grinned. "Professor Taylor's wife is alive and well. Mrs. Robbins lied, which is not a surprise."

I gaped. "Virginia is alive?"

"No, no. She's dead, God rest her soul. I found the notice of her death and the obituary on *The Courier* website. A sweet woman, from all accounts. Well liked. Devoted to her six cats."

"Are you going to tell me who it is?"

"Gina Taylor is Georgina Taylor."

"Georgina Taylor." I gaped. "Do you mean Georgie? Sorry, but I asked her what her full name was, and she said Georgette, like that flaky woman on *The Mary Tyler Moore Show*."

"What have I told you about believing everything you're told? Didn't you ever wonder why she never wanted to give her last name? She always responded with, 'Call me Georgie.'" He smirked. "You know, Nicholas, you were walking around with a major clue."

"I was?"

"According to you, one of the last things Professor Taylor said was mwif."

"Mwif? That's a clue?" I thought about it, and then my jaw dropped. "You mean he was saying, My wife? Who'da thunk. Wait a minute. Do you mean we wasted all this time because Taylor couldn't speak more clearly?"

He pulled out his cell phone and called Sykes, explaining his logic and asking him to meet us at Georgie's. When he hung up, he had a hunter's gleam in his eye.

"Did he believe you?"

"He said he was on his way."

"I'm game." I stood. "Let's go get her."

CHAPTER 43

W hen I pulled up to the curb in front of Georgie's house, it looked like we had missed the action. Ours was the only vehicle around. I got out and joined Edward on the sidewalk. We climbed the three steps to her front door, and Edward knocked. He tried twice more without getting a response before he gave up.

"Maybe Sykes was already in Citrus Grove when you talked to him. They could have patched the call through to his cell phone. That's what they say, isn't it? Patch the call through? Or maybe that's a military term. I seem to remember hearing it in an old war movie."

"You're babbling, Nicholas."

"Because we don't know the location of the woman who has killed two people. Maybe she's at Mort's showing him her oleander plant. The sooner she's in custody, the better I'll feel."

My brother nodded his agreement but kept walking. "We'll go there next. As soon as we make sure she's not here."

I trotted to catch up. "Of course, since I know you as well as you know me, it's possible you, feeling vindictive about the way she ruined your book party, want to take her down yourself, which is fine by me, but let's get it over with."

But she wasn't in the garage. The stacks of boxes I had made in the corner against the back wall had grown another level. The loose papers and knick-knacks had been put away.

Edward let out a low groan.

"I know you were hoping to be in on the kill, but—"

"I didn't say anything."

A prickle ran up my spine. This is how it went down at the bookstore when Taylor shouted at us. And then he died.

The groan sounded again. It came from behind the rack of vintage clothes. Edward pulled back the dresses like a curtain, and I dropped to my knees to give Regina Robbins a few pats on the cheek.

She moaned and moved her head back and forth. When her eyes popped open, she struggled to sit up. "She hit me! I can't believe she hit me!"

Edward, by my side now, gently pushed her back to a prone position. "You need to lie still. Nicholas, phone for an ambulance."

I was already gone.

As I drove, I pulled out my cell phone and called Hattie's number. There was no answer, so I headed for the Happy Chicken. The Amazon hostess informed me Hattie hadn't shown up for her shift.

"Another emergency?"

"I don't know. She didn't call in, but I can't reach her at home." She lowered her voice. "If this keeps up, she'll lose her job."

I headed toward Apple Street next. I reasoned I had phoned first, and that cleared me for stopping by. This time, I tapped lightly on the new front door and kept my volume down when I called her name.

Nothing.

I looked around to make sure the neighbors weren't peering out their windows with binoculars, which they might be inclined to do after the scene I'd caused yesterday. There was one woman across the street with her nose pressed to the window making half-hearted swipes at the glass with a paper towel. When I waved at her, she ducked behind her curtains.

I stepped off the porch, sidestepped in the space behind the bushes and peeked in the windows. Through a haze of white sheers, I could see the living room furniture, but it wasn't being used by anyone. Unlike the last time I looked through these windows, all the cushions were in place on the couch.

Since I try to avoid repeating my mistakes if possible, I tamped down my anxiety and moved down the side of the house to the backyard to see if Hattie was there. The clothes-line, charred in the middle, hadn't been replaced, and the rollerblades had migrated to the opposite side of the back stairs. Then I saw the remains of a pitcher of iced tea and two glasses on the picnic table.

After a few taps on the back door, Hattie opened it the width of her face and peered outside.

"Nicholas." Relief flooded over her features, but then they stiffened. "You should have phoned first."

"I did. You didn't answer." When she didn't open the door wider, I said, "May I come in?"

She responded by narrowing the gap to a few inches. "No. Not right now. That wouldn't be a good idea."

"Why not?"

She lifted her chin. "Do I need to give you a reason?" Her gaze flickered sideways, to her left, and it occurred to me she might have a guest.

"I see. You have company. How's Mike?"

"That's none of your business." She rubbed her forehead. "Look, Nicholas. Remember our discussion the other day?"

"I told you, I phoned first."

"Not that. About your vivid imagination. Thinking I might be in danger, like some character out of a book. I—I warned you about interfering. About trying—trying to rescue me."

I nodded. "I remember it well. It feels like a scene out of fiction."

She slowed down her delivery and stressed her points as if I were a five-year-old in a remedial classroom. "Well, this is not make-believe, Nicholas. It's real. Don't rescue me. Don't break down my door again. Just leave."

She was sending mixed signals. Her words were telling me to go away, but her eyes were wide—not narrowed in anger—and her forehead wrinkled above the bridge of her nose. Then her eyes darted left again.

"Fine. This shining knight is off duty. I've parked my stallion in the garage and left my armor beside it. I just wanted to tell you I'm leaving for good."

She drew in a shaky breath. It was too much. I moved to step inside, but she pushed the door until it was only open a crack. I reached out for her, but when she backed away, I let my hand drop.

"Goodbye, Hattie."

She gave me a final, desperate look. "Bye." And then she closed the door.

I stepped off the stoop and walked around the corner of the house, passing the windows without looking inside. Once I got to my car, I drove it around the corner, parked, and got out.

Either I was a sap or Hattie had been trying to tell me she was in trouble. The way she stressed this is not make believe. She was attempting to tell me the danger was real. I admit in the back of my mind a small voice told me I was a sap, and that I was about to give her a sample of my overactive imagination, but it was worth the risk.

I came at the driveway from the neighbor's yard.When I got closer, I approached the house in a crouched position. Standing off to the side of the kitchen window, I leaned in to peek through the curtains. No one was in the kitchen. I made my way around the back of the house, sticking close to the siding just in case. When I got to the bay window off the dining room, a movement caught my eye. I pressed back against the house and inched close enough to the window that by leaning sideways, I could peer through a gap in the curtains. Hattie sat at the dining room table and looked up at someone. She had her arms folded under her chest in a pose of defiance. *That's my girl*, I thought.

When the curtains pulled open, I jerked back in time. I hoped. When they dropped back into place, I risked looking again. The person inside stood with her back to me. She had a gun in her hand, but she held it at her side. The site of a weapon relieved me from any worries I was suffering from a hero fantasy.

The woman stood about two feet from the window. If I went through, I might surprise her before she thought to use the gun on me, but at least it would provide a distraction so Hattie could get away.

Taking five steps back, I bent my knees, took a deep breath, and prepared myself for the worst. This was going to hurt. Leading with the shoulder I'd used on the door because, what the hell, it was already injured, I put on a burst of speed and, covering my head with my arms, I leapt through the glass.

In addition to the spectacular shatter, I heard a scream. Because of the angle of my jump, I came up short and made a grab for the woman's legs as she spun around. I yanked hard, and she went down. As I wrestled with flailing limbs and a solid kick in the back from a hard-soled shoe, I called out.

"Hattie, run!"

But she didn't run. The gun had flown from the woman's hand and now rested against the wall. Hattie picked it up and pointed it down with shaking hands while I flipped my struggling victim over.

"Pleased to meet you, Mrs. Taylor," I said as I hauled Georgie to her feet.

Hattie lowered the gun and stood there, trembling and fighting off tears. If I hadn't had my hands full, I would have taken her in my arms and kissed her.

"This is what you were hinting at, right?"

I shouldn't have made her laugh because her giggle dissolved into tears.

CHAPTER 44

By the time Edward arrived, Sykes had already carted Georgie away. I didn't see him arrive because I had my eyes squeezed shut while an EMT picked glass out of my hair and face. My forearms and shoulders had taken the brunt of the breaking window, and I had the bandages to prove it.

We were at the kitchen table because Mike was in the dining room boarding up the broken window, while Hattie supervised. I didn't see the workman arrive either, but I couldn't miss hearing the manly rumbles of laughter that complemented Hattie's giggles. At least he didn't bellow like Edward.

"Nicholas! Nicholas! Oh, there you are. What on earth have you been up to?" Edward demanded. "You took the car, so I had to call for an Uber. Mrs. Robbins and I had to squeeze into that Ned person's pickup truck. She insisted on coming with me."

I peeked out of one eye. He ran his gaze over the bloodstains and the shredded condition of my shirt. "Nicholas? Explain."

"Georgie tried to eliminate a loose end. Hattie. I got here just in time."

"I see." He slid over a chair and sat down while the EMT continued to work. He made a fist and slammed it on his knee. "Dammit! We should have come here first, but I didn't think there was any danger. Georgie already knew about Hattie, so an attack seemed pointless. I underestimated how crazed the killer had become. I apologize."

Hattie walked in just then followed by Regina Robbins.

Edward stood and inclined his head at Regina. "You're too late. I'm terribly sorry to have to tell you your sister has been arrested for the murders of Jonathan Taylor and Jeffrey Babbitt. And assault with a deadly weapon on Miss Channing, I assume."

Regina's lips pressed into an unforgiving line. "Good. I came with you to make sure Hattie was all right."

"Yoo-hoo!"

Hattie opened the back screen door, and the entire council, minus Georgie and Mort, greeted her with cries and questions. Hattie invited them in.

"We heard the sirens," Flora said, and then she saw me. Her mouth kept moving, but no sounds came out. Dora gasped.

"Oh, you poor young thing. Did you run into the glass doors?"

"Run into them? Let me guess. You had a farmhand who did the same thing."

She nodded with vigor. "He was running down the hill after a loose lamb. The clever little thing darted left at the last minute, but Robby couldn't stop himself in time. Went right through."

"Get your head out of your butt," Flora said. "Hattie doesn't have a sliding glass door."

Ned leaned over to peer into the dining room at the

chaos. "Nope. You couldn't trip your way through that window. Not from the outside. All the debris is on the inside."

Edward couldn't make me or the female EMT give up our chairs to the ladies, so my brother retrieved some extras from the dining room and got Dora, Flora, Regina, and Hattie situated around the table, while the men remained standing.

"They have arrested Georgie," Regina said, as if making an admission.

There were nods and murmurs of assent. Dora moved over and patted her shoulder.

"Sisters can be difficult."

I jerked forward, and the EMT pushed me back in place. "Did everyone here but Edward and I know the two of you were related? I want a show of hands."

Dora and Flora raised their hands. "We've lived here all our lives." The sisters exchanged a glance. "We probably know everybody's business."

"And you didn't think to share that information?" I demanded.

"You didn't ask," Flora said. "It wasn't a secret."

"Then how come I never knew?" Ned demanded. "I've lived here all my life, too. Weren't no Robbins or Taylors around before Regina and Harold moved here."

Edward gave Mrs. Robbins the kind of tolerant look you might give a delinquent four-year-old. Enough to let the kid know he'd been naughty without putting the fear of God in him. "You led us on. Keeping away from your sister so we wouldn't connect the two of you. Perhaps notice shared facial features or characteristics. Very clever."

Regina let out a hoot of laughter. "You give me too much credit. Georgie was a snob. I've never cared for her much.

We've never had each other over to dinner or anything like that."

Edward stroked his beard. "I should have guessed. You were still involved with the Culinary Arts Council, vetting cookbooks for them. That shows you enjoyed the group, and yet you left. You were there when the cookbook came out eleven years ago. Georgie and Mort met at a meeting approximately ten years ago."

I gaped. "Is that what you wanted to know when we went to Mort's house? How long had he and Georgie had been dating? I thought you were just babbling."

"I was working out a timeline," he snapped, irritated that I had interrupted him. He turned back to Regina Robbins. "Did you leave the council because of her?"

"The Cooking Club of Citrus Grove." She nodded. "That's what we called the Culinary Arts Council before she joined it and tried to make it fancy. Those members who rebelled formed the Sweet and Sour Book Club, but I'd had enough by then. And I had the bed-and-breakfast to run."

Since my chair faced away from the table, I leaned my head back and over to make eye contact with Hattie. "Did you know?"

She stared at Mrs. Robbins, still absorbing the information. "No. Certainly not."

"I bet Georgie killed Johnny." That came from Dora.

"Head is still up your butt," her sister said. "What do you think we've been talking about?"

Hattie paled when Professor Taylor's name came up. "Does someone want to explain why Georgie barged into my home with a gun and what she has to do with Jonathan Taylor?"

"She didn't tell you?" Regina Robbins snorted. "Just like her to make assumptions. Georgie was his wife." She reached out and squeezed Hattie's arm. "Now don't you go feeling guilty. She knew he was a rotter before she married him, but she was too proud to leave him. A college professor's wife. La-de-da. Thought she was the homecoming queen all over again."

"Has she always known that I—that Laurie—" Hattie rubbed her forehead.

Mrs. Robbins nodded. "She didn't blame you, but I'm sure you noticed she wasn't all kisses and flowers with you. Fact is, I don't think she thought about you much at all. She's selfish that way."

"This is so embarrassing," Hattie whispered. She blinked back tears and looked at her guests. "Did you all know about Laurie? That Jonathan was her father?"

Ned blushed. "No, but we've all done stupid things we'd rather not have on the front page of *The Courier*, so we didn't ask about her dad. Wasn't our business."

I relaxed when a giggle burst through Hattie's tears.

"I apologize for being so inquisitive about such a sensitive matter, but what made your sister finally leave him?" Edward asked.

"Me," Hattie whispered.

Mrs. Robbins barked out another laugh. "Hardly. She finally asked him, just out of curiosity, why he wanted to stay married, since he preferred other women. He told her to her face being married kept him from having to marry any of the other women. That gave her pride a big blow, so, when our mother got sick, she packed her bags and moved to Citrus Grove to help take care of her."

I raised the hand the EMT wasn't working on. "That still doesn't explain why Dora and Flora didn't mention the relationship, at least to the police."

The sisters looked scandalized. Dora said, "It wasn't our place."

"For Pete's sake! She told me her name was Georgette and you didn't say anything."

"We thought she was having fun with you, though, now that I think about it, Georgie wasn't known for her sense of humor."

The General cleared his throat. "I, for one, am shocked. Comes as a surprise. Had no idea."

"There's no *for one* about it," Ned cackled. "Mort doesn't know either. Well, maybe now he does."

Edward used his gentle voice. "Did you suspect your sister was the killer?"

Regina Robbins blushed. "At first, when Johnny died, I couldn't believe it of her. He had come to town a few times to see her. I thought they might have patched things up enough to be friends. They even had dinner before the book event." She looked around at all of us. "She told me he had finally agreed to sign the divorce papers. He refused all those years ago, and she didn't want to spend the money on lawyers to fight it. She stuck her head in the sand and pretended the problem didn't exist, which is how she wound up married to him in the first place." The blush deepened. "He made a pass at me when they were dating. When I told her, she said, You wish. Like I'd want anything to do with that man."

Edward arched a brow at me to drive home the point about not believing what people said. "I'm afraid the professor had decided to tell Mort and anyone else who would listen that she was still his wife, and he was going to do it at the book event. He announced it on social media."

"She wouldn't have liked that." Regina Robbins perked up. "Jonathan Taylor was a fool to give her a warning. He should have expected she'd respond poorly. Really, it's his own fault he got murdered."

The EMT scratched me with a shard of glass and I winced.

Mrs. Robbins seemed comforted by the idea her sister wasn't responsible for her actions. I guess family is family, even when you don't like them.

I pointed out that it didn't explain Jeffrey Babbitt's murder.

"What do you remember about Mr. Babbitt?" Edward asked.

After a minute, I said, "He was an excellent businessman. He was painfully free with his opinions. And he had a wicked sense of humor. He agreed with me when I told him murder might be a new marketing plan."

"Exactly the kind of man who would have taken advantage of the situation." Edward turned to face Mrs. Robbins. "Did he know your sister and Professor Taylor were married?"

"He did."

"Did you tell him the professor was coming to town to have dinner with your sister?"

She shook her head. "Not something I cared about enough to repeat. I only told one person, and she had a right to know."

"I'm afraid that might be my fault." Hattie pushed her hair behind her ear. "Jeffrey was a good friend. Easy to talk to. He knew about my history. When I found out Jonathan was coming that night, I told him. He said with a few changes to my hair and wardrobe I would be unrecognizable after thirteen years."

I pursed my lips. "How come you didn't know Georgie was his wife?"

"My parents only moved here when I was a teenager. They knew Regina through church, but Georgie wasn't living here then. I moved back when I got pregnant, but I didn't get involved in the Culinary Arts Council until Laurie was in third grade."

Regina Robbins sighed. "Poor Jeffrey. Like you said, Jeffrey was easy to talk to. He knew Georgie and Jonathan had been married. That man had a wicked sense of humor. I wouldn't put it past him to have teased Georgie about the sudden appearance of her ex-husband without knowing they weren't divorced."

Edward grunted. "And Georgie thought he knew more than he did. That she wasn't a free woman, and yet she was planning an advantageous marriage to Mort the banker. After she murdered Professor Taylor, she thought he would put it together and realize she was the killer."

"He did get upset when I joked with him about Taylor's murder." I pulled the conversation from my memory. "I asked if he felt any responsibility, though I meant for helping to catch the killer, not for the murder. He said nothing he did or said could have any bearing on the murder. I wonder if you're not right about him teasing Georgie."

Edward continued the story. "And then Charlie's son Zackary, while playing with his father's camera, took a few pictures of Georgie and the professor having an argument in the hallway near the washroom. Georgie had her back to the wall and must have seen little Zachery playing with the camera. The wonder is she didn't—"

"Don't say it!" Regina Robbins held her hands in front of her face. "I don't want to think Georgie would be capable of hurting a child."

Hattie gave her a pitying glance.

"All finished," the EMT said, putting her tools away. "You may find bits of glass for a while, but I got the majority."

I thanked her, and when she left, Edward stood.

"Why don't I pack our bags, settle up with Mrs. Robbins, and pick you up in an hour."

Everyone took the hint and reluctantly cleared out.

When Hattie and I were alone, we looked at each other for a minute and then broke into grins.

"That was exciting."

"Nicholas," she began. "I can't thank you enough. Georgie was waiting until Laurie got home before—" She shuddered. "The thing is, Laurie is everything to me. She needs a quiet, stable environment."

My stomach tightened into a knot, but I kept my voice light. "It's not as if there will be a murder every week."

She made a slight gesture toward the window, or maybe it was to indicate the front door. Or both. "Laurie's had enough excitement. Me too. I'm sorry."

I pulled myself to my feet and kissed her on the forehead.

"Window's done." Mike stood in the doorway. "It will hold for the night. I'll be back tomorrow to install the new one." He grinned at me showing those stupid dimples. "You sure are good for business."

"Glad to help."

I left the two of them alone and walked back to the B&B. When I arrived, Bill was waiting. Edward moved to leave us alone in the foyer, but she told him to stay and got right to the point.

"I need to know if you're going to say anything."

I smiled, pretending not to understand. "Nice to see you?"

She didn't smile back. "About the checks."

"Oh. I did wonder how Cecil Brown managed to cash his from the grave, but I didn't care enough to ask you about it. You can see I don't think it's my concern."

She flushed. "I don't want you thinking we're just a bunch of greedy cheats. Those men and I served together through a very rough patch. When we got back, there wasn't a lot of support, not from the communities, nor from the government. After all, it wasn't a war. It was an unpopular police action. One by one they seemed to drift into my bar until they formed a support community. We all pitched in and helped when anyone had troubles. Sometimes a man needed a place to stay because the wife couldn't take the night terrors and personality changes. Sometimes they needed help finding a job or paying the rent while they found employment."

She glanced at me. I nodded to show I understood.

"Cecil was the first to suggest it. He said he was leaving everything he had to the men who served with him. Of course, that wasn't much. There was a partnership agreement regarding the bookstore. Cecil lived a simple life. I remember he said, 'Guys, I worked hard for those military benefits. I worked hard for them. I earned them. So, I don't plan to die.' And then he winked at us. We knew what he meant, especially when he changed his mailing address to the bar's address. So, when he died, we just didn't report it. He didn't have any family members to worry about. His checks went into a pool. Whenever someone had a need, there was money to help him out. The other men did the same thing. A few are gone now, so the pool just keeps growing. No one plans to get rich off it. We just wanted the funds to help pay for emergencies, like medical care."

I reached out and shook her hand. "Nice to know you, Bill. By the way, I have something in my ears and didn't hear a word you said."

After a moment's hesitation, Edward shook her hand, too. "Pardon me. I wasn't listening. I've got a lot on my mind. It was a pleasure to meet you. Now, if you'll excuse me."

I swear she blinked back a tear or two before she nodded and left.

~

We were five miles shy of San Diego before Edward broke the silence.

"Will we be seeing more of Miss Channing?"

"We will not."

He sighed through his nose, and I knew he was feeling sorry for me. I was feeling a bit sorry for myself. I glanced into the rearview mirror.

"What's wrong with me, Edward?"

"Nothing, Nicholas. There is absolutely nothing wrong with you. I have Mother's word for it."

"You actually asked her?"

"Around the time you shot my football full of B-Bs."

"I guess it's good to have confirmation." I tried to leave it at that. Really, I did. "Why is it every woman I like is either a murderer, murder victim, or potential murder victim?"

"Miss Channing is at a different place in her life. She has a child. Are you prepared to raise a child?"

"I don't know. Can you prepare for something like that?"

"No. I suppose not." He cleared his throat. "Look how long it took me to find Claudia."

"Not helping."

"Okay. You want to know what's wrong with you? You're impulsive, argumentative, and you lack self-confidence, which you compensate for by being cocky."

"I have self-confidence." I gave him a quick glance in the rearview mirror to see if he was laughing at me.

He leaned forward and squeezed my shoulders.

"You are my brother, Nicholas. You're fine."

That would have to do for now.

THERE'S MORE

Continue Reading for Book Club Discussion Questions, and more.

AND DON'T FORGET to download your free story

THE CASE OF THE COOKED GOOSE
A Harlow Brothers mystery prequel

When Nicholas Harlow accompanies his brother, Edward, to a conference at the Deer Stalker Hotel, he discovers his childhood idol, Sammy Spade, starring in the hotel's production of *Jekyl and Hyde*. During the evening performance, Sammy keels over onstage, poisoned. Unfortunately, Nicholas was the last one to see him alive, and the detective in charge is ready for an arrest.

Go to www.jacquelinevick.com/subscribehb

THANK YOU FOR READING BAD BEHAVIOR

If you enjoyed this book, please consider leaving a review. Reviews help readers discover new books, and the author, who socializes mostly with dogs, appreciates the human feedback.

ACKNOWLEDGMENTS

Many thanks to my support group of brave souls willing to read proof copies and give me feedback and advice, especially Andrea Voirin and Kim Taylor Blakemore.

To my parents, Albert and Beverly Voirin, who taught us to write Thank You notes.

Also, to my husband, Foster, for his support, bright ideas, and unconditional love.

Finally, thanks to the Mystery Buffs, a community of readers who love mysteries as much as I do.

ALSO BY JACQUELINE VICK

Other novels by Jacqueline Vick

Frankie Chandler Pet Psychic Mysteries

Barking Mad at Murder

A Bird's Eye View of Murder

An Almost Purrfect Murder

What the Cluck? It's Murder

A Scaly Tail of Murder

A Scape Goat for Murder

The Harlow Brothers Mysteries

Civility Rules

Bad Behavior

Deadly Decorum

Standalone Novels

Family Matters

The Body Guy

An Unhealthy Attachment

BOOK CLUB QUESTIONS

The trouble begins when Nicholas lies to Edward about a public appearance. If someone tricked you into doing something, would you walk out? Or forge ahead rather than cause a scene?

Professor Taylor was a pill. He seduced female students and sabotaged those who might succeed where he had failed. Did you have a teacher who was especially difficult? How about one who inspired you?

When Hattie Channing became pregnant by Professor Taylor, she felt pressured by doctors and friends to not have Laurie. It is the author's opinion that Motherhood is the most important job in history. Have you experienced people denigrating motherhood? Especially as a full-time job?

When Nicholas discovers his brother told the Detective Jonah Sykes about Hattie Channing and Professor Taylor's relationship, he feels Edward betrayed him. Did he? Or did Edward do what was right, even though it was difficult?

In his anger, Nicholas accidentally knocks Edward down. Have you ever done something in anger you didn't intend? Something that was misinterpreted?

Zali complains that others don't treat her as an adult. Does she have a point? Or should she have limits placed on her for her own good?

Charlie Grant, the reporter for *The Citrus Grove Courier*, says he isn't interested in the attention of national newspapers because *The Courier* has been good to him. Which would you choose? Prestige and fame at a price, or less exposure at a company that is good to you?

Bill, the owner of the local bar, was scamming the government to help her veteran clients. Did Edward have a duty to report her? Or is it okay to let illegal activity slide if it's for a good cause?

ABOUT THE AUTHOR

Jacqueline Vick writes the Frankie Chandler Pet Psychic mystery series about a woman who, after faking her psychic abilities for years, discovers animals *can* communicate with her. Her second series, the Harlow Brothers mysteries, features a former college linebacker turned etiquette author and his secretary brother. Her books are known for satirical humor and engaging characters who are reluctant to accept their greatest (and often embarrassing) gifts.

Visit her website at www.jacquelinevick.com.